Pam
So nice to meet
fellow wine lovers
all the best & hope you enjoy

Death
of a
Warrior

Stephen M Hannemann
11-03

Stephen M. Hannemann

HARA
PUBLISHING GROUP

Hara Publishing Group, Inc.
P.O. Box 19732
Seattle, WA 98109
425-775-7868

Hannemann, Stephen M.

Death of a warrior / Stephen M. Hannemann. --1st ed. -- Seattle, WA : Hara Publishing, 2003.
    p. ; cm.
    ISBN: 1-887542-09-4

    1. Terrorism--United States--Fiction. 2. Northwest, Pacific--Fiction. 3. Self-realization--Fiction. 4. Spy stories. 5. Suspense fiction. I. Title.

PS3608.A655 D43 2003
813.6--dc22

Cover Design: Laura Zugzda
Senior Editor: Vicki McCown
Interior Layout: Stephanie Martindale

To My Children

Shayne and Troy

Larry and Shannon

and

Stephen Christopher

NOTE FROM THE AUTHOR

Death of a Warrior is purely a work of fiction and any similarity to actual people, organizations, or events in this work is coincidental. I have the utmost regard for our men and women in the armed forces and on our police forces. I did however, thoroughly enjoy the liberties taken during the writing of this story, but only for your reading pleasure.

Stephen M. Hannemann

August, 2003

ACKNOWLEDGMENTS

Only writers truly know how many people contribute to their work and encouraged them on to success. I am indebted to the following, and pray for understanding from anyone I may have failed to mention.

My heartfelt gratitude goes out to Maurice Cassidy, Rob Pyle, Jay Thomas, Sue Thomas, Joyce Booth, Debbie Foushee and Patti Lucas for taking time to read and comment on my manuscript. To Pauline Vorderstrasse for not only reading, but for providing weekend retreats for uninterrupted writing.

To Herb and Marilyn Helsel from Langley Clock & Gallery, for teaching Jason the finer points of his regulator wall clock's Grande Sonnerie movement.

To Laura Zugzda for her inspiration and commitment to excellence in the execution of a stunning cover design.

To the wonderful women at Hara Publishing, Sheryn Hara, Yvonne Grosjean, and Charlotte Opitz, who are responsible for pulling together the finished product that you hold in your hand. And especially my editor, Victoria McCown, who has mentored me to become a better writer and has taught me that less is better, although at nearly 500 pages, I'm not sure she's convinced that I got it.

To my special friend, Lori Goolsbey, who twelve years ago took me by the ear and led me to her keyboard and encouraged me to write. And when I did begin to write, she never once doubted that this work would one day be published. And also, to Ray, Lori's husband who has kept my Mac updated and purring.

But especially to you, the patron of the written word, I am grateful, for without you, word craft would not endure.

PROLOGUE

There comes a time in a man's life when an event of great magnitude rends the soul—a time, if only for a moment, that brings one to a precipice facing the chasm of despair.

"Sanctuary" is the word that defines Jason's Seattle loft. His escape from the madness that had been his life's work brought him here to these high ceilings and expansive interiors that displayed his love of the old and the beautiful. The richly patterned oriental carpets whispered good taste, but they also hinted at the complex mosaic of the man's soul. For Jason was a man in the throes of change, in the purgatory that most of us reach when we are between youth and maturity.

With a scotch and a cigar, he stretched out on his sofa and reflected on his life. He had retired from an outstanding military career, accumulated wealth and retained his good health. He had one friend who cared enough to see that he did not disappear into oblivion before he could ripen his intelligence and talents into something that would sustain him to the end, beyond the threshold that he could only just now make out in the fog of time.

C H A P T E R   O N E

A man's ultimate despair rode layers of stale tobacco and alcohol fumes that permeated the dreary room. Weeks of newspapers, litter, and ashtrays filled to overflowing covered the cheap coffee table and two mismatched end tables. Shafts of sunlight stole through the cracks and tears in the window blinds in their tenacious attempt to bring light to a dismal hour. But faint shafts of light can do little when filtered by the haze of dust and dense cigarette smoke. They died on a dingy floor.

The solitary figure slumped on a stained and frayed brown sofa, gazing longingly at Polaroid photographs of a woman. With quivering hands, he studied the pictures one at a time, then set them in his lap. The leotard she wore fit her body like a fuchsia-colored coat of paint, leaving nothing to the imagination. The long dark hair, the small but full firm breasts, the narrow waist and long, tapered legs—she epitomized the woman most men only dream about, a woman he would never see again. She had been caught in various poses—standing, kneeling, lying on a white bear rug, smiling and happy with eyes full of sparkle and hope. Hope . . . hope was contradictory to the surroundings and mood of the moment.

Eventually, the last picture found his lap. He stared blankly for just a moment, then reached for his drink. A badly shaking hand caused the ice in the tumbler to jingle, a faint surreal music in the macabre setting, a fitting requiem in the painful silence. Emptying the contents with three long swallows, he sat motionless, then without warning, hurled the glass. It hit

1

the wall and exploded with a deafening bang as shards flew in all directions, followed closely by light sounds of tinkle and chinks as the last bits and pieces came to rest. Then again, an eerie quiet.

The man slouched, brooding and still, appearing suspended in time. Then he rose to his feet and slowly walked across the room to a cluttered, scarred dark wood buffet, distressed from years of abuse. Opening the top drawer, the man removed two objects and returned to the sofa. In the heavy gloom of despair, sweat and tears streamed from a face devoid of hope.

After a time the man turned his attention to contents from the buffet. After balancing a red cardboard box on his left thigh, he placed a four-inch barreled Smith & Wesson 44 magnum on the sofa cushion next to his right leg. He opened the red box of cartridges and removed one, then exposed the cylinder of the revolver and dropped in the cartridge, which made a dull metallic sound as it slid to a stop. A loud click-snap followed as he swung the cylinder home, secured in the heavy frame. With his hands still shaking, he drew the hammer back, rotating the loaded cylinder into firing position. Slowly, deliberately he placed the muzzle of the gun against his temple.

The 44 magnum exploded with a thunderous roar.

At that same moment, the telephone rang in Jason's living room. He flinched at the trill of the phone and his hand knocked the half-full mug of Guinness to the floor.

"Dammit!" he swore. He pushed the pause button on the TV remote and reached for the telephone.

"Brisben!" He barked into the receiver as he surveyed the mess on his floor. The video he'd been watching had made him angry and the anger continued to roil and build. He was angry—angry at the notion that a man would take his life because of a woman; angry at the untimely interruption; angry that he had flinched at the peal of the telephone. Jason did not flinch.

"Now *there's* a friendly greeting." He recognized the voice of his friend Jack, his only friend, the one who always made the effort to stay in contact, the one who continually ignored or at least overlooked Jason's mood swings.

Jason Brisben lived within a dichotomy of passion, a jumble of anger and gentleness. In the past, he had seldom allowed himself to show his gentle side in deference to the anger boiling like molten lava beneath the surface of a sleeping volcano. Jason had been working on the demons that fueled his anger, and although they had considerably diminished, he had not yet overcome them.

"I just called to see what's happening. We haven't talked in over three weeks—when *I* called *you*, by the way. How about getting together tonight down at The Box Car?"

Jason barely listened, uninterested in the gibe and the invitation, instead focused on the pool of dark beer on his immaculately maintained hardwood floor and trying to identify the root of his anger. It certainly wasn't the mess; that could easily be cleaned up.

"Can't buddy, I just spilled a beer. Gotta big mess here to clean up."

But Jack was not to be dissuaded by Jason's curt response. "You getting clumsy in your old age?"

"No, I was watching that stupid video you gave me a couple of months ago. The dumb sonofabitch blew his brains out just as you called. I got a whole pint of Guinness on my floor. Looks like a damn brown lake."

Jack let out a snort of laughter. "You telling me, Jason Brisben, man with nerves of steel, is getting jumpy?"

Jason's face reddened at Jack's quick and accurate assessment. "I guess that's what I'm saying, smart ass."

"So clean up the damn mess and pull your head out of the sand, you ostrich. I'll see you at The Box Car in an hour." Chuckling, Jack disconnected, leaving no time for a response, knowing his friend would deduce the challenge and rise to it.

Jason returned the receiver to its cradle, then turned his attention toward the paused video. Is that what had rekindled the anger I've been working so hard to bring under control? he wondered. Was it possible to be filled with enough hopelessness and despair to take your own life? He picked up the remote and clicked the screen dark.

With a past immersed in death, betrayal, and sorrow, Jason Brisben was a man whose dark secrets relentlessly pounded his soul. Yet, unlike the man on screen, he had never given in to despair.

Shrugging off his dark mood, Jason thought of Jack and how he had instantly found humor in Jason's situation. Smiling, he went to the laundry room for the bucket and mop.

If being handsome were cause for imprisonment, Jason Brisben would have been eligible for life without parole. He stood six feet tall, with a dark complexion and curly dark brown hair, came packaged with broad shoulders and a narrow waist, and weighed in at a lean, muscular, one hundred ninety pounds. He was forty-eight years old. Most people who didn't know him well would have bet a month's paycheck that he was not a day older than thirty-five.

For all Jason's good looks, something behind his deep blue eyes revealed he'd lived more years than his body let on. Even Jack, who was closer to him than anyone, didn't know much, and Jason did not offer to ease anyone's curiosity. After a four-year friendship with Jason, Jack had learned only that he had been twice married and twice divorced, the latter being somewhat devastating, although no details had been shared. He knew too that Jason had been a Navy SEAL, of which he rarely spoke. Other than these few details, nobody knew anything about him.

Clearly Jason did not want for money and no one knew the origin of liquidity, including the IRS. This financial mystery kept several people employed, including an army of IRS folks on the one side, and two lawyers and one accountant on the other, whose job it was to fend off the federal agents.

Jason had never mentioned family, no parents, siblings, cousins, or children. It was as if he had appeared from nowhere, perhaps out of the witness protection program. However, if that were the case, he certainly would be keeping a lower profile. In the past Jason had had several encounters with the local law, although he had never spent time in jail.

No one of small means could have afforded his grand loft overlooking Pike's Market and the Seattle waterfront. Two master suites, a den and office combination, one large room that contained a spacious modern kitchen, dining, and living area, composed Jason's safe haven. His furnishings, an artful blend of antiques and contemporary, Persian rugs strategically placed atop highly polished red oak floors, the carefully placed pieces of art that graced his walls, spoke of a profound appreciation for beauty. Nearly the entire west wall consisted of floor-to-ceiling windows and sliding doors that opened onto a deck running the full length of the loft providing an unobstructed view of Elliott Bay and the Olympic Mountain Range, South Seattle, and Magnolia Heights to the Northwest.

To the left of the main entry, near the kitchen, a protrusion formed a separate vault-like room with a heavy door in the back wall. Jason had affectionately named it his "candy store," but he rarely entered that room any more.

After putting away the mop and bucket, Jason dimmed the lights and paused for several moments to take in the view. Then he strode into the bathroom, turned on the water, undressed, and stepped into his open steam-filled shower.

A twenty-year career as a Navy SEAL had molded an inflexible, intolerant man. But since retirement his years in near solitude had brought about subtle changes. The few people that knew him noticed no outward signs of change. And to him, the metamorphosis was almost imperceptible: a softening, maybe a little less rigidity, perhaps not quite so much of the rogue hard ass that he had prided himself on for so many years. While he steeped in the hot shower, he reflected on these changes but his mind drifted back to the video. Something about it nagged at him, but what? One thing he did know: He had embarrassed himself, flinching the way he did. Maybe that's what triggered the anger. I sure as hell ain't what I used to be, he thought to himself.

Jason emerged from the bathroom with a towel around his waist and walked to the nightstand where he picked up the phone to call for a taxi, leaving instructions for the driver to buzz him from the outside security door. He then disappeared into the closet to dress, unaware that a chain of events had begun to unfold that neither he nor the city of Seattle would soon forget.

CHAPTER TWO

Jason navigated his way through the labyrinth formed by a half train's worth of authentic 1920's and 1930's railroad cars restored to mint condition that collectively made up The Box Car Restaurant and Lounge. Dining cars, bar cars, coach cars, all fit together to form a unique piece of architecture, and three side-by-side box cars in the center of the maze created the roomy main bar.

As he turned this way and that, passing from one car to another, he continually admired the old artisan craftsmanship of the interiors, the meticulously hand-carved gussets, window frames and facades with accompanying polished gingerbread. All of the natural woodwork had been stripped and refinished in the original mahogany and walnut tones. The seats were original railroad, reupholstered in green and brown tapestries and burgundy velour. Ornate lighting fixtures had been polished or replated along with the flower vases that were attached to the window frames. All of the dark natural colors and the dim lighting had the potential for a rather gloomy atmosphere, but the richness and quality with which the restoration had been done afforded a quiet and restful ambience.

Entering the main lounge, Jason saw Jack at the far end of the bar, drink in hand, talking with the tall, red-haired barmaid named Carol. Walking the length of the car, he slid onto a stool next to Jack, who turned and smiled. "We were about to send out a search party," he said with friendly sarcasm. "I thought you said an hour."

"I think *you* said an hour. And what can I say? I made a bigger mess than I thought," he said with a sheepish grin. "Hello Carol."

"What can I get you?" Carol asked as she leaned over for her customary kiss on the cheek. Jason and Jack had met at The Box Car a little over four years ago. It had evolved into their usual meeting place, with Carol serving them often.

"A pint of Guinness," Jason responded with a flirtatious grin. "Maybe I'll finish this one."

"I'll bring it to your table." She smiled a broad, all-knowing smile, then turned away and busied herself filling drink orders. Apparently Carol had been told of Jason's mishap while watching the video.

Carol Dunsmure stood just under six feet tall. Blessed with a perfect complexion, huge green eyes and long, silky, natural red hair that hung nearly to her waist, she commanded attention in any gathering. Tonight she wore a white sweater that conformed to the contour of her upper body. A long silk print skirt hung from her narrow waist and draped provocatively over shapely hips. Medium-heeled, high-top leather boots covered her calves. At thirty-two Carol had been married once and divorced. Her marriage had fallen apart shortly after the disappearance of her nine-year-old daughter, Melanie, from a supermarket near their home in Benicia, California. Her husband had blamed her for the tragedy.

Shortly after the divorce, Carol had left Benicia and moved to Seattle, where she found a job at The Box Car. Jason and Carol had been involved at one time, but the relationship only lasted for a few months. Although they had been close, with Carol spending days or even weeks at a time at the loft, their time together had been stormy at best. During Jason's military career and shortly after, his relationships with women had been pursued for nothing more than physical gratification or simply a release from his tension. At times he had been sexually abusive, almost brutal. But with Carol he recognized that he wanted something different and he had tried to change. He found himself wanting to share more of himself with her, to be a tender lover and loyal companion. But he had lapses during the difficult times of their relationship, and because communication was difficult for him, he often retreated into an angry silence.

Rightfully so, Carol had become concerned and fearful of his behavior. But she too had problems. With no warning, she would fall into depression over the loss of her daughter and become unbearably crabby or sullen. Her radical mood swings resulting from the trauma of a husband's rejection and feelings of guilt took their toll on the relationship.

Realizing they both had demons in their pasts that hindered the lasting relationship they wanted, they parted ways. Yet they had enough regard for one another to remain friends.

Jason and Jack moved from the bar to their regular table in the far corner. Jason took the gunfighter's seat, so he could people watch, observing how "normal people" behaved in public.

"Sorry I took so long to get here. I needed a shower and a change of clothes," he explained.

"No problem. I just got here myself. I had to tuck Tommy in for the night. He's got some kind of a bug again. Debbie wanted me to spend a little time with him before I left."

"Anything serious?"

"Nah, I think it's just kid stuff. Who knows? They're always picking up something. At least I hope that's all it is."

Jack and Debbie, a pixie-like brunette, had three children. Jennifer was their oldest, thirteen, Ashley, ten, and Tommy, the youngest, had just turned four. Tommy had been born just shortly after Jason and Jack had met. He had a history of respiratory problems and seemed to be sick quite often. Jason often wondered whether Tommy suffered from something more severe.

Carol brought Jason's pint of tar-colored beer and another double scotch on the rocks for Jack, his second.

"Thanks, Carol. Start a tab, would you please?" Jason asked. She winked and patted his hand. They watched her long silk skirt sway as she glided back to the bar, then smiled at each other.

Jason returned to his concern, not only for Tommy but also for what Jack was drinking. From past experience, he knew Jack only drank hard liquor when he felt stressed, and his face revealed a weary tension.

"So, what's on your mind?" Jason asked. Jack looked up at his friend quizzically, and Jason nodded towards the scotch. "Looks like something's bothering you."

"I don't know, scotch just sounded good to me." By the look on Jason's face, Jack knew his response had fallen flat. He stared quietly at his drink and drew small T's in the condensation on the glass with the tip of his finger. "Hell, there's a lot going on," he confessed. "The finances are getting tight and my job's not looking too good either. Deb's worried about the money and wants to look for work . . . " Jack paused as if to consider their overall situation.

"And—we're both concerned about Tommy. He just doesn't seem to have any resistance. Seems to pick up every bug that comes along."

"What's the doctor have to say about his condition?"

"He doesn't give out much information. Says he needs to run some tests. I think it's got him baffled."

"Have you had a second opinion?"

"Not yet."

"What's happening at work? I thought things were going well for you."

"I honestly don't know, Jason. About six months ago, Cervicon restructured, if you can call it that. Martin hired a new chief of operations so he could spend more time away. His name is Richard Pathmoor. There's just no pleasing the guy. What makes matters worse, he's really pressuring me to approve a modified design for Suter that has gaping holes in it. He's on my ass all the time and with Martin gone most of the time, I've nowhere to turn."

Jack had been in Special Forces in Vietnam. He had turned out of the service and knocked around for two years until he came across Martin Cray, who had just started Cervicon. Jack hired on and lived ten years on sustenance wages while the company struggled to get established. Now twenty-one years after Jack had joined the company, Cervicon had become the industry leader in consulting and the design of custom security systems, with Jack as chief security engineer.

When Jack and Deb decided two years ago to build their dream house overlooking Lake Union, finances were not a problem since a substantial bonus had been promised on the contract awarded to Cervicon by Suter, a large pharmaceutical company moving into Issaquah. But since then, Martin Cray had unexpectedly taken an early retirement, which brought on the upper-end reorganization. With it came the new COO, Richard Pathmoor.

Two years after meeting Debbie, they married and when Jennifer was born, Deb stayed home to be a full-time mother and housewife. Supporting a growing family and saving for their dream house on one income proved to be an arduous struggle, a worthy effort resulting in a close, beautiful family.

Jason sometimes envied Jack and Debbie and their family. For it was something he never had the good fortune to experience.

Jason took a deep swallow of beer and slowly set the glass down, never taking his eyes from his friend. "What's with the finances, Jack?" he asked softly.

"I needed about fifty grand to finish the house, and rather than wait, I signed a note with the contractor to have it paid within a year after completion. It's past due by two weeks." Jack's voice became heavy with embarrassment as he continued. "The Suter bonus would have more than covered it but the project is so far behind schedule, it'll be at least another six months before completion. I feel like I'm trapped."

Jason saw the stress and weariness in his friend's face. "Jack I'm sorry." He moved his eyes from Jack and stared into his pint, apparently hypnotized by the black brew. After a long period of silence, he again looked into Jack's eyes with compassion. "Tell you what, why don't you let me take care of the note. You can pay it off when the project is finished. It'll take the pressure off you and Deb."

Jack's eyes welled. "I don't know what to say. I wasn't looking for a handout." He pondered the offer while he slowly swirled his drink in a circular motion, his eyes remaining hooded in embarrassed discomfort. "I have to be honest with you. I may not be at Cervicon by the time this project is finished. If that happens, I won't have a job or a bonus." He met his friend's eyes.

"You mean the sonofabitch would fire you?"

"He's making noises about it. If I don't get the project wrapped up, it's liable to happen. I'm not going to compromise on the system design, so your offer might turn out to be a poor risk."

"Hell, he'd be crazy to let you go. In any event, you let me worry about the risk. Talk it over with Deb if you want. Just let me know what you decide. I'll write you a check tomorrow."

"I'll talk to Deb tonight, but hold off on writing a check. I'll be leaving early tomorrow morning for Portland. Got a fast-track job down there. Some die-casting company was broken into early this morning. Apparently they're involved in some sensitive government contracts and they specifically asked for me to design a system for them. Probably have to sign a million nondisclosures." He smiled at the thought.

"What kind of stuff do they make?"

"Don't know. But I'm sure I'll find out tomorrow." Both men sat in silence for a moment, then with some timidity Jack said, "Jason, I—I really appreciate your offer. I'd rather work this out on my own but I just don't see how I can swing it right now. I think I'd like to take you up on it. It's a relief knowing my butt's covered."

"Jack, relax. You just tell me when."

Carol had begun her rounds again and was headed in their direction when Jack excused himself to go to the restroom. She slid into the chair that he had vacated and leaned across the table toward Jason. "Is Jack all right?" she asked, her brow knitted in concern. "He looks a little worried to me."

"Only because he is. Things are a little hectic at work for him right now," he answered, downplaying Jack's dilemma. "We talked it through; he'll be okay."

Carol's huge emerald eyes hypnotically drew Jason in and held him. He felt as though he were swimming in deep pools. He missed those eyes. He missed her, and wondered if there would be another chance for them. The moment became awkward and he realized he was staring. He forced himself to look away for a second, then looked back. "How have you been? I haven't seen you in a while."

Carol had sensed something in Jason but wasn't sure what. "That's because you haven't been in for a while. And to answer your question, I've been fine. How about you? You have the look of a man with something on his mind." She restrained a quizzical smile that held a just hint of tension.

Jason's thoughts came to a screeching halt, like gridlock in rush-hour traffic. He felt at a loss for words. He couldn't tell her that he missed her eyes or that he missed her.

"I just got back into town yesterday and hadn't planned on going out. I guess I'm just tired," he lied. He knew Carol's next question would be "Where did you go?" His trips were nobody's business and he cut her off before she could ask. "I heard I missed a hell of a storm."

"You did, and it was a doozy. Three and a half inches of rain fell between ten o'clock on Friday night to noon yesterday and we had wind gusts to ninety miles per hour! A lot of people in the outlying areas still don't have power or telephone service." Carol reached over and patted his hand. "Well, I'd better get on with my rounds." She stood and started to walk away, then turned and looked back. "Almost forgot. You want another?" nodding toward Jason's nearly empty glass.

"I'll have one. Jack's still good." She nodded and moved on to other tables.

Jason leaned back in his chair and watched the quiet, relaxed conversations of the patrons. An elderly couple sat in animated conversation at the opposite corner table. Three tables over, two women talked intently about something. Must be politics, or their husbands, he thought. Two men sat at the bar joking with Carol as she filled drink orders. Jason did a double take as a couple, who had their dinner brought to them in the lounge, stood to leave. Although a woman's legs unfolding from a leather mini skirt first caught his attention, it was the man with his arm tightly around her waist who made him stare. He had the same medium build and height as Jack and he wore a flowered shirt similar to Jack's. For an instant Jason thought it was Jack leaving with the legs.

"You look a bit perplexed, Bud," Jack said with a smile as he returned to his chair.

"Did you see that couple who just left?"

"No, I didn't," Jack said. "Why?"

"For a minute I thought you had a twin brother."

"Who has a twin brother?" Carol asked as she arrived with Jason's Guinness.

"That couple who just left. Are they regulars?"

"No, I haven't seen them before. Why?"

"Jay thought he looked like me."

"Jack, nobody looks like you. You're in a class of your own," Carol answered, with a coquettish wink.

Jason and Jack sank into comfortable conversation. When they finished their drinks, Jack glanced at his watch. "Want to call it a night?"

"I guess so. You'll probably need an early start in the morning.

"Yeah, I suppose so."

"Can I have a lift?"

"What a surprise," Jack said. "Sure."

It had not been an unusual request from Jason and not at all out of Jack's way to drive by the loft, less than two miles from the restaurant. Even though he owned two cars, Jason very seldom drove, unless he left the city on one of his clandestine business trips or on rare occasions, a date. Both his original, black 1965 427 AC Cobra and a new custom burgundy Cadillac Seville with copious amounts of engine and suspension work, spent a good deal of time in the parking garage under his loft.

The two men rose from their chairs. Jason stretched his back, then followed Jack to the bar and paid the tab, including a generous tip for Carol. After a peck on the cheek from her two favorite patrons, she waved them goodbye.

C H A P T E R T H R E E

Jason and Jack walked out into a balmy night, an unusual contrast to the fierce storm that had pummeled the area just twenty-four hours before. Now just after midnight, the temperature hovered in the low seventies. Both men wore light clothes, Jason in a sports shirt and slacks and Jack in a Hawaiian print and khakis.

Jason looked up into a clear sky. "You believe this weather?

"Nope. It feels like July," Jack answered, as they walked to Jack's light blue Ford minivan at the far end of the parking lot. Few cars remained in the lot and Jack's van was the closer of the two, a Jeep Cherokee on the far side. Jack unlocked the passenger door of his van for Jason and walked briskly around the front to the driver's side.

"Omigod!" Jack's voice held anguished horror.

Jason jumped from his seat and quickly ran around the front of the car. He saw Jack hesitate only for an instant, then crouch over the bodies of a man and a woman who lay motionless in a pool of blood between the two cars. The man was curled in the fetal position. The woman, face down next to him, looked like a haphazardly discarded Barbie Doll, her legs apart and arms sprawled in opposite directions. Jason recognized them immediately as the couple who had left The Box Car just half an hour before.

Jack checked the man for vital signs. "He's dead," he said, turning a face white with shock toward Jason.

Jason was already checking the woman, "So's she—no, Jesus! She's still alive. I've got a faint pulse. Help me roll her over!"

Having spent a good deal of time with trauma victims during their service careers, both men knew the drill. Jason went to the top of her head and faced her from above, checking her head, neck, back, and arms, then bringing them to her sides. Jack took her legs and gently slid them together after checking for wounds or fractures. They worked in perfect harmony as if they had rehearsed the procedure a hundred times. Neither one spoke until Jason asked, "You ready?"

"Let's do it," Jack replied, and they gently rolled her onto her back. What used to be a white blouse and skirt were now crimson and they had no chance of seeing the wound or wounds through blood-soaked clothes. Without hesitation, Jason ripped her blouse and bra open to expose her chest. Jack used his pocketknife to cut her skirt, panty hose and panties to expose her abdomen.

"Sonofabitch!" Jason spewed, livid at the sight of the woman's wounds. "Jack, get to the bar! Tell Carol to get out here with dinner napkins for compresses and anything she can grab for warmth. Call St. Francis' emergency and ask for Dr. Thomas Keller. Tell him what we have here and that I need him and the helicopter, like now. She's got to be opened up quickly if we're to have any chance of saving her. Be sure to tell him that I'm here with her. Then call the police and get back here. Oh—Jack—"

"What?"

"What time is it?"

"12:08," Jack said looking at his watch, and taking off in a sprint.

The woman had two visible knife wounds, one at the base and a little to the right of center of her left breast and another one half an inch above her navel. The wound at her breast did not seem to be much of a problem. The one-inch wide gash in her stomach concerned Jason. Her stomach and abdomen were swollen, indicative of massive internal bleeding. With the amount of blood on the ground there couldn't have been much life left in her.

"Come on, sweetheart. Hang on. You can do it. You've hung on this long. Help is on the way. Give us a little more time," Jason softly encouraged to her as he tried to stop the now slow flow of what little blood she had left, by gentle pressure.

"Dammit, Carol, get your ass out here!" Jason yelled in frustration, knowing that Jack probably hadn't reached her yet. The two hardest things for him to deal with were not being in control and the feeling of being helpless. Right now he had a bad case of both.

The old adrenaline juices had returned. Jason could feel the intense flow, carrying with it hate, anger, excitement and passion that washed over him like giant waves. Part of him hated this as he looked at this helpless person; he had seen enough mortal wounds to last a lifetime. But deep down, a bigger part of him loved the excitement, the intrigue. The sudden rush of emotion only served to frustrate him. And, as always, his involuntary protection from what he did not understand was anger.

"Oh God! Carol, hurry, please hurry." There was absolutely nothing he could do until Carol arrived. "Come on, baby, hang in there. You're gonna be just fine. "How fucking long do I have to wait?" he cried with mounting frustration. Each lingering second felt like an hour.

Realizing his energy would be better spent focused on something constructive, Jason began to consider what had happened. While continuing to apply life-saving pressure to the wound, he looked about for any kind of a clue. He saw no signs of a struggle. The woman's shoes remained on her feet, and without scuff marks, meaning no signs of being dragged and dumped. No blood trail, just pools, which meant the two victims had fallen where they'd been attacked. He wished he could get over to take a look at the man but only to satisfy his curiosity. The woman needed him; he was her only chance. Investigating what had happened to a dead man could wait.

He studied the wound by the woman's breast. Jason had been taught every conceivable way of killing in his Navy SEAL training, the position of the wound he saw was all too familiar. Using a narrow, medium-length blade, one can thrust briskly between the second and third rib, upward, causing a direct fatal laceration to the heart. Death is instantaneous. The technique requires surgical precision and is difficult to master, even for the most accomplished assassin. This attempt had been botched, her rib dead-centered, with the knife tip hitting unyielding bone. There had been no penetration. The inexperienced assailant had panicked and stuck her again in the stomach.

"Jason?"

"Over here." Jason yelled with relief.

Carol came around the corner of the parking lot. She hiked up her skirt and ran to him as fast as her long legs would carry her. She had brought anything that might be of some use: folded dinner napkins and white tablecloths. She had even found an old blanket in a back storage area and, of all things, a scotch tape dispenser.

She dropped to her knees beside him, giving no thought to their scraping on the asphalt. "Oh God," she said, turning pale in horror. She swallowed several times trying to gain composure. "What do you want me to do?"

"Use two of the dinner napkins to make a compress." He removed his blood-covered hand from the wound, then took the compress and Carol's hand and placed them over the wound, showing her the proper pressure. When Carol saw the stomach gash, she once again struggled to stay calm.

"Can you handle this?" She simply nodded. Jason gave her a reassuring hug. "That a girl."

He took another napkin to make a bandage. He taped the bandage to the wound under the woman's breast, using some scotch tape from the dispenser. He took some tablecloths and tucked them gently under each side, with the rest he covered her from head to toe, then followed with the blanket. She was so cold, so pale, he thought. After being satisfied that he had protected what remained of her critically low body temperature, Jason rolled the remaining tablecloths into logs and placed them under her knees and calves to elevate her legs. It was about all they could do for her until help arrived.

"Is . . . is she going to live?" asked Carol in a trembling voice, as Jason checked again for a pulse at her neck.

"I don't know. I don't know. I'm still getting a pulse. God only knows why. It's faint, but it's there."

Jason then turned his attention to the man to see if he could determine what had happened to him. He had to be careful not to disturb him. The last thing he wanted to do was compromise evidence at a crime scene. But he wanted to know. He opened the man's shirt, and found a knife wound at the base of the sternum, an efficient assassin's technique that he himself had often employed. Whether the victim knows his killer or is a complete stranger, the technique is the same. The assassin can approach from the front with a knife concealed in either hand. He quickly grabs the person behind the neck with the off hand, briskly pulling his face into his chest, while at the same time plunging the knife to the hilt, in and up from the sternum, moving the blade briskly back and forth, slashing the heart and lungs several times. Again, death is instantaneous.

Jason scanned the area for the woman's purse, nothing. He checked the man's pockets. No wallet either. A mugging? This can't be a mugging, he reasoned. It just doesn't look right. Two people attacked at the same time meant there had to be two assailants! Otherwise, there would be signs of a struggle, or the victims would be farther apart, or there would have been screaming or some commotion. What in the hell had gone on here? Was this a robbery gone bad, or a hit?

Jason stood and backed up so he could get an overall view of the scene. Something bothered him, other than the fact that one and three-quarters dead people lay on the black, cold asphalt. His concentration was interrupted as Jack returned at a fast run.

"The life flight helicopter should be on the way," he said, slightly out of breath.

Jason looked up at Jack and froze, seeing again Jack's uncanny resemblance to the man lying in the parking lot. The height and build, the shape and look of his face even the Hawaiian print shirt worn by each—one man could easily have been mistaken for the other. Jason felt a stab in his heart and silently prayed he was just being paranoid. Still, the scene took on new meaning.

"You look a little peaked. You all right?"

"You have any trouble with Keller?" Jason asked, avoiding the question.

"Not a bit, once I explained our situation and what you needed. He said they'd be on their way in less than five minutes." Jack wanted to ask how Jason knew Dr. Keller but it seemed unimportant as he looked down at Carol. "Do you need help?" he asked.

"No, I don't think so," Carol replied, unsure, her voice weak and shaky.

At 12:15 a.m. the city was very much alive and Fourth Avenue traffic, although lighter, cut into the night with the constant whine of tires and occasional honking of horns. Even so, they could hear the faint sound of helicopter rotors.

"Thank God," Jason said with relief. A moment later, they heard at least two sirens rapidly closing. "Jack, you have any flares?"

"Absolutely. I'll get them." Jack returned to his van, unlocked the driver-side door and pulled a package of flares from under his seat. Jason took half of what Jack offered.

"Let's mark out a landing zone." Jason, followed by Jack, headed toward an unobstrusted area of the parking lot. They quickly lit flares as they ran and formed a crude circle large enough to accommodate the approaching helicopter.

The first police car, a Seattle cruiser, came into view with a second unmarked car, close behind. Jason lit his two remaining flares and ran toward the parking lot entrance, one in each hand, waving them overhead to attract the approaching police cars. First one, then the other turned sharply into the parking lot, and sped directly toward him. Their tires squealed in complaint as they came to an abrupt stop, one on either side of Jason.

An officer in plain clothes exited the passenger side of the unmarked car. "What's the situation?" he yelled, to be heard over the rotors of the helicopter that had made a sharp descent toward the circle of burning flares, their ruby light and smoke creating a hazy aura of tentacles writhing toward a dark sky.

"We've got two stab victims, one male, dead, and one female who is hanging on by a thread. Life Flight is about to touch down with a doctor on board. "We'll be available to cooperate in any way we can, but first can we get that helicopter on the ground? The lady's in bad shape."

The officer turned to the Seattle cruiser and gave instructions to help Jack with the landing zone and to barricade the perimeter of the parking lot as a crime scene. He then turned to Jason once again and introduced himself.

"Detective Bob Montgomery. We'll need to get a statement from you," he said.

Jason responded. "I'll be here whenever you need me. But right now I need to meet with the doctor."

Montgomery nodded and climbed in the passenger seat of the unmarked cruiser as it moved towards Carol and the two victims. With the helicopter about to touch down, Jason ran toward the landing zone to meet the medical team.

The helicopter had no sooner made contact with the pavement when the doors swung open and three people emerged on a dead run. Jason's friend, Dr. Keller, led a short, blond RN whose face featured a classic adrenal addiction to trauma work, and a black male EMT bearing an expression of weary passivity. All wore blue St. Francis OR scrubs. Without a greeting, Dr. Keller questioned Jason for pertinent information as they dashed toward the scene. The EMT knelt down beside Carol while Keller settled on the opposite side of the victim.

"OK, ma'am, let me see what we've got here," Keller said with a soothing baritone voice.

Jason called to Jack and asked him to take Carol back inside the restaurant.

"You did well," he said to Carol, giving her shoulder a squeeze. She didn't respond and stared at the woman as Keller uncovered her and began his examination. Numbly, she rose to her feet and slowly backed away. "I'll meet you inside as soon as I finish out here," Jason called after her, but she did not look back as the two turned and walked away.

Necessity dictated that Detective Montgomery take photographs of the victims and the surrounding area. By the time the personnel from the crime lab arrived, the scene would be further compromised but the woman's life dictated the priority.

Jason turned and came face to face with a man in a wrinkled blue sport jacket with an SPD badge displayed from his breast pocket. "Jason Brisben, Officer," he said, extending his hand.

Something in the policeman's face unnerved Jason as he introduced himself.

"Lt. Dailey, Seattle Homicide," came the curt reply. He did not accept Jason's hand but continued to eye him suspiciously. "You've already met Montgomery," he added, nodding towards his partner still busy with the photos.

Lt. Dailey looked to be an overworked and overweight fifty-year-old. His open sport coat revealed a wrinkled white shirt stretched tight at the mid-section; seedy brown slacks, unshined black shoes, and no tie completed his disheveled appearance. A full head of black hair and scruffy black beard generously salted with gray did not disguise a fleshy, bloated face. Detective Bob Montgomery, by contrast, appeared neat and fit, his five-ten frame sporting clean Levi's and a blue shirt under a gray herringbone tweed sport coat, all of which were underscored with neon-white Nike athletic shoes.

"You want to bring me up to speed on what went on here?"

"My friend Jack and I came out of the restaurant and found these two lying in between the cars. We checked for vital signs and Jack ran in to call for medical help and the police."

"Why didn't you call 911?"

"Didn't have time. The woman was—is—just barely alive. Dr. Keller—he's the one working on her—is the head of ER at St. Francis'. I thought it would be faster to eliminate the middle man."

"You seem to know your way around this kind of situation," Dailey commented, still looking at Jason with a critical eye. "What's your background?"

"I did a couple of tours in Vietnam. I had to deal with my share of this shit." Jason, still uncomfortable with Dailey's suspicious demeanor, turned to watch the medical team work with the wounded woman.

"Damn. Her veins are collapsed. I have to cut down." Although a grave situation, Dr. Keller's voice held no hint of panic, simply a calm urgency. "I'm going to plumb her. Let's get some fluids going. Start a saline IV. And I want her on oxygen. As soon as I get her hooked up we'll get her onto the backboard and get the hell out of here." He prepared a syringe and handed it to the nurse. "As soon as I finish, give her this."

"You didn't leave me a lot to work with here, buddy," Keller said to Jason, as he continued with his scalpel and forced a tube into a collapsed vein.

"Well I didn't find a whole hell of a lot. I figure she's been here now for the better part of fifty minutes, counting the time it took you to get here. What kept you?"

"Thirteen and a half minutes to touch down. I got the call at 12:10. I'd say we did pretty damn good."

Jason looked fixedly at the woman. "What do you think?"

"Don't know, Jason. She's bled out pretty good, not breathing very well and she's colder than my ex-wife. Quite honestly, I'm surprised she's still with us."

"That's what I was thinking."

The two nurses and Keller worked with quick precision in preparing the woman for transport. Lt. Dailey and Detective Montgomery continued to take pictures and take notes while the other two uniforms put up stanchions with crime scene tape and marked the dead man's body location with chalk. When Keller signaled he was ready to transport the woman, Jason walked ahead and lifted the tape so the medical team could pass. They placed her on a gurney and rolled her quickly toward the Life Flight helicopter.

"Thanks, Doc. I'll call you first thing tomorrow. Take good care of her. "

"We'll do what we can, Jason." Keller's words were nearly lost to the sound of the helicopter as its rotors paddled the air, as if impatient to leave.

While Jason watched them load the woman into the helicopter, the coroner's wagon arrived, followed closely by the Scientific Identification Detail van. In a short time, the crime scene evolved into a hive of activity with the SID personnel scouring the area. Jason walked quickly over to Lt. Dailey, hoping to defuse some of the tension between them.

"Lieutenant?"

"Yes," Dailey said curtly.

"Is there anything I can do to help right now, or would you like me to keep out of the way?" Both men turned at the noisy turbulence of the helicopter's lift-off. It rotated and banked hard while gaining altitude over the canyons of the city, then disappeared into the night sky.

"Well, I gotta get with the lab boys and the coroner. Hang around a bit, just give me a minute here with the coroner." His voice had lost some of its edge.

Feeling that he had made some progress, Jason decided to penetrate the lieutenant's shell a little further. "If you like, I can mark the exact position of the woman for you. We found her lying on her face nearly on top of him." He nodded toward the deceased. "We had to roll her over to administer first aid. It will be easier for me to do before they remove his body."

"That'd be good. Bob, get him some chalk," Dailey said, nodding toward Jason and then strode briskly away with the coroner in tow.

Montgomery walked to Jason and handed him a fat stick of yellow chalk from his pocket, then followed him to where the woman had been lying. Jason drew an outline of the woman on the blood-covered asphalt and explained how they had found her, while Montgomery wrote the details in his note pad. When Jason finished his description, he and Montgomery joined Dailey who was still talking with the coroner.

When finished, Dailey turned to Jason. "Just a couple of questions and then you can wait in the bar with the others." He opened his notebook. "Have you ever seen these people before?"

"No, not before tonight. They had their dinner in the bar. I just happened to notice them as they were leaving."

"What time was that?"

"I can't be sure exactly. I wasn't wearing my watch, but I'd guess close to 11:30," Jason said, his face knotted in concentration. "Jack might be of some help; he looked at his watch just before we left. I figure we left just before midnight."

"So you estimate you found them at midnight?"

"Had to be close to that time, because we didn't spend more than five minutes with them before Jack went to call for help and that was 12:08."

"12:08? How can you be so sure?"

"I made a point of asking Jack the time."

Dailey eyed Jason appraisingly. "Uh, huh." He made a note, then flipped the notebook closed. "Okay, why don't you go inside."

Inside, Jack and Carol sat at the long maple wood bar, drinking coffee, neither one talking. A waitress Jason did not know was filling in for Carol and taking care of the cleanup.

"Hell of a night," Jack said as he looked up, his face full of distress and fatigue.

"Yeah, isn't it? You two okay?"

Carol looked up at Jason, then turned away. She stared blankly at the counter top, sipping her coffee, her hands wrapped tightly around the mug as if to take comfort from its warmth.

As Jason walked around the back of the bar to help himself to coffee, Jack said, "I hope this doesn't take long. Tomorrow's drive is going to come all too soon."

"Why don't you take off? I'll cover for you with Dailey. I can take a cab later."

"It won't work," Jack replied. "Dailey said the lab people are dusting my van for prints, so I have to wait anyway."

"Can't you call in and take the day off? My God, it's not like this is an everyday occurrence."

"Under normal circumstances, I would, but the way things are going at work I don't want to give Pathmoor any excuses to cause more trouble for me."

Jason moved back around the counter and sat next to Carol. He put his arm around her waist and pulled her to him. She laid her head on his shoulder and let out a long sigh. "God, I felt so helpless, so utterly helpless." Her voice was weak, her body trembling.

"We all did, sweetheart. You did just fine. Believe me, we did everything textbook. There was nothing else we could have done for her. We're the best thing that happened to that woman tonight. Without us, she would have had no chance."

Carol pushed herself into Jason's chest, whether for comfort or protection, she did not know. What she had witnessed in the parking lot took her back to the day she had taken

Melanie to the supermarket. Melanie preferred to look at magazines while Carol shopped, just like always, except this time when Carol came for her daughter, Melanie was gone. She would be fourteen now, a young woman.

If I only knew. Anything would be better than not knowing, she thought. Did Melanie end up like the woman in the parking lot? The thought turned her rigid in Jason's arms. He sensed the tension but mistakenly assumed it was a normal reaction to the incident in the parking lot.

Jason, also preoccupied with his own dark thoughts, looked over the top of Carol's head at his friend and debated whether he should bring up how much the dead man resembled Jack. Before he could decide, Lt. Dailey, Montgomery and another man with a badge hanging from his breast pocket entered the bar and walked directly over to them. Lt. Dailey introduced Cory Benson from SID.

"The three of us will question all three of you separately." Dailey stated, looking around the room. Without asking, he pointed toward the corner, "We'll use that large table over there."

"Mr. Brisben, will you accompany us?" And all three immediately moved toward the corner. Carol reluctantly moved away from Jason and made a fresh pot of coffee for everyone as he left to join them.

Cory Benson began the questioning. Little new information was added to what Dailey had already learned in the parking lot. No, Jason had not known the couple. Yes, he had seen them in the bar earlier. He did not know exactly what time they had left the bar, about 11:30, he guessed. He and Jack had come upon the victims in the parking lot.

Forty-five minutes later Jason became impatient and nearly lost his temper when asked again, to explain why he had called St. Francis' instead of 911. All three policemen took copious notes, asking and re-asking questions they believed pertinent before sending him back to Carol and Jack.

"Your turn, Mr. O'Connor," Jason said upon his return.

Jack departed, without comment. "How are you holding up?"

"Oh, I'm just fine," Carol said, with hostile sarcasm. "It's not every day you get to see two people murdered." She realized how it sounded and softened her tone. "I'm sorry. I'm not okay at all. I just feel so . . . oh hell—I don't know what I feel. I just want to go home."

Jason had seen more death than a thousand people see in a lifetime. This was Carol's first encounter with violent death. He felt sad for her but had no words of comfort. His only thought, hold her, would have to do.

"How long do you think this is going to take?" she asked.

"Not much longer. It's all pretty basic."

Carol released a long, painful sigh. "God I'm so tired. "I just want to go home . . . but I don't want to go home. I won't be able to sleep and I don't want to have to explain all this to Judy." Judy, Carol's roommate, would want to hear the whole gruesome story. "Jason, I really don't want to be alone tonight. Would it be . . . do you think I . . .?"

"You don't have to explain. You know that you're welcome. Besides, I'm not sure I want you driving in your condition. Jack's driving, so we might as well leave your car here. I'll bring you back for it tomorrow."

"I just don't want to be alone," Carol repeated apologetically, "but I don't want you to think that I'm trying to get something started again. Oh shit—Jason, I don't know what I want. I'm sorry I even asked. I'll just go home as soon as Lieutenant what's-his-name says I can go."

"Don't worry about it. It's not a big deal. You've been through a lot tonight. We all have. So relax and take it easy. I have no expectations. So don't worry. It's okay."

Carol relaxed only marginally. The sight of the woman, naked and bleeding, had brought back the mélange of emotions she had lived after the disappearance of her daughter. Although the circumstances were now entirely different, the pain of those same feelings, from the loss of Melanie and her ex-husband's rejection and blame, descended upon her like a cold and heavy fog. Now fatigue had settled in as well. A part of her was disappointed that Jason said he had no expectations. She wanted to feel connected, needed, loved, all of what she had previously been denied during her loss and the far greater and continuing horror of not knowing.

Jason noticed Carol's brooding silence. He could feel her trembling now and she was cold.

"Hey kid, what's going on?"

Carol turned her face toward him. When their eyes met, she unleashed a full flood of tears, her body shaking convulsively. "Jason, please, just hold me!"

Jason stood from his barstool and took her in a full embrace. She gave herself to his arms and buried her face in his chest.

He felt the warmth of her body against him and the wetness of her tears on his shoulders and chest as they soaked through his shirt and realized it felt good to be close to her again.

A few moments later, Jack returned.

"It's your turn in the barrel, Carol."

"Will you be all right with this?" Jason asked.

Slow in pulling away, Carol looked up at him and answered with more confidence than she felt, "I'll be fine."

He touched her arm as she turned away. "What did that couple have for dinner?" he asked.

She looked at him, confusion carving a deep furrow in her brow. Then after a moment, she responded, "Porterhouse steaks and Pinot Noir."

While Carol was away, Jason looked behind the counter for the meal ticket and payment receipt. It took but a few minutes to find a ticket for two porterhouse steaks and three glasses of Pinot Noir. The corresponding Visa slip yielded the pertinent details: Carston Jennings had left a $15.00 tip on a $58.85 tab. A generous man, Jason thought—his last act of generosity. He copied the name and number, walked to the table where Carol was being interviewed and interrupted. "I think I have an ID for you, Lieutenant."

Dailey looked up hotly at Jason, as did the other two investigators. "You? How?"

Jason handed Dailey the two pieces of paper. "The meal ticket and Visa slip, Lieutenant."

Dailey snatched the papers from him and turned to Carol. "Is this what you served them?" Carol nodded. "Well then, Ms. Dunsmure, it looks like we have all we need for the time being. I'm assuming we'll be able to reach you at your home or here at the restaurant."

Again a weary nod from Carol.

Dailey stood; Montgomery and Benson followed his lead. "Tell Mr. O'Connor that we'll go out ahead of him to make sure his van is released to him."

Jason and Carol returned to Jack who sat at the bar, nearly asleep. "We're out of here," Jason said.

CHAPTER FOUR

At 2:45 a.m., the dead bolt's sharp ker-slap pierced the interior silence of Jason's loft. The door opened; Carol entered, followed closely by Jason. He switched on the lights and immediately disarmed the alarm system located in a panel to the left of the entry, silencing the sharp irritating beep. Carol took a few steps into the kitchen area and leaned against the cooking island facing the windows with her arms wrapped tightly around her. Jason turned on the sound system and dimmed the lights to enhance the view. Soft piano music drifted into the room like an invisible fog.

He returned to Carol, placed his hands gently on her shoulders, and looked into her eyes. "Can I get you anything?"

"I don't know. God, I feel like I'm freezing," She vigorously rubbed the goose flesh on her arms.

Jason recognized symptoms of shock. "I'll turn up the heat. Why don't you take a hot shower and I'll make something warm to drink."

"That sounds good but I don't know if I can even move. I just feel numb."

"I'm sorry you got dragged into this; I didn't expect this to be so hard on you."

"What the hell *did* you expect! I'm not used to being around murdered people for Godsake!" She immediately regretted her outburst. Oh God! What's wrong with me, she thought.

Jason, surprised and unprepared for her anger, tensed and pulled his hands away. She could see frustration, pain, and anger written in his face. Before he had a chance to react, she spoke, attempting to salvage the situation. "Jason, I'm sorry. It's not your fault. I had no right to say that. I'm tired and I'm upset by what I saw tonight. I'm not angry with you. Please forgive me."

"It's okay," he lied, still smarting from the comment. "Go take your shower and I'll make us something warm to drink," he repeated. But a note of tension had crept into his voice. Carol knew that she had hurt him. She wanted to work through it, to set it right so he wouldn't stew over it. However, past experience had taught her Jason's limitations. She decided not to press and moved away to the guest bedroom.

Jason watched as she disappeared through the bedroom doorway, then moved to the thermostat. Although the loft maintained a comfortable seventy-two degrees, he readjusted it to seventy-five for Carol and returned to the kitchen. Moving mechanically from fatigue, he prepared some rum-laced hot chocolate, filled a carafe and set it on the island next to the range along with coffee glasses. He dimmed the lights further and went to his room to shower.

His master bedroom and bath were decorated with the same impeccable taste as the rest of the loft. A forest green-and-gold patterned Egyptian cotton comforter and matching pillows and shams covered a stunning carved Honduras mahogany queen-sized pencil post-bed. As Jason entered his room, he opened the floor-to-ceiling sliding glass deck doors, then drew the sheers closed. They gracefully wafted into the room, caressed by the gentle breezes that continually flowed across Elliott Bay.

This was Jason's favorite room. He loved to lie in bed and become lost in the artwork that graced his walls, or to relax in its comfort, reading a good book before falling asleep. Often he would just watch the ferries, container ships, and yachts as they moved silently on the sound.

The shower's hot water pummeled his face and chest and he placed his hands on the tile over his head, still angry, still frustrated with what had happened a few minutes earlier. Why, he thought, why do I shut down when I'm confronted in a relationship? It's as if I become paralyzed. I can't think of a thing to say unless it's aggressive and hurtful. All my life I've been programmed to meet aggression with equal or greater force or energy in order to win. And that's what cost me my relationship with Carol. I can talk with other people and ask them questions; they can share their feelings with me, but when it comes to me, I close up like an oyster. I don't know what I'm feeling. I guess I become frightened and that's humiliating. Then I get angry! I get embarrassed too, he thought.

Jason had in that moment, begun to understand a little bit about himself, about how he processed, or more accurately, didn't process. He realized he had no tolerance for being embarrassed or humiliated. Those two issues had been responsible for more conflicts than anything else in his life, both physically and with relationships. Suddenly, he felt exhausted. He leaned his head against the tile of the shower wall feeling the water skim past his head onto his back and down his legs. After what seemed an eternity, he reached for the soap, washed himself, and turned off the water.

Wearing only bikini briefs and a burgundy kimono, Jason returned to the kitchen and placed the carafe and the coffee glasses on a silver tray. Being preoccupied, he failed to notice Carol wrapped in a towel crossing from the guest bedroom into his bedroom. He picked up the tray and carried it to the coffee table in the living room area and sat down to look at the magnificent view that always seemed to calm him and bring him so much pleasure.

He had no idea how long Carol had been standing behind the sofa looking down to study him before he noticed her reflection in the windows. She wore one of his white dress shirts with green, burgundy, and blue pinstripes. Only the center button was fastened, providing a generous view. The dim indirect light from behind filtered through her freshly dried brilliant red hair and giving the appearance of fire. He turned and looked over his shoulder, drinking in her beauty.

"My God, you're beautiful! Come and sit. Are you warm enough in that outfit?" He took her hand and guided her around the end of the sofa. When she moved to sit, he realized she wore nothing but the shirt.

"I'm plenty warm now. The hot shower was just what I needed. I stayed in there so long I thought I would wrinkle."

Jason leaned forward and poured their drinks from the carafe. He handed Carol hers and leaned back as he tasted his. "Thank you," she said, looking into his eyes. They both stared at each other for some time, sipping their drinks. Then Carol spoke. "Jason, about my outburst. I'm really sorry. I had no right to take out my frustration on you. Please forgive me."

"It's okay," he replied. "You don't need to apologize. It's okay." He wanted to change the subject.

"No, it's not okay," Carol responded, holding his face fully with her eyes. "If you can find it in your heart, I need you to forgive me."

"You asked me to forgive you and I just did, and I said it was okay." Attempting to restrain his frustration, he continued. "Sweetheart, please be patient with me because I don't know what you want." Shock registered as he realized he had spoken what he'd been thinking. Carol mirrored his surprise.

"'*Carol, I forgive you*' is forgiveness," she said softly. You told me, '*It's okay.*' That's patronizing me."

"I don't understand the difference," he said, as he watched tears fill her eyes. Jason set his glass on the coffee table and placed Carol's alongside it. Taking her hand and pulling her to him, he put his arms around her and said softly into her ear, "Carol, I forgive you."

Jason held her tightly while gently stroking her back. Carol, with her head lying on his shoulder, whispered "Thank you" in his ear. They held each other for quite some time, neither one speaking, until Carol pulled away.

"I'm sorry that I took your shirt without asking. I didn't have anything clean to put on after my shower. I hope you don't mind."

"Does that mean that I have to forgive you for taking my shirt without asking?" Jason asked timidly.

"No, just tell me it's okay." Carol looked him straight in the eye with a grin and then they both burst into laughter. It would be some time before Jason realized the significance of what had just happened. Carol's need to be forgiven was as important as Jason's need to learn to forgive. He did now know with certainty, that he felt relieved, clean, free. His frustration and anger were gone.

They chatted, sipped their drinks, hugged, kissed, and petted each other like two teenagers in the back seat of the family car. Soon they realized how much they wanted each other. Jason stood and bent over Carol; she placed her arms around his neck as he lifted her effortlessly and carried her to his bed.

He dimmed the lights to a soft glow, crawled up beside her, gently unfastened the single button of her shirt. Her body responded to his caresses and her breathing quickened. In the past, Jason had been impatient, sometimes rough during sex. Tonight he concentrated very hard on being slow and tender. He no longer simply wanted sex, but to be Carol's consummate lover.

Gently touching with his lips and fingertips, he caressed her as a gifted violinist would relish and fondle his prized instrument. He not only drank in her beauty but her essence as well, and she responded in kind. Her whole body rippled with heightened sensation.

Trembling with expectation, she opened Jason's kimono and slid his briefs from him. When she could wait no longer, she guided him to her wanting embrace, shuddering with longing pleasure as she drew him to her.

The sun rose over the hills far to the east and when high enough in the sky, found passageways between the skyscrapers of Seattle, its reflection dancing on the chop of the Sound. Seven o'clock seemed very early to Jason as he rose and quietly stole from his room, not wanting to disturb Carol. He lovingly watched her sleep for a moment before closing the door and crossing to the guestroom to shower.

A little while later, Jason emerged in his kimono and picked up the glasses and carafe from the coffee table on his way to the kitchen. He brewed coffee, took a bottle of champagne from the wine cabinet, and put it in the refrigerator to chill. He squeezed fresh orange juice for mimosas and tucked it away with the champagne. The aroma from his cup of coffee soothed him as he padded to the sofa and watched the 7:30 ferry from Bremerton glide into the terminal.

* * * * *

Jason sipped his coffee, seemingly mesmerized by the view. But behind his stare he reflected on the past evening's events, examining the chronology: His arrival around 10:15, estimating the couple's departure roughly at 11:20 or 11:30. Jason thought about the time that it took to settle their bill and say goodbye to Carol. We must have hit the parking lot right at midnight. That fits, because we sure as hell didn't waste any time after we found them, and Jack told me it was 12:08 when I asked. That meant the woman had been bleeding for roughly thirty minutes. Way too long, he thought.

Jason went over the picture etched in his mind—Jennings, curled in the fetal position next to the Jeep and the woman sprawled nearly on top of him. If a robbery, why not just mug them and leave? Why kill them? The man's wallet is gone, the woman's purse missing. It has all the earmarkings of a robbery, but the way that they were attacked? No struggle. It looks more like a hit. Either they were taken completely by surprise or they knew their attackers. Well hell, I already figured out that much last night. I wonder who the woman is?

Jason still had an uncomfortable feeling about what had gone down. He retrieved his wallet and removed the piece of paper with the account number on Jennings' Visa slip and looked at the antique clock outside of the office wall—7:45. Too early to call the partners, he thought. I'll call Keller and find out what he knows.

He moved to his office and dialed Dr. Keller's pager number. While he waited for the return call, he sat at his desk and went through his mail that had piled up while he was out of town the previous week. The junk mail he tossed into the zero file, the correspondence and bills he filed in their proper places. After a trip to the kitchen to refill his coffee cup, he retraced his steps to the office. The moment he sat down, the phone rang.

"Brisben."

"You rang?" replied a tired voice.

"Good morning, Doctor. How's our patient this morning?"

"Well, it's a little early to tell. We just took her to ICU about thirty minutes ago. She hasn't regained consciousness. She had massive internal bleeding in her upper abdomen and stomach area. We had to open her up pretty good in order to piece her all back together. I hope she won't be too pissed at me because she ain't gonna look too great in a bikini. And that rib. She took a hell of a shot to her rib. It'll be sore long after everything else is healed up. She may have been oxygen starved, but it's too early to make a determination about brain damage, although I don't think there will be any. She was breathing on her own until just after we got here." Jason could hear a weary sigh. "I can't tell you a whole hell of a lot yet, buddy. I don't expect her to wake up for three or four hours, even if everything goes well. If not, . . . well, we'll just have to wait and see. You have any ideas on what happened out there?"

"No not really. We just found them on our way home."

"Lucky for her."

"Well, let's hope so. Say, Tom, one of the reasons I called, you have any idea who she is?"

"Yeah. We did get an ID. Apparently the Jeep belongs to her. They ran the plates through DOL. As far as we know, she's single. Her name is Lori Phillips. Date of birth, May 14, 1969, height: 5'- 4". Weight 112 pounds. Blond hair, blue eyes. Sound familiar?"

"Yeah she does," Jason replied in a depressed tone. He turned the page on his desk calendar and looked at the new date, Monday, May 15. There was an instant of sorrow as Jason realized that Lori Phillips and her friend had probably been celebrating her birthday. "Hell of a birthday present."

"Yeah, no shit."

"Have any info on her family?"

"Nope. Nothing on relatives or friends yet. We're working on it here and so are the police. I don't have anything on the John Doe and I don't expect to get anything from the police. My main concern is getting her medical history. I'm sure we're going to need it."

"Well, the John Doe is Carston Jennings. Picked his name off his Visa slip. Don't know anything about him other than his name. Say, do you have an address for our friend Lori?"

"Oh no, you don't! I've got my ass hanging out a mile, and I'll tell it to you straight, *we never had this conversation!* I've got a memo on my desk ordering me to meet the hospital director at 11:45 this morning, something about hospital regulations and the unauthorized use of a helicopter. I don't need to add breaking patient confidentiality to the list. This meeting has all the makings of a real party."

"I'm sorry, buddy."

"Ah hell. If she pulls through, we'll all be heroes. If not, you may end up with a roommate."

"If there's anything I can do . . . "

"Nah, you've done enough," Tom interrupted, laughing. His clashes with hospital brass were legendary. "I've got to get some sleep before my meeting. What's your schedule this afternoon?"

"I'll be taking Carol home some time today and I want to check in with my friend Jack. Other than that, no plans."

"Well, take your mobile with you. When she comes around, I'll call you with an update."

"Thanks, Tom, talk to you later."

"Count on it."

Jason returned the receiver to its cradle, rocked back in his chair, and stared off into space. He sat motionless for a few moments. His desk clock displayed 8:15. It shouldn't be too early, he thought, and picked up the phone again to dial Jack O'Connor's number. "Debbie, this is Jason."

"Jason! How are you doing? Jack told me what happened last night. It must have been awful."

"I'm doing okay. I thought I'd give Jack a call and see how *he's* doing."

"Well, he must be doing fine. He showered after he came home, only slept for an hour and a half, made a pot of coffee and rolled out of here at six o'clock."

"I thought he might take the day off, considering the circumstances."

"I tried to talk him into staying home. I don't know if he talked to you about what's been going on at work, but things are a little tough for him right now. He didn't want to give anyone an excuse to cause trouble."

"Yeah, he told me a little of what's been happening, but I can't help but think once his new manager gets his pins under him, he'll realize Jack's one hell of an asset."

"I hope you're right," Deb said with reservation. Changing the subject, she asked, "Have you heard any news about the woman you found?"

"I just got off the phone with her doctor. She's in intensive care and he's not making any bets. Apparently, she was on the operating table until around 6:30 this morning." Jason relayed the conversation he had had with Dr. Keller. He also told her about it being the woman's birthday. "If she comes out of this, we'll have to throw her one hell of a party."

"Count me in on that one," Debbie said. "What do you think about sending her some flowers? I have to take Tommy to the doctor later this morning. I could stop by the florist on my way home."

"That's a great idea," Jason said. "Well, I have a couple of calls to make and I want to check on Carol. She came a little unraveled last night, so I let her stay over."

"Oh, are you two on again?"

"It's a little early to tell yet. But I wouldn't mind giving it another try. As a matter of fact, that's one of the calls I have to make. I'm going to give Laura Mathers a call. Spent some time with her after Carol and I called it quits. Maybe she can keep me on track."

"Well, you'd be a great catch, Jay. You may have a couple of chinks in your armor but you're no different than the rest of us."

Jason wished that were true, but he knew better. "Thanks for the vote of confidence. Anyway, tell Jack I'll call him tonight. What time do you expect him home?"

"He didn't tell you? He won't be back until Wednesday."

"Oh, that's right, he mentioned something about that. I forgot. I'll wait until I hear back from Keller, then page him in Portland."

If you call him before he gets in touch with me, would you give him a message for me? While he was out last night, Martin Cray called and wanted Jack to call him when he got home. Oh, by he way, did some guy catch up with you two at The Box Car last night?"

"No", Jason answered guardedly.

"Well some guy called, wanted to see Jack last night. He said he worked with him so I told him where you were. He didn't leave a name. Jack came home so late, and after he told me what happened, I completely forgot about his messages."

A chill rippled through Jason. All of the uncertainty, the nagging feelings of the previous night converged. Now alert, his mind became a torrent of activity at the implications. His twenty-some years as a Navy SEAL had trained him to be suspicious of everyone and everything, and the nine months of de-programming at the end of his career had not quelled the skills he'd honed over two decades. Just cause for Jason feeling that he was nearly impossible to live with, another unfortunate side effect of his former profession.

At that moment, his training flashed through his mind, as if stimulated by an electric probe. He willingly embraced all that descended upon him, because someone he cared for might be in danger. During his career in the service, Jason had lost comrades to whom he'd been close. But to lose someone he loved in civilian life to an assassin would be intolerable. He would not allow it.   After mentally replaying the parking lot scene, the wounds, the victim's positions, he was positive now: the attack had been a hit—with Jack the target. He desperately wanted to quiz Debbie further but resisted the temptation for fear of alarming her.

"Jason are you still there?" Debbie's voice held humor tinged with concern.

"Yeah, I'm still with you. Just distracted for a minute. He hadn't realized he'd retracted into his head. "Anyway, that guy never showed, but it doesn't mean anything. He might have gotten lost. Don't worry, I'll give him the messages."

As he spoke, he felt two cool hands caress his face and a tender kiss on the top of his head. "Well, I'd better get started with my day," he said.

"Thanks for the call . . . and Jay, good luck with Carol."

Jason thanked her, and once again, returned the receiver to the cradle. He swiveled around in his chair to find a towel-clad Carol.

"Good morning," Carol said. She plopped into his lap, definitely in a playful mood. She flopped her wet hair back and forth across his face and chest and asked, "So, what have you been up to this morning?"

He did his best to disguise the turmoil brewing within him, undecided as to how much to tell Carol of what he now knew. She saw it in his eyes and immediately stopped her teasing.

"What's wrong?" She had read something in his face, plus he had yet to answer her original question.

He resented ruining her playful mood, but he could not lie. Jason relayed the essentials of his conversation with Keller and some of what he and Debbie had discussed. But he kept his suspicions about Jack to himself, wanting more information first, in particular, more information about Carston Jennings. Then he wanted to concoct a way to approach Dailey with his hypothesis. Abruptly, he changed the flow of the conversation, leaving no time for a response.

"Did you sleep okay?" he asked.

Carol eyed him suspiciously. "I slept fine. And you?"

"Like a baby," he said. He could smell the sweet scent of shampoo as she bent close to him. Her green eyes seduced him, and he could feel himself being carried away. They kissed, softly at first, then passionately. But, unfinished business still nagging at him, Jason fought to regain control of himself. "Okay—uncle! Look, I have one more phone call to make. It'll only take a minute. There is a bottle of champagne in the fridge and I've made some fresh o.j. Why don't you make mimosas and I'll finish up in here."

Aware that she had been dismissed, Carol accepted it with good nature. With a quick hug she left to mix the drinks.

He pushed speed dial, then said, "Joe Castellano, please."

Castellano, DiAngelis, and Partner was the law firm that Jason retained to handle his offshore accounts and to fester the ulcers of the folks at the IRS. In return, Jason provided covert investigation services from time to time. Joe Castellano and Benjamin DiAngelis had worked intelligence in Vietnam. The

"Partner," one Sobahr Taharin, had been previously a bean counter for the oil cartel and an ex-CIA operative in his former life. As the accountant and financial investigator for the firm, he kept a low profile. With their knowledge and connections, these men could access unpublished information on the Pope.

"Castellano."

"Joe, this is Jason. I need a favor. Would you run a credit card number for me? I need all the information you can get on a Carston Jennings." He briefly explained what had happened in the parking lot earlier that morning.

"What do you think you're into, my friend?"

"I have no idea, Joe. What I *do* know is the victim looked enough like my friend Jack O'Connor to be his twin. Same features, same build and they were wearing damn near identical shirts." He filled in the details including what he had learned from Debbie. "I'd just like to know what you can dig up."

"You think someone's trying to off Jack?"

"I don't know for sure, but it sure as hell has me thinking."

"All right, give me an hour."

Jason thanked him and hung up. He started to dial Lt. Dailey, then stopped, deciding to wait until he heard back from Joe.

Carol sat on the couch with two mimosas in flutes waiting patiently on the coffee table. Jason joined her, held his glass up to toast, and said resolutely, "To our relationship."

Carol, her mouth open in surprise, stared for a moment at Jason. "You're serious aren't you?" her voice cracking slightly as she asked the question.

"Yes, I'm serious."

"I don't know what to say," she said after another long hesitation. "I thought . . . I mean, when we called it quits, you told me you didn't think you would ever be able to handle a close relationship." Carol paused again, then added, "Honestly, I didn't stay here last night to try to get something started again."

"Shh—shh." Jason tenderly put his finger to her lips, leaned over, and kissed her cheek. He took her drink along with his and set them on the coffee table, then took her hands in his. As he began to speak, he could feel the mystery surrounding Jack gnawing at his subconscious, but, as before,

Carol's hypnotic emerald eyes drew him in and he soon forgot about everything but her.

"I know what I said about our relationship, but that was because I felt I'd never learned to communicate. When it comes to dealing with my feelings, I become frightened and frustrated. My mind just goes blank and that makes me angry. So rather than risk a blunder, I stay silent, and that hurts you. But last night, you prodded me, but you were patient and helped me understand just a little of what Laura encouraged me to work on in our sessions two years ago. I know you have some issues to work through too, because of the loss of Melanie, but as frightened as I am of your moods, and my not being able to understand, I really think I'd like to try our relationship again. Carol, I think I love you, and I guess I want to find out for sure—if you're willing."

Carol's face flushed with emotion and her eyes filled.

"I'm not suggesting that we live together," he continued. "I just would like to find out if we could make it work, and if we can, I think I'm ready to commit to something more."

"Jason," she said through her tears, "do you know that you have never told me that you love me before?"

"I never thought about it, but it makes sense. I wanted to tell you several times, but telling you 'I love you' made me feel vulnerable. Now, it scares the hell out of me because I don't want to let you down. I think I'm ready to see Laura again; maybe she can help me understand and work through some of this."

"The hardest thing for me to handle was your silence," she said with tears streaking her cheeks. "It made me feel like I had done something wrong or that I was being punished again. I'm frightened too, Jason, and you're right—I haven't gotten over Melanie or worked through all my emotions and anger. But—but I don't want this to slip away from us again."

Jason handed Carol her glass, then took his, and they solemnly touched them together. As Jason leaned back against the sofa cushions, Carol turned so that her back rested against his chest, her head against Jason's cheek. "This feels good," she said, "the mood, the drink, the closeness, and it feels good just to be held."

They continued their private thoughts in silence, slowly sipping the subtle mixture of orange juice and champagne. Jason watched the marine traffic on the bay and inhaled the sweet fragrance of Carol. He wondered where his sudden bold-ness had come from, wondered what he had gotten himself into. With his commitment to their relationship, he was break-ing new ground, and while he wanted it, it also unnerved him. He had to smile at the irony. He had faced situations when he thought he would go to prison. Hell, he thought more times than he could remember that he was about to die. He'd killed people, stared into their faces and watched their eyes become vacant as life abandoned them. It never affected him like this. It just didn't seem to make sense, and how could he share those things with Carol?

Carol must have sensed something and broke the silence. "You're awfully quiet."

"Yeah. Just thinking. This is a big step for me. I don't want to screw this up," he confessed.

"Stop fretting. We'll take it slowly . . . and we'll work through it together, with lots of patience, love, no pressure. We have the rest of our lives. We'll be just fine. I promise."

Her words were encouraging but at the same time they filled him with apprehension. He wished he could believe. He gave her a squeeze of appreciation and leaned back with her in his arms. She took his hand in hers and placed it under her towel. They sat in silence, watching boats and ferries in the sound with Jason's fingers lightly tracing her contours.

"That feels nice." She loosened her towel allowing it to fall open. Her body became sensitized to every caress as she lay relaxed and contented in Jason's arms. Contentment, she wondered? Something that she had had precious little of in her life.

Carol responded to the soulful feelings of being protected, cared for, a sense of oneness, and completeness, all becoming reality as their love-making intensified. Once again, the sym-phony of love continued building to its crescendo as the two frolicked, intoxicated in their union. Then came the quiet throb-bing afterglow of two spent lovers, peace and tranquillity wash-ing over them as they basked in mutual love.

The two lay together in a sort of suspended animation for some time before Jason rolled his head back and looked at his wall clock upside down. The pendulum swung back and forth like a metronome in slow motion. Jason treasured the clock, a 150-year-old, three-weight regulator with a porcelain face and a Grande Sonnerie movement. He traced the antique clock's lines with his eyes as it struck the quarter-hour signature— 10:45. Should he take Carol to lunch, then to pick up her car at The Box Car? Yes, that way he could spend more time with her. Suddenly, visions of the restaurant's parking lot and the gruesome murder pressed in on him, bringing him back to reality.

He needed to call Dailey, to voice his theory about Jack.

He turned his face back to Carol and watched her for a moment. Eyes closed, the corners of her mouth turned up slightly, she seemed at peace.

"I'm hungry," he whispered in her ear. "Shall we dine in or out?"

"Hmm?" Carol responded drowsily. She turned her face toward Jason, her eyes opened as if coming out of a deep sleep. "Did you say something?"

"Uh-huh." Jason replied with his face now right in front of hers, brushing his lips softly against her cheeks. "I'm hungry. Shall we dine in or out?" he repeated.

"Gee, I think I'd rather stay right here . . . for about a week. Do we have to move?"

"Yes, we have to move. I have things to attend to this afternoon."

"Oh, okay." Carol rolled over on top of Jason and gave him a passionate kiss. "Will you wash my back?"

"Right. That'll save a lot of time," he laughed. They struggled to their feet. "Go get the water started. I have to make a phone call, I'll be there in a minute."

Jason went to the office and found a message from Joe Castellano.

"Carston Jennings is from Vermont," his voice mail said. "Thirty-eight years old, single, forty-four K annual income. Three credit cards, zero balance every month. The guy's a school teacher, some kind of sha-hooty in special ed. Your boy's a genuine Eagle Scout. Not even a traffic ticket. No reason we can find that someone would want to take him out. Call me if you need any more info. Have shovel, will dig."

When Jason finished listening, he called Dailey. He was unavailable, so Jason left a message that he needed to talk, along with his cellular number.

Jason and Carol emerged from the master bedroom looking like models for a *GQ* unisex clothing ad. He wore light gray-green linen slacks, a burgundy and green print silk sport shirt and bare feet in Bally loafers. Carol sported Jason's latest—pinstripe navy slacks, blue-and-white pinstripe dress shirt, without her bra, (a nice touch Jason thought) a yellow blue-spotted tie and Jason's authentic Japanese bath-house thongs that he acquired in Japan while in the service. Carol had two wardrobe choices, the previous day's clothes, or Jason's finest. She opted for the latter.

The elevator opened in the parking garage and they walked toward Jason's cars. "Well, it's a beautiful day. You pick the car."

"That one." Carol pointed to the canvas-covered car sitting next to his burgundy Seville.

He removed the cover with its velour lining, exposing an original black, hand-rubbed, 1965 AC Cobra that reflected light like a contoured mirror in the dimly lit garage. He folded the cover and placed it in the trunk of his Seville, while removing his cell phone that he often stored there. They buckled up and Jason turned the ignition key. The motor hadn't turned over three full revolutions before it exploded to life. The finely tuned exhaust system resonated through the garage as the engine's radical camshaft made the big 427 engine roll and lope like a fuel dragster hunting for an idle range.

They eased out of the garage onto Virginia Avenue and up the hill toward the northbound freeway entrance to I-5. As they waited at the red light at the freeway entrance, the powerful engine sent harmonic vibrations through the car, transmitting them to the seats. The phenomenon awakened Carol to the not yet subsided tingling between her legs, a pleasant residual from the morning's activities. She began to smile.

Noticing her happy smirk, Jason asked, "What?"

"I like this car!" Carol replied, laughing.

At the first sight of the green light the Cobra bolted onto the freeway, off to lunch at the Mukilteo Ivar's just five minutes west of Carol's Everett home.

C H A P T E R　　F I V E

Only 187 miles separated Jack's home from Portland, but it seemed a long and arduous trip. He had been exhausted before he left home and now the tedious merging with the 8:30 a.m. Vancouver commuter traffic headed across the Columbia River into Portland made the trip more tiring. Biddwell Die Casting, located at the southern end of the Portland metropolitan area, required Jack to travel through the city during the crush. He had overshot his nine o'clock appointment by fifteen minutes when he rolled into the Biddwell Business Park's lot. He inched his van into the last visitor spot next to a Portland police cruiser. Tired, frustrated by traffic, and running late, Jack found his morning not to be shaping up as well as he would like. A spectacular sunrise and the fresh green of spring had been the only saving graces of the drive.

Jack opened his door and lethargically forced himself from the van, took a long stretch, picked up his briefcase and walked to the reception area. At forty-five years old, five feet ten inches tall, 175 pounds with brown hair and blue eyes, Jack was a handsome man by most standards, his only flaw a nose that seemed just a little small for his face. He had good posture and kept himself fit. His silver satin flight jacket with Cervicon embroidered on it reflected the morning sunshine as he entered the building, a striking accent to his navy slacks, white shirt and tie.

The reception area sat in a spacious glass enclosed atrium canopied by tall tropical trees. A dramatic black-lacquered desk and counter combination surrounded the petite brunette receptionist in a half circle. The nameplate on the counter identified her as Lisa. She looked up from her computer monitor and greeted Jack with a comfortable smile.

"Good morning. May I help you?"

"Yes. My name is Jack O'Connor with Cervicon. I have an appointment with Peter Hargrave and Donald Biddwell."

"Oh yes. They've been expecting you." Retaining her smile, she asked him to sign the visitor registry while she made him a badge.

"I'll see if I can locate Peter," Lisa said, rising from her chair. She winked at Jack, handed him his badge and quickly disappeared down the hallway to announce his arrival. Jack took a long look. Easy, big fella, he thought to himself as he watched her buns shimmy away in her tight, bright, flowered print mini dress. She reminds me of the telephone company— every line is busy.

A large burly man, appeared in the hallway and moved full stride toward Jack. He wore his sandy-colored hair clipped short, his attire casual with loafers, khaki trousers, and a golf shirt.

"Good morning." He extended his hand and smiled broadly. "Peter Hargrave, General Manager." Though the greeting seemed enthusiastic, Jack picked up on the subtle way in which Hargrave appraised him.

"Jack O'Connor," he returned, trying to muster the energy to match the vice-like grip of Hargrave's handshake. "Pleased to meet you, Peter."

They exchanged business cards, Peter giving Jack's a cursory glance before sliding it into his shirt pocket. "We've been expecting you. How was your trip down? Did you fly or drive?"

"I drove. It wasn't too bad, and the weather doesn't get any better than this."

"Well, you're just in time. The cop just got here, so now we won't have to hash over all the information twice. Come on back. I'll introduce you around and we can get started."

Jack followed Hargrave down a long hallway into a spacious conference room. Four men sat comfortably in blue cushioned chairs around an oval, black walnut table. The off-white walls of the brightly lit room displayed several large photographs of several sophisticated die castings. A large window at the far end of the room overlooked a garden in full bloom, filled with red and pink rhododendrons and azaleas.

"Gentlemen, this is Jack O'Connor, our security consultant from Cervicon," Hargrave said. Introductions ran around the table: Donald Biddwell, the owner and president, Bill Velrose, the COO, Tim Halderman, the shop foreman, and Todd Buckwalter, the investigating Portland police officer. Jack seated himself and Hargrave joined them after closing the door.

Jack asked for permission to use his tape recorder to facilitate an accurate record. There were no objections.

Todd Buckwalter, the police officer, a short, stocky man with curly hair, his kevlar vest making him look rather pudgy, opened the proceedings. "This is the beginning of the formal investigation of the break-in. First, I'll be asking pertinent questions, then everyone will adjourn to the shop for a walk-through. Afterwards, we'll return here for questions and answers. Also the SID, that's an acronym for Scientific Identification Detail, people completed their fingerprint sweep during the preliminary investigation last evening. However, because of the hostile environment, mainly oil, grease and smoke residue, they felt that it would not yield much. Also, I've asked the Monday first shift to stay home until noon in order to preserve any evidence that still may be recovered."

Bill Velrose, COO, explained to Buckwalter and Jack that Biddwell Die Casting had a Sunday maintenance man who came in every Sunday afternoon at 3:30 p.m. to do the weekly maintenance of the die casting machines. His responsibility also included preheating the dies that were in the machines to ensure they would be hot and ready to run Monday mornings when the crew arrived. He had been the one who discovered the break-in and had phoned the police and the chief of operations. Velrose in turn called Peter Hargrave who contacted several alarm companies. Two of them had recommended Cervicon, Hargrave said.

They reviewed the initial report and a list of known damaged and missing tools and equipment. Based on the information presented, it began to look like sabotage to Jack. It became apparent that whoever perpetrated the exercise was familiar with the die cast process and machines.

"I have three possible scenarios running through my mind," Jack said interrupting—"a competitor, an ex-employee, or someone still in your employ."

"You may be on to something," Peter Hargrave, added. "The plant key lock box was jimmied and all the keys are missing. A disgruntled employee or ex-employee looks promising."

"We have in excess of $100,000.00 in government orders due in just two weeks," Biddwell stated, with grave concern. These concurrent projects for the Navy F14 Tomcats, Air Force F15 Fighters upgrades, and smart bomb components, represent a quarter million of our billings for the next two months. From the damage report I've heard here, six of our ten dies have serious damage. Forgive me if I seem a little panicky, but we have our backs to the wall here. Let's focus on how we recover and make our deliveries and worry about how it happened when we have a little breathing room. And, I charge you Mr. O'Connor, to make damn sure this doesn't happen again."

Immediately upon completion of Biddwell's statement, the group of men adjourned to the casting shop in an attempt to ascertain exactly what had happened. Jack would use the information to develop a security plan, Hargrave and Halderman to form a recovery stratagem.

They entered a plant that normally would have been a hive of noisy activity. This morning an eerie quiet prevailed. Ten die cast machines ranging from the size of a small car to a large semi truck stood silent.

Tim Halderman spoke as he led the small group. "The die cast machines' sizes are designated by tons of mold platen clamping pressure. The mold platens hold the die halves in the machine during the metal injection process. The clamp tonnage is important to keep the die from 'squirting or flashing' the parting line while introducing thirteen-hundred-degree metal into the dies at high velocity at 9,000 to 20,000 pounds of injection pressure."

Trim presses stood at the end of every casting machine as well as strategically placed second-operation machines for sanding, drilling, and so on. A CNC shop, for post-machining the castings in the building across the parking lot afforded Biddwell customers the option of complete finished goods. The efficiently laid out shop allowed materials to move in one door and out another. After seeing the operation, Jack understood Buckwalter's reservations about obtaining usable fingerprints. All the tools, equipment, ceilings, and floors had a thin oil film from the die spray being atomized as it hit the hot dies.

Jack felt affirmed in his suspicions regarding sabotage. The person or persons who wreaked the kind of havoc he witnessed were either angry or wanted to shut Biddwell down, and possibly both. He took notes, made sketches, and used his recorder. Halderman pointed out extensive damage to the six dies scheduled to run that morning. All for the defense project. Every toolbox had been broken into, so none of the die casters would be able to do their jobs effectively. The keys, all missing from the jimmied lock box. The fact that all of the expensive measuring instruments and computers remained untouched, appeared odd. The offices had been rifled but nothing had been taken, or so it seemed.

At eleven-thirty, everyone returned to the conference room. Hargrave called Lisa in to take orders for sandwiches so they could continue with business.

After Lisa left, Jack spoke first. "I'd like to make a few suggestions if I may."

"The floor is yours," Peter Hargrave said.

"First I'd like to ask a couple of questions." A nod of approval rippled throughout the room. "How many people do you have who are capable of die cast machine maintenance and repair?"

"Four, maybe five," answered Halderman.

"Good. How long would it take them to purge the hydraulic systems on all of the die cast machines and trim presses?"

"What are you getting at?" Donald Biddwell asked, looking confused at the question.

"What I'm getting at, Mr. Biddwell, is that I believe you've been raided. I am aware that you hired an alarm company. However, Cervicon is a bit more. We are a full service security company, which means we do complete investigations and analysis before we design a system. What I *did* notice during our walk-through was the hydraulic fill ports on several machines had oil pooled around them, like they had been over-filled. It's entirely possible someone has contaminated your hydraulic systems with sugar, sand, or any number of chemicals. I have a feeling that what we've seen this morning might just be a smokescreen. I think someone is trying to cripple you or even put you out of business."

"I sure as hell don't understand any of this," Biddwell lamented. Why would anybody want to shut us down?"

"I can't answer that, Mr. Biddwell. But I can tell you, from what I've observed this morning, I'd say there's more here than meets the eye. Just take a minute to look at a couple of things that we know for sure: You have defense contracts that are on critical path. You have die damage to the tooling that you need to fulfill those contracts. I contend, and mind you, it's just speculation, the machines used to run those dies may have been compromised as well. It's entirely possible that whoever did this is betting that you will be too preoccupied with the damage and getting back to normal production to take the time to check out the equipment. It could be disastrous. And there's one more issue that hasn't been addressed. Is there any product missing?"

"Not to our knowledge, but we haven't had time to do a full sweep," Hargrave answered, then turned to his COO. "Bill, I want that checked out as soon as we're finished with this meeting."

"We've got product right now that we're already late on," Biddwell interjected. "We'll be down for a week!"

"Not necessarily," Jack continued. "Tim, how many hours will it take for two men to do a complete check on a machine?"

"Oh, I'd say about two to four hours per machine," the shop foreman answered.

"How long for a complete system purge?"

"Six to eight hours."

"That means the machines that check out with a clean bill of health could be running by the time the second shift is scheduled," Hargrave said.

"And the ones that don't check out could come on line at the rate of two per day beginning tomorrow's first shift, providing you can get a crew to work through the night," Jack added.

"Now I understand why Cervicon came so highly recommended." Peter Hargrave nodded his approval across the table to Jack. He looked at his watch and turned to his foreman. "It's five to twelve; you have your crew coming at noon. I want you to get started now. I'll bring you up to date on the rest of this meeting later." With a nod to Jack, Tim rose and left the meeting.

"It's a sound plan," Biddwell complimented. "We won't have to worry about the equipment. Peter, you handle the plant issues, and I'll take care of damage control with late deliveries."

"There's one issue that we haven't covered," Jack said.

"Yeah, the perps," Todd Buckwalter, interjected. "The way I see it, you have two possibilities. One, a pissed-off employee, or two, a pissed-off ex-employee. You folks had any confrontations with any of your people lately? Any people been turned down for raises, anything like that?"

"We have very little turnover with our employees, Officer," Hargrave said. And as far as ex-employees, we haven't let anyone go for a long time."

"Well, it's something you might want to review in your personnel files, because this wasn't done by kids looking for pot money," Buckwalter said.

Todd Buckwalter finished his investigation and report, then excused himself from the meeting. Jack began his preliminary proposal for the new security system and arranged for a complete lockdown.

Lunch and the locksmith arrived, and as locks were rekeyed and sandwiches inhaled, Jack laid out a plan to shut the plant down from Friday afternoon to Sunday afternoon in order to install the internal monitoring portion of the security system. That brought on more questions from Mr. Biddwell who was justifiably concerned about the loss of production. Another explanation and tough sell. But that was okay with Jack, who spent a good deal of his time in the field working with the customers.

At 3:30 in the afternoon, Kevin the maintenance manager entered the room with a grim announcement. "We've detected contaminants in the hydraulic systems of machines one, two and eight. I'll bet we'll find the same in at least two more of the machines. The machines we predominantly use for the government parts." Someone knows Biddwell's operation well, Jack observed.

Donald Biddwell, Peter Hargrave and Bill Velrose all went to survey the latest development, leaving Jack alone in the conference room. He continued to work on the security system design, made arrangements for materials, a crew for the weekend, and hired two night watchmen for the interim until the system would be fully functional.

At 4:15, Jack's pager went off. He puzzled momentarily at the number, then leaned back in his chair and closed his eyes, suddenly exhausted. After resting for a few minutes, he collected his notes, order forms, tape recorder and laptop, dumped it all into his briefcase and walked out into the shop.

He found the management group gathered by machine number one, staring at buckets of hydraulic oil with the consistency of cottage cheese.

"Have any ideas what it is?" Jack asked Hargrave.

"Not yet, but it's some nasty shit," he replied. "Whatever it is, it's corrosive as hell."

"Has it had enough time to do any damage?" Jack asked.

"I don't think so. We owe you one, Mr. O'Connor."

"I'll be checking in at the Holiday Inn across the freeway, you can reach me there if you need me," Jack informed the group.

Ten minutes later, Jack stood in his room examining his weary reflection in the mirror.

"Ain't you a sight." He slowly backed up and fell backward onto the bed, looking up at the patterned ceiling for only a moment before his eyes closed.

C H A P T E R   S I X

The warm weather made the forty-minute drive to Mukilteo a pleasure. The heavy traffic moved briskly along and Carol's hair whipped in the wind like a campfire dancing in a stiff breeze. Carol felt a closeness to Jason, but sensed his growing preoccupation by the time they reached the restaurant. After being seated, Jason excused himself to make a phone call.

"Lieutenant Dailey, please. Yes, I'll hold." It took nearly five minutes before Dailey picked up.

"Homicide, Dailey."

"Lieutenant, this is Jason Brisben."

"Yes, Mr. Brisben, what can I do for you?" he said brusquely as if in a hurry.

"It's about last night, Lieutenant." He hesitated for a moment, not quite sure how to proceed without sounding as if he were an alarmist. Just get it out, he told himself. "Since last night, I've discovered some information that leads me to believe that someone is trying to kill my friend Jack O'Connor. In fact, I think the man in the parking lot may have been killed by mistake."

A long pause, then, "What information would that be, and why do you think it was a mistake, Mr. Brisben?" His voice projected a guarded interest.

But Jason wanted to leverage the situation and glean information about the police investigation. "First, let me ask you a question, Lieutenant. Didn't you find it strange the way the man and woman were found, and the nature of their wounds?" After he heard the question he'd asked, Jason could have kicked himself. It sounded as though he were questioning Dailey's competence as an investigator.

"You haven't answered my question, Mr. Brisben. What information?" Dailey said, without a hint of hesitation.

Jason hesitated, realizing that if he told Dailey about his conversation with Debbie, the lieutenant would be over there questioning her in a heartbeat. He could not let that happen. He wished he had thought things through a little better before he made the call. Now he would sound like an idiot.

"Lieutenant, if you examine the photos that were taken at the scene last night, I'm sure you'll notice that the victim bears an uncanny resemblance to Jack O'Connor. I know there was no purse or wallet at the scene, but that was probably just to make it look like a robbery." Jason realized the more he talked, the deeper was the hole he dug for himself.

"Mr. Brisben," Dailey said. His patience obviously wearing thin. "You still haven't told me what *relevant* information you seem to think you have."

"Stupid, stupid, stupid," Jason muttered to himself. "Lieutenant, Carston Jennings was a school teacher from Vermont. He's practically a canonized saint, some big-wig in special education. He was single, had no debts, and didn't gamble. Probably on a date celebrating Lori Phillips' birthday. There is nothing to suggest that there'd be a reason to contract him."

"Whoa. Whoa. Whoa! Where the hell did you get your information on Jennings?" Dailey said hotly. "Where the hell are you now?"

Jason realized he had just kicked a sleeping tiger, and he had no tail for leverage. "We need to talk, Lieutenant. I'm . . ."

"Now that's an understatement. Where are you?"

"I'm up in Mukilteo. I'll be back sometime around two-thirty. I'll call you when I get in."

"I got your message earlier; I'll wait for your call . . . and, Mr. Brisben, a piece of advice: Don't be mucking about in a murder investigation." With that said, the line went dead.

Carol glanced up from the menu as Jason slid into the booth. She knew immediately his call had not gone well. "What's wrong?" she asked.

Jason wrestled with two problems, first the way he had blown the conversation with Dailey, and now how much, if anything, to tell Carol. "Nothing," he lied. So much for honesty in a relationship, he thought.

The look on her face said it all. What had promised to be an intimate lunch suddenly took on the feeling of something else, and he knew where to place the blame.

"Jason, you've been brooding about something for the last twenty minutes," Carol said. She decided to press, knowing full well from past experience a volatile encounter might follow.

It hurt Jason to look into Carol's eyes and see not only her strength, but also the fear and pleading. He decided to tell the truth or at least part of it. "Look, I can't talk about it until I have more information. It's about last night. Something's not right about what went down, and I don't want to involve you in it, at least until I figure it out."

"It's something you found out this morning, isn't it?"

He simply nodded. Carol's frustration mounted at not knowing the details but did her best to let it go. Curiosity is an ugly beast to control when trust has been destroyed by a tragic past.

* * * * *

Jason turned from Western onto Virginia Avenue and as he did, he spotted the unmarked police cruiser double-parked next to his parking garage gate. His rowdy engine and loud exhaust brought mixed reactions of envy and annoyance from the pedestrians as he pulled to the entrance. While waiting for the remote-activated gate to clear, the doors of the police car flew open disgorging Dailey and Montgomery. Dailey did not look happy. Carol glanced questioningly at Jason but he remained silent, his eyes focused only on the gate. He too did not look happy. The garage reverberated at the low resonance from the Cobra, and finally with the car parked and the engine now quiet, the silence became nearly as painful as the noise, the tension even more so.

Jason opened Carol's door just in time to be greeted by a hard-faced Dailey. "Miss Dunsmure, Mr. Brisben, you remember Detective Montgomery."

Jason had not expected Dailey to show up on his door-
step, and immediately copped an attitude, not so much visible, but Carol felt it, the old Jason, a cool hardness emanating
from every pore. He quickly took control. "Lieutenant, Detective, you're just in time for coffee."

"You're probably aware that this is not a social call, Mr.
Brisben," he stated harshly. "We have a lot to talk about."

The folder Dailey clutched tightly in his hand did not go
unobserved and Jason instinctively knew its contents. He
quickly glanced at Carol who looked unnerved at the now palpable tension.

"Well, Lieutenant, I guess we'll go upstairs and deal with
that," Jason said, nodding toward the folder. Before Daily could
respond, Jason turned on his heel, took Carol by the elbow
and walked her to the elevator.

Once in the loft, he protectively guided Carol to the sofa,
and moved two chairs across from her for Dailey and Montgomery. "I'll make some coffee."

Carol resented sitting on *that* sofa across from two detectives, where only a few hours before she had made love to a
man who made her feel so loved and protected. Now she felt
fear and bewilderment at the near malevolence between Dailey
and Jason.

Jason french-pressed four cups of coffee and brought them
to the coffee table, then moved in next to Carol and took her
hand. She was rigid and unresponsive. He could hardly blame
her, but he didn't know how to stop the spiral. He had blown
it with Dailey and, more importantly, he had blown the relationship progress with Carol. Old habits die hard.

Dailey began without preamble. "Mr. Brisben, would you
be more comfortable if Mss. Dunsmure left the room?" Carol
quickly looked at Jason who, unlike her, appeared to be unaf-
fected by the question. His steely gaze never left Dailey.

"No, Lieutenant, I prefer Carol to stay." Jason turned to
Carol. "Unless you want to leave."

"I'll only stay if you want me here," she answered honestly.

"I want you here." She nodded, still bewildered.

"Mr. Brisben, I have some questions for you regarding
your friend, Mr. O'Connor. Actually, questions for both of you,

Miss Dunsmure, if you feel up to answering," he continued. "How long have you known Mr. O'Connor?"

"A little over four years."

"And you, Miss?" Dailey queried.

"Actually, Jason and I have known him the same length of time. I was on shift at The Box Car the night Jack and Jason met." Carol answered.

"Mr. Brisben, what is your relationship with Mr. O'Connor? Are you close?"

"I guess we're about as close as I've ever gotten to anyone. We knock around together and go out a couple of times a month or so. They have me over for dinners and birthday parties, you know, that kind of thing."

"Does he gamble?"

"No."

"Now, you mentioned, 'they.' I assume from that he's married. Is he a good husband? Does he sleep around?" Carol's mouth fell open at the questions being asked, but she said nothing. She never would have had a chance, as Jason's answer came instantaneously.

"Hell no! He's a devoted husband and father. He loves his wife *and* his children. Where the hell are you going with this, Lieutenant?" Jason demanded, visibly irritated.

"Well, Mr. Brisben, you're the one who suggested that someone might be trying to kill Mr. O'Connor. I'm simply looking for a motive."

Carol looked over at Jason, in shock. "Is that what this is about? Someone's trying to kill Jack and you didn't think you could tell me?" A scarlet flush of anger colored her face.

Dailey looked surprised realizing he had let something slip.

He quickly came to Jason's defense. "Miss Dunsmure, we're not sure of anything at this point. Mr. Brisben was right in not telling anyone." This admission did little to temper Carol's anger, but the lieutenant continued.

"Since I let the cat out of the bag, so to speak, I need a little more information than you gave me earlier today," he said, looking at Jason again. "If you'll indulge me with a few more answers, it would be much appreciated." Jason nodded and Dailey resumed his questioning.

"What does Mr. O'Connor do for a living?"

Jason explained Jack's job with Cervicon in detail, how he had started with the company, worked through the lean years, and now enjoyed the position of chief security engineer.

Montgomery and Dailey aggressively took notes. "How is he doing financially?"

"Fine," shrugged Jason. Then he remembered about Debbie's worry about money and Tommy's medical bills. He decided to keep that information to himself.

"So, he's not in any kind of trouble that you know of, financial or otherwise?"

"No, not to my knowledge."

Jason was caught off guard by what Dailey did next. "What I'm going to tell you must be considered confidential. Is that understood?" Jason and Carol both nodded.

Dailey leaned back in his chair and began talking about Lori Phillips. Jason had already learned much of the information, but kept his mouth shut in order to protect Keller. "The woman whose life you saved this morning, is still unconscious as of 2:30 this afternoon, and according to the doctor, her chances of survival are slim at best. Her name is Lori Philips, a schoolteacher at Edwards Elementary School here in Seattle. We interviewed the principal and her co-workers at the school, but they didn't seem to know a lot about her personal life and had no idea who she was out with. She has no next of kin that we've been able to locate. We have no motive, no suspects, no murder weapon or weapons and no leads. And that, Mr. Brisben and Miss. Dunsmure, is what we do know about Lori Phillips.

"Now we come to the male victim," Dailey continued. "You, Mr. Brisben, apparently have more information on Carston Jennings than we do." Carol turned toward Jason with a surprised look, but he focused on the file Dailey had placed on the coffee table, which Dailey noticed. "Don't worry, son, we'll get to that soon enough. First would you care to give us the information that you have on Mr. Jennings?"

"Well, I gave you all I had when we spoke on the phone: He was thirty-eight years old, a school teacher from Vermont, and single. He earned forty-four K, had three credit cards, which he zeroed out every month, and had no debts. He had some involvement in special education. And that, Lieutenant, is the extent of my information."

As Dailey and Montgomery busily scribbled notes, Carol slowly shook her head in disbelief. She didn't know whether she was more hurt by him for not confiding in her or more angry for his lack of trust. But she was struck by the realization of how little she *did* know of Jason Brisben. That frightened her.

"Bob, give Mr. Brisben what we have," Dailey said, referring to the events of the early morning in the parking lot.

Bob Montgomery paraphrased from his notebook. "Because of the close approximation of the two victims and the similarities of their wounds, we believe they were attacked simultaneously, meaning there had to be two assailants." Jason nodded at this, affirmed in his evaluation of the situation. "The coroner confirmed our hypotheses during the autopsy when he stated that the wound was inflicted by a person well trained in the use of knives. An eight-inch blade was used, approximately three-quarters of an inch in width. In an interview with Dr. Keller this afternoon, we learned it's a possibility that the second assailant may have tried the same technique on Miss Phillips but botched the attempt. Her first wound would have been fatal if the assailant hadn't connected with an uncooperative rib. Dr. Keller suggested Miss Phillips probably fainted from fear or shock and that's what saved her life. When stuck again, she went limp; the assailant assumed that she was mortally wounded."

When Montgomery finished, Dailey looked at Jason and smiled wryly. "You see, Mr. Brisben, we are not totally inept in the art of investigation." Then he surprised Jason again. "My compliments on your powers of observation. You might have made a good cop." It would have been a compliment had it not been for the heavy tone of sarcasm.

"Your intuition about this not being a robbery was also correct. We canvassed the area and at 4:15 this morning our people found Mr. Jennings' wallet and Ms. Phillips' purse in a drop box behind a mini mart a couple of blocks from the restaurant. Their money, credit cards, and ID were all intact.

Whoever did this, didn't fence the cards, didn't want to leave a trail."

The adversarial tension had all but disappeared. Jason knew he was being set up and waited patiently for the kicker. Dailey made his request with an eloquent preamble.

"You didn't give me all the information that you had during our phone conversation. I could tell you were holding back. You're protecting your friend and I respect that. However, we are still investigating a murder. The jury is still out as to whether someone was actually making a try for Mr. O'Connor, but if they were, that information is critical to our catching these bastards. Now, we've been forthright with you and I'd appreciate the same consideration."

Jason committed himself to protect Jack no matter what. In order to do that effectively, it would help immensely to know from whom. To do that he needed Dailey's help. The tricky part would be getting Dailey to cooperate, without his knowing.

"I talked with Debbie, Jack's wife, this morning to see how Jack was doing," Jason said, leaving out the part about his conversation with Keller. "During our conversation, she told me Jack had already left for a job in Portland. When I mentioned I would try to get in touch with him later in the day, she asked me to give him two messages she had taken last night after he left to meet me.

"The first message was from Martin Cray, the retired owner of Cervicon. I didn't give that one a second thought." Since then, however, Jason had changed his mind. He began to wonder if Cray's call and the mystery man might have some unknown connection.

"The second message is the one that bothers me. A man called, wanting to talk to Jack. When she told him that Jack wasn't home, the caller said that he worked with Jack and asked if she knew where he could get in touch with him. Without thinking, she told him we were at The Box Car."

"So to your knowledge he never showed?" Montgomery said.

"That's the point, Detective. I think he did, the result being Jennings and Phillips. Jennings looked enough like Jack . . ." Jason's unfinished sentence hung like an ominous cloud.

Dailey closed his notebook. "I think we had better pay Mrs. O'Connor a visit."

"I was afraid you would say that," Jason said. He informed the two detectives of his conversation with Jack the night before, explaining Tommy's health problems, and Debbie's fragile emotional state. He omitted the issue of finances so he would not be caught in a lie after direct questioning about them. "I just hate to get her all upset with all she's had to deal with."

"She'll be a hell of a lot more upset if her husband ends up on a slab at the morgue," Montgomery quipped.

Jason could not argue with the logic. Taking a minute to think, he said, "How about this: What if I call Debbie and put her on the speakerphone. I'll ask her the questions and you can take notes. It'd be the same as an interview and, if we were careful, she'd never suspect a thing."

"It'd be worth a try," Montgomery said. "If it doesn't work out we can always go bang on her door." He glanced at Dailey for a response.

Dailey looked back to Jason. "Why don't you get Mrs. O'Connor on the line."

They all stood around the island as Jason dialed the O'Connors' number. When Debbie answered, he made the excuse that he was cooking and put her on the speakerphone. "I called to find out how things went with Tommy today."

"Well," she hesitated, sounding unsure of how to answer. "I don't know what to think. The doctor doesn't have a clue as to what his problem is and they're not giving me any information or any encouragement. It's really getting to me, Jason. I'm frightened for him."

"I'm sorry, sweetie. If there's anything that I can do, please let me know."

"Thanks, Jason, I will."

"Say, Deb, I haven't called Jack yet. I've been running all day. I'll be calling him in a minute. Can you give me any more information about the mystery man who called for him last night?"

"Gee, I don't know. Why? What's up?"

"Oh, nothing really. I just thought because he didn't leave his name, I wanted to have as much information as possible to help Jack figure out who it might have been."

"Well, let me think. First he asked if this was the Jack O'Connor residence, like maybe he wasn't sure. Then he asked if Jack was in. I told him no and asked if I could take a message. He said no, and then he said that he was a friend from work and needed to get in touch with him. I thought about it again, after you called this morning, and did think it strange that he wouldn't leave a message or at least his name. Anyway, he asked if I knew when Jack would be home. I told him no, but if he really needed to speak to Jack, he might find him at The Box Car. Oh, I told him that he should be easy to spot because he was wearing that obnoxious Hawaiian shirt that I hate. I guess that's about it. He said thanks and hung up."

"Well, that won't be a whole lot of help, but maybe he'll figure it out. Thanks, Deb."

"Oh, before I forget, I sent the flowers to Lori Phillips. I hope she'll be all right."

Jason put his hand on his forehead and closed his eyes momentarily. He could feel the heat from Dailey's angry stare. "I hope so too. Last I heard, she still hasn't come around. I'll let you know if there's any change."

"Thanks, Jason, I would appreciate that. After hearing about her, I guess my troubles aren't so bad after all," Debbie said, almost as an apology. "Oh, by the way, I spent sixty-five dollars on the flowers. I hate to ask, but we're a little strapped right now. Would it be all right if we split the cost? We're not using our credit cards. I put it on our account, so they could bill us."

Damn, Jason thought, he could feel more heat radiating from Dailey, regarding the O'Connors' finances. "I'll take care of it, Deb, you've done enough." Jason asked for the name of the flower shop and said he would mail a check right away. "Oh-oh, my brandy sauce is getting hot, better go. I'll talk to you soon. Bye-bye." Jason pushed the disconnect and slowly looked up.

Dailey glared at Jason, red-faced. "What else haven't you told us?" Referring to how Debbie knew so much information about Phillips, and also to his direct question about money.

"I think that's about it, Lieutenant," Jason said, flippantly.

"Mr. Brisben," Dailey said in a controlled voice, "earlier today, I gave you a warning about interfering in an investigation. If I find that you are withholding any more information that would remotely hinder this investigation or anything that I determine relevant, you'll not just find your butt in jail, but I'll personally take pleasure in throwing so much legal bullshit your way, you'll never see daylight. Am I clear on that?"

"Perfectly, Lieutenant," Jason answered, coolly, realizing he had lost credibility. He learned from past experience that a fine line existed between helping or hindering the police. He had crossed that line before and it had turned ugly. Conversely, he knew he could be an asset to his friend and the police, but to this, he would need access to the department's information. In turn, they would demand uninhibited cooperation from him. Based on today's performance, they had no reason to trust him, and discipline, they knew, was not his strong suit. Jason needed to convince them they could work together. But how? With his resources he could move faster, unencumbered by police regulations, and that would be a source of conflict. He was not as interested in catching the murderers as he was in saving Jack's life.

Or was he?

CHAPTER SEVEN

A t Carol's suggestion, they took a break, which helped diffuse tension. Everyone moved to the kitchen area where she made fresh coffee and set out biscotti. Dailey asked when Jack would arrive back in Seattle.

"Probably late Wednesday," Jason said. "I suppose it'd be good it he returned sooner."

"Not necessarily," Dailey replied. "If it turns out that he *is* in danger, he's probably better off in Portland. At any rate, we need to talk to him. From your conversation with Mrs. O'Connor, I assume you have a way to contact him."

"I have his pager number." Jason punched the number into his telephone and replaced the handset.

"Well, while we're waiting for him to call, we'd better get started on another issue." Dailey nodded toward the file that lay on the coffee table.

Carol's stomach knotted as she witnessed dread wash over Jason's face. His blue eyes turn cold and granite hard. She wondered what the file contained to cause such pain. She wanted to comfort him, but simply stood beside him, paralyzed with fear.

Jason turned to face Dailey, "Let's get to it," he said, the tone in his voice razor sharp.

Dailey glanced toward Carol and then to Jason with a questioning look as if to say, You want *her* here? Jason turned toward Carol and held out his hand. "You need to be here for this," he said.

"Are you sure you want me here?" she asked.

"If we have any chance for a future together, it starts now. You need to be here," he assured her with an unexpected tenderness. Seating her on the sofa, they again faced the two detectives. Carol sat rigid and upright; Jason leaned back in what appeared to be a relaxed defiance.

Jason knew why Dailey was sitting across from him with the file. He had known the minute he'd seen the detective get out of the car with it. He understood why Dailey had worn the quizzical look earlier that morning in the parking lot when Jason had introduced himself. Dailey hadn't placed the name then, but he had now. He put it together after Jason called him from Mukilteo, and knew from past history that Jason Brisben would become involved.

"Mr. Brisben," Dailey said sternly, "the reason this file is here . . ." He hesitated, then went on. "I have to make you . . ."

"Lieutenant, I know why the file is here. I know why you're here, and I also know that you read the file and probably know it verbatim. But the file is incomplete. Am I right, Lieutenant?" He didn't wait for a response. "Well, now you'll hear the complete story."

Jason spoke to Dailey and Montgomery rather than to Carol. "Born and raised in Denver I graduated from high school in 1966 at nineteen. I was expelled my senior year in sixty-five for fighting and had to repeat the following year in a different school, finishing a year behind."

"Fighting?" Dailey grunted. "Says in the file, you beat up a teacher so bad he spent three days in the hospital."

"The guy had me in a strangle hold, if I hadn't done something he would have killed me. I defended myself."

"Go on."

"More trouble came a year later and this time a bit more serious. A couple of so-called friends wanted to take someone's car for a joy ride. I guess that's the politically correct term for stealing a car now days. I wasn't buying into it; we'd been drinking, and one thing led to another. We fought, two on one. One of them ended up in the hospital with brain damage. The other kid told the court that I had attacked them.

"A year later, the hospital released the kid and the truth finally came out, but by then it was too late. I was supposed to do some hard time, but my loving father used his money and clout, pulled some strings, and cut a deal to get me off if I went into the service. When the dust settled, he told me he never wanted to see me again and to never set foot on his property."

"Jasper Brisben, Brisben Mining?" Montgomery asked.

"The one and only," Jason answered with disdain.

"You know him?" Dailey inquired of Montgomery.

"Know *of* him," Montgomery responded. "Owns a lot of land, big into silver and copper mining. Bought up everything he could get his hands on in the forties through the late fifties, pretty ruthless from what I heard. Sorry," he said, nodding at Jason apologetically. "I remember my uncle talking about him. I guess they bumped heads from time to time."

"Then it sounds like you've got the gist of the situation," Jason said stoically.

Carol reached for Jason's hand to show support. She took in every word, having never heard any of it before. No one in Jason's immediate life knew what the three people in the room were now hearing, although Carol had asked Jason several times during their previous relationship about his background but received the same curt response: "What's in my past doesn't concern you *or* me anymore. It's not something I care to talk about."

"I joined the Navy in '67 and, after I finished boot camp, I applied for the Navy SEAL program. A year later, after going through all of the various schools offered, I spent nineteen years in the teams as a team leader from about '70 on. I did two tours in Vietnam, and in about '75 we (the U.S. Government) became interested in anti-terrorist training. The Iranian kidnappings brought that to a head in the eighties. We worked in counter-terrorism for several more years; then I retired from the Navy in '87. Most of that should be in the file."

Dailey nodded. "Says here that you won some medals— quite impressive—Silver Star, three Bronze Stars, a couple of Navy commendations, fourteen confirmed hand-to-hand combat kills. Very impressive indeed. "

Jason continued without comment to Dailey's commentary. "A month later a man from the Pentagon contacted me and requested that I meet with him regarding a new program they wanted to introduce, something to do with national security. I met with him and two others the following week at which time they swore me to secrecy.

"What I am about to tell you is dangerous information and it's crucial that I have your word it won't leave this room. I will give you the name of a contact who can verify the information. I'm hanging my ass out a country mile, gentlemen. Do we have an agreement?"

Montgomery quickly responded. "If this information is so delicate why share it with us?"

"Because without it, I won't be able to clear my record with you. Because there are three fucking years of my life that aren't in that file you're holding in front of me. Because there are two deaths with my name attached to them the government has so graciously red-stamped DO NOT INTERFERE, which leaves you and me hanging. And because I want you to trust me so I can protect my friend without your trying to put me in a box, which you will soon realize will be easier said than done. So, do we have a deal or not?" Jason raised his voice only slightly in asking the question, but his tone left no doubt of his determination.

In her emotional confusion, Carol pulled her hand from Jason. The fact that he didn't notice only added to her tension. A part of her wanted to comfort and support him; the other wanted distance.

Dailey, his worst fears confirmed, met Jason's eyes, and the look that passed between them could melt steel. Dailey had to make a decision. The rules of investigation dictated that a police officer could tell someone anything for the benefit of an investigation without recrimination: the truth, a half-truth or an even an out-and-out lie. Being a man of principle, those tactics did not sit well with him. He wanted to ask Jason what he could do that the Seattle Police Department couldn't do. He knew the answer. With budget cuts and tight money, they didn't have the resources to afford O'Connor full-time protection. Jason could maneuver much faster outside the rules of police protocol than he and his people could. He felt a growing respect for Jason, and yet the man brought on an influx of acid to an already raw stomach. He feared he was about to make a deal with the devil.

"Whatever you tell us from this point on will not leave this room. You have my word on that," Dailey said.

Jason continued as if there had been no interruption to his story. "The three men from the Pentagon laid out a plan for evaluating the security of our military bases, federal agencies, airports, elected officials, and so on. I was supposed to pick a team of twelve men, train them, then systematically invade specifically targeted facilities considered to be our most secure and expose their weaknesses. That was the fun part." Jason allowed himself a brief smile. "God, we had some great paint ball wars and raised a lot of hell.

"Now, the not-so-fun part. There were some concerns within the intelligence community about the activities of various militia and survivalist groups. Those operations were deadly serious because some of the groups were not wanna-be adventurers playing paddy-whack. If you got caught on their turf, you could wake up dead. That in itself wasn't too bad; it just made the exercises interesting. The bad part was, if we got caught, the three fucks who conceived the concept would deny knowledge of the operation. And get this, we could be prosecuted."

"And you agreed to this?" Carol asked in amazement.

Jason turned toward Carol. "I was one month out of what's considered to be the elite fighting force and full of patriotism. At that time, I thought I was making a supreme sacrifice for the safety of the American people. If you knew of some of the acts of terrorists and their results that I've been exposed to in other countries, you could better understand my motivation. I would at the time—and still will do—anything in my power to keep those kinds of activities off American soil. They're not pretty—and only a fraction of what really goes on makes it into our media. But we won't get into that.

"I selected twelve of the best men available and spent six months training and molding them together into the best of the best. By August of '87, we were ready for our first mission. I notified my Pentagon contact that we were ready. We spent the first six months having a ball. Some of our supposedly most secure facilities ended up with egg on their faces—or, more accurately, paint ball paint—and ringing ears from flash-bang grenades. We never so much as took a hit and proved that the best attempts at 'terrorist-proofing' were lacking at best.

"Then we moved on to the good stuff, raiding select camps that we had ferreted out. We started infiltrating the militia groups about mid-year in '89. The tricky part of a covert activity is they can't know that you've been there. Everything went along real smooth until we hit a camp in southern Georgia. This place had all of the makings of a full-blown guerilla training center. We knew we were on to something and went in, undetected, two more times. There was some serious shit in the works at that camp. They were in the final stages of preparation for a raid.

"I got in touch with my contact and gave him the report on what we found. I'll never forget his words, 'That *is* very disturbing. If what you say is accurate, it appears they're preparing for an all-out offensive.' Three days later the brick-butt, yellow piece of shit told me to cease all activity regarding intelligence-gathering on the militia groups. Not only cease the operation, but disband the team completely. We were to have no further contact with him, or any militia groups."

Jason's eyes became cold and hard, his voice deliberate and guttural. "I went back and reported to the team. We all had the same question: Why the hell had we been doing all our training, going through all of the bullshit for a year and a half?

"We agreed to find out what was going down. I contacted some people I knew who worked intelligence in Vietnam, Iraq, Turkey, had them do a little snooping. In the meantime, we infiltrated the camp again. We learned that there were going to be simultaneous attacks on three different locations within three weeks' time. We could only guess at the locations until the 'intell' group confirmed them for us—three refineries. Come to find out there're bigger profits for some U.S. oil maggots by keeping the pot stirred in the Middle East. They were setting up a good guy-bad guy scenario and a couple of hundred innocent rag heads were about to get dead. All for thirty more cents a barrel for crude.

"I tried one last time to contact the Pentagon geek but got stonewalled. Within three hours, I got a coded message—a warning to back off. I went back to the team and laid it out. We took a vote. The way we figured it, if they were going to deny we existed, no worries. We went in and took out the camp. Shut it down completely. We destroyed all weapons and buildings. They went up in smoke in a period of fifteen minutes, along with a few of the camp's personnel. We let the people who were collecting the money do the cleanup and covertly monitored the activity, and learned the source of the camp's funding."

Jason slowly shook his head, his eyes unfocused as if he were watching it happen all over again. "You know, what we stopped was illegal as hell and could have touched off an international incident in an already volatile part of the world. It violated every international law ever written. Politically, it could have been a disaster for this country. Yet nothing ever surfaced in the media. The only thing we accomplished was postponing the Gulf War a few years, and that cost somebody big money."

Jason looked through the windows of the loft, his face inscribed with a mixture of sorrow and subdued anger as he remembered the experience. "All that and for what?" he said slowly as he continued to stare off toward the Olympic Mountains. "The only thing we wanted was to show how vulnerable our country is and to help the appropriate people to learn that. We hoped, given our experience, we would be afforded the chance to develop programs that would make our country a safer place. We were never given the chance.

"Things turned ugly. Within two weeks, six of the team members were murdered. Real pro jobs. Bobby Denton was the first. It was made to look like an all-night store robbery gone bad. Keith Hohner fell asleep at the wheel—of course the car went over a bank and burned. There wasn't enough left of his body to bury. Paul Daniels went two days later. Now get this—a Navy SEAL—he drowned, a nighttime swimming accident. The next day they got Michael Daniels, Paul's brother, and Chris Hammond and Rod Peters, in a motel fire. Even though we were on the move, they were doing a good job of tracking us. The three team members had just arrived at the motel that afternoon. The pros had gotten to our Pentagon dweeb, gotten our names, ID's, photos, the works, and went headhunting. We were being systematically eliminated.

"While all this was going on, two of the original designers of the plan died, people whom I had met at the Pentagon. One of a heart attack, the other in another one-car accident south of DC. And, of course, my contact was nowhere to be found. I set my intelligence trio after him and they came up with zip. The intell hypothesis was that after they got to him, he ended up at some Texas oilman's barbecue as plump kosher hot dogs."

Carol looked perplexed, but Dailey had picked up on the nuance.

"What Mr. Brisben meant, Miss Dunsmure, is someone murdered him and ground him into sausage." Carol stared at him wide-eyed in disbelief. "It's been known to happen," Dailey said, with a shrug.

"So, we went to ground, vanished," continued Jason. We were down to a six-man team and needed to be careful. First rule: Any time we moved, we moved in pairs or threes, never alone. We kept a low profile. We got help from our intell trio to get a fix on who we needed to get to in order to stop the bloodletting. It took us three months to get a complete workup on the operation, from the bottom to the top. Some heavy hitters were involved, three U.S. senators, and some people in the Pentagon, along with two Texas oilmen. The oil money flowed into campaigns, creating a tight, well-oiled fraternity. No pun intended.

"Next came the strategy to get to them without compromising ourselves. We prepared documentation, one hundred forty-three pages containing names, dates, a complete description on the camp personnel and who they answered to, and so on. We also prepared a well-documented record of all requisition orders for supplies and equipment for the team. This we did to get help from the military boys. Without the proof, the whole situation could blow up in our faces.

"We prepared the documents to be sent Federal Express on a specific date. Three senators, two oil maggots, one general, and one admiral were to receive fat, overnight letters on the same day, before ten a.m., just like it says in the ad. Everything was in place including our insurance policy. Key people at the *Washington Post* and the *New York Times* who were willing to put their careers on the line had been contacted, people who could get the story out without it being spiked.

"Right about now, you're wondering why we didn't go public with what we had. In a nutshell, these people we were up against were very powerful people entrenched in our political system and the military. Their images may have gotten tarnished a little, but more than likely a whole butt-load of innocent people in their organizations would have taken the fall. All that we wanted was to come out of the situation with our hides, not turn the whole country on its ear. You can understand, with this kind of crap going down, why militia groups are springing up at an alarming rate. I don't agree with them, but some have a modicum of legitimacy.

"The letters stated that they would be contacted within twenty-four hours. We wanted to make sure they had ample time to get in touch with one another. We contacted them the next day and set a meeting for the following morning, which didn't allow them time to cover their butts.

"Two years and eight months after the operation began, we met in a Washington, DC, safe house. The meeting proved to be interesting. Three nervous senators and their bodyguards, two arrogant oilmen with their personal security, as they described them, an army general who looked to have a high alcohol content in his blood, Admiral McNairy, write that name down, because he's your contact," Jason said to Dailey, "and three uptight and angry Navy SEALS.

"The meeting was short and to the point. We told them to call off their dogs and let us get on with our lives. Clearly the oilmen were in charge. One of whom's first comment was 'You've bitten off a large chunk of meat, son. Best be careful you don't choke on it.'

"That's when McNairy broke in and said, 'All right, this bullshit stops right here. It's finished right here and now.' His comments were directed to the oil money and the senators.

"My reply to the oil money was: 'That little remark just cost you twelve million dollars.'

"Oil money jumped to his feet and slammed his fist to the table and said, 'When hell freezes over. And what makes you think you'll leave this town alive?' He face burned with fury, but we had them by the balls. Obviously he didn't know squat about chess.

"'Check mate, dickhead. How many of my team do you see sitting here, you ignorant piece of shit?' I unfolded the morning editions of the *Post* and *Times* and opened to page three. It was blank, with the exception of bold letters that read: **FEATURE ARTICLES TOMORROW ABOUT,** and it listed the names of the guests of honor who were present at the meeting. The subject: **OIL, POLITICS, AND THE MILITARY. . . Don't miss it!** I checked my watch, it was 7:45 a.m. I knew with the schedule that I'd set, they wouldn't have had time to read the papers. 'It's seven forty-five,' I said to the oil money and the senators. 'By five o'clock Eastern Standard Time, I'll expect to see two million dollars in each of these accounts.' I handed the account numbers across the table. 'If the money isn't secured in the accounts, you'll read your epitaphs in tomorrow's sunrise edition. Believe me, gentlemen, as you well know, it's well documented. Once the money has been transferred, we'll submit short articles for each of you, on stabilization strategies for troubled oil regions.

"One of the senators complained that it was blackmail. 'Yes it is, and a damn fine job of it too,' I told them. 'And another thing, if any of the remaining six of us happen to die of anything but old age, we go to press, and I swear to you, there will be no place for you to hide. You can confirm with your military colleagues here that we are capable of compromising any security.' One senator wanted to put us into the witness protection program, which we immediately rejected. I explained to them that under no condition would we hide out like a bunch of fucking Mafia stoolies. We had been involved in a secret operation for the benefit of our country, and his solution was unacceptable.

"Apparently, the oil money had hired the hits with no way to call them back in. I told them they had a real problem on their hands and they had better deal with it. If any contractor made a move on any of us, the oilmen would wish they were dead. I also waved the *Post* at them.

"After more grousing they agreed to our conditions and the meeting adjourned. Admiral McNairy cautioned us to keep our heads down for a couple of months until they could be sure the hit contracts could be rescinded. The money was transferred that afternoon and the following week we went our separate ways. I put my money in an offshore trust in the Cayman Islands, and spent the next two months in Mexico. That's where I met my second wife. We moved to a little place in Edmonds. You pretty much know the rest."

"The rest of what?" Carol asked looking from Jason to Dailey.

Dailey looked to Jason for the first time with compassion in his tired eyes. "Do you want to tell her or shall I?"

Jason sat silently, his eyes dark with grieving. Taking a sip of his now cold coffee, he stared at Dailey and quietly answered, "Be my guest. You can take it from here."

Dailey began. "The Edmonds Police received a call that there had been a disturbance at the Brisben address. When the officers arrived, they found Mr. Brisben sitting on his couch, his wife in their bedroom with a bullet in her head, two men in the dining room, one face down on the floor with his throat cut, and the other tied in a chair with a broken neck. The man in the chair had been tortured before he died."

Carol, with a shaking hand to her mouth, looked back and forth between Jason and Dailey in disbelief, but said nothing.

"Mr. Brisben refused to give a statement, which left the officers no choice but to take him in for questioning. By the time they arrived at the station, the police had received a message from the Department of the Navy that they had a man on the way from Washington, DC, and this incident was a matter of national security and not to interfere. Would you fill in a couple of gaps for us?"

Jason slowly raised his eyes; grief and anger hung hauntingly in them. "Well it's pretty simple, Lieutenant—I came home, found that those two jerk-offs had killed my wife and wanted to know the locations of the rest of the team members.

They got careless. I took one of them down and interrogated the other, and then put him out of his misery."

"Interrogated?" Dailey interrupted, taken aback by Jason's calm demeanor. "Jesus! The only bone in his body that wasn't broken was his head."

"I wanted some answers. He was stubborn. Can we get on with this?" Jason asked, his anger no longer masked. Dailey nodded and Jason continued. "When I finally got the information I needed, I called Admiral McNairy, told him what was going on. I also told him that I wanted immunity because I would be cleaning up their fucked-up mess, and if I didn't get it, there would be some interesting reading in the morning papers. It took him about fifteen seconds to make his desision. I think you can finish it up from here, Lieutenant."

"Basically, what he's telling us," Dailey continued, "is that he'd been promoted to a vigilante with government protection. Mr. Brisben here beat the information out of the surviving hit man, information pertaining to the identification of the remaining three contractors, and was able to systematically eliminate them over a period of the next two and a half months. It kept the Seattle and the Salt Lake Police Departments busy for a while. He was a good boy, though. He always let the authorities know where to find the bodies. Oh, and a rather wealthy Texas businessman disappeared about the same time. Quite a media circus, as I recall. You wouldn't happen to . . ."

Jason interrupted. "I'm afraid I don't have any information that will ease your curiosity, Lieutenant."

"You've been on pretty good behavior for the past four years. But the question that I have to ask myself is, why in God's name would I want to wake a sleeping lion by letting you get further involved in this current mess?"

"All I want to do is protect my friend," Jason responded quietly. "I don't suppose you would want to hear my I-have-that-right speech."

"No, I don't, but you do have to understand that we can't condone private citizens nosing around in police business. That kind of thing can get the department into a lot of trouble."

"What kind of trouble?" Jason asked. I will be strictly on my own. There will be no liability if I get hammered. It's my problem, not yours. All I'm asking is that we share information."

"Ah-ha, it's the information that you want! Now we're getting somewhere."

"That's right, but look at it from this perspective: I have resources, I can get into places that you can't and, with help, I can get to them quicker."

"He's making sense, boss," Montgomery interjected. "He's already undercover. I mean nobody knows him. We can feed him information and he can do the legwork. Seems simple."

"Oh, hell yes, it's simple all right. It's a simple way for me to lose my pension if this thing gets out of hand and blows up in our faces, not to mention the fact that you'll be back on the street and they won't even give you a bicycle."

Jason looked at his watch. "Look, I fully understand that this puts you in an awkward position. Believe me, I know what it's like to be screwed over and I'm not looking to do it to you. The last thing I want is to get you into trouble, but this can work. I'll check in with you every day and we'll work through it. If it doesn't work, we'll bag it. Besides who's going to link us? I sure as hell won't. Just think about it for a few minutes while I try to contact Jack again."

Jason moved to use the kitchen telephone. As he tapped in Jack's pager number, he glanced over to Carol who sat with her hands in her lap staring blankly at the coffee table.

Jason returned the receiver to the cradle and waited for Jack to answer his page. Lieutenant Dailey stood and stretched and faced the windows to look at the view. Nobody spoke during what seemed like an eternity of uncomfortable quiet. Suddenly, the silence evaporated into the startling trill of the phone.

Jason quickly gathered up the receiver. "Brisben."

"Jason? What's up?" Jack asked while yawning.

"I've been paging you for over an hour. Where the hell ya been?"

"Sleeping."

"Sleeping! I thought you were supposed to be working."

As if as one, Carol, Dailey, and Montgomery moved to the kitchen area to be near the phone.

"Yeah, right. It's not like I've had a lot of sleep lately. How's the woman we found last night?"

"Hanging on by a thread. She hasn't regained consciousness yet. It's too early to tell. But that's not why I called."

An obvious curiosity crept into Jack's voice. "What's up?" he asked a second time.

Jason, suddenly faced with the reality of having to tell his friend that someone might be trying to kill him, now found it harder than he had expected. "Jack, we have a troublesome situation here," he said, groping for the right words. "I'm not quite sure how to put this."

"Well spit it out, or I'm going to go back to sleep," his voice held a fragile mixture of humor and irritation.

"Jack, I guess there's no easy way to say this—there's a possibility that someone is trying to kill you."

"What! Are you nuts?" The response came loud and instantaneous. "Hey, buddy, I'm exhausted and I'm not in any mood for a practical joke."

"Jack, listen to me. This is no joke," Jason said, trying to recover the situation. "Lieutenant Dailey and Detective Montgomery are here; I'm putting you on the speaker." Jason pushed the button, then replaced the receiver.

"Mr. O'Connor, this is Lieutenant Dailey. Your friend Mr. Brisben here has some ideas about the activities of last night. Now there's no hard evidence as yet, but I have to admit his theory has merit. I think you should hear him out and for the time being we should be taking some precautions."

Jason explained that the photos of the crime scene had documented the physical similarities between Jack and the victim. Then he related his conversation with Debbie, being particularly careful to give all of the details regarding the two telephone messages, the one from Martin Cray and the man who wouldn't leave his name. "This is for real, my friend. I know the evidence looks slim, but I'm not willing to take any chances, nor is Lieutenant Dailey."

Feelings of confusion and disbelief flooded through Jack when he realized Jason was serious. The fear would come in due time. After a full minute of silence, he finally said, "You're not joking, are you?"

Carol read the bewilderment in his voice. "Jack, this is Carol. I just found out about this a few minutes ago, so I understand your shock. But I can tell you, Jason is as serious as a heart attack, and the police are looking at this as a real possibility."

"Oh God," Jack said with a sigh of frustration. "I can't believe this." He paused again, then asked urgently, "What about my family? Are they safe?" His mind filled with a firestorm of questions. "How can I tell . . . Deb's . . . . Debbie's absolutely going to have a nervous breakdown!" The gravity of the situation settled in like a weight from hell.

"I don't think it's necessary that she know just yet," Dailey said, "and I don't see that your family is in danger, at least for the time being. And again, there's no solid evidence to support this theory, so until we have something concrete, just sit tight. But we wanted you to be aware." He paused. Mr. O'Connor, do you have any thoughts about anyone who would benefit by your being out of the way? Mr. Brisben here says you've got a situation at work. You think that might be a place to look? Or what about success stories? Any of these systems that you've designed, have they been responsible for putting anyone away? Those are the kinds of questions you need to ask yourself. I know I'm bombarding you with questions and you haven't had time to process any of this, so I'm not expecting immediate answers. But for the present, do you have any thoughts on the two phone calls your wife received last night?"

"I honestly can't think clearly about anything right now, Lieutenant. It's true, things aren't going particularly well at work, but it's not enough to create a situation like this. About the calls last night, I have no idea what Martin Cray wanted. I haven't heard from him in several weeks. As for the other guy who called, I have no idea what he may have wanted. I'll give Martin a call. Maybe he can shed some light on this. It's probably all a mistake and we're getting excited over nothing."

"Well, that's certainly a possibility and I hope you're right," Dailey answered.

"Jack, does anyone know where you're staying?" Jason cut in.

"No . . . uh . . . come to think of it, I told Peter Hargrave, the GM at Biddwell, in case they needed to get in touch with me."

"I want you to change hotels. Don't tell anybody. Then, when you get settled in, call me and let me know where you are," Jason directed.

"Aw, come on, Jay. Aren't you overreacting?"

"It may sound like overkill, but I think it's a good call at this point," Dailey agreed. "Who knows, by tomorrow maybe we'll all be laughing about this . . . . Let me ask you this: Your job in Portland, you finding anything unusual about it?"

Jack remained silent while he pondered the question before answering. "Well, from my perspective there's always something weird about a break-in, but yeah, there is." Jack went on to explain about the vandalism and the out and out attempt at sabotaging the machines that ran the military work.

"You think there may be a connection in all this?" Dailey asked.

"I don't see how," Jack answered."

"Well, keep your eyes open and be careful," Dailey advised. "We'll be in touch."

"Jack, get yourself moved and call me when you get settled," Jason said, then signed off.

Everyone retreated into their own thoughts for a moment, then Dailey spoke.

"Well, that wasn't a hell of a lot of help." He turned to Jason. "I know you want to help, son, but we'll all be better served if you leave police business to the police." But a synergy had developed between the two nevertheless, and Dailey knew without a doubt that Jason would be involved, right up to his now sparkling azure eyes. "If you would, forward Mr. O'Connor's number to me when you get it," he stated as an order not a request.

"We probably had better get back to the office," Dailey said to Montgomery. He turned to Carol and nodded as he spoke, "Ms. Dunsmure, good day."

CHAPTER EIGHT

"Well, that went better than I thought it'd go," Jason said, after Dailey and Montgomery left the loft.

Carol leaned against the kitchen island looking out through the windows, her arms folded tightly against her chest not from cold but from anxiety. The strongest of emotions—fear, anger, and love—burned in fierce conflict within her, tearing at her soul like a rabid dog. She had always wanted to know more about Jason, but this . . . this she had not expected. At the moment, she both feared and loved the man, but anger was winning the war that raged within. Her eyes welled but she did not speak, afraid she would be unable to control the tears. She felt the protection and love that she had so coveted earlier that day, slipping away.

Jason read the struggle of emotions in her face. "Tell me," he asked quietly.

She turned to face him. Tears now ran freely down her cheeks and dripped onto her blouse. "You're going to get in the middle of this, aren't you?" Her voice choked with the pain. Anger had clouded her thoughts because it was not what she wanted to say. Jason's past frightened her. He was a dangerous man and she wanted to ask—something. She didn't know what to ask or how to ask.

"I *am* in the middle of this. I got in the middle of this when I walked out into that parking lot this morning."

"No, Jason. I watched you put yourself into this situation a few minutes ago. Lieutenant Dailey asked you to stay out of it. I could see it in your eyes. You have no intention of letting this go."

"Look, all I want to do is make sure Jack is safe," Jason soothed, trying to downplay the situation. But Carol was right; he wanted something more. The excitement he had felt, the adrenaline coursing through his body as he worked over Lori Phillips and his mind racing to figure out what had happened had acted like narcotics. He wanted what Carol wanted, but he also wanted this challenge. "Carol, honey, I don't want our day to end like this. Can't we . . . ?"

"Just how is our day supposed to end, *honey*? My God, I've been making love to—to someone with ice water in his veins. Most people get queasy taking a pet to the pound and having it put to sleep. You . . . you and Lieutenant whatshisname talk like killing is just part of a normal day at the office. God, I don't believe this!"

Her sarcasm cut Jason and stripped his resolve to de-escalate the conflict. "I don't believe this either. What are we talking about here? The war, my wonderful time in terrorist control, what?" As always, when things got tough, Jason attacked. "Let me tell you something: War is about killing. People don't seem to understand that. And I have to deal with it every night when I go to bed. It's not a game, sweetheart! . . . Damn! . . . I don't need this shit, I just—"

Carol cut him off. "I don't need this shit either! I guess I'm going to need a little time to get used to . . . ." She hesitated briefly, then her eyes widened as a new thought came to her. "It's . . . the killing . . . . " She stopped. A look of enlightenment spread over her face. "I don't think you're done. I think you're going to hunt these people down. That's what I saw when you were talking to the lieutenant. I didn't know what it was at the time. You're going to hunt these people down and kill them. That's it, isn't it?"

"Wait a minute," Jason said, attempting to justify himself. "I remember you saying that if you ever caught the people who took Melanie that you'd kill them." He realized the second the words came out of his mouth it had been a cruel and hurtful thing to say to Carol. The roller coaster of emotion had taken control but at the moment he no longer cared.

"That was different!" she screamed.

Carol's scream put him over the top and into a free-fall. "You're right," Jason retorted. "Yours was fantasy. Mine is reality."

Carol went rigid with anger and pain.

In the midst of the melee a spark of sanity struck Jason. "Look, I'm sorry about what I said. Can we just take a break for a minute and try to calm down? We can work through this."

"Be my guest," Carol said, coldly.

Jason left the kitchen escaping to his master bath, hoping to calm himself and collect his thoughts. He splashed cold water on his face, then toweled dry while looking at his reflection in the mirror. He did not like the man looking back at him.

* * * * *

"Carol, I'm sorry," Jason said, as he came from his bedroom doorway. He stopped when he realized that she was no longer in the kitchen. "Carol?" he said again as he looked hopefully through his office doorway. He walked back toward the kitchen and, as he did, he noticed a scrap of paper on the counter. He picked it up and read the barely legible scribble: *I took a cab to pick up my car. I need a couple of days.*

Before the pain and the sense of loss could register, Jason felt his involuntary defense mechanism take hold. He could have intercepted Carol before the taxi arrived, but he chose to do nothing. Growing up with an abusive father, he had learned not to let the hurt in. *No one will ever hurt me again* had been his motto from the age of eight. Anger had served him well.

* * * * *

Jason sat on the sofa, staring blankly at the sound as he finished his second scotch, trying to sort out what he really wanted. His first reaction, to hell with her, I've gotten along fine without her, he knew deep inside to be a lie. He also felt a commitment to Jack and his family, and there lay the dilemma.

The jangle of the telephone interrupted his reverie.

"I'm at the Marriot Courtyard, just down the street from Biddwell," came Jack's tired voice. "Jay, I want to apologize for the way I acted today, I guess I'm more shaken than I thought."

"I understand buddy, it's no problem." Jason looked at his watch, which read 7:15. "You get anything to eat?" he asked, attempting conversation, his mind still muddled by the confrontation with Carol.

"Dinner's on the way. Room service. I don't suppose you've heard anything, like maybe this is a false alarm?" he asked.

"No, not yet, and I haven't heard anything new on Phillips either. You get anything out of Cray?"

"I called, but he wasn't home. I left my pager number and told him to call ASAP. So, what do I do now?"

"I'll probably drive down to see you tomorrow. Right now just sit tight and call me if you hear anything from Cray. Oh, and, tomorrow while you're at Biddwell, make sure you stay with groups of people. Don't go off by yourself. I'll call you within a couple of hours with a plan of action. And, Jack, not a word about this to anyone."

"All right, all right, I'm too damned tired to argue with you anyway. How's Carol? She seemed pretty shook up last night and now with this . . . she holding up okay?"

Jason had just begun to clear his mind and now Jack had brought her back to the forefront of his thoughts. Maybe it would help to talk about it, he thought. He told Jack about their wonderful morning and then how quickly everything had changed.

"Debbie and I went through some of those same things in our early years during my readjustment from Special Forces," Jack reminisced. "Tell you what, I'll call Debbie and let her in on what happened. Maybe she can give Carol a call and help out, discreetly of course." After hanging up, Jason found, to his surprise, he actually felt better.

Jason poured himself another scotch, then picked up the phone and punched in a number he had not used in nearly two years. "Laura Mathers' office," the recording said. "Our office hours are from ten a.m. till six p.m."

"Damnit," Jason said to the piece of tape.

"Tuesdays through Thursdays. If there is an emergency, please call," and the machine gave the number. He disconnected and called the new number.

A buttery soft voice cooed, "Laura Mathers' answering service. May I help you?"

"This is Jason Brisben. Please have Laura call me as soon as possible."

"Is this an emergency, Mr. Brisben?

I called the damn number, didn't I?"

The attendant had Jason spell his name and took his number, and still with the buttery voice said, "I will see that she gets the message. Thank you Mr. Brisben."

He scrunched his face at the receiver, mouthing her confirmation before hanging up the phone, then moved past the kitchen to the entrance of the vault-like enclosure and entered the code of the electronic combination lock. The bolt released with a buzz-click, the door opened just enough to get a handhold to pull it open.

"Welcome to my *candy store*," Jason said aloud.

The "candy" was actually one of the largest private collections of small arms in the country. Nearly all of the world's weapons manufacturers were represented: Colt, Grand, Smith & Wesson, Bren, Browning, Mauser, Heckler & Koch, Uzi, Ruger. There were handguns, sporting rifles, sniper rifles, submachine guns, assault rifles and shotguns, not just one, but several of each variety with ammunition for all. The vault also contained progressive loading presses with dies, brass casings, primers, bullets and powder for the various calibers.

Jason moved to his display of handguns and paused momentarily, then picked up one of three Browning High-Power pistols, a Belgian-made 9mm semiautomatic, then opened a drawer under the shelf where the Browning had lain and pulled out an inside-the-belt holster and three loaded clips. He inserted one of the clips, chambered a round, and released the hammer into the safety position.

"Just pull the hammer back and you're ready to rock and roll," he said aloud to no one. Moving half a step to the left, he picked up a 10mm Colt Delta Elite, opened the drawer below and again took three clips, slid one home into the base of the grip. He worked the slide, chambering a round, then clicked on the safety. After looking at several options, he selected a shoulder holster for the Colt and put everything into a black satchel just as the kitchen telephone summoned him.

"Jason, it's Laura, returning your call. How are you?" Laura Mathers, the therapist he used during his first try at a relationship with Carol, sounded genuinely pleased to hear from him.

"Well, I thought I was doing good until today." He gave an abbreviated version of the events of the previous twenty-four hours, with more detail regarding the confrontation with Carol. "I would like to see you as soon as you can fit me in," he concluded, hoping she would see him that evening.

"Wow. You were never one to keep it simple," she said with concern. "I have a full schedule in the morning and early afternoon. How about five o'clock? You'll be my last appointment. We'll have as much time as you need."

"Any chance of meeting tonight? It's this thing with Carol that I'm struggling with."

"I can imagine, but it will take some time, Jason. You'll have to take it slow with her. The situation is too volatile for you to approach her right now. Patience will be your most important ally right now. Can you trust me on this? Now, I'm assuming you're not going to do anything stupid before tomorrow."

He let out a long sigh. "No, I guess not."

"Jason, I know patience isn't your strong suit, but please trust me. If you push right now you will just drive a bigger wedge between the two of you."

"You're the doctor," he said, but not enthusiastically.

"Yes, I am," Laura said, picking up on his disappointment. "Trust me, and I'll see you at five tomorrow."

Jason had no more than set the phone down when it rang again.

"Lori Phillips regained consciousness about forty-five minutes ago," Dailey reported. "I'm sorry to say she confirmed your suspicions. We were only able to have a couple of minutes with her because she was in and out of consciousness. She said two men came from behind the blue van, which would have been O'Connor's rig. The only man she remembered was the one who attacked Jennings, a husky blond guy with curly hair. What he said confirmed your theory, and I quote, 'Well,

well, Jack, does the little lady know?' Apparently he assumed O'Connor was stepping out on his wife. She said the other man grabbed her, but she didn't get too good a look at him. Then she felt a sharp pain in her chest and that's all that she could remember, nothing else until she woke up in the hospital."

"Did she give *any* kind of description of her attacker?" Jason asked.

"The only thing she said was that he was dark."

"That really narrows it down. Do you think she got enough of a look at the blond guy who attacked Jennings to help you with a composite sketch?"

"Probably in a day or two. She'll be too drugged to be much help before then," Dailey said, then paused. "Well, I just thought you would want to know."

"Thank you, Lieutenant. I appreciate the call."

"So, with this latest development, what are your plans?" Dailey asked, now fishing, wanting to know if Jason would take his advice and stay out of the situation.

"Well, I'll be honest, I'm planning to drive down to Portland tomorrow to meet with Jack, kinda watch his backside, so to speak. I'll call you when I get back in town."

"You do that," Dailey said with a tone that communicated a lack of trust. "Brisben . . ."

"Yes, Lieutenant?"

"In view of this latest information, you keep your eyes open. If you see anything out of the ordinary, you keep me informed."

"Lieutenant, you'll be the first to know."

"Yeah," Dailey said, and the line went dead.

Jason sat at the bar in the kitchen and pondered the conversation he had just had. Aside from wanting information, Dailey had a concern for my safety, good sign, he thought. He looked at his watch again and went to his office to get Joe Castellano's pager number.

While he waited for Joe's return call, he made a mental list of information he needed. Within three minutes the telephone rang.

"Brisben."

"Castellano here," Joe said.

"Joe, I need you to get in touch with the team."

"Who you gonna kill?"

"Not funny, Joe. I just received confirmation from Lieutenant Dailey that my friend Jack O'Connor was the target in The Box Car incident. I need the first two available bodies and I need them in the Portland area sometime around noon tomorrow."

"Okay, sorry about the flip remark. Jason, I do need to warn you: There could be some serious ramifications if you get caught." Part of the amnesty agreement with the government had stipulated that none of the team members were to associate with one another.

"Ancient history. The way I figure it, who's going to tell? There's some serious shit going down and I don't have a lot of time. Will you be available tomorrow?"

"I have to be in court all afternoon, so from 11:00 on I'm booked. I can't say for sure, but I think Bennie's free all day."

"Bennie's never been *free*," Jason quipped.

"Good point," Joe laughed. "I'll see what I can do."

"Joe, I want Sobahr in on this. I need some financial profiles on two companies, a Cervicon, they're local, and a Biddwell Die Casting. They're located in Portland. I also want personnel records for both. I'll see you about eight in the morning. And call me back tonight with names of two team members and how I can reach them."

"My God, you're a pushy sucker."

"Yeah, but my money's good."

"Another good point. We'll see you at eight."

At 9:30 Jason called Jack. He made the decision to put off telling him about Dailey's interview with Lori Phillips until tomorrow, seeing no reason to add to Jack's burden. "You hear from Martin Cray?" Jason asked.

"Nothing yet. He's probably out on his boat. It's not unusual for him to take long weekends, or he could be checking on it after the storm. Oh by the way, I talked to Debbie about your situation with Carol; she said she'd call her tomorrow, maybe invite her over for lunch."

"Thanks, Jack, I really appreciate that." It impressed Jason that Jack would take time to think of his troubles in the midst of everything that had befallen him. Jason thought it time to reciprocate. "I'm getting restless; I think I'll drive down tomorrow, give you a little moral support. I should be rolling in sometime around one o'clock."

"That's not necessary. There will be plenty of people around. I don't think there's anything to worry about . . . I suppose you'll come anyway."

"Yeah, I will. Jack, have you thought about what Dailey asked? Any ideas at all of anyone who—"

Jack cut him off in mid-sentence. "That's all that I've been thinking about since you talked to me the first time. I haven't a clue." His frustration clearly apparent.

"What about this Path—Pathfinder character? What's with him? Do you think he'd make this kind of a move?"

"Richard Path*moor* is a certified weasel, but he's not stupid," Jack said with resentment. "He doesn't have the connections or technical background to make Cervicon fly on his own. Everything we do is a custom design. If we need something that's not an off-the-shelf item to integrate into our systems, we design it and have it manufactured under the Cervicon name. That's what makes us unique. With Martin out of the picture, he needs me, although he'd be the last to admit it."

Jason thought for a minute. "Has anybody been fired recently?"

"Jay, I've been through every possibility and I've come up with nothing. Quite honestly, I don't think I really know where to begin. This just doesn't make any sense. Like we said before, maybe it's a false alarm and tomorrow we can all laugh about it.

"That'd be nice," Jason agreed. He still chose not to tell Jack about Dailey's conversation, hoping he would get a good night's rest. "You get some sleep. I'll see you tomorrow."

* * * * *

Later that evening Jason received a return call from Joe Castellano, his message brief and to the point. "Two of five are available for tomorrow," he said. "The meet will be south of Portland at the Aurora Airport at 1250 hrs. Steve Honeycut will be driving up from Eugene and Dave DuPonte will be flying in on a private. I hope you know what you're doing," Castellano cautioned. "Oh, by the way, Sobahr would just love to do some snooping for you. He'll be at the office at eight sharp. I'll be a little late, and I haven't been able to get hold of Bennie yet, but he generally shows about that time. See you tomorrow."

CHAPTER NINE

A good sleep, a shower, and the aroma of fresh-ground coffee beans rejuvenated Jason. While the coffee steeped in the French press, he quickly scanned the first few pages of the morning paper. What he found on the bottom corner of page six brought great disappointment.

"Dammit," he said aloud as he read:

Stabbing Victims Identified

Late yesterday, a Seattle Police Department spokesman released the identity of the male and female victims of a brutal knife attack in the parking lot of The Box Car Restaurant late Sunday night. The fatally stabbed male was identified as Carston Jennings, a Vermont resident. The woman victim, Seattle resident Lori Phillips, was taken by Life Flight to St. Francis' Hospital where she remains in critical condition. "At this time a motive has not been determined," the spokesman said, "but it is the subject of an ongoing investigation."

"Dammit," Jason said again. With the names of the victims revealed, the perpetrators would know they had killed the wrong person. In addition, they now had the location of a surviving witness. "Dammit to hell."

He immediately called Dailey, whom he knew would not be in at that hour, and left his home phone and cell phone numbers. With that done, he pressed the coffee and made breakfast. Jason enjoyed cooking as a hobby and took pride in his culinary abilities. But he did not enjoy eating alone, so his commercial range received little use. This morning, however, he had time before his meeting with the partners to whip up some crepes and grill a small portion of his homemade country sausage.

*   *   *   *   *

Jason strode through the door to the offices of Castellano, DiAngelis, and Partner at precisely 8 a.m.

"Well, Mr. Brisben, what's the occasion?" Gwen inquired. Gwen, the feisty mainstay in the office, appeared to be at least seventy, but didn't look a day over one hundred and one. Her shriveled-apple-sculpture complexion was the likely result of spending the first sixty-five years of her youth as a sun worshipper and dedicated chain smoker. Nobody quite knew why the sun worship had gone by the wayside, but the smoking habit burned as hot as ever.

"I just thought I'd stop in to see how the big dogs are getting on."

"The IRS on your ass again, huh?" she said, priding herself on her intuitiveness.

Jason, having a soft spot for Gwen, didn't have the heart to disappoint her. "It's just incredible how you know these things, Gwen. You're truly clairvoyant. Is Joe in?"

"No, he called and asked me to remind you that he'd be in about eight-thirty. But Bennie D's in. He'll meet you in the conference room with Sobahr. Go on in. They're expecting you. I'll let them know you're here, and I'll bring in some coffee."

Jason thanked her and saw himself to the conference room where he stood at the window admiring the view of the Seattle Harbor and West Seattle. The offices of Castellano, DiAngelis, and Partner were plush but not overbearing. However, their offices and those of their support staff took up a good portion of the 43rd floor of the Columbia Center Tower.

"Ah, Jason, it is good to see you, my friend," Sobahr said upon entering the room. "Benjamin will be along momentarily. How have you been?" he asked, as the two men shook hands.

Sobahr Taharin was of Turkish ancestry and one of the few ex-CIA operatives who, while having made the transition into the private sector, remained very well-connected and moonlighted for the "company" from time to time.

"I've been fine, Sobahr. And you?" Jason asked, as the handshake lingered.

"I am truly fine, my friend. Things could not be better." Sobahr, a small, frail man with a dark complexion and rapidly graying hair, had coal black eyes filled with exuberance. As always with him, things could not be better. "And," Sobahr looked quizzically to Jason, "why this visit, my friend? No trouble with Uncle Sugar, I trust?" Uncle Sugar was Sobahr's sarcastic term for the IRS.

"No, not this time. I've come on another matter entirely. But in the interest of time, I'll wait for Ben before I get into details."

"Ah, of course, Jason, always the expedient one. We shall wait. Benjamin will be along in a moment."

Gwen brought in a tray with a carafe of coffee and cups. "Thank you Gwen. Fresh coffee, Jason, I just made it a few minutes ago," Sobahr said beaming. He took great pride in brewing nearly undrinkable Turkish-style coffee.

Jason had met Sobahr during the development of the anti-terrorist team. He had been loaned to the team because of his experience and knowledge in the field of Middle East terrorism. As a mild-mannered bean counter, he had infiltrated camps in Iraq, Libya, and Iran, and his expertise had proven invaluable. Jason had introduced Sobahr to Joe and Ben at the time they also were gathering intelligence on Libya.

Prior to the 1980's, Joe and Ben had been army cryptologists in Vietnam. Jason would bring them information from his raids. At one time, Jason and his SEAL team had rescued Joe and Ben, when, because of a communication screw-up, their outpost had been left undefended and fell under attack by VC. Jason and twelve men, being outnumbered thirty-to-one, went back for Joe and Ben and brought them out safely. The two men felt they owed Jason a debt of honor.

Joe, Ben, and Sobahr had been invaluable to Jason and his surviving team members during the persecution of the anti-terrorist team because they fed him information and provided safe houses. The debt of honor continued when they set up the offshore trust (Jason's nest egg), sheltering it from taxes.

Since the war in Iraq, CD&P had become a notoriously successful hired gun in helping companies combat hostile take-overs. They had become legendary folk heroes on the wave of public disdain for the corporate greed of the eighties. All of the partners were still doing a considerable amount of consulting for various government agencies. Bennie D and Joe specialized in anti-trust and tax law and Sobahr in, as he termed it, manipulative accounting. These three men could make Boeing look like a dime store on the brink of bankruptcy.

As the verbose Sobahr prattled on, Jason's mind drifted to concerns for Jack's safety. His thoughts were interrupted when Benjamin DiAngelis entered. Jason and Ben shook hands and, after briefly shared pleasantries, seated themselves at the conference table along with Sobahr. "Why don't you bring us up to date," Joe said. Jason relayed the events in the parking lot and Dailey's information from Lori Phillips confirming that Jack was the target.

"I will be meeting David DuPonte and Steve Honeycut later today in Portland. They'll be with him 24/7, and also be snooping for the reason someone might want Jack out of the way."

"It doesn't sound like you have a hell of a lot, Jason. Joe said last night that you wanted some information on a couple of companies. What exactly do you need?" With his easy manner and broad face full of smile lines, Benjamin DiAngelis, a six-foot-six, three hundred-pound Greek with a full head of black, curly hair, always set his clients at ease. He casually leaned back in his chair lightly tapping his pencil on his notepad while his dark eyes searched Jason's.

"I want the full meal deal," Jason answered. "Jack has no known enemies. That leaves me only one logical conclusion—it's work-related." Jason explained what he had learned from Jack about Richard Pathmoor. "I want Pathmoor checked out thoroughly. Also, check out companies that Cervicon has done work for over the past three years. Look for anything adversarial that might have come out of any of those relationships. Jack's working on a job in Portland at Biddwell Die Casting. There was a break-in with a considerable amount of damage. They do some government contract work. See if anything raises a red flag with their financials or anything else you can think of. While I'm in Portland, I'll see if Jack can help with Biddwell's personnel information. That sort of information may narrow the field."

"My God, Jason, you're talking about copious hours of work here," Ben stated bluntly. Do you have a time frame?"

"Yeah, I do, and you're not going to like it. After this morning's paper, whoever attempted the hit will know they whacked the wrong guy and will probably try to correct their mistake. Right now we have one minor advantage; they don't know that we suspect anything. We may have a chance to collar them if they make another run at him. Jack will be in Portland for a couple more days. That will give David and Steve time to settle into a routine with him."

Joe Castellano joined them as Jason concluded. Castellano, very Italian, average height, olive complexion, dark eyes, and black hair slicked back, could pass on any given day for Al Pacino.

"Hell, man, you needed this information two days ago," Joe said, after being briefed. "You have anything big going on?" he asked looking sideways at Ben.

Ben slowly brushed his lips contemplatively with his finger tips. "Nothing that can't wait," he said, as he removed his hand from his mouth with a discernible smirk. "Just like old times," he said. "Except last time, we knew our enemy. This time, we got squat. What about the police, you think they'll work with us?"

Jason shook his head. "Nothing we can use at this time, and I think we can move faster than they can."

"I've got to tell ya, you bit off a big one," Ben said matter-of-factly. He turned toward Sobahr. "How much time do you have left on your project?"

"Two or three days," Sobahr replied after a moment's thought. "But I do not think our client is in a rush. I have time for my friend."

"I have at least two more days of litigation. After that's wrapped up, I'll have time," Joe advised, glancing back and forth from partner to partner. "So, do we take on this project?" he asked. Joe and Jason both received affirmative nods from Ben and Sobahr. "Then let's roll up our sleeves and get to it." Joe picked up the phone and buzzed Gwen, asking her to bring everyone note pads and to hold all calls.

Sobahr spoke as Joe and Ben removed their suit jackets. "Jason, you have undertaken a very difficult task. We will not be able to get everything you ask of us very quickly."

"With Jack in Portland, we will have an advantage, but it will be short-lived. I know Jack, and he won't to go into hiding without putting up a fuss. So my hope is that we'll get some sort of a break before tomorrow night or talk him into staying in Portland longer. It's imperative that we keep his wife from finding out about this. Hopefully, I'll hear from the rest of the team; that will give me the resources to cover their house."

Gwen entered the room with legal pads, pencils, and a carafe of drinkable coffee and inquired about any further needs before taking leave.

"We still have The Kennel in Tukwila," Sobahr volunteered. The safe house that CD&P had provided for Jason and the surviving team members several years back bore the code name, The Kennel. "We could have it cleaned for you very quickly."

"I appreciate that," Jason responded, "but I think his family will be okay at least for a couple of days. If it becomes necessary after Jack finishes in Portland, I can move them to my place on the Island." Jason owned a summer cottage in Oak Bay near Victoria on Vancouver Island.

"Jason, I gotta tell ya, I think you need to rethink this and get them the hell out while we still have the edge," Joe cautioned.

Jason explained Tommy's condition to the group and the pressure Debbie was feeling. "Jack is adamant about not informing her unless it becomes absolutely necessary but I'll bring it up again when I see him.

"Weapons and transportation?" Joe queried.

"I have everything I need," Jason said.

Joe interrupted, "When I spoke to David and Steve last night, I told them to bring their foul-weather gear, so God only knows what all they'll show up with." Foul-weather gear usually meant weapons and body armor. "For transportation, I told Steve to rent a car. He'll be driving directly to the Aurora air strip."

"Okay, gentlemen, if there's nothing else," Jason said as he stood, "I have to check in with Dailey. I'll call you with any developments. Thank you, my friends, I appreciate your help." Before he reached the door, Joe called to Jason. "Keep your eyes open and watch your back."

"Count on it," Jason answered. The two men held eye contact for a moment, then he turned and left.

* * * * *

"Lieutenant Dailey, please," Jason said into his cell phone as he merged onto the I-5 freeway heading south. A moment later Dailey picked up. "Lieutenant, have you read the morning paper?" his tone communicated his displeasure at having Carston Jennings' name made known to the public.

Jason's subtle abuse did not go unnoticed by Dailey. "Yeah, I have. And just so you know, I gave our public affairs nitwit a royal ass-chewing. Now, with that out of the way, what can I do for you?"

"Well, in view of the circumstances, I was hoping you could find someone to keep an eye on O'Connor's house until I can collect the resources to cover it. And I'd like someone outside Phillips' too."

"Probably not a bad idea," Dailey agreed. "I'll find out who's available and see if I can get an appropriation for the manpower."

"It will be some time tomorrow before I can have my people in place. I should know by the time I return from Portland this evening."

"Oh, by the way," Dailey said, "I forgot to mention this last night. Lori Phillips asked me to have you stop by to see her. She wants to thank you for saving her life and also for the flowers."

"Will do. I'll stop by the hospital on my way home. Thanks for the help, Lieutenant." Jason disconnected feeling he had made a little more progress with Dailey. An inch at a time, the thought brought a smile.

He glanced briefly at the phone still in his hand as he drove. Even though Laura had cautioned him to give Carol some time and space, he called in spite of the warning but only listened to the cheery greeting on her answering machine. He thought she would want to know about Lori Phillips' regaining consciousness and felt disappointment at not being able to reach her. However, after a moment's thought, he realized he just wanted to hear her voice, maybe check the pulse of their relationship—if there was a pulse. As his disappointment turned to frustration, he decided to call Jack's home. He knew that Debbie would be happy to hear about Lori.

When she answered, he passed on the good news. "I'm planning to visit Lori this evening. You're welcome to come along. Maybe Jennifer could watch the kids for an hour or so."

"I'd really love to, Jason, but I have plans for this evening. Actually, I think you'd rather I stood you up. Carol's coming over this afternoon and I asked her to stay for dinner tonight. I just talked to her about fifteen minutes ago."

"Thank God! How does she sound? I just called her a minute ago and didn't get an answer."

"She's angry, scared, frustrated, and confused. I can really understand what she's going through. She'll be all right. Just give her a little time," Debbie said, reinforcing the advice he had received from Laura. "She wouldn't be having all these feelings if she didn't love you. Believe me, I know what I'm talking about. I went through the same kinds of doubts and fears when Jack and I were first together."

"I'm sorry you were dragged into this, but I sure appreciate your help. If it's any consolation, I have an appointment with my counselor tonight, so I guess we'll both be working on it. I hate to cut this short, but I'm on my way to an appointment. I'll call you tonight after I visit Lori and let you know how she is. And, Debbie, thanks again for your help."

"Don't mention it, and try not to worry. It'll all work out, you'll see. Take care and we'll talk tonight."

A sensation of relief washed over Jason. Even though he had doubts, he hoped Debbie would help Carol understand. It comforted him just knowing that she cared enough to help. As the miles peeled away beneath clear blue skies, a contemplative spirit settled in, and for the second time in less than two days, he became aware of his frustration, his unsettledness, a grating at his soul. Never before had he worried about a woman. Why now was it so important that he talk to Carol? The epiphany came in an instant: He feared losing her. Not that he had her, but the fear of her loss *was* a first.

With the car on cruise, he drifted back in time to painful memories. As a child, he had had to fight the abuse of his father, the trouble toward which he seemed to gravitate, and eventually the law. He had been an angry loner ever since. The elite fighting force, the SEAL teams, and later the anti-terrorist team had been a natural fit for him, his surrogate family of sorts.

His sense of belonging had suddenly evaporated during the demise of the anti-terrorist team. Now he felt like a misfit. With his service pension and the buy-off money, he had no financial worries, but he was bored and unfulfilled—until this situation with Jack. He thought it important to protect Jack and his family, and, in the process, realized that he envied what Jack had—the love of a mate, a more stable way of life. Conversely, his fearless craving for excitement, his fast cars and boat, the abusive way in which he kept his body in shape and rock hard, opposed that lifestyle 180 degrees. Although exhilarated by what Jack had stumbled into, part of him wished to leave that life behind.

Something deep inside coveted the peace and tranquillity, expressed in his classical music, his library, his loft, the furnishings—they all breathed serenity and he sorely wished Carol would have a part in it.

In the past, he had fought for his life, and done so very effectively. He had looked forward to combat, even reveled in it. But now, now he faced the possibility of losing two people for whom he cared deeply, one possibly to murder, and one because of what he'd become. Jack and Carol were as close as he had ever come to real family. And he could see one or the other, or both, slipping away. These issues kept him unsettled, his subconscious relentlessly rendering them to the surface.

Decision time, Jason thought. What do I want to do with the rest of my life? I'm forty-eight years old, able to plan the rest of my life without having to worry about the daily struggle of finances. I'm strong, healthy, I can do anything I want. All I need to do is figure it out.

Jason did not want for personal possessions—his loft, the Cobra, his thirty-eight-foot twin-engine 2,500-HP offshore race boat, the Seville that quietly and comfortably encased him as he closed the distance to Portland at nearly ninety miles per hour. But they were not that important to him in the grand scheme of things. He appreciated more the simple gifts of life, watching sunsets from his deck—and what an uncomplicated thing, what a contrast to his past. But what does it matter if I'm not happy?

He continued to burn away the miles, pondering the mysteries of his life. After another twenty-five miles, he came to the sobering conclusion that although Carol, Jack and his family, plus good health, were important, they were only embellishments to life. They could not bring what he yearned for. Fulfillment he would have to find for himself. It would have to come from within.

CHAPTER TEN

Jack opened his eyes and rolled instinctively toward the bedside clock. He blinked several times; a digital display of 7:15 slowly came into focus, its image filtered through a foggy brain. Sleep had been an elusive commodity, which his weary body willingly confirmed. The previous night's conversations had taken their toll. Awake most of the night, Jack tossed and turned with worry, hoping and praying that Jason's and Dailey's suspicions were a mistake, but he suspected they were not. He did not fear for himself, but for Debbie and their children.

In his thirteen years of marriage, Jack had done his best to insulate Deb from undue pressure. While she had never been shielded from the realities of life, and took an active role in the decision-making process, Jack always assumed the responsibility of stewardship, affording her the uninhibited freedom to be a devoted full-time mother. Jennifer, Ashley, and Tommy were their testament to the value of family and active parenting.

Then Tommy's illness crept into their lives, bringing with it an emotional drain on them both. Then medical bills, for one reason or another, were not covered by their medical insurance. If they did not obtain the proper referrals, the claims were denied. If tests were not pre-approved, the claims were denied.

But The Suter bonus would have solved their financial woes. They had planned to pay off the note to the contractor, pay down their mortgage and refinance at a lower interest rate, giving them an extra five hundred a month. But the breakdown at Suter occurred, and Martin Cray had retired, leaving Jack to deal with Pathmoor. Although Jack tried not to talk about his situation, he knew it all took a toll on Debbie. And now he feared this latest development would put her over the top.

His thoughts returned to the present and he rolled onto his back for a moment and stared at the ceiling. "Who" and "why" plagued his tired mind. What the hell have I stumbled into, he questioned. Does it have something to do with this job at Biddwell?. . . with Suter?. . . God forbid, with Cervicon? It all pressed in on him like a suffocating blanket.

Jack forced himself to an upright position. He had never been one to feel sorry for himself, and he did not think to start now. He set himself to see the thing through, and whatever it happened to be, he would make sure that Deb would not suffer because of it. She always would be his first priority.

* * * * *

"Good morning Mr. O'Connor," Lisa said, as he walked into the atrium of Biddwell Die Casting. Jack's freshly hotel-pressed clothes looked stellar, but the man inside them did not match. His tired, worried face, and blood-shot eyes had not gone unnoticed.

"Good morning, Lisa."

A naturally cheerful enthusiasm radiated from her, even though her face clearly communicated her observation of Jack's weary appearance. "It looks like you're heading into a busy day," she advised. "You have two messages and one appointment waiting in the conference room. Maybe we should put you on the payroll." Lisa looked up smiling. Jack unknowingly displayed a puzzled expression. "Here you go," she said as she handed him the phone memos. "You have a message from a Dwight Sheffield and one from a Richard Pathmoor. And Karl Denton arrived about five minutes ago. He's in the conference room. You can use the phone in the conference room and I'll bring you coffee. Is there anything else I can get for you?"

"No, that will be fine, and thank you," Jack said, as he took his messages. "You're a gem." As he walked the hall to the conference room, he looked over the messages.

Jack greeted Karl Denton as he entered the conference room. Denton, one half of the two-man night security team Jack hired, agreed to meet in the morning to give his recommendations on the security system monitor placement. A fair amount of the Biddwell operation went on during the second shift and Jack wanted to make sure that his monitors were positioned for optimum coverage. After Lisa brought in a tray with coffee, the two men spent an hour reviewing the rough sketches Jack had prepared the day before and finalizing the materials and equipment list.

After Denton departed, Jack picked up his phone memos and called Dwight Sheffield, saving Richard Pathmoor for last. Jack used Sheffield regularly for Cervicon's Oregon accounts rather than bringing a crew down from Seattle. He scheduled an appointment early the next morning when he would give him a full equipment list and a tour of the plant in order to facilitate adequate preparation for the system installation.

His conversation with Sheffield completed, Jack poured himself another cup of coffee and sat back in his chair. The combination of stress and lack of sleep had not only extracted his energy, but his enthusiasm as well. He leaned his head back to rest his eyes for a few moments, a failed attempt to fight off the exhaustion. Once again, his eyes settled on the message from Richard Pathmoor. "I might as well get it over with," he said aloud, and picked up the phone. But before calling Pathmoor, he pushed the extension button to the front desk.

"Lisa, it's Jack O'Connor. Will you see if Mr. Hargrave would be available for lunch today?

"Peter is on the phone. I'll check as soon as he's finished."

"Thanks, Lisa." With that accomplished, he could think of no other reason to stall. He took a deep breath and called Cervicon.

"Good morning, Cervicon, this is Marcy."

"Hi Marcy. Is Richard P in?"

"Well, good morning, Jack. Oh yeah, he's in. It's 'P' as in 'pissed off.' I take it you called in for some self-inflicted pain?"

"I guess. You'd better put me through."

"Okay, but when you're finished, have Mr. Pissed Off transfer you back to the switchboard, I have some messages for you."

"Will do." While Marcy transferred, Jack thought back to how he had eagerly poured himself into Cervicon for nineteen and a half years and now he hated to go into the office or even call in any more. It was—

"Pathmoor."

"Good morning, Richard. I got a message that you called."

"What the hell takes you so long to return my call, O'Connor!"

"What took so long is that we have a company in a crisis down here and I've been in a meeting this morning."

"Well, we have a goddamned crisis up here! Mr. Sloan from Suter called me, and he's hot. He says if you don't sign off on the final system approval, he'll sue. I don't give a damn what you're working on down there, get up here and get the system approval signed and on my desk."

"Dammit, Dick, I talked with him last Friday. He knows there is no way we can assume the liability for the testing facility without the changes. Our butts will be hanging out a country mile. You ought to know that by now. How many times do we have to go over this thing?"

"They're financially at risk because of the delays. We have to relax some of the requirements. You need to get back here and work this thing out."

"They're at risk because they changed the plans after our designs were completed and approved. We can't allow their financial problem to become our liability. We've been through this, God knows how many times, with our underwriters. The way Sloan wants this thing written, we'll be assuming all of the risks. Our underwriter won't give us liability insurance on their terms. And if they have an accident, you know as well as I do, they'll come after Cervicon, and there isn't enough money in Seattle to cover the settlements. Why is that so damned hard for you to understand?"

"Maybe you didn't understand me. They're going to start legal proceedings if they don't get the approval by 9 a.m. Thursday morning. I want you back up here this afternoon."

"It isn't going to happen. Whether I come back or not, I'm not going to sign off until they comply with the safeguards. You'd better get used to it or get someone else to design their damn system, because I cannot come back today."

"That just may happen sooner than you think, O'Connor."

"GO FOR IT!" Jack slammed the receiver into the cradle. "You ignorant jerk," he said much louder than he had intended.

"Friend of yours?" Peter Hargrave asked smiling, as he poked his head around the conference room doorjamb.

Jack spun around, startled. "I'm sorry," he apologized, his face flushed with heat, "some company politics. I hope I wasn't too disruptive."

"Not a problem," Hargrave said, good-naturedly. "So, you're up for lunch, I hear. I'm buying. It'll make up for the dinner you missed last night."

Jack looked puzzled. "What dinner?"

"I called your hotel, wanted to get together for dinner. They said you had checked out."

Jack felt his face flush again, he did not lie well. "There was a mix-up with the reservations. I stayed at The Courtyard down the street," he said trying to recover. "Lunch it is. I hope you don't mind a working lunch," Jack said, still unnerved.

"Working lunches are good," Hargrave said. "And it will give you an opportunity to bring me up to date on the system design. Also, I can get some preliminary numbers from you for a capital purchase requisition. How about eleven-thirty? That way, we'll beat the crowd."

"Eleven-thirty works for me." Jack welcomed the relief when Hargrave finally left the room.

* * * * *

At eleven-twenty-five, Lisa stopped Jack and Peter Hargrave on their way through the lobby. "I have a Marcy on hold for you, Mr. O'Connor. You can take it right here if you like."

Damn! I forgot to call back to the switchboard, Jack thought. "Thanks Lisa," he said as he took the receiver from her. "I'm sorry, Marcy. Things got a little out of hand and I forgot to call back. What do you have for me?"

"It sounds like I'm gonna have a termination check for you if Pathmoor doesn't calm down. He's on a rampage. What the heck is going on?"

"I can't go into it right now; I'll fill you in later. What about those messages?"

"Okay, here you go. At nine-ten this morning, Paul Terrell from Quays Construction called, needs to talk to you ASAP about the Suter Research plans. Brenda from the drafting department asked me to let you know that the Watson plans are ready. She wants to know if you need to see them before she sends them off."

"Tell Brenda to send the prints." Then musing aloud, "It looks like Sloan is working all the angles. He's probably trying to pressure the Construction Company into finishing without the updated clean room system. I'll call Paul Terrell right after lunch. Is there anything else?"

"Nope that's it . . . Oh, wait a minute, some guy called about a half an hour ago. He sounded a little strange. First he wanted to talk to you. I told him that you were out of town and wouldn't be back into the office until Thursday morning. He asked for a phone number where you could be reached. I told him I couldn't give out that information. He interrupted me, asking where you were, and I told him that I couldn't give out that information either, but if he would leave his name and number, I would have you return his call when you checked in. He seemed angry and just hung up. Weird, huh?"

"Is that all he said? Are you sure he didn't say anything else?" Jack asked, fighting to retain his composure. He could feel droplets of perspiration forming on his upper lip and around his temples. He knew now that Jason had a valid concern and felt weak at the confirmation.

"That's all that he said. I've repeated everything practically verbatim," Marcy replied.

Well, the goons figured out their mistake, he thought. "Marcy, if anyone else calls, be sure to get a number, but whatever you do, don't give out my location." Urgency filled Jack's voice.

"Jack, is everything all right? Did I do something wrong?"

"You did just fine. I'll check in with you later today. You don't need to worry—everything's fine," Jack said, wishing he believed it. He handed the receiver back to Lisa.

Jack returned to Hargrave who sat in the atrium area reading a *Business Week*. "Sorry for the delay, Peter. Hope we can still beat the lunch crush."

"You all right, buddy? You're looking a little peaked."

Jack knew how he must have looked and could do nothing about it. "I'm all right," he said weakly. "Let's have lunch and tie up some of these loose ends."

During lunch, Hargrave imparted the progress on the purging of the hydraulic systems and the repairs to the machines and dies. "It's all taking longer than our original estimates. The good news is, only eight of the ten machines have been contaminated and at this time we have four machines operating and will have another two up and running this evening."

"That is encouraging," Jack responded with disguised enthusiasm. Because of his personal situation, he found it difficult to concentrate on the information. However, he did hear enough to carry on an intelligent conversation. "Although it's taking longer than you thought, you're still ahead of the game. The perpetrators assumed that you would look at external damage and not find the sabotaged hydraulic systems."

"Well we have you to thank for that brilliant bit of intuition," Hargrave commented sincerely.

They talked leisurely during lunch about fishing, golf, and their families. After dessert and their coffee had been warmed, Jack presented the rough layout of the system he proposed. His presentation began to have a therapeutic effect, a diversion that took his mind off the bad news he had received prior to lunch. He continued on enthusiastically for an hour and a half feeling pleased with the design he had created in such a short time. "So, what do you think?"

"I think you've done your homework and a great job," Hargrave said, obviously impressed. "How soon can you get this down on hard copy with firm numbers? You can consider it a done deal, but I would like you to present a dog and pony show to Donald Biddwell before we start."

"Not a problem," Jack said eagerly. "If you can get me on a computer with a modem, I can have a hard copy of the materials and equipment, plus firm numbers in proposal form tomorrow morning. The actual project prints will take longer. I don't expect to have them much before Friday. However, I think I can get our drafting department to piece some preliminary stuff together."

"Whatever you need. I'll have Lisa set you up when we get back," Hargrave said as he picked up the check.

While Jack had lost himself in the Biddwell project during lunch with Hargrave, on the short return trip, his personal problems slithered into his thoughts like a serpent stalking its prey. The situation with Richard Pathmoor was becoming intolerable. I need to get in touch with Martin, he thought. I need to know if I have a future with Cervicon. After this morning, it's questionable. He made a mental note to make a call to Martin his highest priority upon his return to Biddwell. Then another thought entered his mind; someone's trying to punch my ticket. So how in the hell do I deal with that on top of everything else?

The silence did not go unnoticed by Peter Hargrave. "You're awfully quiet, Jack."

"I'm just thinking about all the details that need to be handled by the Friday shutdown," Jack lied. "But I probably don't have nearly as much going on as you do," he continued, trying to turn the focus of the conversation.

"Yeah, we do have a lot to do, but I just do what I can, and the rest, well—you just do what you can."

As they entered the building, Hargrave arranged for Lisa to set Jack up in one of the offices with a computer so he could begin work on his proposal. Lisa led Jack to an office, turned on the light and booted the computer for him.

"This is Jessica's office, our accountant," she offered. "She's on maternity leave, so I don't think she'll be bothering you," she laughed. "If you need anything, you know where to find me."

The accountant's office, Jack thought to himself as he looked around the room. This has got to be the mother lode. It would be relatively easy to do a little snooping into the electronic bowels of Biddwell Die Casting. He navigated around in the computer for a few minutes, then sat back in his chair, unable to concentrate. I have to get this thing with Pathmoor settled once and for all, he decided. Jack did not believe in ultimatums, but he couldn't help but feel one brewing. He took a minute to compose himself, to think of how to best present his case, so as not to appear subversive. One way or another, he would know where he stood with Cervicon.

Jack picked up the telephone and angrily punched in the numbers to Martin Cray's home and waited.

CHAPTER ELEVEN

The sun flashed off the silver wings of the needle-like Lear jet as it made a wide arc in a southerly approach into the Aurora airport located twenty miles south of Portland. It glided effortlessly, touching down on the runway in front of Jason and Steve as they waited on the tarmac. They watched in silence as the small plane streaked past, then slowed and exited the runway onto the taxiway at the far end of the field a half mile to the north. It had been almost five years since Jason had seen both the man standing next to him and David, who was aboard the approaching private charter with its engines now spooled down to a low whine, a thoroughbred cooling down after a brisk run. David and Steve were two of the remaining six anti-terrorist team members, the two men to whom Jason had been the closest during his twenty-two-plus years of service.

Jason had arrived at the little airport just minutes before and it had afforded him little time to visit with Steve before they spotted the aircraft on its approach. Both men shared an unspoken excitement at their reunion as the plane pulled to a stop in front of them with just a slight dip of the nose, a subtle salute. Jason wondered what David would look like. With the exception of thinner hair, Steve had not changed. He had been a fearless man with uncanny instincts and macabre sense of humor, which had endeared him to Jason. Steve Honeycut, now fifty-three years old, five-ten, a hundred-sixty pounds of muscle and sinew, still had his broad shoulders and his enviable size-thirty waist. Although Jason stood at least two inches above Steve, he never considered him small, probably because pound for pound he was stronger than anyone on the team. Steve dressed in multi-colored baggies, a SEAL team tee shirt, and a light warmup jacket. His jacket did not serve to warm him on this sunny day, but to conceal the weapon carried under his left arm in a shoulder holster.

The plane had only been stopped a moment before the door opened and the stairway extended. David DuPonte appeared, filling the door with his six-foot-four, two-hundred-twenty-pound frame. He needed to bow low in order to exit, then climbed down the steps to greet his two-man welcoming committee. David hadn't lost his John Wayne walk. The only movement of his body took place from the waist down; his head and torso seemed to glide with no perceptible motion. He had added about fifteen pounds and a full, shortly cropped beard that matched his strawberry blond hair. He wore a pink golf shirt, khaki Dockers, and loafers without socks, and carried a small duffel bag.

"I knew that bullshit amnesty agreement would never hold," David said boisterously as the three men embraced. David referred to the same condition about which Joe Castellano had cautioned Jason: The team members must have no contact as a part of the twelve-million-dollar amnesty deal. "So, Commander Brisben, what's so damn important that you needed to interrupt my golf game?" He tried unsuccessfully to conceal his conspiratorial grin.

"He figured you needed some real exercise. You're looking a lot like Moby Dick," Steve interrupted.

"Who asked you, runt?" David rejoined, with a failed attempt to look perturbed.

"I see nothing has changed," Jason said, and the three men laughed. David and Steve had been in a feigned adversarial relationship since their first meeting, but had adopted each other as team partners almost instantly and remained so during their tenure. Jason suspected they had been in contact in spite of the amnesty rules. "Let's get your gear and I'll brief you over coffee."

A few minutes later, David's two large duffel bags, plus the one he carried off of the airplane, were stowed in the white Taurus stationwagon that Steve had rented. They now sat around a table in the coffee shop and Jason gave a detailed account of Jack O'Connor's situation, the morning meeting with the partners, and his en-route telephone conversation with Lt. Dailey. Then he described the hit in the parking lot and the content of the phone message that Jack's wife had received.

"I want you two glued to Jack like ugly on an ape," Jason directed. "As far I can determine, these guys are 'walk up and do it' people, so keep your eyes open. You know the drill—it's just like secret-service duty—eyes open, run interference, and take prisoners. Then we sort it out. What about weapons?"

"Just issue stuff for me," David said. "I brought my Beretta 9mm and a Smith 357. Oh, brought along my night gear just for the hell of it."

"Same here," Steve added, "except I brought an HK my recon bag, and night gear. I talked earlier with Sobahr. He told me The Kennel would be cleaned and ready for use by tomorrow afternoon."

"Okay, sounds good," Jason said, contemplatively, his brow knitted while he weighed all contingencies. "We'll get moving—I need to be back in Seattle by five. I want you packing going into Biddwell. I don't think anyone knows where Jack is yet, but let's not take any chances." The three men returned to their cars where David slid his weapon into a hip holster and covered it with a golf sweater.

* * * * *

The three men walked into the reception area of Biddwell. Jason introduced himself to Lisa and asked for Jack O'Connor.

"Oh yes," she responded cheerfully. "Mr. O'Connor has been expecting you. I'll let him know you're here." She left the reception area and disappeared down the hallway.

It wasn't but a minute before Jack appeared, talking with Lisa as they walked toward the reception desk. Jason introduced Jack to David and Steve, then Jack led them to the conference room where he had set up his temporary office. Jason closed the door and cut directly to business.

"I'm afraid I have bad news, Jack," Jason said. "Dailey interviewed Lori Philips last night, and she confirmed you as the target." Jason looked a bit surprised by the lack of response from Jack, until Jack recapped his earlier conversation with Marcy regarding the man who called Cervicon and would not leave his name.

"I knew then that you were right all along," Jack said calmly. "It didn't take them long to figure out they blew it."

"It wouldn't, with the help they had from the newspapers," Jason said with disgust. He explained about the morning's page-six article. "I think it would be a good idea if we moved your family out of the area until we get this sorted out." Jason could see by Jack's expression that his suggestion did not sit well.

"Absolutely not. The last thing I want to do is drag Debbie and the kids into this. It's me they're after, not my family."

"Yeah, well that's real noble," David said. "The truth is, the fastest way to you just might be through your family." David never minced words, not caring what people thought of him or his tatics.

But Jack did not intimidate easily. "No," Jack reiterated, looking back at David with a no-nonsense glare of his own. "I won't involve them—at least until I can be with them."

Jason knew that they were going nowhere on the present course, and after telling Jack that Dailey had committed to the surveillance of his house, he changed tack. "I'm having the partners check out Biddwell. They'll be looking for anything that might not look quite right, no matter how obscure. We could use a little help from you if you're up for it. Information on personnel, financials, all that type of information you can get your hands on."

"Your timing couldn't be better. Peter Hargrave set me up on a computer in an office down the hall to help speed the system design. In fact I've already learned my way around their system. If you provide me with an e-mail address for CD&P, I could have some information to them before you get back to Seattle."

Jason gave him Sobahr's name. "He'll be your contact at the partners."

As they planned their strategy, Jason observed an uneasiness in Jack, something bothering him other than the morning's business. He wanted time alone with Jack to find out what. "Jack, does anyone know where you're staying?"

"Only Peter Hargrave," he answered.

"That's one person too many." It provided the excuse Jason needed to send David and Steve on an errand. "David, Steve, on the way in, I saw a Phoenix Inn. I want you to get back there and rent a two-bedroom suite. Put it in your name," he added to David. "Get Jack's gear out of The Courtyard, but don't check him out. Leave some toiletries and some underwear lying around. If anyone comes looking for him, it'll appear that he's simply not in. Jack, you're about to disappear. And you two," Jason said, speaking to David and Steve again, "when you get back, make sure that at least one of you, and preferably both of you, are with Jack at all times. I don't want him out of your sight. No exceptions." The two men acknowledged the directive and immediately left the conference room.

Jason looked across the table at his friend. Jack looked bad. His broad shoulders appeared to be hanging loosely from his neck, as if attached by string. The usual enthusiastic sparkle had disappeared from his pale blue eyes; fear and fatigue now stared back at him.

"Jason," Jack began, "I know you have the best intentions in the world, but my situation with Cervicon is tenuous at best, especially after today. I just had a confrontation with Pathmoor and I don't know if I'll have a job when I get back. I can't leave all this hanging and simply disappear. I have a family to think of and bills to be paid."

So that's it, Jason thought. "What exactly is going on between Cervicon and Suter? I remember some sketchy information from Sunday night, but how about some specifics? It seems to me the biggest bone of contention between you and Pathmoor is this issue with Suter."

"The project at Suter has been dragging on like a bad case of hepatitis. We won the bid on that project over two years ago, and they're just now about 75 percent complete with the construction. They are expanding and moving their whole operation from Chehalis to Issaquah."

"What does Suter make?"

"Generic prescription drugs. They have a line of pharmaceutical supplies, syringes, tourniquets, certain surgical supplies too, but their main business is the drugs. However, they're also starting a whole new division devoted to AIDS and Eboli research. That's what makes the whole project so complicated—keeping the manufacturing and testing separate. You can imagine the potential for a catastrophe, having the most contagious of communicable diseases contaminating some off-the-shelf drugs. It's not just a safety and liability concern, but a major public opinion concern. About 80 percent of the security system is devoted to internal safeguards and only 20 percent to external security for breaking and entering. To top it off, the project is about six months behind schedule. I haven't had a warm fuzzy feeling about any aspect of the project."

"Who's responsible for the schedule slip?"

"It gets really complicated. Because of the liability of the disease research, I wouldn't allow Cervicon to guarantee internal security against contamination unless the disease research and the drug manufacturing areas were put into separate facilities. They could be on the same site but in different buildings with a proper quarantine area of separation, whatever that is. That caused a considerable redesign. Two years ago they hadn't committed to the research, so there was no consideration given to it in our original proposal."

"Let me guess. That's when the tension started on the project."

"Exactly. And it escalated after Pathmoor arrived on the scene. There's a lot of money at stake, big money, and, of course, Suter is capitalizing on government subsidies for the research facility."

Jason nodded. "I wasn't going to tell you this, but I'm having the partners check out Cervicon and, in particular, Pathmoor. But now, it might be a good idea to throw Suter Pharmaceuticals into the mix. Maybe you can help speed up the process. Is there a way to get into the Cervicon computers externally?"

"Absolutely, but it's complicated. I designed the safe-guards." Jack's face brightened at the thought of getting information on Pathmoor. Enthusiastically, he said, "I can talk Sobahr through the roadblocks. I'll call him as soon as we're finished here."

"While you're on the phone, give him as much information on Suter as you can. Maybe there's something there as well. Jack, I've given this a lot of thought: Your situation has got to be work-related. It's the only thing that makes sense."

"In that case, it doesn't make my situation with Cervicon any better, does it?" Jack looked down at his hands, then back to Jason. His momentary enthusiasm had all but disappeared.

"No, I'm afraid it doesn't." The two men were silent for a moment. Then Jason spoke, "What's Martin Cray have to say about your situation?"

"Hell, he must be out on his boat or out of town. I haven't been able to reach him," Jack said, with no attempt to mask his frustration.

Jason became silent again, then asked quietly, "You ever think about quitting Cervicon?"

A flush of anger turned Jack's face crimson. "I've spent twenty years building that company, working shoulder to shoulder with Martin. It's my life. I love what I do. This is what I do." He made a sweeping motion around the Biddwell conference room with his hands as a demonstration. Jason started to say something, but Jack continued. "I know what you're going to say, so save your breath. There are other jobs out there, I know that, but I'd rather see this through. And this thing with someone trying to kill me, I'll get through this too."

The fact that Jack never referred to the chance of losing the Suter bonus money, impressed Jason. Money was an issue, but the fulfillment of doing what he loved clearly came through. There's a lesson in that, he thought. Without taking his eyes off Jack, Jason reached to the floor and picked up the satchel that he brought with him, and set it on the table.

"What do you want for yourself; what's your highest priority?"

"I'm not sure that I know what you mean," Jack answered.

"It's not a trick question," Jason said. "Think about it for a minute. What's your most important responsibility?"

"Well. . ." Jack hesitated for a moment, "taking care of my family. Why?"

"You're going to have to trust me if that's truly your goal, and you sure as hell can't take care of them if you're feeding maggots," Jason commented quietly, his eyes cold and penetrating. "I know what it's like to be hunted, Jack. But I had at the very least some advantage—I knew why. You, buddy, are at a double disadvantage. You don't know *who* and you don't know *why*. I also know what it's like to be betrayed, and that's what it seems like Cervicon has done to you. It doesn't sound like there's a whole lot you can do to change Pathmoor's attitude toward you right now.

"I'll talk to Dailey when I get back this afternoon. We'll see how hostile Pathmoor is after Dailey throws a little investigation at him, and see just what crawls out from under *that* rock.

"But, about being hunted, on that I'm an expert and you *are* going to disappear. You can finish up down here, but then you are going on a vacation." Jason pulled a check from the satchel. "Take your vacation time, anything beyond that I'll cover." He slid a check across the table to Jack. It was dated and signed, but the amount was blank. "This is for the note to your contractor. Pay it. This is not a loan. That note is the last thing you need to be worrying about on top of everything else right now." While Jack looked at the check, not knowing what to say, Jason again went into the satchel and removed the Browning High Power. He slid it across the table. "It's locked and loaded. There's a pill up the spout; just pull the hammer back and you're ready to rock and roll."

Jack slowly stood, overwhelmed by the situation. "Jason, I—I can't accept all of this . . . ." He slowly slid the Browning from the small holster and admired the gleaming custom-blued piece as he held it. "It's beautiful . . . I don't know what to say—but—I just can't."

"Sure you can, and don't say anything. Just listen." Jason stood and held him by the shoulders with outstretched arms. After hesitating, Jack looked up from the weapon; their eyes met. "I don't have a lot of friends. As a matter of fact, I can't think of any outside of you and Deb. I'm not complaining. That's the way I've kept it, for whatever reason. You call and bug me every couple of weeks even if you don't hear from me. You've hung in there with me, never trying to dig into my past, never asking about how I spend my time or where my money comes from. You've just accepted me and let it go at that. I guess I've taken it for granted until this situation came up. If something happened to you, Jack, I'd really miss you. I think if you were gone there'd be a gaping hole in my life. So, my friend, this is a labor of love. I have the time and the money, so just accept it as a gift to you and your family."

Jack's eyes were beginning to well with emotion; he turned his head to keep Jason from seeing. After a moment to regain his composure he looked again into Jason's eyes. "Thank you. I won't forget this."

CHAPTER TWELVE

Jack O'Connor's predicament presented Jason with many issues to ponder on the way back to Seattle and plenty of time in which to do it. He reached for his cellular phone and called Laura Mathers' office at a quarter to five. From Olympia north, he had been embroiled in twenty to thirty-mile-an-hour traffic. It would be impossible to meet with Laura at five o'clock. Radio station KBSG's Fast-Lane Phillips had announced that a semi truck had jack-knifed near the Tacoma Dome and Jason just now could see the accident. When the receptionist answered, he identified himself and explained his situation. He learned that Laura had been behind schedule all day and the receptionist assured him that being late would not be a problem. Jason thanked her, then called his answering machine, again hoping for a message from Carol. There was none.

At five-twenty-nine he parallel parked in front of the little brick office building where Laura Mathers shared her practice with two other therapists, off of Admiral Way in West Seattle. Laura did not usually see clients this late. She purposely kept her workload light, never more than six hours a day, four days a week. Quality, not quantity, was a maxim she seldom violated.

Jason announced himself to the matronly receptionist named Marian and seated himself in one of the plush over-stuffed leather chairs.

Jason had no sooner picked up a magazine when Laura's office door opened and she came forward to greet him. Laura Mathers, fortyish, attractive, with dark brown hair highlighted with gray flecks, smiled enthusiastically. Her hazel eyes sparkled. She wore a white embroidered peasant blouse, a long royal-blue skirt, and high burgundy boots. The color of the rich boot leather matched the embroidery on her blouse.

"Jason, it's so good to see you." Laura reached out and took both of his hands. Her hands were warm and communicated genuine sincerity. "Believe it or not, I've made a list of people that I have been wanting to get in touch with and you were at the top of the list. I was so pleased when you called. I hope you weren't put off by my not seeing you last night."

"Well to be honest, I was at first, but, as usual, you were right. I wouldn't have been able to concentrate anyway. I had a lot going on last night."

"You look great as usual, but you're awfully tense. I can feel it," she said, squeezing his hands lightly. Laura had an uncanny ability to decipher people's energy. She could accurately determine internal stress levels within her clients by simply holding a hand or lightly touching her fingertips to their temples. "Come into my office and I'll make you some herbal tea. It will relax you."

Jason followed her into her office and sat in another of the comfortable overstuffed leather chairs and watched in silence while she made his tea. Simply by being in her office, Jason felt some of his tension wash away, like dust in a warm shower. The subdued natural light provided by northern skylights and light tubes, the warm-toned antique furniture, and soft background music, all contributed to an atmosphere conducive to complete relaxation. The old, well-polished furnishings, a walnut desk, matching desk chair, the two overstuffed burgundy leather chairs and a matching love seat all sunk into plush, forest-green carpet.

Laura brought him the tea, then moved her chair directly in front of him. She never conducted sessions from behind her desk. "Jason, before we start, just close your eyes and let the tea work for a few minutes."

Jason leaned his head back into the soft leather. He'd been running on pure adrenaline with no food since his early breakfast. Until that moment, he hadn't realized how tired he was. The tea soothed as it slid down his throat, refreshing and nourishing. After much too short a time, Laura spoke softly. "Do you want to talk about what's been going on?"

Not really, he thought, but with his eyes still closed, Jason began to speak. "As I told you last night, I thought things were going well, until Sunday night." He described in detail the events of two hurricane-like days. "But with all this," he said, "there's something else. I can't put my finger on it. It's like I'm unsettled or uncomfortable inside, or—" He slowly shook his head. "It's like I don't know who I am anymore." Then he went back to describing the confrontation with Carol the night before. He told Laura how he had planned to call her after his previous night with Carol at the loft because he wanted some help on how to work through his feelings and how to communicate better, particularly with Carol. He recounted their lovemaking and the strong feelings, then asked: "How can we be so close, then five hours later she's ready to rip my head off?" His voice and face were filled with frustration and anger.

"Well, you certainly do have a complex situation," Laura said softly and with compassion. "It sounds as if you have two separate issues: First, there are some changes happening, or, more accurately, about to happen in you. Second is the issue with Carol. The changes in you we can deal with at a later time, because they will be ongoing and will happen over time. The issue with Carol is the *now* issue. I guess my question would have to be 'What are you going to do about Carol?'"

"I don't know. That's why I came to you," Jason answered, just then opening his eyes.

"So I could tell you what you should do?"

"I guess, or at least give me some advice," he said hopefully, now alert and somewhat suspicious of her question.

"Jason, I can't tell you what to do, and I can't fix this situation with Carol for you." Laura could read the disappointment in Jason's face and decided to slow the pace. "Let's back up just a bit. Just minutes ago, you said that she left the loft, leaving you a note. What did you feel then?"

"Anger," he said, matter-of-factly.

"What is it about this that makes you angry?" she continued.

"I want to know what set her off or why she's so pissed off. I don't know what I did and I haven't been able to talk to her about it," he said, both exasperated and angry.

"Okay, we have established that you're angry. Anger can be considered a state. What I really want you to tell me is how you feel about your present situation with Carol."

"I have no idea what you're fishing for here. I told you I'm angry," he repeated adamantly.

"So, you're pouting because Carol won't play fair? Is that what's bugging you?" Laura knew that Jason was genuinely frustrated and truly didn't know how to identify his feelings. She understood many men's difficulty with understanding feelings because of their years of programming and macho role modeling. She could see his neck redden and his anger intensify. But she continued to lead him to the goal of discovery—first, discovery of his feelings, then, understanding that it's okay for men to feel, that feelings are neither right nor wrong, simply a part of what shapes who people are.

"I'm not pouting, dammit. I just can't stand being—"

"Come on, you can say it," Laura said with excitement and motioning with both hands, trying to draw him out with encouragement. "Come on, spit it out. What's the feeling?"

"I—I feel—hel—helpless. Hell, I don't know," he stammered, unsure of himself and unsure of what Laura was really after.

"Bingo!" Laura said. "And if you're helpless, you're not—come on don't stop now," she encouraged.

"I don't know. I guess I don't have any control. Hell," he said shaking his head with a look of timidity and frustration.

"Very good! " Laura said with enthusiasm. "I could have told you those two words but it would have just been information. You, on the other hand, struggled hard to find them. Do they feel truthful to you? Are they accurate? In this situation, are you feeling helpless and out of control?"

"Yes," Jason replied, feeling less angry and much relieved that she was no longer badgering him, but also not quite realizing the significance of what he had discovered. "So now that I know that I'm helpless and not in control of my situation, what good is it?"

"Good question. Let's slow down for a second. You just said that your discovery felt truthful. Then you have just acquired knowledge, not just information that you may or may not remember because someone told it to you. Now the plan is to take that knowledge, understand it, then apply it to your situation."

Finally, this is beginning to make a smattering of sense, Jason thought. He could relate to it, if he compared it to the seeming mountains of information that he had gathered while working with intelligence reports. None of the information had value unless it could be applied to a specific situation, then evaluated, and, from that plans developed. Well, this is kind of like that—well maybe, he thought.

"Jason, we as adults can't be in control of much in our lives, and that includes a mate. We'll qualify that statement in a later session. When you were in the service, everything was controlled: training, meals, operations, you name it. But now, people in real life have free will. They can do pretty much what they want, including being angry. You cannot be responsible for or control someone else's feelings or actions. You can deliberately hurt them, but that's not what we're talking about, and I think you understand that." Jason nodded in agreement.

"Carol learned some hard facts about you and reacted to them," Laura continued, leaning forward in her chair in an encouraging posture. "You're reacting to her reaction, and if you're not careful, she'll react to your reaction when you do get together to talk. So, what's your plan, what are you going to do with your newly discovered knowledge?"

Jason thought for a long time before speaking. "Could I have some more tea?" he asked.

"You're stalling," Laura responded bluntly. "Let's keep this moving."

Well, that didn't work, he thought. "I guess in my situation with Carol, I plan not to react, because I have no control of the situation. But how do I get in control?" he asked sincerely.

"Jason, you don't," Laura responded adamantly. "There is a difference between taking control and taking the initiative. You *do* understand the difference. I think that's what you meant. Isn't it?"

"Yeah, but how do I establish communication?"

"You won't have to. My guess is that she'll call you sooner than you think." Laura paused briefly to leave Jason a moment for her last statement to register, then continued. "Let's move on to the next part. What do you think made Carol react to what she learned about you?" Laura asked, moving into the tougher part of the session. She now leaned back in the chair, looking relaxed and confident.

"Well, she seemed to tense up when she found out that my second wife had been murdered." Jason hesitated for a moment as he realized how stupid that statement sounded. Any normal person would have tensed up at hearing *that* news. Laura smiled as she observed his recognition, but kept silent. He continued, "And I guess maybe because she found out that I've killed people. Or—maybe because of some of the things that she's had to go through in her personal life. As I think about it, several issues could have set her off." He frowned as he pondered his answer.

"Jason, I know a little about Carol's background from our sessions a couple of years ago. I know that she has some issues that she undoubtedly needs to work through, and she may never get over grieving the loss of her daughter. If they had found her dead, it would be easier than never knowing what happened to her. That could be an issue, but I don't think it's the issue here. Carol is not stupid; she knows you were a SEAL and that you were trained to kill and probably did." Laura spoke softly and gently and guarded against sounding accusative. "What was your motivation for not telling her about your background?"

"I honestly don't know how to answer. I guess it's—I don't talk about my past, partly because I don't *like* talking about it and I suppose it keeps people guessing, kind of like a mystique."

"We're not talking about just anybody," Laura interrupted, still speaking softly, guarding against putting Jason on the defensive. "You've told me that you want a relationship with this woman and you may consider marrying her. You have shared yourself intimately with her. Do you think you would have ever told her?"

"I don't know if I would have or not. I guess it doesn't make any difference now. Does it?"

"Jason, for future reference, I want you to figure out the answer to that question. Because if your relationship with Carol continues, the question will come up and you *will* have to deal with it. Now describe the circumstances when Carol learned of your past," Laura directed.

"Well, we were at my loft with Lieutenant Dailey and his partner." Jason's first impulse was to make it sound as if the information about his past just happened to come out. But to what purpose? he reasoned. It's time for the bare-bones truth, he decided.

"When Dailey got out of his car outside the loft I knew where we were headed. He had the file tucked under his arm and I knew what it contained. We got into the discussion about whether or not I would be allowed to be a part of the investigation. And when that subject turned into a contest of wills, Dailey thought it prudent to let me know that he knew about my past. Basically he wanted to know, given my past, why he should let me be involved. And that's how Carol found out."

"And Lieutenant Dailey and Detective Montgomery were present?" Laura asked, the instant Jason finished speaking.

"Well, yeah," Jason said, as if it were a stupid question. "Both Lieutenant Dailey and Bob . . . Montgomery . . . ." His voice suddenly trailed off.

"What is it?" Laura asked.

"Boy, I really blew it. Didn't I?" She learned all about my past with two strangers in the room."

"You're a good student, Jason," Laura said, not making any attempt to console him. Did you make an attempt to discuss the matter in private with the police officers?" she asked, offering Jason an out, testing to see if he would take it.

"No, I didn't, but Dailey gave me the option of having her leave the room. And come to think of it, Carol even asked if I wanted her to be there. I gave the macho answer: If we were going to have a relationship, she would need to know. I know this will sound like a contradiction, but although I don't like to talk about my past, I am proud of my service career and

I guess I wanted her to know that. Now *that's* a mixed signal," he said with remorse.

"With hindsight being twenty-twenty, I guess we can safely say that you blew it," Laura said smiling warmly. "I am pleased with your honesty in not using the excuse that you didn't know Dailey would bring up your past. There are, however, a couple of other things going on that we need to explore."

Jason studied his mishandling of the situation and wavered as to whether he wanted to continue looking for anything else that might make him feel worse than he already did.

Laura quickly read Jason's facial expression and body language. She moved into the subject without hesitation, encouraging and helping him to understand, gleaning the good from his predicament. "Jason, let's look at some of the positive aspects of the situation. First, we've learned several things that contributed to Carol's anger. This is information we can look at, understand, and then turn it into knowledge for the good of the situation. So, what's the good stuff you've learned?"

"I don't know, it doesn't sound like a whole lot of good stuff to me," Jason replied, sounding discouraged.

"Stop pouting!" Laura responded quickly. "If you can't find the positive in the situation, you will have a hard time in any relationship, not just this one. When you were in the war, did you roll over when something didn't go quite right? I don't think so. If you had, you'd be sleeping between dirt sheets."

Jason blinked a couple of times and now looked attentive and embarrassed. "Guess I don't understand what you're looking for," he said, his voice more controlled.

"Okay, I can accept that," she said, confident that he now knew she would not patronize him. "I know that you have a lot on your mind and that you must be tired after the last two days, so I'll give you some help. Carol has lost a daughter. That anger and frustration will always be there, festering just below the surface, looking for an excuse to vent, a contributing factor to her reaction. Sunday night, she was in close proximity to a murder—another factor. Monday afternoon, she discovers your past—another factor. During the meeting at your loft, she learns that you're willing to put yourself in harm's way by wanting to protect your friend, and the police agree to it—well, more or less. We'll come back to that one. But that's another factor contributing to Carol's reaction. That's four in all. That's a lot, I'd say. Now let's make some sense of this and use it for the good of the situation.

"Carol's past, although a contributing factor, we'll call neutral, because for the time being you cannot have a positive or negative effect on it. The same with her having been exposed to the situation in the parking lot. It's neutral. There's nothing we can do about those, but it's important to file them away in our memory banks. We will be able to use them for future reference, which *will* be a positive. Now we get into the good stuff. What about Carol finding out about your past? Is it positive or negative?" Laura asked, giving him an encouraging smile.

Jason laid his head back, closed his eyes and rubbed his left hand lightly across his chin and mouth as he pondered the question. "Well," he said after a few minutes, "guess it's both positive and negative. The circumstances were bad, but now she knows the truth and I see that as being good."

"Very good," Laura commended. "Now let's look at some of the negative aspects of Carol finding out about your past. What, besides finding this out in front of strangers, did she react to?"

"Killing?" he asked.

"Could be. What else?" she questioned, wanting him to dig deeper.

"I can't think of anything," he said, genuinely puzzled.

"What about trust?" Laura prodded.

Jason took his time before speaking. "That I didn't trust her enough to share my past with her, and I didn't trust that she would accept me?"

"Very good again," she encouraged. "Now what can we learn from that?"

"That an intimate relationship is based on trust and acceptance. But when she found out, she reacted. She threw the killing in my face, so that means that she probably doesn't accept me."

"Possibly, but she had lot of other input that afternoon, don't forget. The killing was the easiest for her to grab onto.

That's why she hasn't called you. She doesn't fully understand. She's still trying to sort it all out. Put that in your memory bank, and let's keep moving forward. You're on a roll. Didn't you say Carol reacted when she assumed that you were going on a hunt for the assassins?"

"Yes, but I—"

"Come on, think, Jason," Laura encouraged. "Didn't Carol react when she found out that people were trying to kill you five years ago and also again when Dailey couched his 'no' on your offer? What do you think it means?"

"I think it frightened her," he answered.

"You're damned right it frightened her. And why do you suppose that is?" Laura questioned, with her come-on, tell-me look.

Laura, in her infinite wisdom, made a quick decision to have compassion. "She loves you, Jason," she said softly with a smile. "And she doesn't know if she can deal with your being in harm's way or the possibility of losing a loved one again, or, whether she can trust you, trust you to not be taken away by someone bad. She may be wondering if there are any more surprises in your life. That's my take on this, but it's something that you will have to confirm with her. You need to give her a little time to sort through it."

Jason just sat with a dumbfounded look on his face. Then he rested his head back onto the chair. "Wow—I sure have a lot to learn," he said, with a sigh.

"We all do, Jason. We all do. But look at what you learned in the last hour. Do you think you can recap it for me? Remember, in spite of the way it looks, it's all positive. Want to give it a shot?"

Jason sat quietly for a moment, then said, "I can't always be in control. In this situation with Carol, I need to consider her past and present, and her perspective. That she loves me. To be patient. And to file all of the mistakes and negatives into my memory bank so I can use them to avoid future screwups."

"You've done well and that's enough for today," Laura said smiling. "I'll make you another cup of tea. You've had a hard session and a hard day. I want you to relax for a few minutes. Then I want you to tell me something positive."

When Laura returned with the tea, Jason relaxed with his eyes closed and sipped it quietly. Again it seemed quite refreshing and rejuvenating. Laura took her seat across from him and remained quiet. After five minutes, he opened his eyes and said, "I think I'm beginning to understand a little about wisdom."

"Would you share it with me?" Laura asked.

"Knowledge must be tempered with experience for wisdom to be born."

CHAPTER THIRTEEN

Jason drove down from the West Seattle Freeway, snaked his way over to Fourth Avenue and headed north. Not a proponent of fast food, but tired, in need of sustenance, and considering himself to be nearly comatose, he pulled into a Jack in the Box at six forty-five. It wasn't really on his way to St. Francis' Hospital, but he was desperate. He stopped at the drive-through speaker and ordered a cheeseburger and a coke, then pulled forward to the window and waited impatiently. Nothing irritated Jason more than waiting, and waiting at a so-called fast-food gut bomber was intolerable.

With his anger mounting, he tried diligently to balance his thoughts. Although he did not want to forget the substance of what he had just learned during his session with Laura, he realized the need to concentrate on the remainder of his evening: visit Lori Phillips, meet with Dailey and Montgomery for their courtesy update with what he had learned from Jack in Portland. He wanted to paint a picture of cooperation with the police, hoping that Dailey would reciprocate with shared information. Although he knew that Dailey would not have had time enough to produce useful information at this juncture, it certainly wouldn't hurt to fertilize the garden.

When the unsuspecting, pimply-faced young man finally *did* appear at the window with a bag and cup, Jason rudely snatched it away and drove from the parking lot without so much as a word. While en route to the hospital, he placed his drink between his legs and ate his sandwich with his left hand.

He had just gotten into a coordinated rhythm—take a bite with the left hand, steady the steering wheel with the knee, sip the coke with the right hand, when his cellular phone rang. Damn! This has to be a test, he thought. He set the drink back between his legs, set the burger on top of the cup, grabbed the wheel with his left hand and reached for the phone with his right hand.

"Brisben." he said, with a measure of satisfaction. His frustration level diminished as he silently complimented his dexterity.

"Keller here."

"Hi, Tom, how's our patient doing? Dailey called last night to tell me that she had regained consciousness."

"She's not out of the woods by any stretch of the imagination, but she's a fighter. I apologize for not calling you myself last night, but things are always hectic around here. Anyway, I just left her and she's been asking for you."

"Apology accepted, and I should be there in less than ten minutes."

"I'm about ready to leave, but if you're that close, I'll wait. Our gal's pretty weak, so you won't have much time with her. I'll see you when you get here."

Jason disconnected and continued his dexterity drill, finishing his cheeseburger at about the same time he reached the hospital. After driving what seemed endless levels of the hospital parking garage, he finally found a spot and called Lt. Dailey before going in. Dailey was unavailable, but he did reach Bob Montgomery and made a dinner appointment for later that evening at Cutters Restaurant. They agreed on a time of eight-thirty. Jason made the reservations, then went in to meet Lori Phillips.

* * * * *

Dr. Thomas Keller's shoulder-length, dishwater blonde hair whiffed off his shoulders and neck as he walked. He looked like a throwback from the late sixties, a tall, slender man with a full handlebar mustache and blue, penetrating eyes. Although branded as somewhat of a maverick in the medical community, Keller was without a doubt one of, if not *the* most respected of the northwest's trauma physicians. He had attained a reputation for gutsy, sometimes untried surgical procedures on critically injured patients who had little or no hope. His attitude in the OR of "Let's try it. They're not going to make it anyway" had proved a bit dicey with his superiors, although he had a very good batting average—a case in point being Lori Phillips.

Jason knew what he was doing when he had summoned Keller to the crime scene and his decision had been correct. Both men were believers in the "golden hour," knowing what happens in the first hour is critical. Phillips would not be alive had Keller not been there.

The two men met during their tours in Vietnam. Keller had been out on several patrols with Jason's team, and from that experience the two had developed a long-standing but intermittent relationship. They felt fortunate that fate had landed them in the same city, even though they might see each other only once or twice a year.

They approached the room at a brisk pace. Keller acknowledged the police officer stationed at the door as they entered. The doctor walked quietly to Lori's bedside and Jason hung back just a bit to survey the scene.

Forty-four hours had passed since the attack, and Lori Phillips lay on a hospital bed looking as if she were dead. Jason remembered the warm, tanned glow of her face and arms from his brief observation of her as the couple left The Box Car. Now she looked gray and emaciated. Her arms were black and blue from God only knew how many IV's. Her vibrant blonde hair of two days ago now lacked luster and lay matted and limp. Monitors with IV's invaded both arms. Drain tubes appeared from under the light blanket. As he stood in silent observation, a moment passed when, he realized he felt a mixture of anger and joy—anger at what had happened to this woman and joy that she was still alive. Jason wondered how she would recover both physically and emotionally. He remembered her as being beautiful and vibrant, and now . . . .

Keller bent low over the bed and spoke softly. "Lori . . . Lori." Her breathing quickened slightly, followed by a slow deliberate blinking of her eyes. "Lori," Keller repeated again, "there's someone here to see you." It appeared to be a struggle for her to focus. Finally she seemed to be somewhat coherent and looked into Keller's face.

"Cap?—Oh, hello, Doctor." Cap, Jason later learned, was her nickname for Carston Jennings.

"Lori, Mr. Brisben is here to see you," Keller said in a voice just above a whisper. Jason watched in admiration at the display of tenderness and patience. In spite of his shortcomings, Tom Keller had a great bedside manner. "You've been asking for him." Her eyes focused on Keller's face, then slowly began to search the room until her eyes found Jason. She stared as if trying to find some sort of reality before speaking.

"Come here," she mouthed, with no sound.

Keller moved back slowly when Jason approached her bed. "She's heavily sedated," he whispered as Jason moved to the spot the doctor had occupied.

"It's good to see you," Jason said, struggling for something to say. "Don't try to talk just yet. You just listen for a bit until you wake up. Doctor Keller here says you're a real scrapper and that you'll be fine in no time."

"Thank you," she said. This time her voice could barely be heard above the circulating air from the air-conditioning vents.

"He said that you're *one* pretty tough lady."

Lori looked up quizzically at Jason as she struggled to get her thoughts organized through her drug-clouded brain. With slow and labored speech, she said, "No, not very tough . . . ." Then again in her weak voice, "Thank you for saving me—and thank you for the beautiful flowers."

"You're very welcome for both. My friend Jack and I are just thankful we came along when we did." Jason looked down at this emaciated person and into her confused, glassy eyes and wondered how he could do what he was about to do. He wished earnestly for a bedside manner.

"Miss Phillips," Jason began. "I know this is not a good time and it's hard for you, but I need to ask you some questions about last Sunday night. I'm working on the investigation with the police. I know you have already talked to them, but they may not have told you that we suspect the men who attacked Mr. Jennings mistook him for my friend, Jack

O'Connor. We need your help so we can protect Mr. O'Connor and apprehend the people who attacked you.

"To make this as easy as possible for you, I will ask you questions that you can answer with a yes or no. If you can provide any additional information, and you feel up to it, please interrupt at any time." Lori said nothing but nodded in agreement.

"Did you see the men who attacked you?" She nodded yes.

"Were there two of them?" She nodded yes.

"Did you see them in the restaurant earlier in the evening?" Lori moved her head slightly from left to right, indicating no.

"Did you notice if they followed you or Mr. Jennings?" Again, a negative response.

"Were you able to get a look at the faces of the men who attacked you?" At this question, her eyes teared and her face seemed even paler than before. She nodded yes.

"Would you be able to describe them?" Again, a nod of yes. Tears were now trickling from the corners of her eyes.

"Do you think that you can talk enough to describe them to me now?" Jason asked, trying not to push too hard.

The words came slowly, only a few words at a time, her speech weak and labored. "One man was blonde—curly hair—stocky—he attacked Cap." Jason leaned forward with his ear close to her mouth. Her eyes were closed now and tears flowed as she relived the horror of Sunday night. "Didn't see the man who attacked me very well—I was watching Cap." She began to sob and shake at her thought of Jennings. "I think—man who stabbed me—smaller—dark— Mexican—Philippino maybe, I'm not sure."

"Did they say anything?" Jason asked, continuing to press as he felt a tug on his arm from Keller.

Once again, an affirmative nod. "A van—next to my Jeep—I think they were behind it—they came up to us." Her words came stronger now and were full of loathing. "The blonde man said, 'Well, well, Jack—does the little lady know?'—then, 'See ya, Jack.' And he stabbed Cap. "They appeared—so quickly—I felt—sharp pain—in my chest—and that's all I remember."

Lori was now shaking profusely, her eyes still closed trying to blot the scene from her memory, the tears flowing even harder than before. She turned her head away. "Everything went black—all I remember."

"That's enough for now," Jason said. "You've been a great help. If there's anything you need, please let Dr. Keller know and I'll see that you get it."

Her mouth said "thank you" but, as before, she could not be heard. She slipped into unconsciousness and Jason gently patted her arm. It surprised him that it felt so warm. He glanced at Keller with a questioning look and Keller motioned to follow him out of the room.

"Why is she so damned hot?" Jason asked, as he walked with Keller back toward his office.

"That will be our biggest hurdle—infection," he replied, turning toward Jason as they walked. "The fever is from the infection. She was cut up pretty badly internally, released a lot of garbage into her abdominal cavity. We cleaned up as best we could, but she's going to have to fight for the rest." Keller stopped in the hall and looked at Jason, shaking his head. "It was a real mess in there, Jason."

Keller and Jason moved out of the hallway into his office. Jason sat in the chair across from the desk. Keller poured coffee for them, handed Jason a cup, then sat on the desk in front of him. "Lieutenant Dailey came in to see me last night and again this morning," Keller began. "He told me about the theory of mistaken identity, told me that you would be around this evening. What love potion did you use to wangle your way into his heart? Seems as though you'll be helping out with this mess."

"As far as Dailey's concerned, my only function will be to protect Jack," Jason said. Then he went on to give his account of the previous afternoon's meeting at the loft. "No magic in it. I just made them realize that they couldn't protect Jack as well as I can," Jason concluded.

"Well, to hear Dailey tell it, there must have been some unspoken communication, because he's under the impression that you're going to be a royal pain in his ass. And from the sound of your interview a minute ago, you're getting a little more involved than providing personal security for Jack. I assume he's aware of your capabilities and contacts."

"Painfully," Jason said.

"So what's your take on this? Why are they after your friend?"

"Haven't a clue. He hasn't a clue. The only thing I can figure is, it must be related to his work. He's stumbled into something. So far we're grabbing at straws. There's no real place to start. I've got the partners going over the Cervicon accounts and looking into a couple of customers with work in process. Maybe they can ferret out something, but for now, nothing."

"The partners," Keller laughed. "Well, if they can't find something, nobody can. Once they get their teeth into someone's ass they're as relentless as a pit bull. They never let go," he said.

Jason smiled his knowing acknowledgment. "You know anything about Suter Pharmaceuticals?"

"They're big. A lot of our supplies come from them— drugs, dressings, surgical supplies. Why do you ask?"

"Jack O'Connor has designed a security system for their new plant in Issaquah. Why would they get into AIDS and Eboli research?" Jason asked.

"Money. There's a lot of government money available for that kind of research. I heard that they were headed in that direction. I asked myself why, the same as you, but I guess a billion-dollar-a-year company can do anything they want including pulling big money from Uncle Sam. You think there's a connection?" Jason shrugged.

"This friend of yours, O'Connor is it? How's he holding up?"

"As well as can be expected, I suppose. I've got David and Steve watching him. He's out of town on business. He'll be all right for a couple of days at least."

"What about the family? They gonna be all right?"

"I think so. Dailey's got some bodies covering them." Jason took the last sip of coffee, then looked at his watch. "Speak of the devil, I have a meet with Dailey and Montgomery at eight-thirty. I'd best be moving. I need to swing by the loft and grab a quick shower."

Jason stood to leave and the two men left the office to walk to the elevator. He looked at Keller. "Keep our patient alive." He said it as an order more than a request.

Doctor Keller's crow's-feet around his eyes disappeared along with his smile. "Doing everything I can." His face and eyes turned cold as well as the tone of his voice. "Do me a favor."

"Name it."

"When you find the motherfuckers, make 'em suffer."

"Count on it," Jason said, coldly.

* * * * *

Jason stood in his shower and let the hot water massage his weary body. He had checked his answering machine, hoping for a message from Carol, but nothing. Leaning with his arms against the tiles, he wished that he could stand there for an hour, then just crawl into bed. But, remembering the way Lori Phillips looked on that hospital bed renewed his resolve. He still had work to do. And besides, he knew he had a good meal waiting at Cutters, just catty-cornered across the street from his loft.

Since his service days, Jason had been fastidious about his personal appearance, always considering himself the picture, his wardrobe the frame. He stepped from the shower, toweled dry, and went into his room where he dressed in a white shirt and a lightweight navy blue linen suit with no tie. On his way to the entry door, Jason glanced at his 10mm and holster on the kitchen island. Pausing for a moment, he decided he didn't need his weapon for dinner. Besides, he would be dining with cops, for crying out loud. As he armed his security system, the telephone rang. He walked to the counter in the kitchen and answered, "Brisben."

"Jason, this is Carol," she said, a note of urgency in her voice.

"Thank God, you finally called. I've been worried about you," Jason said, wishing he hadn't sounded so concerned. After all, he still needed a modicum of pride.

She made no comment about his being worried. "Jason, I think someone is watching the O'Connors'."

"What makes you think that?"

"I went over to Debbie's this afternoon," Carol began. Her voice wavered and Jason read the failed attempt to mask her fear. "When I got there, I noticed a car parked about half a block away with a man just sitting in it. I drove right by him on my way to their house and didn't think too much about it until an hour later. We were in the kitchen, Debbie, Tommy, and me. Debbie said she wondered if the medical insurance papers were in today's mail. I volunteered to check the mail for her because she was busy preparing some things for our dinner tonight. Tommy and I went to the mailbox, and while we were outside, I looked down the street and another car pulled up and parked, and the one that had been there, left. I went to the window just before dinner and the first car was back again."

"What kind of cars are they?" Jason asked.

"The first one was a green Toyota two-door and the other one is kind of a pyucky beige four-door Tempo."

"I guess the police are using their own cars these days," Jason said.

"What do you mean?" Carol asked.

"Early this morning, I asked Lieutenant Dailey to send someone around to keep an eye on the place. Sounds like he's doing a good job."

"Well, I guess I got all upset for nothing." Carol said with tension remaining in her voice. "Oh well," she continued, "at least Debbie and I will get a bottle of wine out of the deal."

"How's that?" Jason asked.

"I didn't want to take a chance calling from their house, so I made up the excuse that we should have a bottle of wine with dinner. I'm calling from the store."

"Clever girl," Jason commended. What he really wanted to say was, if you'd called me you wouldn't be in a tizzy right now. However, the session with Laura flitted through his brain, and he recalled something about not reacting. He chose to bite his tongue and see how the time factor Laura had talked about would work out. "I have a meeting with Dailey and Montgomery in a few minutes. Do you suppose that I could come see you afterwards?" he asked hopefully.

"Oh, I'm sorry, Jason, we're having such a good time, Debbie and the kids invited me to spend the night. Could you call me tomorrow? I don't have to be at work until six. Maybe we can talk before work."

He was about to press the issue when patience again came to mind and then control. An opportunity had been provided, he could make a choice. He could push Carol or he could be patient and take control of *his* emotions. He chose the latter. "Well, whatever works," he said, with his disappointment filtering through. He'd used about all of the self-control that he could muster at the moment.

His reward came immediately when she said, "Thanks for not pushing, Jason," now sounding less tense. "I'd better get back, I really want to talk tomorrow. Okay?"

"Tomorrow's fine," he returned. He wanted to tell Carol about the latest developments regarding Jack and Lori, but thought it could wait until tomorrow. It wasn't worth the risk of causing more tension. "I'll give you a call. Bye, hon," he said and hung up.

Jason paused, looking at the phone for a moment. He had taken control of his emotions, but he still felt out of control. Carol had determined *when* they would talk and that bothered him. However, he had made a conscious decision to take control of *himself* and not react. Good, he thought, hoping that, in time, he would understand all of this new information.

good deal of patience, of which, I suspect, you have very little."
He took a sip of pinot, then swirled the wine staring into the
glass appreciatively. "These two guys that you have watching
O'Connor, they any good?"

"They're good. We trained with the Secret Service while I
put the anti-terrorist team together. Why?"

"Just interested in how well-protected your friend is."

"I've given a lot of thought to that lately, believe me. When
you care for someone, no amount of protection seems adequate.
I—I don't know," he added, shaking his head.

"We still have the advantage of their not knowing that we
know O'Connor's the target," Montgomery encouraged. "I
know that's not much consolation. It would help to get the
composite sketches to your people before these people make
another try."

In the back of Jason's mind lay the knowledge that someone had called Cervicon trying to get information about Jack.
If I were a hit man, Jason thought, I'd be damned careful about
doing a walk-up again. There are too many long-range options
available. The thought gave him a chill, as he wondered about
the effectiveness of his guardians.

The three men continued to discuss several scenarios
until the meals were served. The presentations, as always, were
exquisite. Lt. Dailey ordered the Apple-wood Grilled Fresh
Wild Hoh River Steelhead; Montgomery, the Garlic Roasted
Black Tiger Prawns; and Jason, the Apple-wood Grilled Dunge-
ness Crab. Jason poured more of the pinot to accompany his
guests' dinners.

Once dinner had been completed, he took the liberty of
ordering dessert and coffee for the table. Full to the point of
pain, they sipped their coffee and again returned to discussing options to deal with the investigation and the situation
with Jack. Beverly faithfully made frequent stops with the coffeepot until Jason held up his hand in submission at eleven
o'clock and asked for the check. He had had his well-deserved
meal and now was tired and ready for the comfort of his bed.

Dailey and Montgomery thanked Jason for their dining
experience and the three men stood from the table. "Getting
hooked up with you might not have been too bad an idea,"

Dailey said again with his quirky grin. "Of course, my waist-line may not be too appreciative."

"You don't have a waist," Montgomery interjected. "It's a waste zone, and should be classified a Northwest containment disaster." Montgomery and Jason laughed, while a red-faced Dailey feigned anger, but only briefly, before joining them in laughter.

"You're not gonna be laughing so hard when you find your butt on that bicycle patrolling Pike's Market, wise guy," Dailey said. "I still deserve a modicum of respect, sonny—" He paused with a look of surprise and glanced down as he removed the vibrating pager from his belt.

"Speaking of respect," Jason said. "I want to thank you for keeping an eye on the O'Connors' house. I really appreci-ate it. I didn't expect twenty-four-hour coverage."

"What's that?" Dailey looked up from his beeper. "Excuse me for a minute, this looks important. I'll be right back."

The three men walked from their table to the pay phones by the parking garage elevator. Jason and Montgomery waited on the opposite side of the glass doors to the elevator access while Dailey used the telephone. In silence, they watched him hang up and make a second call. After a brief conversation, he returned the telephone to its cradle and turned around. He did not resemble the jocular man of moments before.

"What's up?" Montgomery asked, reading the trouble behind his partner's eyes.

"I just got off the phone with Dr. Keller. Lori Phillips just died a few minutes ago," his face filled with a mixture of sor-row and anger. "He wants to see me."

Jason stood dumbfounded. "I was with her not more than three hours ago," he said in disbelief. "She had a fever but it couldn't have gotten out of control this fast."

"I'm sorry to cut this short, gentlemen, but this whole evening just turned to shit!" Dailey said tersely. "Dr. Keller thinks Miss Phillips was murdered."

"What?" Jason and Montgomery said in unison.

"He seemed pretty aggravated. Wouldn't give any details over the phone. Just said he wanted me ASAP."

"I'll meet you there," Jason said.

"Hold on, Brisben," Dailey said sharply. Jason turned to protest, but Dailey cut him off before he could speak. "You mentioned twenty-four-hour surveillance at the O'Connors'. As far as I know, the only surveillance we could spare is a cruiser every hour or so. If somebody has set up twenty-four-hour surveillance, it's not us."

"Dammit, you've got to be kidding!" Jason's words burst forth vehemently. Anger at himself came instantaneously for not making sure that Dailey had in fact provided adequate surveillance. He had let his frustration with Carol interfere with good judgment.

"You want to tell me what's going on?" Dailey asked. Jason explained the phone call from Carol prior to dinner. "I don't think there's any harm done yet," Dailey speculated. "After the call to Cervicon, they know he's out of town. They're probably waiting for him to come home. I don't think the family is in any danger. Remember, they don't know that we suspect anything yet. "This is the break we're looking for. Now that we have someone to watch."

"Not for long," Jason retorted. "I'm going to get Carol and Jack's family out of there."

"We've got a break. Let's not get our knickers in a knot and blow this by being in a hurry," Dailey protested. "Now that we have something solid, I can put some men on the people who are watching the house. They sure as hell will lead us somewhere."

But Jason would not be calmed. "If what Keller says is true, these creeps have balls the size of bulls. Lori Phillips *was* under police protection. You had a guard supposedly watching over her. What the hell happened?"

Dailey's face turned crimson.

Montgomery spoke. "Hold it! Hold it. We can still use this to our advantage," he said in desperation, trying to calm the two reactionaries. "We can do both," Montgomery continued, "Jason's right. We really don't know anything about these guys. It's a real possibility that the O'Connor family is now in danger. How about if I go pick up the guy in the car and haul his ass in for questioning. While I'm doing that, Jason can move in and get the family out to a safe place. The creeps won't be able to follow and the family will be out of harm's way. We can follow whoever shows up in the relief car."

"What the hell are you going to pick this bozo up for? Parking?" Dailey scoffed.

"I'll think of something," Montgomery replied.

"Lieutenant," Jason said, after having a moment to control his emotions. "We've lost the only witness that could identify Jennings' killer. And I apologize for making it sound like the police were at fault. That wasn't my intention. I realize that if Bob picks up the guy who's parked in front of O'Connors', they'll know we're on to them, and we may lose some ground. But this is Tuesday. The kids have school for three more days this week. If they get impatient, these people could snatch one or both of them for leverage to get at Jack. I, for one, am not willing to take the risk. If Bob picks one of them up, at least we'll have a place to start. I know that this is a lot to give up. But we're caught on the horns of a dilemma here. I don't see that we have a choice."

Dailey looked thoughtfully at Jason, then to Montgomery, weighing the merits of the two men's persuasive input. "I have to concede to your logic, Mr. Brisben," Dailey said, running his hand contemplatively through his beard. "The safety of O'Connor's family must be our first consideration. And, like you said," he turned back to Montgomery, "we can still follow the relief car, Bob. I'll drop you at the precinct. Pick up a car and have Thompson and his partner follow in a separate car. I want you to converge on this scum. Do it right; we can't let him get a warning."

To Jason, Dailey said, "Bob and a couple of uniforms will meet you at your place in twenty minutes. You can plan your strategy once they get there. Now that we have that settled, where are you going to stash O'Connor's family?"

"I have a cottage in Oak Bay on Vancouver Island. I'll bring them back to my place for the night, then take them to the island tomorrow."

"Once they realize the family has split, they may be watching the airports and ferry terminals," Montgomery said.

"If they're at all organized, I'm sure they will. But I have a boat, and I'll take them over myself."

The two detectives moved toward the elevators, and as they did so, Dailey became preoccupied with his thoughts regarding this man Brisben. Resentment began to fester. He had worked his whole life protecting the citizens of the great city of Seattle and for what reward? After nineteen and a half years, by necessity, he still adhered to a tight budget. Hell, he drove a piece of shit car that would die two years before the payments, with which he struggled. No way in hell could he afford to dine the way he had this evening. And this . . . this handsome, this cocky . . . person, for lack of a better word at that moment, who was out looking for something to do with himself, seemed to have it all: a beautiful apartment, cars, and now a boat! And what irritated him the most? He was beginning to like the sonofabitch!

"So then, are we all clear on what we're doing?" Dailey asked as he looked back. Jason gave an affirmative nod. "All right, Mr. Brisben. I'll be off to see Dr. Keller, and Bob will be back to you in about twenty minutes. I want to see you in my office after you get everyone settled at your place. Maybe we'll have some information from the man in the car by then."

* * * * *

Jason removed his jacket as he entered the loft. By eleven-thirty he had made a pot of coffee and found the city map to familiarize himself with the layout of streets in Jack's neighborhood. He unfolded it on the island counter and set out cups for the police officers who would soon arrive. Then he picked up his weapon and spare clips from where he had left them before dinner and hurried to his room to change into black Dockers and a black turtleneck. He attached his Bianchi pistol pocket to the inside of his pants on his right hip and took his 10mm Delta Elite, checked the clip, loaded, locked, and stuffed it into the compact holster. He also inserted two full clips into a leather clip pouch and attached it to his belt on his left hip.

After making several subtle adjustments to his gear, he took a black leather jacket from the closet and viewed himself in the full-length bedroom mirror. Nothing showed. It looked right. It felt right.

While he waited for Montgomery and the uniforms, Jason considered calling Debbie to let her know he would be coming, but decided against it. She would have plenty to deal with soon enough. And her phone might be tapped. So he just waited, impatiently.

The buzzer from the loft's security door brought him back from his musings. Two minutes later, he showed Montgomery and the two accompanying officers, Thompson and Dolan, into the loft. Thompson appeared to be an ordinary young man in a policeman's uniform, brown hair, blue eyes, five foot ten. But officer Dolan was anything but ordinary. Out of uniform, he could have been a poster boy for the local gym. He stood not more than five foot eight, but his shoulders gave the illusion of being four feet wide because of his short height. Attached to the shoulders were biceps the size of baked hams that stretched the fabric of his short-sleeved uniform blouse to the limit. With his blonde hair and brown eyes, he should have had fair skin but looked painfully tan from spending as much time in the tanning booth as he did in the gym.

Jason served coffee, then immediately immersed the three into situation planning, formulating the strategy to snatch someone they hoped would give them their first real lead.

From the beginning of the planning session, it became obvious to the police officers that Jason was an adept strategist. After circling Jack's house on the map, Jason insisted upon everyone having a clear understanding of the neighborhood, as many of the streets on the east face of Queen Anne Hill were only a few blocks long or they dead-ended abruptly.

Within a few minutes, they had memorized all of the access streets and adjacent avenues. After studying Jason's plan to converge on the unsuspecting car from two directions, they felt confident they could carry out the exercise without incident. They also developed contingency plans for the unexpected.

* * * * *

Jason's Seville sparkled under the night lights of Virginia Street as it passed beneath the parking garage gate. He would lead the way to the O'Connors' neighborhood, then separate and park on a dead-end side street where he would remain out of view until the suspect was apprehended.

As he turned into the designated side street, Jason extinguished his lights. He drove to the end, turned around in a driveway, and slowly and quietly moved to the intersection from which he had just come, where he parked facing east a half block south of Jack's home. From his vantage point, he could observe Jack's house and a good portion of Taylor Avenue, the street on which the O'Connors' lived. Although the Seville was screened by a sickly hedge with sparse foliage, Jason had nearly an unobstructed view of the Ford Tempo a block to the south.

Jason had only been parked a minute or two when he saw the headlights of the first of the unmarked cruisers slowly approach from the south off Howe Street. It continued on, passing the suspect's car and Jack's house, rolled north two blocks, and turned left up Crockett Street and out of sight. Five long minutes passed before another set of headlights appeared from the opposite direction from Crockett, turned right onto Taylor, headed south past the car and out of sight onto Howe. The two cars rendezvoused a few blocks away to confer and compare notes, making sure they would converge on the correct car. They made physical rather than radio contact, so as not to risk being picked up on a scanner.

Five minutes later, the two cars approached at moderate speed from opposite directions, abruptly hemming in the Tempo and its unsuspecting occupant. The lights came on and all three officers jumped from their vehicles. Montgomery opened the driver's door of the Tempo and Dolan reached in and literally lifted the occupant from the front seat. In less than a second, he was spread-eagled over the hood. Dolan frisked him while Montgomery and Thompson stood about five feet apart with their weapons trained on the man at point-blank range. Dolan handed Montgomery something, then handcuffed the man's hands behind his back and ushered him unceremoniously into the back seat of Montgomery's car.

Unfortunately, no one noticed a green Toyota with its lights off, just west of the intersection of Howe and Taylor streets. It had stopped, turned around, and beat a hasty but silent retreat. Jason's ever-vigilant eyes never saw it because it had taken place a few feet beyond his field of vision. Montgomery holstered his weapon and without a word slipped into his cruiser with his suspect tucked safely in the rear. He turned right and disappeared, unaware he was being followed.

Thompson and Dolan returned to their car and drove onto the little side street where Jason waited. They drove past, turned around, and parked directly behind him.

Jason promptly started his car, pulled forward onto Taylor and up a half block into the O'Connors' driveway. Thompson and Dolan were to remain behind to cover his back in case the green Toyota showed up. If that happened, the officers were to remove the driver from the area before Jason and Jack's family could be spotted leaving.

At ten minutes to one, Jason knocked quietly on the O'Connors' front door. He could see a light still on somewhere in the house through the stained glass on either side of the entry door. A figure ghosted toward the door a moment later.

"Who is it?" a timid voice asked from the opposite side of the door.

"It's Jason, Debbie," he replied. "May I come in?"

The door immediately opened and Jason faced a bewildered Debbie O'Connor. "What on earth are you doing here at this time of night?" she asked, the tone matching the look on her face.

"May I come in?" Jason asked once again.

"Oh, I'm sorry, of course. Please come in," she said, trying to collect her composure. "Carol and I are visiting in the kitchen and having a little wine. Would you care to join us?" she asked, the question and tone echoing her confusion. Jason stepped inside, closed the door after himself, and followed her to the kitchen.

At first sight of him, Carol frowned at the intrusion but her expression softened as she realized Jason's errand must be important. Conversely, Jason mirrored surprise when he looked at Carol, scantily clad in one of Jack's large tee shirts that barely covered her panties.

"Carol and I were having so much fun, I asked her to spend the night. Obviously, we weren't expecting company," Debbie explained, nodding toward Carol with an impish grin.

Jason felt a deep relief at the sight of Carol. The urge to take her in his arms and hold her gripped him, but he fought it back, yielding to the patience about which Laura spoke so often. Debbie once again offered wine but he declined. "I would rather have coffee, if you have it."

"Sure, there's some left from dessert." Debbie answered cordially, and turned to the counter to pour him a cup.

"Jason," said Debbie, as she turned from the counter to hand him his coffee, "you still haven't told me why you're here."

Jason's jacket opened at the waist when he reached for the coffee, and Debbie caught sight of his weapon sitting high on his hip and immediately backed away. "Jason, what's going on?" she demanded, looking into his eyes with a no-nonsense expression.

"Sit down, Deb," Jason answered softly. Taking time to marshal his thoughts he slowly took a sip of coffee, then seated himself at table across from Debbie. How do you tell a person that someone is trying to kill her husband? he wondered. He took her hand and simply said it. "Honey, we've just learned that Jack and maybe your whole family is in danger."

Debbie turned pale and blinked in disbelief. "What are you talking about?" she barely squeaked putting her free hand to her mouth.

Jason relayed the chain of events of the last two days, being careful not to say anything that would intimate that Carol already knew of the possibility. Carol started to speak, but he cut her off with more of the details, not wanting her to mention anything about the house being watched.

"Jack is safe in Portland," he continued. "I've been working with the police and we didn't want to alarm you until we had proof. I went to Portland today to see Jack and to introduce him to two bodyguards. I promise you he is safe and it's better that he's there for the time being."

"Why hasn't he called me to tell me? And why are you just telling me all of this now?" she asked vehemently. Speaking from sheer panic, she shot questions in rapid succession. "You must have known about this long before now if you've had time to find bodyguards and drive to Portland. You must have known about it this morning, for godsake, and—and you didn't tell me?" She shook violently and burst into tears. Carol quickly moved to comfort her but her compassion seemed to go unnoticed.

Suddenly Debbie's eyes widened with horror as she realized the knife in the parking lot was meant for her husband and not Carston Jennings. "Who would want to kill Jack?" she sobbed. Fangs of grief buried themselves deep into her chest at the realization that a part of her, her husband of fourteen years, could be snatched away. Breathing no longer came as an involuntary act; breath became a commodity she fought for. With hands firmly to her breasts, she tried unsuccessfully to quell the sharp pain in her heart. Jason remembered Laura telling him about stored or pent-up frustrations lying beneath the surface, and then something triggering an eruption. Debbie had had her share as of late: Jack's situation with Cervicon, the pressure with the finances, Tommy's health, and now this. The fullness of it exploded forth like ash through the top of Mt. St. Helens.

Jason reached across the table to comfort her, but she shrank back as if repulsed. Standing in the face of such agony became more difficult than he had ever imagined. This was no longer an adventure. He had confronted the possibility of losing a friend; but now, after Debbie's display of grief, the situation took on new meaning.

Jason searched for words of encouragement, a word of comfort, but none seemed appropriate when delivering that kind of news. He stalled for a time, hoping that Debbie would pull herself together or that some pearl of wisdom would come to him before he had to lay on her the additional burden of having to leave her home. He *would* have to tell her about the men watching the house after all. He could assure her that the police were moving as fast as they could. He could give his personal guarantee that he would keep Jack safe. Oh hell, just say it, he thought.

"Deb, listen to me. Two hours ago we learned that some people have been watching your house. We think they're waiting for Jack to come home. The police just picked one of them up a few minutes ago and I have to get you and the kids out of here before they can regroup. That's why I'm here."

"I can't believe this!" she wailed. Bad news begat bad news and Jason felt like the angel of death.

Carol looked at Jason accusingly and mouthed, "I thought . . . ."

He simply shook his head and gave a stare that let her know this was not the time for discussion. "Debbie," Jason said more firmly. "You've got to pull yourself together. We have to leave quickly. We don't have much time; we *must* be out of here before they send someone back. I don't want to give them a chance to follow us. Do you understand?"

Debbie sat motionless, looking at Jason with a blank stare. Finally, she slowly stood and stared down at him with teeth bared, her face transformed by the anger born of grieving.

"Where will we go? What about school? And Tommy, he has a doctor's appointment for tests on Thursday." Her voice had risen to a shriek as she teetered on the verge of hysteria.

Jason at a loss for words, thought, Simply tell her what you'd planned.

"Deb, everything will be fine. I know this is a lot to handle on short notice, but we'll get through it. We'll all spend the night at my place. Tomorrow, I'll take you to my cottage on Vancouver Island. As for Jennifer and Ashley, they will only be out of school a few days. It will be like a second spring vacation. You can call Tommy's doctor tomorrow and make arrangements to have the tests done in Victoria, or I can fly the doctor to Victoria, or Tommy back here for the tests. All of it can be worked out, but for now just get the kids and enough clothes for tomorrow and let's get the hell out of here."

"Come on, Debbie," Carol said, encouraging her. "I'll help with the kids." Carol supported Debbie with an arm around her shoulder as they moved slowly from the kitchen.

Jason emptied his cold coffee in the sink and refilled his cup with fresh. After a moment of leaning with his back to the counter, he walked through the dining room and opened the French doors to the deck that faced Lake Union. The fresh air felt good as he made his way to the rail. He looked down onto the lake and understood why Jack and Debbie had fallen in love with the place. He could see the lake and the east shore with all of the streets and homes now mostly dark, only shadows accented by streetlights. Light traffic moved along Interstate 5, and occasionally a car could be heard moving along on Highway 99 two hundred feet below.

The temperature had dropped a bit over the last two nights and Jason's thoughts rode the cool breeze to the memory of Lori Phillips and how frail and weak she looked on the hospital bed and then to the image of her in the parking lot. He had wanted so much to see her live. She had fought so hard and now she was gone because of some sonofabitch whom he would dearly love to meet. If Keller suspected foul play, Jason believed it to be true.

Anger bloomed full, and he wanted to avenge the woman's death, but now after his encounter with Debbie, it would be secondary. Jack and his family must be the priority.

"Jason, we're ready," Carol touched his shoulder and Jason flinched. He possessed the awareness of a cat, so it was unusual he had not heard her. He had heard her voice, but it did not register even though she had called his name twice before touching him. Her voice had belonged to a dream. Suddenly alert, he turned slowly and faced her.

"I'm sorry I startled you," she said softly. "I'd better get going. It's going to take me at least forty-five minutes to get home."

"We all have to stay together. You have to come with us," Jason said.

"Why? Why can't I just go home?" she asked sharply. "I'm tired and I just want to go home!"

"Carol, please!" Jason said, feeling the fullness of his fatigue. "Please don't argue. Can't you just trust me?" he pleaded. "I'll explain everything when we get to the loft. Debbie and the kids can use the beds in the guestroom and you can sleep in my room. I'll take the couch. We need to talk. A lot has happened since Monday afternoon."

Carol gave him a questioning look, but said nothing as she left Jason to join Debbie and the kids, who stood in the entry hall with their overnight bags and backpacks. When Jason joined them, they all moved to Jason's car with the children trundling behind in a semiconscious state. They huddled together in the back seat with their mother. Carol sat rigidly in the front, while Jason stowed their gear in the trunk. He returned to the house, checked all the doors, and armed the security system.

They backed out of the drive and drove south on Taylor Street, passing Thompson and Dolan who were still parked on the side street. Immediately the cruiser's headlights came on and turned in behind the Seville, then stopped beside the brown car. Thompson and Dolan would search the Tempo, then wait out of sight for Montgomery to relieve them.

* * * * *

They arrived at the loft at one-thirty. Jason went quickly to the guest bedroom and turned down the covers of the two queen-sized beds. Debbie carried Tommy; Jennifer and Ashley followed like a pair of zombies. She directed the two girls to their bed. In silence they crawled up and flopped down, making no attempt to cover themselves. Debbie tucked Tommy in on the opposite bed, then covered the girls. She stood looking after them for a moment before seeking out Jason, who had since returned to the kitchen.

"Would you like some juice or something?" he asked.

"No thanks. I think I just want some sleep. Do you mind if I just turn in?"

Jason stood stunned at the dramatic change in Debbie's physical appearance. In less than an hour, the stress of fear and grief had transformed a cute pixie-like woman into a gaunt, exhausted waif. Her hair lay limp and her eyes, accented by dark circles, were red and swollen. He started to answer, but before he could, she hugged him tightly and buried her face in his chest.

"I'm so afraid, Jason. I'm scared to death. Please forgive me for attacking you. I do appreciate what you're doing."

"There's nothing to forgive," he answered softly. "You're safe now. Go on now, get some sleep."

"Please don't let anything happen to Jack," she pleaded, with her head still buried in his chest.

Jason tenderly kissed the top of her head. "I won't let anything happen to Jack, sweetheart. I promise," he said, hoping it was a promise he'd be able to keep. Debbie stood on her toes and kissed his cheek, then turned toward her room.

Jason watched the door close quietly behind her, then his eyes went to Carol. They stared at each other, neither one quite sure what to say.

After a moment of awkward silence Jason said, "Carol, I need to meet with Dailey for a while—"

"This time of night?" she interrupted, irritated.

Jason ignored her tone and continued, "Before I leave, I would like to explain what's happened."

"I just don't understand. What's so important that you have to meet with them now?" she persisted.

"Dammit! Will you shut up and let me talk for just five minutes!" Jason snapped, beyond the point of exasperation. "Carol, I'm truly sorry that you've become involved in this mess. Late Monday night, Lori Phillips regained consciousness and confirmed that Jack was the target." He went on to explain, telling about his visit with Lori Tuesday evening.

"I also want to thank you for calling and telling me about the men watching the O'Connors'. At dinner with Dailey I learned that the police were not the ones watching the house. If you hadn't called, all of you might have been in serious trouble," he said, gratefully. The information to this point had been easy to tell, but now it became difficult. "Last night after dinner, Dailey received a phone call notifying him that Lori Phillips had died. Dr. Keller believes she was murdered." Carol brought her hand to her mouth. "Phillips would have been able to identify her attackers, the people who were trying to kill Jack."

"Oh, God!" Carol gasped. Tears filled her eyes.

"Sweetheart, that's why I need to meet with Dailey. I need to find out what happened to Lori and learn all I can about the man Montgomery and the other officers picked up tonight. That information will be important help if I'm to do a good job of protecting Jack. Can you understand that?"

She nodded but did not speak.

"Before I go, there are some things I want to say to you." Jason moved to the sofa and sat next to Carol but made no attempt to touch her. Looking down into his lap, he spoke softly. "I want to apologize for the awkward way in which you found out about my past. I never should have allowed that to happen, and I hope someday you will be able to forgive me."

Facing her, he tenderly took her hands into his own. He looked directly into her eyes and began speaking in a quiet, tense voice that made him sound unsure of himself. "I'm not very good at this and I don't even know how to start, so please bear with me. I guess I'll just start and maybe we'll be able to make some sense of it."

Carol searched his face and saw a mixture of fear, confusion, compassion, and love. She was a jumble of emotion, still angry with him and not sure why, afraid of him and not sure why, very much in love with him and, again, not sure why.

"You reacted to what I chose to do after my Navy career," Jason began. "But, for you to understand, I need to give you some background and the reasons for my choices.

"You didn't learn from our episode with Dailey that I married two weeks before I joined the Navy. Even before I finished boot camp, my wife got lonely and decided that she didn't want to be married to an absentee husband. It was probably for the best. It still hurt. But I masked it with the anger and hate that I carried for my father.

"The SEAL program and its physically abusive training felt good to me. It provided a vent for my pent-up anger. It got to the point where I would look forward to seeing how much more pain I could endure every day. It became an obsession with me, an experience for which I'm grateful because it saved my life several times in Vietnam." Jason shared with Carol his past and some of the horrors of war, and his voice became stronger as he began reliving some of his experiences.

As many times as I've faced death and physical pain, why is this so difficult? he wondered to himself. I still don't understand this thing about feelings. He gave this woman, whose hands he was holding, every bit of information about himself that he knew how to share. Carol, although attentive, sat rigid with no perceptible warmth. "The transition after Vietnam was difficult, coming home to the scourge of the anti-war sentiment. But always, deep in my heart, I believed in what I did, and still do. After my discharge, I felt an emptiness and a lack of purpose. And when I read about all of the terrorist activity in the Mid-East, Scotland, and Germany, and listened to Gadaffi's bullshit, I would become angry because I couldn't to do anything about it. When the opportunity to develop an anti-terrorist team came along, I jumped at the chance, even with all the risks. I've seen the effects of repeated terrorist attacks, and *they are* despicable and sinister.

"Sweetheart, I am a true patriot. I love this country, and my only true desire was to protect our people from the kind of carnage that I saw in Vietnam, Israel, and Lebanon. And yes, the whole thing turned sour, but I still believe that our government isn't bad. Maybe some of the people are, but I believe with all my heart that there are more good people."

"But they tried to kill you, the same goddamned people that set the whole thing up tried to kill you, the ones you were supposed to be protecting," Carol responded angrily. Jason realized Laura had been right. Although Carol had disdain for the violence in his life, she may have a greater fear of losing him. "And because you got yourself backed into a corner, you go off and start killing them?" she continued in a hostile tone. "Where does it end? How can you reconcile setting yourself above the law by becoming judge and jury?"

"I don't pretend to set myself above the law. I admit to a time when I looked forward to the killing. You have to revel in it, like a dog gone mad with the taste for blood, because it's the only way that you'll survive. Those who didn't came home in body bags. After my discharge, I thought I could simply walk away and forget. It hasn't been that easy.

"Carol, I want to share something with you that I've never told anyone, not even Laura. I'm sharing this with you because I think I'm in love with you and I want you to love me." His voice carried the timbre of timidity, again because sharing his emotional vulnerability did not come easy.

"I told you the other night that my past haunts me. I don't know if it will ever stop. I trained for years to do nothing but kill. That's one side of me, but there is another side, a side that has a great capacity to love—and also has a need to be loved. A part of me thrives on danger and adventure, and also a part of me has been trying to emerge over the past several months. I didn't know it at the time but it tried to surface when I married in Mexico. I wanted to learn to love my second wife, the way she loved me. But that opportunity was taken from me by people who are not all that much different from me, except they have no cause, no morals. They kill for money. The five remaining team members were in danger. I could eliminate that danger, and did."

"Jason, why did you tell people your second wife divorced you?"

"Because that's the way it had to be. She was an orphan and had no family. We hadn't lived in Edmonds long enough for anybody to get to know us. If you tell people that your wife died or was killed, they ask questions. If you tell people that she divorced you, they leave it alone.

"What I want to explain is, I'm trying to allow this thing to evolve, to find out what's inside that's good that hasn't been destroyed. But the warrior in me is still very much alive and I'm not sure if it's bad or good. I know I've changed. I don't hunt any more. Killing an animal doesn't appeal to me. I'll take my boat to Bainbridge Island and simply walk in the woods over there. Sometimes I'll just lie down in the quiet and listen. Sometimes I think that I can hear the trees and the grass breathing. I've come to realize all of creation is alive, it's becoming sacred to me.

"But this war continues to wage inside. The warrior doesn't want to relinquish his hold on me. He still wants to be fed. The only thing I can do is to be patient and let the warrior die at his own pace.

"Then something like this comes along, and I realize that I'm an enigma. Although I covet life and all living things, I know I still have the capacity to kill another human being without remorse. I can kill men who care nothing for the acceptable boundaries of coexistence, men who would walk up to someone in a parking lot and simply snuff out his or her life for a paycheck. Carol, I would kill again in an instant to protect someone I love."

Carol continued her gaze into Jason's eyes. She could see them welling with emotion and marveled at his hunger for understanding himself and his tenacious capacity to endure. He had made a real effort to be gentle and tender toward her.

She remembered times when he had not been tender. But it had been his silent brooding, his intense anger that had frightened her away in the past. Never before had he shared himself in this way, and for the first time, she understood why he acted as he had. His use of the term *enigma* was accurate.

"With that said, I hope you understand why I have to see Dailey. Go, take my bed, and get some sleep. I'll see you in the morning. And again, I'm sorry you've been involved in this mess."

Carol did not want him to leave. Never before had they had such a revealing conversation. But his last statement distracted her. "Involved? You keep saying I'm involved. How am I involved?" she asked with a bewildered expression.

"You're involved because they've seen you."

CHAPTER FIFTEEN

"Morning," Jason said, after weaving through the maze of cluttered desks, arriving at Dailey's cube.

"Brisben," Dailey replied tersely. He slouched in his chair with his feet on the desk. A contorted face and posture revealed a boiling fury.

Thompson and Dolan were standing at the cube with coffee in hand, discussing the contents of the Ford Tempo. Thompson looked to Dailey for direction; when he didn't receive one, he spoke on his own.

"The suspect had no identification and a 357 Colt Python when we rousted him. A loaded Canon 35mm camera with a telephoto lens and a police band scanner were found when we later searched the car. Also, there were no plates on the vehicle. We're waiting for word from the legal department as to how to proceed."

All in all, it looked like a good score to Jason. Why the testy atmosphere, he wondered?

Jason knew enough about the law to understand a part of Dailey's predicament. Although a combination of vagrancy, a concealed weapon, and possibly a stolen car, could be levied, the evidence had been obtained after apprehension. Even a wet-behind-the-ears law student would know enough to scream "Illegal search and seizure." There had been no hard evidence of wrongdoing before the guy was picked up, only suspicion. But hell, they knew all that before they rousted the guy. So what's the big deal?

Jason soon found out. Only minutes after Montgomery returned with the suspect, an attorney had shown up looking for a Samuel Wellington. This attorney knew the guy had been hauled in before Montgomery and Dailey had even learned his name. Dailey was furious, but had resigned himself to the fact that picking up the man was the only way to generate a break in the case without jeopardizing the O'Connors' safety, in spite of the legal fallout. By morning, this move would provoke action by his superior akin to a pit bull dining on Dailey's backside. He had gone out on a limb and knew it. He had cause to be angry.

Although Jason listened to the conversation, his real interest lay with what had happened to Lori Phillips. Exercising discretion, he decided to wait a few minutes before broaching that subject, instead jumping into the current discussion.

"So, where's Wellington now?"

"He's in an interrogation room down the hall, with his fat-ass attorney," Dailey said. "I'm trying to figure out just how far I'm willing to push this thing. We've nothing substantial enough to charge him with. I can hold him for twenty-four hours if I want to stretch it, but what's the point? Pisses me off, I don't mind telling you."

"The point is information," Jason said.

"What? What are you talking here?" Dailey asked, perturbed. The two officers looked puzzled.

"Well, the way it looks to me," Jason said offering his hypothesis, "the worst thing that can happen is you turn him loose." Dailey looked up to protest but Jason held up his hand. "Hold on a minute, Lieutenant. We know why the sonofabitch was there, whether you had any evidence to pick him up or not. We also know from Phillips' description that he wasn't one of the hitters, so he's either there to watch the house for Jack or to snatch some leverage in the form of one or more of the family. If I had to guess, it'd be watching the house. Hell, open up that camera and see what's on the film. The worst thing that can happen is, you give it back, turn him loose and follow him. When you have what's on the film, you won't have any trouble getting the authorization for manpower to follow him."

"Just what do you think is on the film?" Dailey asked gruffly.

"Photos of the O'Connors' house, the kids, or anyone who has been coming or going," Jason said confidently.

"He's got a point," Thompson said in agreement. "We can take the film down to the lab and have it processed, see what's on it, and have it back in forty-five minutes. We keep the photos and put the film back in the camera. They certainly won't open the camera to check for fear of exposing the film. I guarantee once he's out of here he ain't gonna come back and make a fuss, especially if we have proof that he was watching the house. To hell with Legal. Who needs 'em?"

"Yeah, it's not a bad idea," Dolan said soberly. "Give me the camera and let's get this film developed. Then we can make a decision that's based on something. What d'ya think, Lieutenant?"

"What I think is that I'm too damned tired to argue. Let's get on with it," Dailey barked. Dolan picked up the camera making a note of the number of exposures. After the lab processed the photographs he would have the lab technician reinstall the processed film into the canister, return it to the camera and advance the film to the proper exposure number. It would look as if no one had tampered with it. With camera in hand, he disappeared to the lab.

That issue taken care of, Jason decided to bring up the subject of the second murder. "So Lieutenant, what gives with Lori Phillips?"

Without altering his slouched position, Dailey looked up at Jason through tired, bloodshot eyes. "Well, I'm not sure what to think. Dr. Keller is convinced of foul play, but so far there's nothing to substantiate it. I just have to say, I can't argue with his suspicion. At nine-thirty, the guard outside her room was called to the nurses' station for a phone call. When he got to the phone, no one was on the line. He got suspicious and ran back to Ms. Philips' room and she looked all right as far as he could tell. He checked the hall again and—nobody in it. When he initially ran back to her room, he thought he might have seen the stairwell door closing. He ran to check it, but by then, it was empty. He went back and checked Miss Phillips again and she seemed to be fine. She apparently slept through the whole episode.

"Ten minutes later, she flat-lined. They tried to defibrillate her, but she never responded. They paged Dr. Keller and he showed up twenty minutes later. He went over the printouts of the monitoring equipment. When I arrived he told me what he found didn't make any sense. As far as he could tell, her heart just stopped with no apparent reason. There will, of course, be an autopsy. I'll let you know what they find."

"Somebody wanted the guard away from her room," Jason said irritably.

"Looks that way," Dailey said. "But so far there's no proof. We'll just have to wait for the autopsy, see what they find."

Jason, deep in thought, still fumed over the loss of Lori Phillips and only heard the conversation between Dailey and Thompson as so much noise in the background. He needed sleep, but understood himself well enough to know that he wouldn't get any, at least until he found out what images were on the film.

The telephone on Dailey's desk rang, and after a gruff "yeah," Dailey handed the phone to Thompson. He responded with a series of okay's, uh huh's, and humph's while scribbling furiously on his notepad, then handed the receiver back to Dailey. "The car was a one-owner vehicle we traced by the serial number to seventy-eight-year-old Jake Benham of Enumclaw," Thompson reported. "The reason the car hasn't been reported stolen is Mr. Benham died three months ago of a heart attack. The DOL in Enumclaw issued the temporary permit we found in the back window at 8:10 a.m. yesterday. I guess we'll be looking into it first thing this morning when the DOL opens. We better have someone go up and impound the damned thing."

"Why? So we can give it back at our expense?" Dailey groused. "You seem to have forgotten, the only thing we had to go on, was that he was parked a few houses down from the O'Connors'. Not a reason for picking someone up, or even questioning them."

After long moment of silence Dailey spoke again. "Okay, this is the plan, gentlemen. When Dolan gets back, we'll take a look at the pictures, then question the twerp. I doubt if he'll give up anything with his attorney sitting in, but I'll go through the motions. It won't go anywhere, so we'll turn him out. Your theory about him not making a stink may be correct, Mr. Brisben. Thompson, be ready to tail this guy. I hope to hell he'll lead us somewhere."

Jason wanted to suggest that he wait for Wellington outside. He knew he'd be able to get the information he wanted, but also knew it was just the tactic Dailey feared. He decided not to jeopardize an already tenuous relationship. Instead he retreated into himself and thought of the day ahead, things that needed to be done in order to deliver the people in his charge safely to Oak Bay. But fatigue had taken its toll, and Jason struggled to concentrate. His boat hadn't been in the water since summer's end, he remembered. The marina crew would have to prep the boat and have it ready by mid-morning.

Jason jolted to the present with Dolan's return, and he lazily looked at his watch: three-forty-five. "Anything good on the film?" Jason asked, with a rigidly clenched jaw, stifling a yawn.

"They were there for only one reason," Dolan said, as he handed a set of photographs to Dailey, then a second set to Jason. "I had 'em make a set for you."

Jason looked at the photographs one at a time, and each one brought a successively sinking feeling. A picture of Debbie and Tommy in the front yard; Deb grooming a bright red azalea with Tommy's assistance; Tommy and his lime-green wheelbarrow. Another of Deb again, putting mail in the mailbox. Then another of a familiar silver Toyota pulling into the drive, and, with the next photo, a full head-and-shoulder shot of Carol getting out of the car, looking sideways at the O'Connors' house. One of the last two pictures was an image of a beautiful ten-year-old girl with a backpack, bending over to smell a tulip at the edge of the O'Connors' property—Ashley. And the remaining picture showed a full-face shot of Carol at the mailbox with Tommy looking directly up at her. Jason studied the photos carefully for several minutes.

"Interesting pictures," Jason said. "The first picture, that's Jack's wife and their four-year-old son, Tommy. Notice where the shadows are: The back of their house faces east. Look at how most of the front yard is in the shade and the long shadows. Those are nine or ten o'clock shadows. In the next picture, the shadows are much shorter, the one of Debbie at the mailbox. Now look at the later pictures, the one of Carol getting out of the car. Looks like about a two o'clock shadow. The shadows are very short and going the other way. And the last one of Carol and Tommy, it's a little longer. The sun is high in the west. When Carol called me last night, she told me that when she went for the mail, one car came to replace the other. From her description it seemed to be happening about every two hours or so. That matches with some of the changes in the shadows."

"That's a brilliant discovery," Dailey snapped. "So what? What's the point?"

"The point is, Lieutenant, that there were two cars and two cameras. Carol also told me that she had gone for a walk with Deb and Tommy. There are no pictures of them during that time, and also, there are no pictures of Jennifer on her way home from school. Those are in another camera. There're more pictures out there somewhere. Let's check with Montgomery and find out if there's any sign of the other car up there."

"That makes sense," Dailey said grudgingly. "If your estimate of a two-hour shift change is correct, Bob should have reported some activity by now—unless—any of you see that green Toyota?" he asked of Thompson and Dolan.

"Not even a hint," Thompson replied.

"Shit. I'll bet that's how they knew we picked up Wellington. Somebody saw us grab him. You see anything?" Dailey asked Jason.

"Negative. I didn't see a green Toyota or anything that looked like surveillance."

Dailey removed his feet from his desk and reached for his telephone. "Well, it's probably an exercise in futility, but Thompson, Dolan, get on up there and relieve Montgomery," he said while waiting for Montgomery to answer his cell phone. They were on the way to the door but stopped when they heard Dailey's contact with Montgomery. "You see anything up there?" he asked. Dailey shook his head and motioned the two officers to continue on. "Bob, Thompson, and Dolan will be up there shortly to relieve you. I want you back here when I pay Wellington a visit."

Dailey wearily hung up the phone and turned to Jason. "You may as well go home and get some sleep. Call us tomorrow. We'll let you know if we come up with anything."

Jason did need sleep. The simple act of rising from his chair made him aware of the effort required to lift his tired body. He stood and straightened his back, then stretched. "What time can I expect an update call?" he asked somberly.

"We won't be on until three in the afternoon," Dailey replied.

"Well, I'll be in Victoria long before then." Jason returned.

"Why don't you call me at home before you leave," Dailey offered.

"It won't be before ten," Jason said, "but I do want to be under way before noon to take advantage of the warm weather. I'd like to have as much information as possible before I leave. It will help me with my plans for Jack when he finishes in Portland."

"Ten o'clock will be fine," Dailey said. "If we learn anything before then, I'll give you a call. Now get out of here and get some sleep."

* * * * *

The four-fifteen quarter-hour strike of Jason's antique regulator greeted him as he quietly closed the door to the loft. The soft sound drifted toward him in light, friendly tones. The only lights illuminating the loft were in the kitchen area and Carol had dimmed them to a comforting glow. From there he could see her wrapped in a blanket, almost curled in a ball on the sofa, sound asleep. It disappointed him that she hadn't taken his bed. It's just as well, he thought.

He walked to the sofa and stood above her, looking down at her for a moment, then bent over and gently kissed her cheek. He moved quietly to the kitchen, then to the office and turned off the telephone ringers so no one would be disturbed by an early morning call.

Jason prided himself on being a fastidious housekeeper, but tonight his clothes lay where they fell as he removed them. After stripping to his briefs, he moved the bedroom telephone ringer to the low position and turned back his covers. Sleep came the instant his head landed on the cool pillow.

CHAPTER SIXTEEN

The ring of the telephone continued for some time before sleep relinquished its hold and Jason slowly opened his eyes. He rolled over and picked up.

"Brisben," Jason said sleepily into the receiver. The clock radio sitting next to the phone indicated 7:45 a.m.

"Jason, this is Bob Montgomery. Sorry to wake you, but I thought you'd want to know—we lost our lead."

"And just how did we manage to do that?" Jason asked, still semi-conscious.

"We turned Wellington loose at six o'clock this morning. He went to the lobby, made a phone call. Thirty minutes later, believe it or not, the green Toyota showed up in the parking lot and picked him up. Our friend got in on the driver's side and they left. Thompson and Dolan followed them to the East Marginal exit. They headed west down toward the Boeing museum. At the stop light at East Marginal and Interurban, the passenger hopped out and our boy Sammy made a U-turn and headed back onto I-5 North, then east on I-90.

"Just past the I-90/405 interchange, he pulled off into a McDonald's. Probably wanted to eat or piss or something. Anyway, Thompson, wanting to keep his distance, parked across the street. The guy parked, turned off the ignition, looked like he was getting out of the car, and pow! Instant fireball! The hood and doors landed about ten feet from the car . . . Wellington's toast."

The fog of sleep abruptly lifted from Jason's mind as he shook his head and sat up hanging his feet over the side of the bed. "Did you get any more information on Wellington?"

"Nah, not much. We're still checking."

"I take it you didn't get anything on the guy who got out, down by Interurban?"

"You take it right," Montgomery replied. "That's something we didn't expect."

Jason, now fully awake, realized their plan had backfired; with their hot lead up in smoke, they were back to square one. "I don't suppose you got any information out of Wellington before you released him?"

"Nada. It went as we suspected. He'd been well-schooled. We gave him his camera back and told him and his pant-load attorney to have a nice day, though we didn't expect it to be so short."

"So now what?" Jason asked, puzzling over the latest development. "We have three people dead and we still know nothing."

"Yeah, well one thing's for sure, our boss is not a happy man. And now with this car blowing up in our faces we're gonna have the Feds nosing around. There'll be a lot of pressure to get answers. Daily asked me to tell you to keep your head down."

"Well, you can tell the good lieutenant that nobody wants answers more than I do. My head will be down until I get back tomorrow afternoon. After that, I'll be looking hard. Thanks for the call. I'll be in touch."

Jason looked long and hard at the telephone after the call ended. What next? he asked himself, sliding off the bed. He put on his kimono and shuffled to the kitchen. On the way, he paused over Carol; she was still asleep on the sofa, still curled in a tight ball. Just for a brief moment something stirred in his chest but he moved on. He pushed the feelings back, knowing too much lay ahead. He could ill afford distractions. As he ground the beans for coffee, he heard water running in the pipes. A glance at the sofa let him know Carol had quietly slipped into his shower. With the coffee maker set, he moved to the office to make his telephone calls.

He first called Hard-Ship Marine to make arrangements for getting his boat prepped and in the water. After brief and somewhat heated negotiations, Jason obtained conformation that the boat would be de-winterized, cleaned, fueled, and on the water by eleven-thirty. Next he called Dr. Tom Keller. The phone only rang once.

"Keller."

"What the hell happened, Tom?"

"I have no idea. Her heart just stopped."

"You trying to tell me, after all she's been through she died of a fucking heart attack?"

"That's what's got me baffled. Her heart was strong as a bull's. It stopped like a wheel with a bar through the spokes. I'm telling you, man, her rhythms were like a metronome. Then flat line! End of report! We tried to jump-start her and got no response to defib, not one thump. Zilch. That's unusual. I've been up all night analyzing her blood and there's something weird, something I've never seen before."

"Like what?"

"That's just it, I'm not quite sure. There's a very subtle, almost imperceptible difference in her blood from the time we checked her for a match. I'm working on it with two specialists and none of us knows what to make of it."

"So, you think somebody injected her with something while the guard was gone?'

"That'd be my guess," Keller said. "There were no additional needle marks on her body. They must have injected it into her IV access. But at this point, we have no idea what it is. It's nothing any of us have any knowledge of. Whatever it is, it's some stealthy stuff."

"How long d'ya think it'll take before you know anything?"

"Jason, I have no idea. We'll keep on it until we find it. You know me. When I get pissed, I don't let go. I find out something, you'll be the first to know. This is personal now. When we brought Phillips in, she had zero chance. I'm telling you, man, we worked miracles and I think she would have made it. Find these bastards, Jay. I'd like to see some justice for her, and I don't mean some bullshit five-year court battle."

Jason's anger flared as he listened to his friend vent his frustration. They shared not only anger about Lori Phillips' death, but also about the danger to Jack and his family. "You can bet your ass I'll give it my best shot," Jason responded hotly.

"You'll be the first to know when I have some answers. Talk to ya."

"Thanks, Tom." He hung up and leaned back in his chair, trying to assimilate the disturbing information he had just received and the challenges that lay ahead. But his thoughts were interrupted when he heard the sound of muffled voices from behind the walls of the guestroom. Better be getting some breakfast on, he thought.

Jason wasn't territorial about too many things, but he guarded his kitchen jealously and he had precious little patience for anybody messing about in his domain. Only wooden spoons and spatulas were allowed to touch his carefully selected pots and sauté pans. And his prized cutlery, when slicing or dicing, came to rest only on the custom maple cutting board. He pulled a handful of mushrooms, a large onion, a green pepper, a dozen eggs, some cheddar cheese, and smoked bratwursts from the refrigerator, setting them on the large island cutting board. His sauté pan rested over a medium flame on the cook-top while he lost himself in the dicing of the vegetables. Unexpectedly, someone tugged on the hem of his kimono.

"What are you doing, Uncle Jason?"

Jason looked down into a pair of wide-open blue eyes set above a wide pie-faced grin.

"Well good morning, Tommy. I'm making something to eat. You hungry?"

"Yup," Tommy said, matter-of-factly. "Can I help?"

Jason's first impulse was to say no, but after a moment of staring into pleading eyes the size of soup plates, he thought he'd better find something for Tommy to do. "How are you at breaking eggs?"

"Don't know. I never did that before."

"Well, then, I guess it's about time you learn." Jason moved one of the bar stools up close to the counter, set a large stainless bowl in the sink, then hoisted the expectantly helpful child to his perch in front of the sink. My God, he's frail, Jason thought. Tommy beamed with pride as Jason patiently showed him the fine art of cracking eggs.

Jason watched as his small apprentice labored intently, his face serious and filled with purpose. Jason's concern was not for shells in the eggs, but for the health of his little friend whom he had not seen in several months. Tommy didn't look good. It seemed to be an effort for Tommy to breathe. He'd talk to Debbie when they settled in at Oak Bay. Jason returned to his chopping and dicing, smiling to himself when he heard an occasional "Ooops" from his kitchen partner. A little crunchiness couldn't hurt, could it?

"All done, Uncle Jason," said a proud lad, with a considerable amount of egg on his blue blanket sleeper.

"Wow, Tommy! You did good. Now go tell Mom that you need to get cleaned up and ready to go. Then you come back and help me cook up a gourmet breakfast."

Tommy responded by jumping down from the stool with a thump and an "Oh boy!" then disappeared to the guestroom.

Jason poured clarified butter and the chopped ingredients into the pan, sautéing them until they were tender and setting them aside. He had just finished removing the larger bits of shells from the eggs and cleaning up a little when Carol reappeared wrapped in a towel.

"I hate to bring this up, but if you're going to keep a woman against her will, you'll need to provide some sort of a wardrobe," Carol said, as she took a cup from the cupboard.

"I guess I'll have to, or buy myself a new one. Too many days of this and I won't have any clothes left," Jason replied.

"I don't suppose there's any chance I can go home and get a few things,"

"Negative. As soon as breakfast is out of the way, I'll sit down with you and Deb and fill you in on our situation."

The tensions of prior days were absent or at least held in check, so it seemed. Carol sipped her coffee, complimented Jason on the aroma in the kitchen and offered to help. He thanked her but declined. "Tommy's helping me."

Carol raised her eyebrows and tilted her head in surprise; she had asked only as a courtesy, knowing Jason preferred cooking solo.

After brief but pleasant conversation Jason volunteered his wardrobe. "Breakfast will be ready soon and we'll need to leave shortly after. You'd probably better get ready, take any of my clothes you like." Carol thanked him and with coffee in hand Carol sauntered back to his bedroom. Jason felt a stirring as his eyes followed after her until she disappeared behind his bedroom door.

With the sautéed ingredients tucked in the oven to keep warm, Jason returned to his office to inform the partners of the latest developments. With that accomplished, he retraced his steps to the kitchen and was nearly run over by Tommy, closely followed by Debbie in her unsuccessful attempt to contain his enthusiasm.

"What's this I hear about Tommy helping with our 'gomer' breakfast?" Debbie asked.

"Well, I hoped it might be 'gourmet,' but who knows?" Jason laughed as he scooped up Tommy, positioned him on the barstool, telling him he would be the keeper of the bratwurst. He set the flame on the front burner and heated a large cast iron skillet.

Meanwhile, Debbie set the table as Jennifer and Ashley appeared one at a time, both demonstrating confused expressions as to why they were there. Jason put the sausages into the skillet and showed Tommy how to turn them with tongs. He then told Tommy he had just been promoted to head chef. Tommy, ecstatic about his new position, set his mouth in a purposeful grimace as only a four-year-old can while turning the sausages one by one with great care.

Jason cajoled Ashley into making the toast, but gave Jennifer a wide berth. She seemed in a bit of a sour mood. He poured juice, whipped the eggs and continued on with breakfast. Five minutes later, everything came up together and on time. Life was good at the loft.

During the time of keeping a low profile after the anti-terrorist debacle, Jason spent a good deal of time in Portland at a little French café called Du Berry. It was there Jason learned many of his cooking skills while watching Mike, the owner in the kitchen. Jason remembered the times when Mike would hand him a knife or a sauté pan and put him to work. The tasks were never too terribly important, but he felt complimented all the same. Jason and Mike became culinary soul mates of sorts and continued to share fine wines and recipes when they were in their respective towns.

Carol emerged on cue. Once again, she wore some of the finer items from of Jason's wardrobe: navy linen trousers and a white dress shirt with French cuffs. The cuffs flashed a pair of Jason's solid gold monogrammed cuff links. Another unisex fashion plate.

The breakfast went well and no one made disparaging remarks about two of the sausages that were a little closer to black than brown. When everyone had finished eating, Jason had Tommy stand in his chair and take a bow for cooking a real 'gomer' breakfast. He bowed and grinned from ear to ear, jumped down and ran over to crawl onto his mother's lap.

"Was it really good, Mommy?" he asked for reassurance.

"It was really good," Debbie told him.

While Jennifer and Ashley cleared the dishes and loaded the dishwasher, Jason directed Carol and Debbie to his office. "I'm sorry, Debbie, about your situation and in particular how it's affecting you and your family," he began.

He reiterated they had wanted to wait until they had proof before telling her about what they knew. Jack, he continued, had only been apprised of the situation late Monday night. As Jason spoke, he could read the fear returning to Debbie's eyes and, considering her emotional state, he decided it best to give her only the essentials. He mentioned that Lori Phillips had died, but gave no details. He told her they had questioned the man, Samuel Wellington, who had been watching the house, and he brought out the photographs they had obtained from his camera. He did not tell her about the car bomb and Wellington's death.

Debbie's hands shook as she looked at the pictures. Jason was grateful for Carol's presence and knew she would be a source of support for Debbie in the days ahead.

"Why are they doing this?" she moaned, staring at each picture.

"At this point, we have no idea. What we do know is these people are organized and they move fast. They must have learned from the newspaper that they'd killed the wrong person. Yesterday morning, someone called Cervicon attempting to locate Jack. And from these pictures we learned someone has been watching your house for most of the day. But we've had less than forty-eight hours with this," Jason continued, "so we need to be patient. You'll just have to trust us."

Trust, was the wrong word to use.

"How can I trust when I don't even know what's going on and neither do you? My God, whom should I trust? I have a sick child; the doctors can't tell me what's wrong with him. Jack's about to lose his job. Then you barge in during the middle of the night, practically kidnap us, and tell me that someone is trying to kill Jack. And—and I'm supposed to be patient? I'm supposed to trust?"

Tears welled in Debbie's eyes as she fought for control. Jason, too felt as though he were losing control because he had no answers to give his friend, or words of comfort to ease her anxiety.

How can I tell her everything is going to be all right? he thought, with the compassion of a friend. Simply tell her what you've planed, he counseled himself.

"Debbie, I have two of the best men I know with Jack. They won't let him out of their sight. He's as safe as we can keep him. Now that we've removed you from your home, they have no way of tracking you. They can't use you or your family as a means to get to Jack."

He continued to impart his plan, trying his best to sell it as a vacation on Vancouver Island, while all the time Debbie fidgeted with the corners of the pictures. She never looked at Jason or Carol. With downcast eyes and shaking hands, she asked all the questions Jason had expected. "How are we supposed to live? What about clothes? What about school?" And, of course, and most importantly, "What about Tommy? He's been getting worse over the past few weeks. What if he needs a doctor?"

"All legitimate questions, Deb," Jason said calmly. "Don't worry about the expenses. I'll take care of whatever's needed for Tommy's medical needs. The most important thing for us right now is to get out of this city. So with that in mind, let's try to make the best out of a lousy situation and do whatever we can to keep it together. Let's not waste energy fussing and stewing over things that haven't happened yet." Jason opened his hands in supplication, "So far, we're all safe and that's what's important. So, can you hang in there? Can we all hang together? If we can, I'm sure we can weather this out."

"For how long, Jason?" Debbie looked at Jason with teary bloodshot eyes. "How long do we do this?"

Jason took a slow, deep breath, partly from frustration and partly to buy time to think. He had no easy answers. He had no answers, period, other than: "As long as it takes. I don't know what else to tell you. And, Debbie, as soon as we get settled this afternoon, I'll sit down with you and we'll talk about Tommy. Please try not to worry."

Debbie angrily slid her chair back and stood. "I'm going to get the kids ready. How soon do we have to leave?"

"Within the hour," Jason answered.

Carol remained seated. "Debbie, I'll be out in a minute to help with the children, but first I need a minute with Jason." She sat silent for a moment with her eyes searching Jason's face, a face that revealed nothing. "Why do I have the feeling you haven't told us everything?"

"Because I haven't," Jason said evenly. He massaged his chin with his hand while trying to decide how much he should tell Carol. He wasn't at all sure how she would respond if he told her everything. One angry woman was enough. He didn't need two.

"Come on, Jay, I have a right to know. Like it or not I seem to be up to my eyeballs in this mess. So please, don't jerk me around."

"Samuel Wellington was the name of the man we picked up watching the house. Dailey had no legal reason to hold him and had to let him go this morning. Less than an hour after they released him he was blown up in a car bomb." Jason waited for a response but Carol simply stared at him. "Also, I talked with Keller this morning. He's definitely convinced someone murdered Lori Phillips. Whoever these people are, they're well informed, well organized, they move quickly, and they're dangerous as hell. And we still know nothing. We do know that you have been spotted and that puts you at risk. I'm sorry, that's all I have. We're working under the assumption that there was another camera and they have photos of everyone. They're still in the driver's seat, and we're on the defensive—at least for the time being."

Carol had no perceptible reaction. "So, from what you've said, we just hide out until you get a handle on whatever is going on. That's it?"

Jason shrugged and sighed. "Unless you have a better idea."

"What am I supposed to do about my job?" Carol asked calmly, apparently having resigned herself to the situation.

"Do you have any time coming, vacation or sick leave?"

"I work in a bar, Jay. They don't give sick leave," she said, with an ironic laugh. "I do have two weeks' vacation saved, but this isn't quite how I had planned spending it."

"Well, can you call in and tell them you have an emergency? I'll make up your wages. That way you can save your vacation."

"I know that you're financially well set, Jay, but you just can't go around paying everyone's way. Some people might take offense to it."

"Well, this seems to be a bit of an emergency, now, doesn't it?" Jason said, trying to keep his voice even, then instantly regretted his sarcastic remark. The last thing he needed or wanted was an argument over money. "I'll spend every last dime I have, if that's what it takes to keep you and the O'Connors safe. Now, are you telling me you're taking offense at my generosity? If you are, by all means use your vacation. I won't be offended." That wasn't any better, he thought. "I'm sorry," he said, shaking his head.

Carol softened her expression. "I didn't mean to give the impression I'm offended by your offer because I'm not. Why don't we see how it goes and I'll make my decision as the need arises. How does that sound?" She paused and looked away for a moment before speaking again. "Thank you for trusting me with the information on what's happened. I really appreciate it."

She hesitated again before going on. "Where are you and I? I lambasted you pretty good Monday night and I wasn't too cordial last night either. I guess what I'm asking is, did I screw everything up?"

Her question set him a bit off-balance, and during an uncomfortable silence that followed, Jason formulated a careful but honest response.

"I have to tell you I was pretty damn angry yesterday. But I also understand why you were angry, as I already explained earlier this morning. I haven't changed my mind about what I said to you on Monday. I still want to have a relationship with you. But right now I'd like to get Deb and the kids to Oak Bay. Does that answer your question?"

"Yes, and thank you again for being honest." She arose from her chair. "I'm glad I didn't scare you off." Carol's eyes no longer carried the fire of anger from the previous day.

"I'd like to stay in Oak Bay until tomorrow afternoon. Can we make time to talk after we get settled on the island?"

Carol leaned across the table and kissed him. "I would like that." She silently studied Jason, then, without a word, left the office. Jason sat, sipping his coffee as he gave thoughtful consideration to the dynamic of what had just transpired. That stuff Laura's been foisting on me ain't too bad, he reflected.

Jason showered and dressed, then went out onto the deck from his room. The Bainbridge ferry barked loudly from a quarter mile out. He watched intently as it silently glided to its mooring. People disembarked on foot, then in cars, at a frantic pace. For a brief moment, he felt thankful that it wasn't necessary for him to be a part of the rat race. Thank God, he thought, that I have the time and resources to help my friends.

As he continued watching the scene, It occurred to him that some of those people, if they knew his situation, might feel sorry for him. Most of those people he watched were scurrying to their jobs. They were toiling to achieve their goals with great anticipation. They probably had purpose in their lives, families to go home to at night. Who was the less fortunate? Jason wondered.

He continued watching the people from the ferry streaming out across Alaskan Way and suddenly became aware of a void within. He pondered what it would be like, having a family and purpose in life. Well, he certainly had purpose now, didn't he? But what about after this business with Jack? What then? Another periodic job for the partners? What was it, three of them last year? And what about family? He had never known family. He had been just four when his mother had died, and he remembered only snippets of her. He had no recollection of what she looked like. Childhood memories consisted mostly of beatings from his father. Those beatings, he remembered, seemed to be the only time spent with his father.

He had a stepsister from one of his father's brief marriages, but she had disappeared from his life when he was ten. His father, Jasper Conrad Brisben III, had died about nine years ago of cancer, he'd heard. Jason was twenty when his father had told him to leave and never return. He hadn't seen the old man since.

Jason did not realize a smile had crept across his face as he remembered briefly the scene of the morning's breakfast. Never before had he shared his kitchen, let alone with a four-year-old. In the past Carol had offered to help but had always been relegated to a barstool to watch. He had realized with a sudden shock that he had enjoyed the whole morning's experience.

Family? As he refocused his attention toward the Elliott Bay ferry terminal watching the people begin their day, the question this time seemed less fleeting. Indeed, who was the less fortunate?

CHAPTER SEVENTEEN

Caretaker of Jason's boat had not been part of the package Leon had envisioned for his yacht maintenance enterprise. Leon Black owned Hard-Ship Marine, a facility for the service and repair of high-end yachts, not permanent storage. He had the only publicly accessible crane on the north end of Elliott Bay in the heart of Smith Cove. Without hesitation, Jason had seized the opportunity to buy his way onto Leon's pier.

Even though Leon thought it inconvenient at times, today's situation being a good example, Jason had paid handsomely to raise a building to house his boat. The facility, complete with a fifteen-hundred-gallon tank for special high-octane racing fuel and custom cradle, provided dry storage. Jason required dry storage for his boat to keep the bottom from fouling. A wet-moored boat's bottom grows algae and barnacles that rob boat speed Jason had spent a great deal of money to attain. The cradle allowed the ten-thousand-pound boat to be rolled out of the building, picked up by Leon's crane, and set on the water in a matter of minutes. *Strictly Business*, Jason's custom-built, thirty-eight-foot Fountain powered by two supercharged 1,250-horsepower Hawk Marine engines, had been clocked at 117 mph on radar.

The temperature hovered at nearly seventy degrees. A hint of breeze from a clear azure blue sky drifted across the pier as Jason's Seville rolled silently along on the weathered planking toward the boathouse. Tommy let out a squeal, his eyes alive with excitement when he caught sight of a metallic, cobalt-blue, knife-shaped hull suspended some thirty feet in the air by a huge crane. The sun reflected painfully bright from the polished stainless steel, razor-sharp surface propellers hanging aft of the twin Speed-Master stern drives.

"Look at that boat, Uncle Jason!" Tommy exclaimed wide-eyed. "Boy, I bet it goes really fast."

"Well, Bud, you're about to find out."

"Oh boy! Is that your boat? Is that really your boat, Uncle Jason?"

"That'd be my boat, bud," Jason replied. Tommy's enthusiasm elevated everyone's mood. Even Jennifer smiled until she caught herself when she made brief eye contact with Jason in the rearview mirror—a typical moody teenager.

The car rolled to a stop and they all watched in silence while the crane effortlessly swung five tons of boat in a slow arc over the edge of the pier, gently lowering it onto the placid water some twenty feet below. Two men on the dock manned the lines from the bow and stern.

As the group spilled from the car, a mountain of a man lumbered towards them. His gray sweat-soaked shirt strained against the weight of huge arms and stomach. A sudden wind gust carried his shiny black-shoulder length hair wildly. Dark eyes, set in a ruddy pock-marked face, made him look fierce, but when a warm smile enveloped his round face he appeared more like a three-hundred-fifty-pound teddy bear.

"Morning, folks," said Leon Black, a full-blooded Duwamish Indian. His high voice seemed incongruous for a man his size.

"Morning yourself. Sorry about the short notice, Leon," Jason replied, as he faced the gentle giant, greeting him with a handshake. "How's everything look?" Jason inquired.

"Everything looks good. She's clean, dry, not a speck of mildew. I went over every inch of her myself. We flushed the fuel lines, found no condensation, and filled both tanks. She's full to the gills. Took on 395 gallons of 125-proof gold. We changed the oil, pulled the mags, and just finished running the oil pressure up to ninety pounds on both engines. She's ready. You want us to fire it up, or you gonna do it?"

"Go ahead," Jason replied, "I wouldn't want to spoil your man's fun."

"Tony," Leon yelled. One of the men on the dock turned and looked up toward Leon, who made a circular motion with his hand over head. He turned back to Jason. "Changed a little since you've been here. Tony's living here permanent now. Built him a three-room house; tacked it on to the back end of your boathouse. He makes a good watchdog. If there's trouble, got someone right here to work it. Tony's a goodun' to have around. Don't ask for much. Just does his job real good. Never have to worry."

"Pretty shrewd, adding a house onto the boathouse. Saved you the cost of a wall," Jason said.

"You're plenty smart too, Jason. You noticed that right off."

Jason acknowledged Leon's compliment, handed him the keys to his car and told him to park it in the boathouse. "Keep it out of sight. I'll be back tomorrow afternoon."

"Where you headed?" Leon asked.

"For a cruise. If anyone comes asking, you haven't seen this family."

Leon eyed him suspiciously. Jason had never been tight-lipped with Leon. "What's up?" He asked. "I don't want trouble. Don't need the cavalry coming down here. Don't want trouble."

"There shouldn't be any trouble," Jason said to assure him. "Can we trust Tony and . . . ? Jason nodded toward the man working with Tony.

"That's Roy. They're tight."

"Then tell them that they haven't seen me. It's important."

Leon eyed Jason uncomfortably again for a few moments. "Done," he said, having come to his decision. Jason had never given Leon a reason to mistrust him.

The starboard engine fired with a pop followed by the roar of unchambered exhaust. Tommy jumped and grabbed his mother's leg. Then he turned round-eyed and looked at Jason who walked over and scooped him into his arms. "What do you think, sailor?" Seconds later the port engine fired, doubling the sound. Tommy quickly looked down at the boat, then back at Jason.

"It's noisy!" Tommy shouted.

"You scared?" Jason asked.

"Nah . . . well . . . maybe a little. I didn't know it was so noisy," he said with a worried look. "Do I still get to ride in it?"

"Sure, you still get to ride."

Jason continued carrying Tommy as the group pulled together and collected their backpacks and suitcases from the trunk to haul to the boat. They were half-way down the gang-way when Tony killed the engines. He waited on board until they came along-side, then took the gear from Roy and helped everyone aboard. With the engine hatch closed and the gear stowed, Jason passed out foam earplugs to everyone and installed Tommy's for him. Once all the children were fitted with life vests they were ready to get under way.

Jason started the engines and turned on the exhaust baffles as Tony went over the side to cast off. The throttle levers were pushed forward and the sleek boat slid away from its moorings. Once they were a safe distance from the pier, Jason gave the helm to Carol to hold steady while he pulled in the mooring lines and fenders and stowed them. He returned to the helm and brought the boat up on step, a speed at which the boat planed. Once away from Elliott Bay and a good distance from Seattle, he increased the speed and cruised at sixty-five.

They passed the southern tip of Whidbey Island and entered the Admiralty Inlet. A friendly northerly breeze kicked a one-foot chop on the water that aerated the surface of the hull, which made the boat's progress effortless. Jason frequently glanced to his companion sitting on the bolster next to him as she appraised their rapid transit through the inlet. Carol's hair pulled tightly then flailed against the stiff breeze in syncopation with forward progress, her bright yellow windbreaker accentuating the brilliance of her hair. As he caught his reflection in her aviator sunglasses, he wondered about their relationship. Would it end as abruptly as it had started, or would it endure the present trials and those to come? He returned his attention to staying on course knowing they would break out of the inlet soon to make their run to Oak Bay across the Strait of Juan de Fuca. Once they reached the open water of the strait, the tranquil water conditions might be only a memory.

Debbie made her way forward and slid next to Carol. A petite woman whose bright eyes always communicated the best of expectations, today carried a weariness that betrayed the fear and anxiety she struggled to mask. Apparently restless, she remained forward only briefly, then gave Jason a rueful smile and returned to her family on the stern bench seat.

When they broke out of the inlet, the southeastern tip of Vancouver Island came into view about twenty miles to the northwest. Much to Jason's liking, the water conditions held and their progress remained unhampered. In spite of the fortuitous conditions, a feeling of melancholy came over him, unusual for him. He flashed back to the thoughts of watching the ferry passengers disembark earlier that morning. In his past profession, the uncertainty of life necessitated taking one day at a time, with little consideration for the future. But now, the future *did* seem important. As he gazed down the seemingly endless foredeck of his boat, their destination appeared to move along ahead of them, as if they were making no headway even at sixty-five miles per hour.

After joining the service, his goal in life had been purely patriotic—to keep his country free and safe. Had that goal eluded him? Have I really accomplished anything of a lasting quality, or was my goal so nebulous that it moved along ahead of me? he wondered.

He looked to the stern, checking on his passengers. As he did, he saw the wake curl away from the transom as five tons of deep vee hull knifed along, straight and unwavering, parting the water like a farmer's plow through rich earth. He continued to watch as the wake widened and then disappeared on the horizon behind. A mile behind the boat, the sea had returned to the way it had always been. Will anyone ever know if I've passed this way? he asked himself.

CHAPTER EIGHTEEN

Jason, Carol, and the O'Connors walked the stone path to the front porch of his cottage situated only half a block from the marina. The little two-story saltbox sat in the midst of a beautifully maintained yard filled with rhododendrons, azaleas, and an array of spring plantings. The pageantry of emerging spring color, intensified by the bright sun, provided the illusion of walking through the pages of a fairy tale.

Once inside, Jason and Carol opened the screened windows to let in the offshore breeze. The stale air, held captive for months, rapidly gave way to pungent spring scents mixed with salt brine. The cottage seemed larger inside than its outward appearance. Natural wood beams supported the ceiling and the second story. An open staircase led to three bedrooms and another bathroom on the second level. The floors throughout were made of oiled, straight-grained fir planking, doweled at the ends, generously accented with handmade native Indian rugs. Walls that were not paneled with natural knotty pine were plastered and painted with a creamy off-white background, then hand-painted with light pastelIndian designs. White curtains on the windows brightly contrasted with the warm wood tones, providing an inviting and relaxed atmosphere.

Before leaving for lunch at the yacht club and shopping for clothes and groceries, Jason went to a corner of the living room area where a small, oak, rolltop desk holding stationery and a telephone sat in the light of a window. His first priority would be informing Jack of the latest developments, a call he dreaded. He made the decision to put it off until Debbie and the children were safe. Also, he knew Jack would naturally want to be with his family as soon as he found out about their situation. The difficult part would be convincing him that he and his family would be safer if they remained separated and Jack stayed in Portland as long as possible.

Jason picked up the phone, then frowned. No dial tone. Even though the cottage remained unused a good deal of the time, he never interrupted the phone service. He checked the connection to the phone, then the wall jack; they appeared to be intact and connected properly. The storm, he thought. He walked outdoors to the side yard where the phone line should have been attached to the cottage. A limb from his birch tree had broken and torn the wire loose. The limb and severed wire lay in the yard. He would have to make his call from the boat during his lunch at the yacht club.

* * * * *

Their lunches ordered, Jason and Debbie left Carol and the children at their table while they walked to the boat to use the telephone. When Jack came on the line, Jason chose his words carefully.

"We had a bit of a situation develop up here, Jack. We caught someone watching your house so I moved everyone out. They're fine. I'm on my cell, though, so I'll give you their location, some time tomorrow, when I get to a secure phone." He did not mention the deaths of Lori Phillips and Samuel Wellington in the presence of Debbie.

"I'll be finished down here this afternoon. I can join you this evening," Jack said, his words clipped by impatience and anger.

"Not a good idea," Jason quickly replied, disappointed he'd be finished so soon. "Both you and your family will be safer if you remain separated, at least for the time being. David and Steve will take you to a safe house and I'll meet you there tomorrow afternoon." Jason could read Jack's displeasure writhing in the silence.

"How's Debbie?" Jack asked quietly.

"She's fine and she's here waiting to talk to you." Jason turned to Debbie and handed her the phone. "Don't give out our location over the phone," he cautioned, and he disappeared above deck, leaving her some privacy.

"Hi honey," Debbie said weakly, keeping her voice neutral.

"How are you holding up, honey?" Jack struggled at hearing her pain and fear, blaming himself for her difficult situation. He battled, too, with the guilt of not being with them. "God, I'm so sorry about this. I have no idea what the hell is going on. I wish I had listened to you and taken Monday off. At least I would be there with you."

"Oh, Jack, I'm so scared," Debbie confessed in a flood of tears. "I want you here so bad, but I'm glad you went to Portland. If you hadn't, these people, whoever they are, would have found you. If you'd stayed, they might have . . . ." Debbie sat on the lounge and sobbed and shuddered in silence, fighting for control. "Jason's right. You're safer in his care. Please do as he says. Don't worry, we'll be fine. Besides, Carol's with us; she'll be a big help with the kids."

Jack steeled his courage to comfort her. "Well, you don't need to worry about me. These two that Jason has baby-sitting me seem to know what they're doing. Probably by the time I finish up down here, the police will have the whole thing figured out. It's probably all a mistake anyway."

"Jack, do you have any idea at all why anyone would want to . . . ." She could not finish.

"No, I haven't a clue. Like I said, it's probably all a big mistake. And again, don't be thinking about it. Jay and the police will have it figured out soon."

Debbie also picked up on her husband's frustration and tried a little encouragement of her own. "You're safer in Portland, and you're working. Pathmoor should be happy."

If she only knew, Jack thought.

Jason returned below deck and sat beside Debbie on the lounge, placing a reassuring arm around her shoulder while she finished her conversation. "I need to get back to the kids, hon. Please be careful. You take care of yourself and don't worry about us. We'll be fine."

Jason watched in silence as Debbie communicated a bravado that she had to have dug deeply to find. With her face awash with tears she urged her husband to stay away when she truly wanted to be held and comforted in the safety of his arms.

Jason had little experience with compassion, all traces of it having been trained out of him for twenty years. But metamorphosis does not happen with the turning of a switch. Transition is a slow, gradual, sometimes imperceptible process, often more visible to others than to oneself. These new feelings, triggered by the scene before him, brought gray areas with them, and gray was a place Jason had never been. Things seemed different. Nothing specific he could point to, just different.

"Jason . . ." Debbie handed him the phone. "Jack wants to talk to you."

Jason blinked back to the situation at hand and took the phone. "What do you need, partner?"

"When do we meet tomorrow?"

"How about three in the afternoon?"

"Well, in that case, I won't rush to leave Portland. We can leave first thing in the morning. It will give me a little more time to do a better job of finishing up down here. Oh, Jay—I want you to know I appreciate what you're doing for me. It's just that I'm really worried about Deb and—"

Jason interrupted his friend. "Jack, it's okay. You don't need to apologize for being worried. You're in a hellish situation and I understand. And I'll call you later this afternoon. Is Dave there? I need to talk to him."

Debbie laid her head on Jason's chest and he circled his arm tightly around her, giving her what encouragement he could. He wanted her to hear the instructions he gave to David, so she would be confident he and his team were capable of protecting her husband.

"When you leave Portland tomorrow, take Jack directly to The Kennel, and David, I want you both with him at all times."

Jason pushed the end button and drew Debbie into his arms. "Everything will work out just fine," he assured her. "Jack's been in tougher situations than this in the service, and he came through without a scratch."

"But *I* haven't, Jason. I don't know if I can stand this. I feel like I'm coming apart, or drowning. I can't think of the food we're supposed to buy, the clothing we need, I—I feel like I can't open my mouth without losing control."

"Shush . . . shush," Jason quieted her. "You don't have to think. That's why Carol's here. She can make those decisions. You just relax and enjoy a vacation. And don't worry, we will take care of Jack. You don't have to worry."

* * * * *

Lunch passed quietly. Tommy and Ashley were oblivious to everything but their food and the enjoyment of their surprise vacation. Jennifer, however, seemed somewhat skeptical of the situation. The yacht club's peaceful restaurant provided an unmatched view of the harbor and the San Juan Islands off in the distance. It all worked together to create the illusion of being seated in the midst of a watercolor.

The shopping in Oak Bay Village also went well in spite of Debbie's deplorable situation. Jason noticed the brief moments when she lost herself in her children's excitement at their new acquisitions. This being Jason's first encounter with family shopping, Carol thought he would be bored with the process, but he turned out to be quite the opposite. He was more the culprit than the victim, dragging the procession from one shop to another and carrying armloads of the latest summer fashions to the dressing rooms for the bewildered recipients to try on.

By the time they finished, they had barely enough arms to carry the boxes and bags back to the cottage. Tommy rode proudly on Jason's shoulders, hands clasped to his forehead for stability because Jason had no free hands to support him. He carried a box under each arm and two bags, full to overflowing, in each hand. The rest had their share as well. At times during the excursion, Jason had difficulty reminding himself of the reason for being in Oak Bay.

The electricity of excited children filled the cottage as they all showed off their new clothes. Jason drank it in and savored it as he would vintage wine, the taste unforgettable, then gone, the memory often more remarkable than the experience. This was like all of the Christmases he had never had and it fostered a new happiness. As a child he had been taught to see Christmas as a social crutch, a lie—he now knew the truth. The happiness consumed him, even if only for a few brief moments.

After indulging himself for the better part of an hour, Jason turned his attention to the repair of the severed phone line. He opted for fixing it himself as opposed to calling a repair service, not wanting to draw attention to their presence at the cottage.

With the repairs completed, Jason called Jack to give a detailed account of the past twenty-four hours. "That makes three people now, Jack. I couldn't tell you about Phillips and Wellington in front of Debbie. She doesn't know and I see no reason to burden her with it. There is some serious shit going down, my friend, and they don't take prisoners."

"I can't believe this, Jay. I'm not at all comfortable being separated from Debbie, and now with this . . . I understood your logic, but damn. You sure they'll be safe?"

"Nobody knows where we are, except for Dailey, the partners, and you three down there."

"I'm still worried, Jay. I still have no idea as to what this is all about."

"We're working on it. When you get to The Kennel, Steve will contact the partners. They've been working on the information we've given them. They may have more information by tomorrow. Till then, we wait. I'll see you tomorrow, and try to get some rest. Right now, I have groceries to buy or we'll not be eating tonight."

Carol and Jason returned from their walk to the grocery store to find Jennifer in animated conversation on the telephone. Jason had left specific instructions: "The phone is to be used for emergencies only."

"Deb, what's going on? I thought I made it clear, the—"

"I'm sorry, Jay. I let her call a friend to take care of her tropical fish. I told her not to give out any information about where we are. I'll take care of it." She quickly interrupted Jennifer and asked her to cut her conversation short. After several brief but heated exchanges, Jennifer hung up and stomped upstairs to her room. She wasn't seen again until dinner.

After dinner, Jason made a stockpot of soup for the coming week, while Carol and the children set up the card table in the living room to play Parcheesi. Although Jason had no need for games, he had inherited quite a selection from the previous owners and felt fortunate he'd kept them. While the foursome played, Debbie sat in the bentwood rocker, reading a novel, looking up from time to time to enjoy the levity at the game table. The scene took on the atmosphere of a real vacation, Jason observed, with Debbie beginning to relax for the first time in nearly twenty-four hours.

In the master bedroom on the main floor, Jason turned down the covers, stripped to his briefs and crawled into bed. A gentle breeze blew off the harbor and carried with it the fresh briskness that had drawn him to his cottage at Oak Bay—a mixture of salt from the bay, seasonal flowers and the new green of spring. Jason breathed deeply, letting the fragrances titillate his senses as they replaced the stale air that had been held captive since the last time he had been at the cottage. A key component to a warrior's survival is the development of an acute sense of smell. Being able to smell his enemy before seeing him had saved Jason's life more than once. This was not survival now, but pure enjoyment, discerning the components that seasoned the air in his room: the lilies of the valley, salt brine, the bitter scent of tulips. He analyzed and listened as the ever-moving potpourri rustled the leaves of the poplar tree just outside the windows. Then, sleep.

The intermittent breeze continued to breathe through Jason's room, stealing across his bed like an invisible spirit. Bright moonlight filtered through restless leaves, creating psychedelic patterns that danced upon the walls and furnishings. The air was fresh and his sleep sound, but some time during the early morning, Jason awoke to the subtle sound of someone stealing into his room. Twenty years in his previous occupation made him wary at night. In a stealthy serpent-like motion he turned slowly toward the sound and slid his hand under the pillow, taking a firm grip on his weapon. As his eyes adjusted to the light, a tall figure stopped beside his bed.

"I'm sorry I woke you. I couldn't sleep," Carol said. "May I join you?"

Jason yawned and removed his hand from under the pillow. "Sure. What time is it?"

"A quarter to four."

As Carol entered the bed, he encircled her shoulders with his arm and laid her head on his chest. With the fragrance of her body and hair, blended with the incense of the breeze that still moved in his room, for the moment he felt complete. But only for a moment.

The perplexities of his situation fell upon him: The situation with Jack, his rekindled relationship with Carol. But now something new, a first for Jason—a sense of loneliness. These provided fodder for deep meditation. Silence, save the soft rustling of leaves outside and the rising and falling of their chests as they breathed seemed to envelop the room. Under different circumstances, Jason would have been aroused, lying nearly nude with a beautiful woman, but his musing commanded his full attention. These issues had been festering subliminally for quite some time but had not been forced to consciousness until the failed attempt on Jack's life.

As the warrior, his first priority dictated he devote his full attention to the protection of his friend and family. But his desire for a relationship with Carol seemed to be at cross-purposes with this latest adventure. He could ill afford a distraction, and he knew she did not support his desire to involve himself in the situation. Then there were his musings on the deck the previous morning, wondering who was more lucky. This had all been validated after being with Carol and Jack's family, the lunch, the walk, the shopping. It all provided stimuli that brought a full awareness of the void in his life. He asked himself a question never before considered: "Am I looking for fulfillment or a cure for loneliness?" Everything wasn't black and white as it had been in the past, and his movement toward acceptance of not being in control *was* new and somewhat unsettling, because he knew he could no longer hide behind "screw it, it doesn't matter."

Jason continued to delve into his quandary with the same tenacity in which he approached everything in his life. But in the midst of the deluge of questions, a statement Laura had made came to mind: "Don't get too analytical, just *observe*, take it all in. Eventually the light will come on and the right answer will be obvious." And with that Jason relaxed.

"Are you finished?" Carol asked softly.

There must be something to women's intuition, Jason thought.

"Finished? Finished with what?" Jason asked, unable to disguise the surprise in his voice.

"What were you thinking about? You've obviously been heavily engrossed in something for the past hour."

"How do you know?"

Carol rose from his chest and nuzzled his cheek. Then whispered in his ear. "Because I could smell smoke coming from your ears." She returned her head to his chest. "Would you care to share it with me?"

"I would, if I knew enough of it to share," Jason began. "Things are changing, and I'm not quite sure how to define it or describe it to you. It's almost like my perspective is different. I'm thinking about things that two years ago were unimportant or never mattered to me. I think about my past, about my future, will the rest of my life have any importance. I don't understand why all of a sudden it seems to be important."

"Don't you think that may just be a normal product of age?" she asked. "People's perspectives change all the time. Are you afraid of change, or worried about the future?"

"That's the point. I don't quite know, or have any of it defined. I've simply been thinking about things that I haven't ever thought about before. For example, being with you and Jack's family has made me wonder if I want to spend the rest of my life alone. I'm asking questions like: 'Am I as happy as I think I am?' So far, I haven't come up with any answers. Just a lot of questions."

"That's some pretty heady stuff. But for what it's worth, I have noticed a change in you since our relationship of two years ago. You seem a little calmer. I don't detect as much of your brooding anger. You seem to be a little more willing to confront something that's bothering you. That's really a nice change."

Carol affirmed Jason with a squeeze, then kissed his cheek again. They lay motionless and silently together as the night subtly traded darkness for the light of dawn and the ever-present breeze whispered in the poplar tree's dancing leaves. Both were content to just lie together. Carol once again felt the protection she had felt on Monday morning, something for which she had longed for some time, and Jason basked in the comfort of simply being with someone, and caring.

"Monday morning, you mentioned you would like to have a go at trying our relationship again. Is that still a consideration?" Carol asked softly.

"I haven't changed my mind, but I do have to tell you that after Monday night I've been more than a little concerned about whether *you're* still willing."

"That's understandable. I did a pretty good job of spewing venom at you. This is no excuse, but I was caught a little off-guard. Now that I've had some time to think about it, the two things that upset me were finding out about your past and the thought of you putting yourself at risk again. I've lost a daughter and I've never known what's happened to her. I don't know if I could deal with the same thing happening to you. I appreciate your talking to me about it yesterday. You were on the mark with what you said. I know now that you understand. And I apologize for what I said Monday night. I had no right to say those things."

"Your comments Monday night cut pretty deep. You attacked what I've been for over twenty years, a protector of my country. But I made a commitment to a relationship and I want to give it a chance to work. It's not just a relationship for proving that I can maintain one. It's a relationship with *you* that I want. Your comments also made me think about my past and the validity of it, and I've come to the conclusion that I'm still proud of my career as a soldier. And yes, having a relationship with you is still important to me—so where do we go from here?"

"Forward, one day at a time," Carol whispered softly. Then both slipped into a contented sleep with Carol's fears somewhat alleviated, and Jason's questions, though mostly unanswered, were at least being brought into the light with the coming of the new dawn.

They awoke to the thump-thump-thump of little Tommy's footfalls traversing from one bedroom to another.

"Do we want to get up yet?" Carol asked sleepily as she adjusted herself for a closer nuzzle.

"Not on your life," Jason yawned. "Do you suppose we could just stay here and nobody would miss us?"

The question had no sooner been asked when they heard the thump-thump-thump back into Debbie's room and a rapid firing of questions from the floor above. "Where's Carol, Mommy? I can't find her! Did she go somewhere?" They could not hear his mother's muffled response, but decided to get up and put Tommy's mind at ease.

Jason and Carol had not made love that morning. With an unspoken communication they simply basked in the contentment their honesty and openness had brought to them. Both sensed a hope for the future that had thus far been elusive, but now seemed within their grasp.

CHAPTER NINETEEN

After a shower, Jason called Keller for an update on the substance that had killed Lori Phillips.

"Whatever it is, it wasn't a sufficient amount for me to analyze."

"So, we're right back where we started," Jason said disappointedly. "We got nothing!"

"Not exactly," Keller replied, "I just don't have access to the sensitive equipment necessary for this degree of sleuthing. I've got some help coming from the science center and Center for Disease Control but it'll take a couple of days. We'll get it. It'll just take a little more time."

"Well, time isn't something we have a lot of," Jason said, but he dropped the subject, instead bringing up Debbie's anxiety and Tommy's condition.

"I'll get a prescription to the drug store in the village that will calm Debbie. And for Tommy, have Debbie call me at ten o'clock. By that time, I'll have a chance to locate a specialist on the island. Tommy's pediatrician can make arrangements to fax his files if the need arises."

Jason rang off, then padded to the kitchen, poured himself coffee, and slipped through a set of French doors into the side yard. Moments later, Carol silently appeared at his side. Her blow-dried hair made him think of a lion's mane. She wore one of the new outfits they had purchased the day before: navy blue shorts and a blue-and-white-striped cotton blouse. It had not been a particularly striking outfit on the hanger, but Carol gave it style. Coffee in hand, she circled her free arm around Jason's waist. They stood in silence, finishing their coffee, savoring their companionship.

They needed few words as they thought of the intimate time they had shared earlier that morning. Carol found the new depth emerging in Jason encouraging and comforting. That Jason could change instilled hope for their future relationship. Jason himself felt strangely comfortable after his early morning struggle, although from his perspective, nothing had been resolved. He felt ready to face issues that, in the past, he had stifled, and it created a sense of calm within.

"How soon do you have to leave?" Carol's voice carried an unspoken request to spend more time together.

Jason looked off toward the marina and the islands beyond as they slowly walked to the front of his property. His response came slowly with a vagueness that suggested a portion of his concentration lay elsewhere. "I should be under way by noon. Before I leave, I need to check in with Dailey and the partners. I also want to talk to Jack again."

"That reminds me. I need to call The Box Car and let them know that I'll be taking some time off. Do you have any idea how long I'll be staying here?"

"I have no idea. I wish we had some answers for you, but so far, all we have are questions. We have gathered quite a bit of data from companies that Jack has done work for in the past, but it will take time to get it into a data base, and then they'll have to analyze it. Unless Dailey comes up with something, we may be in the dark for a while. Why don't you tell them you'll check in with them on Monday. By then we should know something."

They fell comfortably silent again as they circled the yard and Jason made mental notes of needed maintenance, mostly cleanup from the storm. Eventually they returned to the kitchen where they found Debbie preparing breakfast with Tommy under foot.

"Hey, bud," Jason said to Tommy, "you want to give me a hand in the yard?"

Debbie glanced toward Jason with a grateful smile.

"Okay!" Tommy yelped, and took Jason in tow to the door.

Jason had cut and stacked the remnant of the culprit tree, while with a rake too big, Tommy did his best to rake the wood chips left by the chainsaw. The little helper struggled and grunted without complaint, stopping occasionally to survey with pride the piles he had made. Just as they finished, Ashley called them to breakfast.

"Where's Jennifer?" Debbie asked.

Tommy looked down at his food, guilt riddling his face. "She went for a walk," he said. "I wanted to go but she told me no. She said not to tell."

To soothe Tommy's feelings, Jason said, "Well, it's a good thing you didn't go, bud; you wouldn't have been here to help with the yard." Tommy nodded and returned his attention to his breakfast.

With breakfast finished, the children asked to be excused to go exploring. Debbie cautioned them to not go far. The three adults were lingering over coffee when Jennifer walked in. "Where have you been?" her mother asked with concern.

"I went for a walk," she returned sharply. "No need to make a big deal about it."

"Jen, will you please be civil? If you're going to go off somewhere, I want to know. That's all I ask."

"Yes mother," she replied sarcastically. "Jeez, I feel like I'm in a concentration camp."

"Jennifer! That's enough! I mean it!"

Jennifer ate her toast and juice, her demeanor making it clear she was in a snit. Soon she got up from her chair and announced that she would be in her room.

"I apologize for Jennifer's behavior," her mother said quietly. "I don't know why she gets in these moods; they seem to come from nowhere."

Jason and Carol exchanged embarrassed glances.

"It could be that she has no idea what's happening," Carol suggested.

"You're probably right," Debbie sighed. The tension of the incident subsided and she eased back into the light conversation. She responded positively to the relaxed, friendly atmosphere.

"You look rested this morning, Deb," Carol commented.

"I have to tell you," Debbie began, "it's nice not to have to hassle everyone off to school. I really appreciate your letting us use this place, Jason. I had no idea it was so beautiful here. I just hope I can stop worrying about Jack enough to enjoy it."

"Well, you can relax. He's in good hands and we won't let anything happen to him. I'll stake my life on it."

"Thank you," Debbie said, giving Jason a hug. "You have been so patient and kind to us. I just can't find the words."

"Your hug is just fine," he assured her, squeezing her in return.

Jason moved to the little rolltop desk to phone Dailey and doodled on a notepad as he talked. He would have gladly taken notes had there been any to take, but the lieutenant had made no progress.

When Jason checked in at The Kennel, Steve confirmed they had arrived safely. Jason thought it would be a good morale builder for Jack to talk with his family. Handing the phone to Debbie, Jason rounded up the children.

* * * * *

Jason and Carol walked hand in hand to the marina. Jason unsnapped the cover from the boat and stowed it along with his gear. He opened the engine hatch and checked the fuel, oil, and battery levels. Instead of spending their last few minutes on board, they agreed to take a walk, as neither one wanted to be in a hurry while making love. The warm sunlight felt good, and their renewed commitment heightened the deep feelings stirring within them. They both felt the rarity of the moment, when the erogenous zones of the spirit are touched in a way that no words can describe.

CHAPTER TWENTY

Four-foot swells opposed Jason as he retraced the path he had traveled just twenty-four hours before, his spirit as unsettled as the surface of the water. With the exhaust unbaffled, engine noise and loneliness were his companions. In the not-too-distant past, he would have reveled in the speed at which his boat now rocketed across the rough water. But not this time. He simply wanted the trip to be over and to get on with finding the people responsible for turning his friends' lives into a living hell. With that accomplished, he vowed to take the time to learn what would bring purpose to the remainder of his life. But now was not the time.

With a quick impulse, he pushed the throttles forward. The huge boat surged forward with the dual speedometers climbing steadily, 85—90—95—100 mph. At 110, the hull cleared the water by some six feet as he peeled off the wake of a container ship en route through Admiralty Inlet. Positive G's forced him violently back into his bolster. With instinctive reflexes and impeccable timing, he backed off the throttles so he would not over-rev the engines when the propellers cleared the water. Then, as the propellers reentered the water, he shoved the throttles forward, hard, to maintain hull speed and keep the boat from plowing upon reentry.

Jason usually ran his boat this hard, when he was venting frustration or anger, but not this time. He found his mind too cluttered; too many issues raced around in his head. This time he used his boat as therapy, a preparation, forcing total and complete concentration. Driving five tons of boat at one-hundred-plus miles per hour and keeping it straight and level compelled him to focus both physically and mentally on one thing only—driving. It would clear his mind of all the distractions he had encountered over the last few days. He now had one singular goal, to maintain an alert mind upon his return to Seattle. Once there, he would be mentally ready to work, to get to the bottom of the situation with Jack.

In a little less than an hour from the time he had cleared the no-wake zone at Oak Bay, Jason idled his boat up to the pier at Hard-Ship Marine. As he looked up, he could see Leon and Tony gazing over the edge of the pier, the crane's boom with the slings still attached, already in motion to pick up the boat. Once on the cradle, the boat would be put through the usual drill: Flush the engines with fresh water for half an hour, clean the hull, check the oil and change the filters, cover the boat. They would not see Jason until the next time he wanted to use his boat.

* * * * *

At the loft, Jason showered, poured himself a scotch, put the Brandenburg Concerto No. 2 on his sound system, and went out on the deck. He would do absolutely nothing for a few minutes, just let the music settle over him and relax before meeting with the partners, who had left him a message asking him to stop at their offices before going to The Kennel.

* * * * *

Joe Castellano ushered Jason to the main conference room that had been transformed into a situation room. The huge rosewood table supported two computers, a fax machine, a copy machine, and two additional telephones. The back of one computer had Sobahr's undivided attention. Ben, at work at the functional station, typed with machine-gun precision while watching the monitor with heightened concentration.

Sobahr looked up as the two men entered. "Ah Jason, we are ready for just about any contingency. What do you think?" he asked, beaming with pride and a sweep of his hands.

"Impressive," Jason said, making no attempt to disguise his pleasure as he surveyed the room. "Looks like you're going all out."

"It's only money, my friend. Only money," Sobahr teased.

"Whatever it takes," Jason said flatly. "Joe, you mentioned something about red flags."

"We came up with two names. I thought they would be worth looking at prior to your meeting with Jack." Jason followed him to the workstation where Ben worked and peered over his shoulder. "Ben, pull up what we've got," Joe directed.

"Things moved a little faster than we anticipated," Ben explained. "I took the hard copy you gave us, and created a data base. We started with the Cervicon files that you gave us for personnel, and entered their entire roster. Then we moved on to Suter Pharmaceuticals and did the same thing. That was a little more difficult. We could get their financials with no problem, but it took us a while to get their personnel records." Ben looked over his shoulder at Jason with a smug smile. "Nobody is safe from us. And the Biddwell information Jack e-mailed was a big help because we didn't have to go snooping for it. Saved us a lot of time. At any rate, we just finished the Biddwell data this morning. I did a search of the personnel data base for any occurrences of the same names, just to test the system, and bingo!"

Ben worked the keyboard for only a moment before two names appeared on the screen, followed by three different company names:

Richard Pathmoor	(Cervicon)
Richard Pathmoor	(Suter Pharmaceuticals)
George Comstock	(Suter Pharmaceuticals)
George Comstock	(Biddwell Die Casting)

"Now isn't that interesting," Jason murmured.

"Isn't it?" Joe agreed. "Correct me here if I'm wrong, but isn't Richard Pathmoor the name you mentioned on Tuesday when you came in?"

"Yeah, it is," Jason said. "And it seems strange that Jack never mentioned Pathmoor worked for Suter."

"He probably doesn't know," Joe hypothesized. "Ben, can you put some dates to these people?"

"Coming up." Ben worked the keyboard as the two men watched intently. Within a few minutes, names began to appear on the monitor. Working backwards, he brought up first Biddwell, then Suter.

	Date Employed	Termination Date
Biddwell Die Casting		
George Comstock	Oct 12, 1991	Dec 4, 1993
Suter Pharmaceuticals		
George Comstock	Dec 18,1993	Nov 12, 1994
Richard Pathmoor	Mar 10, 1989	Oct 2, 1994
Cervicon		
Richard Pathmoor	Oct 30, 1994	

"What's with this Pathmoor character? How does he fit?" Ben asked.

Jason explained to Ben and Joe how Jack's work situation had changed since Pathmoor's employment at Cervicon. "All I know is, and I just found this out Sunday night—when Pathmoor began as operations manager at Cervicon, Jack's life became a living hell. Tuesday when I was in Portland, Jack told me there had been a confrontation regarding Suter. Apparently Pathmoor threatened to fire Jack if he didn't move ahead on the Suter contract. Jack's been designing a security system for the new Suter plant in Issaquah for some time. He's also intimately involved with the wording of the contract, and there's a liability issue that Jack won't compromise on. It was an ugly situation Tuesday morning from what he told me. Just looking at this, I'd say that Pathmoor has an ax to grind. Like maybe a conflict of interest. Jack needs to see this. Ben, can you print this out for me?"

"You have only to ask. Jason, what's your take on Comstock? Do you think there's a connection?"

"Beats the hell out of me. That's a name I'm not familiar with. Jack may have some ideas, but I haven't a clue. I'm still trying to figure out this Pathmoor-Suter-Cervicon connection."

"That's got my attention too," Joe added. "But I'm also curious about Comstock and his connection to Suter, and his relationship with Biddwell. I wonder if they're all related. We'll get a complete work-up on both Comstock and Pathmoor. And I mean everything from the size of their Jockeys to what kind of toothpaste they use. If there's a relationship, I want to know what it is.

"Sobahr," Joe continued, and Sobahr looked up from his work on the computer. "Get your FBI buddy on this. See if he can find anything on these two: military records, prison records, fingerprints, anything and everything they can find. And don't mention what we're involved with. I'm sure Lt. Dailey and the Seattle Police Department wouldn't appreciate their unsolicited help."

"I will do it immediately," Sobahr responded. He took the two printouts from the printer. "I will make copies and fax them right away." Head down, he perused them, speaking in a barely audible mutter as he walked slowly toward the door, "Name, birth date, social security number . . ." until he disappeared from the room.

Jason, anxious to leave and get the information to Jack at The Kennel, moved to follow Sobahr.

"Jason," Ben said. "Before you leave, I think we ought to take a look at what we have at this point." Joe motioned Jason to the cluttered conference table while Ben slid back the panels of a large diptych of the Olympic Mountains, exposing a white board. Using colored markers, he created a storyboard starting from the time Jason had received his phone call from Jack Sunday evening. When completed, Ben seated himself with the others just as Sobahr returned with the information on Pathmoor and Comstock.

The storyboard painted an ugly picture. Whoever these people were, they were well organized and had the ability to react quickly. In a time period of just over three days, three people had been murdered: Jennings, Phillips, and Wellington. Two of the three people had been murdered in a little over twenty-four hours from the time that the newspapers hit the streets Tuesday morning. By mid-morning on Tuesday, the perpetrators, whoever they were, had contacted Cervicon in an attempt to locate Jack and had the surveillance of his home in place. Lori Phillips had been injected with a lethal dose of something that same evening, which meant someone inside the hospital had evaluated the security prior to making a move. That could very well mean Jason had been observed entering the room with Dr. Keller, making Keller or Jason vulnerable as well.

Moving down the board, a mere six and a half hours had passed from the time Samuel Wellington had been picked up until he was overcooked in the green Toyota barbecue just forty-five minutes after Dailey released him.

And so the storyboard read. Four men cycled and recycled the information before them. They sat in silence while pondering the picture. The cycle repeated several times. They certainly were no strangers to puzzles; their backgrounds in articulate intelligence-gathering shined as they worked the board time and again. But they did not have enough pieces to provide a sound scenario. They needed more information and hoped Pathmoor or Comstock would turn the tide.

Jason left the offices and headed south towards Tukwila. While en route he rehashed all of the information, searching for any thread of a common denominator. As his mind worked, he became aware of a tension arising within him, a restlessness, a combination of alertness and anxiety he hadn't felt in a long time. He was salivating for the mission.

CHAPTER TWENTY-ONE

With bloodshot eyes set deep in a weary face, Jack met Jason at the door of the faded and peeling olive-drab house, known to a select few as The Kennel.

"How're Deb and the kids?" Jack asked, in lieu of a greeting.

"They're fine, Jack. How are you holding up?"

Jack caught Jason's perusal of his appearance. "I've looked in the mirror." Jack smiled weakly. "This hasn't been one of my better weeks—but I'm okay."

They moved to the living room where David and Steve watched the pre-game activities of a NHL hockey play-off game on a big screen.

Jack's somber mood did not invite conversation so Jason simply handed Jack the file of information had Ben compiled. "See what you think of this. I stopped by the partners on the way. Looks like they've been busy."

While Jack sat himself at the small dinette table Jason went to the kitchen in search of a beer. He returned just in time for Jack's vehement reaction. "What the hell!" Jack's words drug slowly through clenched teeth, low and guttural as he spoke. "That sonofabitch!"

David and Steve both turned to take in Jack.

"Makes for interesting reading, doesn't it?" Jason said with a calmness he didn't feel. "Wait till you get to the second page." But Jack did not turn to the second page. His eyes stayed riveted to the first page.

"Is someone going to let us in on this bit of information, or do we play twenty questions?" Steve asked, impatiently looking at the file quivering in Jack's hand.

"Richard Pathmoor worked for Suter?" Jack muttered, his jaw tight with furry. Jack's reaction confirmed Jason's suspicion. Jack had been unaware of Pathmoor's former employment.

"Looks like it'll be a busy afternoon," Jason said, as he walked to the TV and switched it off. "Let's get to work."

The four settled around the coffee table while Jack reread the printout on Pathmoor, then with reluctance moved on to the following pages.

"When did you get this information?" Jack asked, turning toward Jason.

"Like I said, I picked it up from the partners on my way from the loft. They'd just put it all together when I got there. The files you sent to Sobahr on Tuesday from Biddwell contained part of the information on Comstock. The rest came from raiding Suter's computer data. The Pathmoor information is a combination of data from the Suter Pharmaceuticals and Cervicon computers."

Jack, without response, turned back to the pages to reread them as if he might find something different the second time through. He rolled the information again in his mind, curious at the possibility of a Pathmoor/Comstock relationship and their previous employers. The more he pondered, the more the bitter anger roiled. Pathmoor had concealed his employment with Suter, and the conflict of interest jumped off the page at him.

Jack looked at his watch and stood. "I'm gona grab a shower and go to Cervicon and confront that SOB," he said with harshness Jason had not seen in his friend before.

Jason, in turn responded with a cool frankness. "Negative! Look, Jack, the worst possible place for you is anywhere near Cervicon. Sorry, buddy, but you're staying here."

Jack faced Jason with an icy, venom-filled stare. "Dammit, Jay! I don't want to hear that crap! What do you expect me to do, sit here on my ass while that bastard harasses my family and screws me out of my job? I don't think so!" Dave and Steve watched with interest to see how Jason would handle the situation.

"This is the way it is, Jack," Jason said, unfazed.

His voice had changed, becoming not louder but more controlled, with a quality that made it clear he would not be challenged. Both David and Steve knew enough to keep their mouths shut. Jack, however, had never seen this side of him.

Jason's eyes narrowed and his facial features turned hard. "I fully understand you'd like to bust Pathmoor's balls, and I appreciate that. But we're not sure that he's the key. The directive here is to find out who's trying to kill you, and to also find out why. To do that, we need your help. We need you alive," he paused for the effect that the word *alive* carried.

Jack's intense stare did not waiver from Jason's. The room turned thick with tension at the threat of physical confrontation. But Jason ignored the dynamic and set his plan in motion. "Finally we have something to work with. I think it's time we get Dailey involved and give him the information on Pathmoor. Let's let the lieutenant question him. How late does Pathmoor stay at the office?" Jason asked of Jack.

"It varies," Jack answered warily. "Could be any time between three to six o'clock. Depends if he plays golf or not. What do you have in mind?"

Jason looked at his watch. "It's four-thirty. He reached for the cordless telephone. "What I'd like to do," he said as he dialed, "is get Dailey on Pathmoor's ass today. And while he's involved with him, we'll be gathering information on Comstock."

When Ben answered, Jason directed him to fax only the information on Pathmoor to Dailey ASAP. "In the meantime, I'll call Dailey and let him know it's on the way."

As Jack watched Jason take control he realized he had little say in his situation. Rather than further fueling his anger, Jason's assertive action had the curious affect of dissolving the tension. He saw the possibility of Dailey making Pathmoor's life miserable and volunteered his help. "I'll phone Marcy and make sure Pathmoor will be there," Jack offered.

"Good. Do it before I call Dailey."

Jack immediately called and learned that Pathmoor, because of Jack's prolonged absence, would be working late. He gave Jason an enthusiastic thumbs-up.

Jason smiled with satisfaction as he dialed. This not only may be a break in the investigation but would also provide an opportunity for him to prove himself an asset to Dailey. "Lieutenant, this is Jason Brisben."

"Yes Mr. Brisben, what can I do for you?

"Lieutenant, we have learned some interesting facts about Mr. Pathmoor, Jack O'Connor's boss. In the next few minutes you should be receiving a file on him." Jason briefed him on when Pathmoor had been hired, the omission of his employment with Suter on the job application, the adversarial relationship with Jack, the continued confrontations concerning Suter Pharmaceuticals, the threats of being fired, and, of course, their last phone encounter prior to lunch last Tuesday. Jason did a masterful job of painting a picture filled with innuendo, probable conflict of interest, and a possible motive for murder.

"Why is it, Mr. Brisben, I get the feeling I'm being set up?" Dailey said sardonically.

"When you see the file, I think you'll agree there are some issues that deserve questioning."

"What about O'Connor? Where is he now?" Dailey asked.

"He's in a safe house. If you need to get in touch with him you can call me. He's close."

"Come on, Brisben, don't play games with me. I need access to him."

"You'll have access to him, Lieutenant, any time you want. Just call me. That's the way it has to be at least for now. I'm being honest with you, and it's not prudent to discuss Jack's location over the phone."

"Have it your way for now, but if I need to, I'll get heavy-handed about this, you can count on it. Montgomery just brought me the faxes you sent. I need some time to go over them before I head over to see your friend Mr. Pathmoor. I'll be in touch." The line clicked dead.

Jason looked at the receiver with a sly grin spreading across his face. "It looks like he's going to put the squeeze on Pathmoor," Jason said as he hung up the telephone. He smiled at Jack. "Vengeance is mine, saith the Lord, but a helping hand never hurts."

Jack enjoyed a moment of vicarious revenge before Jason went on. "Gentleman, let's get to work on Mr. Comstock. Jack, give Biddwell a call and find out what you can," Jason directed.

Jack's expression registered surprise. "What do you suggest I say? That I raided their personnel files and I'd like to know a little bit about one of their former employees?"

"Come on, Jack, use a little imagination," Jason said, impatient with his lack of creativity. "Get on the phone to Peter Hargrave and tell him a George Comstock filled out a job application and listed Biddwell as a former employer. Hell, I don't care, tell him anything. You're in sales, think of something. In the mean time, I'll check with the partners to see if they're getting any help from Washington regarding Comstock."

Jack reluctantly called Biddwell, but asked for Tim Halderman, the shop foreman, rather than Peter Hargrave. Halderman, Jack thought, would be less inclined to be suspicious. "Tim, this is Jack O'Connor with Cervicon. How are preparations for the installation going?"

"They're coming along just fine," Halderman said enthusiastically.

"Well, I wanted to check on the progress. You need anything?"

"Not that I can think of: Like I said everything is going good. I can't believe how fast your people are moving. Dwight Sheffield and the crew showed up this morning, said with any kind of luck they'll have the system fully operational for opening of business on Monday morning. So far, we've been nothing but impressed."

"That's good to hear. Not all our installs go this well, believe me," Jack continued keeping the conversation light.

"I bet they don't," Halderman said good-naturedly.

"By the way, I ran into someone on another job who said he knew a guy who used to work for you. You happen to remember George Comstock?"

"Now there's a name I'd like to forget," Halderman said. "Comstock was one strange dude. He only worked for us a couple of years. Hell, he's been gone for quite a while; and I sure as hell wasn't sorry to see him go."

"Sorry I brought him up," Jack said with a slight laugh, hoping Halderman would volunteer more information.

"Talk about a liability," Halderman offered. "The fat pig was disruptive as hell, always spouting his patriot bullshit and stirring up everyone on the second shift. Spent most of his time preaching instead of working. One of those, oh, what the hell do they call them? Survivalists—or some damn thing, belonged to some of those militia groups, although I heard he got kicked out of a couple for being a radical troublemaker. And there were rumors floating around he dealt drugs, pharmaceuticals I heard, but I never caught him at it."

"Why didn't you fire him?" Jack probed.

"Told Hargrave that I wanted to get rid of the guy, but according to Hargrave, we needed the manpower. I told him, in that case, we ought to replace him with someone who would work instead of preaching his garbage. It didn't set well with our GM, so I let it go. You know how it is, no sense creating problems for myself over the likes of him."

Jack wondered fleetingly why an astute manager like Hargrave would keep someone like Comstock around but focused on keeping the conversation going without being to obvious about looking for information. "So, why'd he leave?"

"Damned if I know. He just didn't show up for work one day and we never saw him again. Just sorta disappeared. Nobody knew where he went and nobody's heard from him since and nobody seemed to care. Funny you should bring him up."

* * * * *

Cervicon's new, two-story building, just off Dexter Avenue, overlooked the west shore of Lake Union. The reception area achieved a pleasant atmosphere with colors of light grays and pale shades of burgundy. An impressive built-in display of their sophisticated systems covered the entry wall with back-lit letters stating, "YOU NEED THE BEST TO BE SECURE."

At twenty minutes past five, Lt. Dailey displayed his badge and identification as he introduced himself to Marcy Dunlap and asked to see Richard Pathmoor. Marcy, a friendly, outgoing woman, talked to Dailey over her shoulder as she led him up the stairs and through the corridors toward

Pathmoor's office. She had an easy beauty about her and wore little makeup. Doesn't need any, Dailey thought. Her dark blond hair framed bright hazel eyes and on their brief walk, Dailey learned Marcy was a single mother, had a five-year-old daughter, had worked at Cervicon for three and a half years, and liked her job—most of the time.

"Mr. Pathmoor, there's someone here to see you," Marcy announced as she entered his office with Dailey at her side. Richard Pathmoor sat in a leather chair with his back to the door. His feet rested on the credenza as he gazed sleepily at the boats gliding on the surface of Lake Union. Startled, he spun around in his chair grabbing at papers on his desk in an awkward attempt to look busy. A slender man in his mid-fifties, with short brown hair and small designer wire frame glasses, he glanced up with the look of a recalcitrant child caught daydreaming instead of doing his homework. After squinting for a brief second at Marcy and the man accompanying her, anger spread across his face like a brush fire in a windstorm.

"Miss Dunlap," Pathmoor began, his eyes ablaze. "In the future, you will inform me— "

"I apologize, Mr. Pathmoor," Dailey cut in firmly. "I'm afraid barging in unannounced was my doing." He turned to Marcy with a knowing grin. "Thank you, Miss Dunlap. You've been most helpful."

"And you are?" Pathmoor snapped as Marcy retreated to safety.

Dailey took an immediate disliking to Pathmoor, needing only a brief observation to determine Pathmoor to be a pompous, demanding autocrat. "The end to a perfect day, in answer to your question. I'm Lieutenant Dailey, Seattle Homicide." He quickly flashed his identification, then returned it to his pocket. Pathmoor, stunned, blinked twice and opened his mouth to speak. His lower jaw bobbed up and down but no words came forth. Ah, good, the desired effect, Dailey thought to himself. "I've come to ask you a few questions."

"Questions! Questions about what?"

"I believe I did say Seattle Homicide, Mr. Pathmoor. More than likely there'll be questions about a homicide," he said as he seated himself, not having received an invitation to do so.

"A homicide? What homicide? Now look, Mr. Dailey— "

Dailey raised his hand to quiet the obnoxious man. Frightened, Pathmoor did his best to hide it by trying to intimidate Dailey. But when it came to intimidation, Dailey reigned supreme. "Ah, ah, ah! It's 'Lieutenant,' Mr. Pathmoor, and you seem to be confused. Remember, I said I came to ask you some questions. Now, I'll give you a minute to collect yourself. Then we can begin this little interview. Just remember, I'll ask the questions and you answer. Otherwise, we may be here for some time, and you already appear to be a bit cranky."

Lt. Dailey, for all of his gruff exterior, always presented himself in a professional manner and usually did not deliberately taunt or play games with a suspect. But the longer he sat in front of the haughty little man, the more he disliked him. Unfortunately for Pathmoor, he reminded Dailey of his freshman English teacher whom he also loathed. Jason's description of Pathmoor and the way he had treated Jack, fed his disdain.

Pathmoor's face turned crimson, and once again his mouth opened and closed without sound. Daily just stared at him and waited until the silence became unbearable for the man before he spoke. "Mr. Pathmoor, you have a Jack O'Connor employed here, is that correct, sir?"

"I'm sure you know that we do," Pathmoor answered belligerently.

"How long has he been employed here at Cervicon?"

"He began working for Mr. Cray when he started Cervicon back in 1974," Pathmoor said matter-of-factly, giving the impression that he himself had a long-standing tenure with Cervicon.

Dailey suspected Pathmoor saw this as a possible opportunity to rid himself of O'Connor, if Jason's account of the O'Connor/Pathmoor relationship were true. He decided to see just how far Pathmoor would take the charade. "And what kind of an employee is he? Conscientious? Reliable?"

"In the past, his work has been okay, I suppose, but lately we've had complaints from some customers. He's become difficult to work with and has put some of our projects in jeopardy."

"How so?" Dailey asked, feigning concerned interest. Pathmoor had taken the bait, and Dailey gave him all the line he wanted before setting the hook.

"Well, he has become demanding to customers, trying to sell them what he wants rather than what they want or can afford. I've tried to talk to him about it, but he's uncompromising with his designs. He's arrogant. I think he's had his way for so long he probably feels it's his way, or no way. And, lately, he takes off on trips, doesn't call in; hell, half the time I don't know where he is," Pathmoor lied. "Tuesday I called him, told him he was needed here because of an urgent situation on a large account—a situation that he created, by the way—I haven't seen him since."

"Sounds like he could be a real liability to your business. How long has this been going on?" Dailey asked with the sympathetic frown of a concerned parent. He knew Pathmoor had assumed Jack was the subject of the investigation, an erroneous notion that served his purpose.

"Oh, I'd say six months or so," Pathmoor said comfortably, feeling he now had Dailey drinking from his load of garbage.

"So—that would be about the time you came to Cervicon, would it not—Mr. Pathmoor?"

The color drained from Pathmoor's face and took on the appearance of a stick of white chalk. And again he went speechless. Dailey, in no hurry to continue, leveled his eyes on Pathmoor for a full minute of excruciating silence until finally the man, in sheer desperation, squeaked out his response.

"What the hell is going on here?"

"What's going on here, Mr. Pathmoor, is we've learned this week that persons unknown to us at this time attempted to kill Mr. O'Connor. And I've listened to your attempt at leading me to believe that you've been a lifelong employee of Cervicon. I've also listened to nothing but innuendo for the past few minutes, slander, I might add, about what a bad employee Jack O'Connor is. Now, with that out of the way, I would like to know, first of all, why you're deliberately trying to misrepresent yourself, and secondly, why Cervicon has no record of your employment at Suter Pharmaceuticals?"

Pathmoor's stony white face contrasted with the fiery daggers of hate emanating from deep behind his eyes. If Dailey knew about Suter, what else did he know? he wondered. Without expecting it, his thoughts came forth audibly. "How did you find—" he hissed.

"M-i-s-t-e-r Pathmoor," Dailey interrupted, sounding much like an exasperated teacher dealing with an incorrigible student. "You must be dumb as a box of rocks. I am an investigator and a detective. That's what I do for a living. When I investigate, I detect things—things that raise flags. Things like incomplete information on job applications, things like the omission of your last employer. When I detect these discrepancies, I have to ask myself why. Why would someone do that? And the answer is for only one reason, because they have something to hide. Now, personally, I don't give a damn about your relationship with O'Connor or Cervicon, or how you got hired or if you get fired. But I do give a damn about the three bodies that seem to be related to this whole freakin' mess, plus there are people still out there doing their best to put O'Connor in the deep six rest home. Murder, is what this is about, Mr. Pathmoor.

"Considering the fact that there is some animosity due to Suter's threats of lawsuits revolving around this security system issue, I'd have to say this office is a good place to start. Wouldn't you agree? And you look suspiciously like Suter's inside man." When Dailey mentioned Suter's threats, Pathmoor closed his eyes in defeat, and dropped his head hiding his face between clenched fists.

With Pathmoor's glaring collapse, Dailey charged forward with a vengeance.

"Since I'm a fairly compassionate person, Mr. Pathmoor, I'll be honest with you. You've graduated from an obnoxious ass to my number one suspect." Pathmoor looked up with a start at Dailey's last comment. He no longer looked cocky and energetic, but tired and old. He had been thoroughly beaten by this man; obviously his adversary had done his homework.

Words needed to be chosen carefully. And Dailey waited—patiently.

"Lieutenant," Pathmoor began meekly, "I apologize for giving you the wrong impression, but I assure you I have no knowledge whatsoever of any attempt on Jack O'Connor's life or any murders. I obviously can't deny that O'Connor and I have our differences, but I certainly wouldn't have anything to do with trying to kill him—or anyone."

"What exactly is involved with this system for Suter and why has it turned into such a nightmare?" Dailey asked.

"Suter had been planning the move before I went to work for them. They planned to keep the Chehalis plant in operation until the new Issaquah facility was up and running. It wasn't until a little over three and a half years ago that Suter found the Issaquah property and started planning. That's when Suter contracted Cervicon to design the security system and oversee construction and installation. Cervicon is also under contract for the maintenance of the system and the staffing of the security personnel for five years after the facility is completed. Jack O'Connor as head designer is naturally the one to head up the project. The architect finished the plans, Cervicon submitted the design of the system and construction began a little over a year and a half ago. Everything was progressing on schedule.

"A year ago, Suter made the decision to get into AIDS research. That's when things broke down. Cervicon would not guarantee security without design changes. O'Connor took it upon himself to go to the insurance underwriters with it and they sided with Cervicon. Suter had to redesign and it set the project back almost a full year. And now, O'Connor is stonewalling on nit-picky issues, claiming the Cervicon insurance underwriters won't give coverage. The insurance company said they would sign off once O'Connor gives his approval.

"Suter is panicked because their lease at the Chehalis plant has expired. It's been extended three times and they're about to be forced out. July first is the drop-dead date. The original plan allowed for a three-month overlap to facilitate the Issaquah facility's operating at 75 percent capacity before closing down the operation in Chehalis."

Dailey listened intently. Other than his obvious bias, Pathmoor was finally telling the truth. The information matched what Jason had previously given him.

"Tell me, why did Suter decide to get into the AIDS research business?" Dailey asked.

"It's a very lucrative business, especially with all of the government subsidies."

Dailey gave a nod that he understood the logic, and continued the questioning. "Explain your job change. I find it hard to believe it's simply coincidence."

"It wasn't, Lieutenant," Pathmoor said bluntly, attempting to restore some semblance of credibility. "It didn't take long for us at Suter to figure out the changes to the new facility would become a major point of contention. Over a period of four months, I courted Martin Cray and convinced him to hire me as chief of operations. Once established, my job was to get the Suter plant back on track. O'Connor turned out to be a formidable stumbling block."

"You appear to be a bit cavalier about this, Mr. Pathmoor," Dailey said, not attempting to hide his disdain.

"Look, Lieutenant, you've obviously done your homework, so there's no sense fencing here. I'm trying to cooperate with you. I'm sure I'll lose my job here at Cervicon, but I'd do that before I'd get involved in some murder plot. I know this interview didn't start off too well, but I assure you I know nothing about three murders or any conspiracy pertaining to Jack O'Connor."

"How did you manage to avoid O'Connor during his research and design?" Dailey asked as a matter of curiosity.

"He never came into contact with my department."

"Which was?" Dailey pressed.

"Market research and forecasting. He didn't know me from Adam," Pathmoor replied, a little too smugly.

At that moment, Dailey understood why good cops occasionally got brought up on charges for brutality. He rose from his seat and leaned across the desk above Pathmoor. "Well, Mr. Pathmoor, this conversation has truly been enlightening. Disgusting, but enlightening." He gave Pathmoor the meanest stare he could muster. "One more thing. Where and when is a good time to get in touch with Martin Cray? Seems he's a bit hard to get hold of these days."

"He's on another one of his vacations," Pathmoor answered without hesitation but with considerable anxiety.

Daily detected his fear and seized the opportunity to twist the blade one more time. "Don't worry, Mr. Pathmoor, I won't rat you out. But I'm sure before this episode is over and the dust all settles, most everybody in the Seattle area will be aware of your little charade. However, in view of the fact that someone is trying to kill one of Mr. Cray's key employees, it probably would be a good idea if we talked to the man. Don't you think?"

The angry lieutenant took a business card, threw it down on the desk in front of Pathmoor, and turned to leave. "I'm sure you'll have Mr. Cray call me as soon as you see him. Won't you, Mr. Pathmoor?"

CHAPTER TWENTY-TWO

"They're gone!" she screamed. The heart-stopping shrill, a quivering combination of hysteria, fear, and grief made the voice nearly unrecognizable.

"Debbie?" Jason propped himself on his elbow and held the receiver to his ear. "Who's gone?" The telephone had awakened him from a sound sleep and he tried to focus his eyes on the bedroom clock he thought displayed 9:10 but couldn't be sure.

"Jennifer and Carol, they're gone!" Debbie screamed, hysterically.

Jason shuddered at the report, sleep's stupor instantly gone. "Debbie, try to get hold of yourself. Take a deep breath and talk to me. What's happened? What do you mean they're gone?"

Jason could feel his own panic rising. If true, their location had been compromised, but how? In the background, he could hear Ashley and Tommy crying and asking, "Mommy, what's wrong?" He knew they were crying from fear, mirroring their mother's hysteria.

Jason climbed out of bed, carrying the phone with him as he leaned against the bedroom sliding door, his weight supported by his head pressed hard against the glass barrier. They had worked until the early hours at The Kennel gathering information on George Comstock. He had not set his alarm, wanting to recover much-needed sleep, assuming for the first time during the long week that he had everything under control. Now, still sleep deprived, he needed to think clearly. He could not let Debbie's panic affect his ability to process logically, but to accomplish that, he needed clear, concise information. On the other end of the line he only heard Debbie's sobbing and her children's fearful questions.

"Talk to me, Debbie. Take a deep breath and talk to me," he repeated.

"I am talking, dammit!" she countered. "Jennifer and Carol are missing! Are you deaf? They're not here!" Debbie screamed again, then lapsed back into uncontrollable sobbing. Jason understood it would be impossible to communicate with her until he could somehow calm her. The more agitated she became, the more frightened the children would become.

This is what I've got, deal with it, he told himself. The unlikely thought came to him that Jennifer and Carol were just out for a walk, but he doubted it. Under the circumstances, Carol would have the consideration to leave a message or tell someone, so as not to cause this kind of grief. Secondly, if Jennifer and Carol had been kidnapped, their exact location might not have been compromised after all. As he thought about the situation, he realized that if these people knew the location of the cottage, they would be calling to notify him they had taken the whole family hostage. He needed help, and had no time to get it.

"Debbie, I understand Jennifer and Carol are missing. Please tell me exactly what happened." Jason kept his voice level and calm, an attempt to talk her down emotionally. No matter what he said, he knew he would be open for attack. After all, he had promised her they would be out of danger at the cottage.

"I don't know what happened!" Debbie retorted angrily, her voice filled with exasperation at his apparent stupidity.

"Debbie, just tell me what you've done since you got up this morning." Jason nearly exasperated as well, still attempted to defuse her anxiety by talking softly. "Tell me exactly what you've done since—" He was cut off in mid-sentence.

"Come here, Tommy. Mommy didn't mean to yell at you. It's not your fault." Jason heard the phone shuffle as Tommy apparently crawled into his mother's lap. "It's okay, honey. I'm really unhappy with Jennifer for leaving without asking.

And she shouldn't have made you promise not to tell. Now I need to talk to Uncle Jason for a minute. Why don't you and Ashley go make some hot chocolate." Again, Jason heard movement as the little boy followed her instructions.

"I'm sorry, Jason; I'm so scared—I've really messed up with the kids. I've just made things worse by yelling at them."

"It's understandable, given the situation," Jason said, trying to maintain a soothing level tone. "You're doing fine, Debbie, just talk to me."

"I came downstairs about a half-hour ago and began to make coffee. Ten minutes ago, I noticed Carol's bedroom door was open, so I asked where she was. Tommy told me she went for a walk. He looked guilty and he appeared to be looking to Ashley for support. That's when Ashley told me Carol went looking for Jennifer."

Debbie paused to maintain her composure. "That's when I found out that Jennifer had taken off. Tommy wanted to go with her, but she told him no, and not to tell. She told him she would only be gone for a half an hour. Tommy said she's been gone for a long time, Jason!" Renewed panic returned at her statement.

"I understand," Jason responded calmly. "You're doing just fine. Now, this is important, and just take your time, you're doing fine. How long has Carol been gone? Do you have any idea when she left?"

An excruciatingly long pause followed, and Jason fought for patience while mentally processing. A round trip to the village would only take forty-five minutes. Where else would a thirteen-year-old girl go at that hour of the morning?

"I really don't know for sure. They were both gone when I got up."

"Would Tommy or Ashley be able to help? This is really important, Deb," Jason encouraged. He found it increasingly difficult to mask his frustration with the time, distance, and lack of an immediate response. He realized they would need more protection. He had only limited resources and he needed to remain in Seattle until he knew for sure what was going on.

In the background, he heard Tommy being questioned. "The big hand was on the six and the little hand was on the seven," Jason heard him say. His heart skipped a beat as he realized that Carol also had been gone for nearly two hours. Even if she had been looking for Jennifer all that time, she would have reported to Debbie. Common sense dictated that Jennifer and Carol had been abducted. Jason went over all the ramifications of his dilemma. In the name of secrecy, the O'Connors were on the island illegally. He could not call the local authorities. Contacting them now would create notice-able commotion. He needed to do something fast, but what?

Debbie interrupted his thoughts with the information he had heard Tommy already give. "Okay, Debbie, I agree. Something's not right. Give me fifteen minutes and I'll get back to you. I'll get some help to you. Sit tight and wait for my call. Can you trust me this one more time?"

"That's what you said before, dammit! How long is this going to continue, Jason? You told me we would be safe here. How in hell am I supposed protect myself now? Answer that!"

Jason knew before the conversation came to a close he would be confronted with those questions, and he had no answers. He could have told her that her damn daughter had jeopardized her family, but to what purpose? They had shielded the children from the fact that someone had tried to kill their father. Although some events in his life were somewhat less than ethical by virtue of the way he had handled them, this situation, he knew, required the truth. As painful as it might be, he would not lie to a friend. "I have no answer for you, Debbie. You just have to know that I'm doing everything I can. I'll have some protection to you within the hour. Can you sit tight for fifteen minutes until I can get back to you?"

"I don't have a choice, do I?" came her stinging reply. "I'm sorry, Jason, but I'm scared to death. Please hurry."

Jason leaned back against the bed as he replaced the receiver in its cradle. He stared blankly through his windows while he tried to think, his mind bombarded with all that made the situation nearly impossible. There were too few options. He needed protection at the cottage. But who and how? He needed more manpower. If, in fact, Jennifer and Carol had been abducted, who were the abductors, how did they find them so quickly, and how would they contact Jack? There was no one at the O'Connor house. Would they leave a message on the O'Connors' answering machine? Would they leave a message at Cervicon? Come on think, dammit!

He hurriedly put on his kimono on his way to the office. Keller, he thought. He's my only hope of getting someone to the island. He dialed Keller's pager number and waited. Thomas Keller, an excellent helicopter pilot, regularly flew training exercises with the Life Flight crews. He also had access to several copters at Boeing Field. While Jason waited for Keller to return his page, he took his cell phone from the charger and called The Kennel to inform David to be prepared for a trip to the island. While he waited for the telephone at The Kennel to be answered, he thought of how best to deal with the manpower issue.

"Evergreen Kennels."

"David, get ready to travel; be ready in fifteen minutes. I also want you to get in touch with Joe and have him get Krieger and Macias up here ASAP."

"What's up?" David asked.

"I just got off the phone with Jack's wife. I think Jack's daughter got picked up this morning."

"Shit—O'Connor's gonna be one mad dog."

Jason's office phone rang. "You're not to tell him. I will. I've gotta go. I'm making arrangements to haul you up to the island. Be ready."

Jason disconnected and picked up his office phone. "Brisben."

"I know who it is," Keller said. "It'd be nice if my sleep could be uninterrupted for once." The joking sarcasm did not disguise the sleepy quality of his voice, indicating he had, in fact, just awakened. "What do you need?"

"I've got a situation, Tom. I need David at the cottage in Oak Bay now." Jason then explained the situation with Jennifer and Carol.

"Who in the hell are these people, and how did they find them so fast?" Keller asked no one. "I'm not on until one. That should give me plenty of time to get up there and back. It'll take me about twenty minutes to get to Boeing Field. Have David meet me there. If I can pick up a fast bird I'll have him to the cottage in an hour from now." Keller had used the cottage several times in the past and could accurately predict their arrival time. "Jason, you sure you don't want me to ferry the O'Connors out of there? It might be safer."

"I've thought about that. If they knew about the cottage, my guess is they would have them all and be calling from someplace where they would feel secure. Also, they won't take the chance that someone in the family might panic and call the locals. I don't think they would risk hanging around. My guess is they're long gone."

"Okay, I'm on my way."

Jason immediately called The Kennel and told David to head to Boeing Field. He himself would leave for The Kennel to meet with Jack within half an hour.

Only a half ring preceded Debbie's pick-up; in that brief moment, Jason predicted accurately what her reaction would be. With anguish, she pleaded for him to send Jack to her in the company of a bodyguard.

"I can't do that Deb. The fact that you haven't heard from Jen and Carol all but confirms their abduction. Jack will be needed in Seattle to respond to the kidnappers. It's the only logical place for them to contact him."

"Jason! My heart is breaking. I need Jack here. With—"

"Debbie," he said sharply. "Pull yourself together. I have to get to Jack. I'll call you when I do. David will be with you soon and I can't help you or Jack by being here on the phone. Jack and I will call you as quickly as possible. Now I have to go." And he abruptly disconnected.

Jason felt a pang for Debbie, a strange new phenomenon that created confused priorities. But he had work to do and he squelched the fledgling spark of compassion. When the call came from the kidnappers, and it would come soon, their demands would not be for money as ransom; it would be for Jack. One simply had to remember the scene in the parking lot to know that once they got their hands on him, he would not survive. Jason would need a solid plan in place and that could not be accomplished while trying to calm and reassure a woman on the verge of hysteria.

* * * * *

The abrasive crunch of gravel ceased under the weight of the tires he pulled to a stop at The Kennel. Jason rested his head against the steering wheel, gathering his thoughts as to how he would tell his friend of the new developments. He remembered little of the thirty minutes that had elapsed since he abruptly hung up on Debbie. He berated himself for his lack of tact in dealing with her; he hoped he had not created an irreparable rift.

The gravity of the situation settled in on him, a suffocating weight as he sat motionless in the car. Jack's family had been compromised; Jason's broken promises of safety for Debbie and the children bombarded him; and Carol now faced real danger. His mind ripped like a tattered flag in a gale force wind by more unanswerable questions: Who had them? Where were they? Would they harm them?

So is the way of hostage taking—the psychological effects of cruelty, of uncertainty—and being helpless to counter it. And still to come—the painful waiting game.

He raised his head from his hands and reluctantly looked to the back entrance of The Kennel. The most difficult task would be facing Jack. Although Jason had had the best night's sleep since the trauma-filled week had begun, he felt exhausted, frustrated, and defeated. When he lifted his hands, perspiration droplets were left behind on the steering wheel.

When Jack opened the door and saw Jason's face, he knew something had gone terribly wrong.

"Oh God, Jay, what now?

"Jack—Jennifer and Carol are missing."

Jason only heard Debbie saying that she felt her heart breaking and remembered his cavalier thoughts, but now, as he confronted Jack, he saw him mirroring not only his wife's pain and grief, but his own. Jack's eyes went vacant and instantly welled as his face turned a pasty gray. No words came, only a low, incomprehensible guttural sound from deep within his chest. Jason fully expected a violent explosion of anger. It never came—he had no energy for it, only the paralyzing pain. Jack's ashen face and eyes were the physical evidence of a breaking heart, his love for his wife and daughter. Even though a hundred miles separated them, he equally shared her pain and anguish with the fear of loss of still another family member. All there for Jason to see in a brief few moments—and he steeled himself against its impact so as not to feel any of it. Jack leaned against the kitchen table for support. Both men stood silent, Jason not knowing what to say and Jack not able. Finally, Jack moved slowly to the sink and splashed cold water on his face and on the back of his neck, then faced Jason and uttered only two words, "How long?"

"I received Debbie's call just shortly after nine o'clock. Apparently Jennifer left the cottage some time before seven and Carol went to look for her, as near as we could determine, around seven-thirty. I called just before I left the loft. There still has been no word." Jason glanced at his watch. "David should be arriving there about now."

"I need to call her," Jack said, and moved off to the living room to make the call.

Jason, alone in the kitchen, looked up when Steve appeared at the doorway. "It's not looking good, is it?"

"No it's not," Jason answered.

"When you called earlier, I went down to the 7-Eleven and checked Jack's answering machine. Nothing. I didn't call from here in case they'd tapped O'Connor's phone. What's the plan—you have any ideas?"

Jason seated himself in one of the kitchen chairs. "It only took them a day and a half to find them. I don't think we'll be waiting long for them to make contact. One thing's for sure, they definitely know that we know it's all about getting to Jack. Another sure thing, they won't let him walk if they get their hands on him."

Steve took a seat at the table across from Jason and waited for him to formulate a strategy. From past experience, he knew Jason would process and reprocess the facts until he could come up with some sort of plan.

"We have to neutralize their leverage by getting Jennifer and Carol back quickly. And that, Steve, is the rub, isn't it? They've spread our resources too thin—we need more manpower. Any word from the partners on Krieger and Macias?"

"Not yet," Steve said, shaking his head slowly.

"Okay, get back down to the 7-Eleven and check Jack's machine for messages. Unless they know more than we think, that'll be their only way of contacting Jack." Jason paused as to if to rethink his statement. "It'll either be there or Cervicon and the receptionist has been telling people that Jack's unavailable for the next few days. At any rate, we should hear something soon. In the meantime, I'll see what I can do about getting us some help, then figure out what we'll do when they make contact."

Steve rose from his chair and turned to leave. He was almost to the door when Jason spoke again, "Steve . . ." He turned and looked at Jason. "They'll only get to Jack over my dead body—and I *will* find Jennifer and Carol."

Steve looked into eyes that burned with zeal set in a face of stone. He tried to think of words of encouragement that would not sound trite in response to Jason's statement. None came to mind, so he simply said, "I'll call when I hear something," and disappeared through the door.

CHAPTER TWENTY-THREE

The elevator door closed with a slight hiss and began its ascent to the Columbia Center Tower lobby from the parking garage. Painful silence rode with Jason and Jack, the tension palpable. Not an hour before, Jack had finished his conversation with Debbie and at its conclusion the anger Jason had expected earlier finally bloomed to nearly a full rage, not necessarily all directed at Jason but at the situation. However, Jason had been handy to receive its thrashing brunt. The helplessness of his predicament, the torment of his wife, and the perceived inadequate way with which Jason had handled the affair frustrated Jack all the more. And Jason, not having the answers, only fueled the passionate fire within Jack.

Jason had decided to move Jack to the partners' offices, then to go to Jack's house to program the call-forwarding feature to advance any incoming calls to Joe Castellano's unlisted number at the office. The six men would wait there for the call. Jason knew the psychology of the wait: the cruel pain it would inflict. But the wait would be tempered by the kidnappers' impatience to get at Jack. Jason anticipated it would not be long although every minute would be eternally painful for Jack.

A morose silence engulfed Jack and a chilling aura like a dry ice fog preceded him as he and Jason stepped from the elevator and made their way down the hall. Jason led the way to the newly created situation room where Joe, Ben, and Sobahr awaited their introduction to Jack O'Connor.

Jack's anger-fueled hot/ice demeanor dissipated only marginally during the brief introductions. He occupied himself with the opulence of the conference room and taking inventory of the two computers, several telephones, and the volumes of freshly printed material that nearly covered the large conference table. Eventually, he focused on the large white storyboard at the end of the room: In meticulous detail, dates and times recorded everything that had happened since Sunday evening when Jack and Jason had met at The Box Car. Jack scanned the chronology, his eyes stopping at the last entry: Friday May 19th—9:10 a.m.—call from Debbie—Jennifer and Carol missing—

In an attempt to offer consolation, Sobahr stepped forward again: "We are so sorry, Mr. O'Connor, for your misfortune. This is, I know, very worrisome, but I assure you that we are doing everything possible to rectify this situation, and I speak for all of us when I say that all of our resources are at your disposal. We will work diligently together and overcome this atrocity, you will see."

Jack's eyes once again on the move, took in information from the storyboard of which he had not been aware. It all lay before him, the conversations with Lt. Dailey; the FBI and CIA operatives that had been contacted in conjunction with Richard Pathmoor and George Comstock, and the contacts for more manpower. After an uncomfortable pause, he turned slightly to acknowledge Sobahr. "Yes, I see that you are." And to Jason he said, "I owe you an apology. I had no right to say the things to you that I said."

"It's understandable given our circumstances. And believe me, I want to find them as much as you do," Jason returned.

Jack simply shook his head, as he continued to peruse the storyboard. "I had no idea how much work you and your friends have been doing. This is—" A ring from one of the four telephones interrupted him.

Joe quickly answered. "Joe Castellano." He first looked at Jason then to Jack as he listened. "Thank you. I assume that you'll be headed this way . . . Good." Joe returned the receiver. "That was Steve, he said to Jack. "They left a message on your answering machine."

Without hesitation, Jack lunged to the conference table and snatched up the telephone nearest him and punched in his number with painful intensity. As he put the receiver to his ear, Joe moved to a recorder sitting near by and pushed the record button. Color drained from Jack's face as he listened to the message. His eyes became vacant as if looking into a great void . . . his shoulders sagged when he returned the receiver to its cradle. He said nothing, reaching for the back of a chair to steady his quaking legs.

Joe quickly rewound the tape and played it back for all to hear.

The message came soft and rather high-pitched for a man's voice, effeminate in a way, with a relaxed delivery. Too relaxed—it flowed from the speaker like soft water over mossy rocks. But the message left nothing to the imagination; its sinister intent conveyed.

"Mr. O'Connor, we have two packages I'm sure you'd be interested in retrieving. I'm positive one of them belongs to you . . . I sincerely hope you're available the next time I call, because you must be aware that these packages are perishable goods. I will expect your voice to be at the other end of the line at six o'clock this evening. And, Mr. O'Connor, a word of warning—don't be talking around. Remember the crucial words are "perishable goods."

* * * * *

Jason returned from the O'Connor home having been gone little more than an hour. He had parked three blocks away and entered the house from the rear, having approached the property from the east crawling up a steep, nearly impenetrable brush-covered bank to avoid being spotted by unfriendly surveillance. He not only forwarded incoming calls from the O'Connor home to Joe's private line at the office, but carefully surveyed the neighborhood in hopes of picking up someone watching the house. This time if he caught someone, he would conduct his own no-holds-barred interrogation—no police, no attorneys. Unfortunately, he spotted no one and returned to the office empty-handed.

In his absence, Joe, Ben, Sobahr, Jack, and Steve had listened and relistened to the tape of the telephone message. It gave no clues, no hint of a location from background noise, nothing as to environment or anything of use. "It's stark and clean, as if spoken from a soundproof studio," Ben said. "You listen, see what you think. Maybe you can come up with something."

Jason took a seat at the table and watched Jack as they listened yet another time. The words once again tortured him. His face mirrored the despair he felt. As Ben had said he found nothing usable, so why force Jack to listen to it again?

"Turn it off," Jason snapped as he turned in his chair and faced the window with his back to his colleagues. He looked down on the city, then out over the bay and across to the Olympic Mountains, still covered with a heavy snow pack. With his mind momentarily adrift, it seemed as though from the forty-third floor of the Columbia Center Tower, he could actually look down on Mt. Olympus. Normally, this panorama would nurture his spirit, but not this time. A wave of deep sadness gripped him.

He thought about Jennifer and the terror she must be feeling and Jack and Debbie's anguish cutting to the depths of their beings. He thought of Carol and the danger she faced. Just as his last wife had been innocent of any part of his past life, so also was Carol in danger because of her involvement with him. He hoped against hope it would not end the same.

For the first time in his life he hated who he was. Pangs of anger began probing for chinks in his armor, but he quickly fought to stifle them. He knew anger clouded the ability to think clearly and react accurately. However, the sadness remained and continued to weigh heavily, as his eyes drifted back to the city. He watched the ant-sized people and traffic scurry at their hectic pace, totally oblivious to the danger in which his loved ones had been placed. And yet someone in the sea of humanity had orchestrated the plight of his friends. But who—and why?

Enough self-pity and pondering, he thought, and pinched these new emotions into submission. He would take the offensive. The who would be known to them soon and the why would follow shortly after. "We need to take away their leverage," Jason said, abruptly turning back to the table. He looked at his watch. "It's one-thirty now. We have four and a half hours to plan our attack."

Jack looked up with a start. "What attack? How can we att—"

Jason held up his hand to silence him. "Our first priority is to locate Jennifer and Carol and get them back, quickly. Jack, when the call comes, I want you to roll over. Sound and act defeated, agree to anything, promise anything. Except don't agree to meet until after nine o'clock."

"Why after nine o'clock?"

"Because you're not going to meet them, I am," Jason said calmly.

Jack nearly flew from his chair. "Now you wait just a minute! I'm not going to allow you to jeopardize Jennifer's life by playing cowboy. End of discussion."

At that moment, Joe Castellano intervened. "Jack, she is already in jeopardy. Jennifer and Carol are in grave danger. Do you think for one minute that if they get their hands on you, they'll turn Jennifer and Carol loose? Look at their track record. Anyone who's been able to identify them has been murdered, including their own. You'll not live, nor will your daughter or Carol. Jason is right in not letting you meet with them." Joe knew Jack would take this advice better from him than from Jason.

"What am I supposed to do, just sit here and wait while all this is going on?" Jack retorted, still highly agitated. "What's to prevent them from killing you when they realize they've been tricked? Then where will Jennifer be? Jason, I'm scared shitless. I haven't a single clue as to what's going on. My daughter's been kidnapped and my wife will probably never be the same. What is it you want to hear? Here's a whole room full of men and equipment, all spinning their wheels doing all kinds of stuff and my daughter's still missing! What good is it? What do we know now that we didn't know Monday night? I'm sorry, Jay, I'm not into this cloak and dagger shit."

Jason understood his friend's anger and frustration, but he couldn't buy into his willingness to give the opponent the upper hand without a fight. "Jack, when we get Jennifer back, she will need both you and her mother for support. Think in terms of *when* we get her back."

"You sound awful damn confident. So far, if you'll excuse my frankness, things haven't gone quite according to your plans."

Jason ignored the gibe in favor of continuing on. Steve, however, leaped from his chair landing face to face with Jack. "Look, mister, if you're concerned about Jason's ability to take care of himself, you needn't be. People better than these have tried to take him out and failed. If he says he'll get your daughter back, he will. And after all he's been doing for you, you better shut the fuck up and listen."

"All right, Steve, that's enough," Jason said calmly. "Let's get on with the plan. I know that we can't prepare fully until we actually hear from them, but, if at all possible, I want you to follow me. I want absolutely no intervention and by all means don't let them spot you. When they realize they've made a mistake, I want you on the outside and not mixing it up with me on the inside, wherever that might be. Understood?"

Steve nodded and seated himself. Jason continued. "I'll use your van, Jack, assuming we can talk them into meeting after dark. If not . . ." his voice trailed off as he apparently thought through the ramifications of meeting in daylight. Then with unexpected suddenness, he turned to Joe and said, "Let's get some food in here. There's no sense spending more time planning until we actually hear from them."

While Joe ordered Chinese food, another of the telephones rang momentarily, captivating everyone's attention. Joe's private line remained silent, but Ben answered one of the two remaining communication lines.

"Ben DiAngelis." He looked at Sobahr. "It's for you."

Sobahr reached along the table and took the phone. "This is Sobahr. Yes, yes, that is very good and thank you so very much." Sobahr handed the receiver back to Ben. "The information on our Mr. George Comstock will be coming through on the fax within minutes."

Page after page rolled off the fax machine and Ben scanned each as they appeared. They seemed to pile up to the thickness of *The Winds Of War*. Ben took the pile and made copies for the others. A cryptologyst and a speed-reader of the first order, Ben had finished reading the entire report while Jason and the others struggled to reach half-way.

"It doesn't get good until page nine," he said, as he went back through the pages once again. "Says here, third paragraph down on page nine . . . he joined the army in 1983, tried qualifying for the rangers and didn't make it. Too big, too fat, and too slow. Ended up in supply. He worked supply several years at Fort Hood, Texas. Then over on page ten, says he got interested in chemical warfare; they transferred him to Fort Lewis, Washington. Take a look at the last paragraph on page ten. Went to Desert Storm as an anti-chemical warfare specialist. Came home in July, '91, shipped back to Fort Lewis, Washington.

"Hello," Ben continued. "Top of page eleven, August 7, '91, received a dishonorable discharge, caught dealing drugs. Sounds like our Mr. Halderman at Biddwell Die Casting had a legitimate beef," he interjected as he looked up to watch the other men scramble though the pages to keep up.

"Will you slow it down," Jason pleaded. "We mortals can't read by osmosis. We have to see the words and then our brains need just a little time to do this electrical impulse thing so the words register, okay? And by the way, where'd you get that too big, too slow stuff on page nine? Are you reading something different than I am?"

"No, just my interpretation of some of the information I gleaned back on page eight, paragraph six. He spent four years on the Pocatello High School football team as the towel boy. Then, look forward to page nine, second paragraph. It gives his physical description: hair, eyes," he said, purposely skipping that portion of the description. "Now look: height, six-feet two and a half inches, weight two hundred, count 'em, and seventy-six pounds. If he wasn't a lazy fat slob, would've been a killer lineman instead of a towel boy. How would you interpret it?" Ben asked, giving an apologetic palms-up shrug.

"Makes sense to me," Steve said. "Wish we had a picture of this overgrown lummox. Look at the last page. There's a note to Sobahr: 'Comstock's military ID photograph and latest Idaho driver's license photo will arrive by courier tomorrow.'"

"Jack, take a look at Comstock's description on page nine." Jason suggested. "Look like anyone you remember from your visits to Suter?"

Jack took his time reading the description. He tipped his head back and closed his tired eyes. After a few seconds his head shook slowly. "No, doesn't look like anyone I ran across. But I only dealt with a few people, and I mostly observed the manufacturing process. Didn't pay too much attention to the personnel. Of course, if I had seen anybody of his size, I think I'd have remembered him."

"Well, think about it. Your life might depend on it," Steve interjected.

Jack nodded his head at the sobering comment. "Point taken," Jack returned. "Like I said, nobody comes to mind."

"We're assuming a lot here," Joe Castellano said. "There's nothing here to prove that Comstock is involved."

A valid observation, Jason thought. But ever since Ben had pulled up and matched the names Pathmoor and Comstock, he'd had the feeling a crucial link had been made.

Ben continued as if there had been no interruption. "He spent most of September of '91 in the Pocatello area, then moved to Tigard, Oregon, in early October, just prior to working at Biddwell. In September, he made one trip to Hayden Lake, Idaho. That's significant as I'll explain in a bit.

"According to our data, he worked at Biddwell for a little over two years, and this profile confirms it. Now, it's interesting that during the time Comstock worked at Biddwell, he made six trips a year to the Pocatello area, and during that same two-year period, he made four trips to Hayden Lake. I wonder what the attraction is?"

"You might be reading too much into that, Ben," Jason said, "He could have been visiting friends."

"True. It's just an observation, not a judgment. I just point out trends—it looks like a pattern. That's why I mentioned it, but we can analyze it later."

"Drugs, maybe?" Joe questioned.

"Or skinheads," Steve suggested, "or both. Isn't Hayden a Mecca for the Aryan Nation? Didn't that fellow at Biddwell, Halderman, say Comstock was preaching radical propaganda and dealing?" The question hung in silence as the men pondered it.

Joe spoke out interrupting the short pause. "I can see Comstock dealing in the Portland area, but Pocatello and Hayden Lake? I have to concede to Ben. What's the attraction?"

"The pattern didn't change when he moved to Suter," Ben began again. During the eleven months that he worked for Suter, he made another six trips to Pocatello, and two trips to Hayden Lake. The dates correspond with the previous years' same pattern. And then nothing. After leaving Suter, he turned into a ghost. He went to ground."

"Somebody's going to have to help me here," Jack said. "How in the hell can anyone get this kind of information in less than twenty-four hours?"

"Easy," Joe answered. "It's not too much different from the way they run a credit check on you when you apply for credit. The first thing they ask you for is your social security number. Now this profile doesn't say how they extrapolated the information, but it usually comes from credit card transactions, social security deposits, tax returns, medical insurance and medical records, car insurance, phone company records, you name it. We'll be getting more complete information."

"But how did they find out about him renting a house in Tigard, Oregon?"

"Simple—bank records," Ben said. "Tomorrow when the photos arrive, if Sobahr's source is thorough, and they generally are, the photos will be accompanied with approximately a hundred pages of information on our Mr. Comstock. What we have here is just a synopsis. The complete version will contain printouts of credit card transactions, bank deposits, medical insurance claims, telephone records, anything and everything with his name or social security number attached to it."

The men in the room watched Jack as he shook his head in disbelief. The realization of the vulnerability of people to electronic information-gathering appeared to stagger him. "Nobody is safe, are they?" he asked quietly, still taking it all in.

"And, Mr. O'Connor, this is, as it is sometimes said, only the tip of the iceberg. This information comes to us in twenty-four hours only. Think what could be accomplished with more time," Sobahr continued, his eyes sparkling with excitement and pride. "Tomorrow, the complete report will come. Then we can use it as a basis for further investigation and build on any segment, or all of it, to gather even more information. When enough information is received and we have a complete and detailed background, we can accurately predict what our Mr. Comstock will do in a given situation. When we save companies from corporate raiding, we do these things. And do not forget, my friend, these people who are looking for you, they may have done these same things to you."

Jack paled at Sobahr's statement. With his head down, he fidgeted with a little metal part he had picked up at the die cast shop, moving it between his fingers like a worry stone. He turned and met Jason's gaze and simply asked, "This is all about drugs, isn't it?"

"It's only one possibility, Jack," Jason offered. "We have no solid evidence to connect any of this to you."

"Yes, but Tim Halderman said they were sure Comstock was dealing drugs."

"That still doesn't connect him to you," Steve said.

"What about the survivalist groups that Halderman mentioned? Maybe there's some connection there. Maybe he was supplying drugs to them." Jack offered, becoming more proactive.

"Could explain all of the trips he took," Ben agreed. But to confirm we'd need to learn his actual destinations. It would certainly fit. The man spent a hell of a lot of time on the road. But it's all moot if we can't connect Comstock to Jack."

Lunch arrived and Steve cleared space on the conference table. While everyone scoped various combinations of Chinese food from paper boxes onto plastic plates, Jason dropped deep into thought. He believed that the call would not come at six o'clock, which meant the meeting would take place after dark. He reasoned that if he were the kidnapper, he would wait as long as possible. The effect would be to create more fear and tension, thus rendering the victim more agreeable. The meeting time would be less than an hour after the call, allowing Jack no time to prepare a defense or devise a trap. What Jason feared most would be their running Jack all over the city from phone to phone. Because they could observe Jack at the various stops, Jason would have a difficult time taking Jack's place. Jason hoped it would dark. Extremely dark.

Why am I bothering to plan? he wondered. This is a suicide mission, pure and simple. There's been no recon, I have no idea who they are, I have no idea how many I will be confronting. I'll be unarmed, and I'll have little or no backup. These assholes don't take prisoners and they don't leave witnesses. What the hell is there to plan? He had never taken on a mission with such formidable odds. In Vietnam at least, he knew the enemy and how they operated.

With his entire being, he focused on clearing his mind, preparing himself to make quick black-and-white judgments and accurate reflex decisions with no looking back. Jason honed in on the objective: finding Jennifer and Carol, rescuing them, and reuniting Jen to her family. The rest he would leave to Dailey and Montgomery. If he failed, the bad guys would keep the hostages alive to get another crack at Jack. If that happened, Jason would have no worries. He'd be dead.

* * * * *

Eternity seemed shorter than the hours that passed after their lunch. Steve played solitaire with a deck of cards he kept in his jacket pocket for just such occasions. Ben entered information from the Comstock report into the computer, while Joe and Sobahr left to conduct company business. Jack failed at trying to be calm, failed at reading magazines, and mostly fidgeted with the little die casting. Jason slouched in the leather conference room chair, head tilted back and eyes closed. A picture of tranquillity. On the inside he struggled to remain focused.

* * * * *

At six the phone did not ring. In an attempt to counter the slow movement of time, Jason suggested that Jack call Debbie to see how things were going, which he did with little prodding.

While Jack visited on the phone, Jason once again turned his chair toward the window and quietly watched the sun set behind the Olympic Peninsula. Although filled with the tension of repeatedly rehashing the odds he would later face, the spectacle of nature enveloped him. He immersed himself in the transition of color from the Creator's palette. The brilliant quivering orange of the fireball transitioned to bright pink in the process of sinking slowly behind the mountains. Wispy lavender clouds stretched halfway to Seattle as dusk backlit the now ebony Olympic Mountain Range. The phenomenon brought brief but welcome physical and mental rest.

* * * * *

At eight forty-five, the ring of the dedicated telephone ripped through the silence. Jack gathered up receiver in the middle of the second ring.

"Hello?" His voice cracked with emotion and fear, his eyes darted with nervous tension as he spoke only three words. "Yes, it is." He sat silently.

Then he said urgently into the phone, "I need to write thi—" Then he flushed red, having been cut off. His face reflected a sense of helplessness. All in the room waited and listened as the reels turned on the voice-activated recorder attached to the line. The call had lasted only thirty-eight seconds. At its conclusion a very pale Jack returned the receiver to the cradle.

"I've got to go," he said, looking directly at Jason.

"Please, one moment," Sobahr said. "We must first listen to the tape recording. It may contain something very useful." He pushed the rewind and play buttons, and everyone leaned forward with acute interest.

"Hello?"

"This is Jack O'Connor, I presume."

"Yes, it is."

"Mr. O'Connor, do not speak; just listen. By now I'm sure you're aware we have something that belongs to you. To ensure the safety of the package, it will be necessary for you to meet two men behind the old boots and hat gas station at the corner of East Marginal Way and Corson on the—"

"I need to write thi—"

"No, Mr. O'Connor, don't write, don't talk. Just listen. East Marginal and Corson at nine-fifteen tonight. That's thirty minutes from now. About four car lengths off of Marginal on the north side of Corson, there will be an open gate. Drive through it and park behind the boots. Two men will meet you there at nine-fifteen.

"And, Mr. O'Connor, there will be an army of men watching from every conceivable angle. Come alone, remembering that your package is perishable goods. Don't try and call your friend Lieutenant Dailey, because we'll know."

The line went dead and the six men listened to the click of Jack hanging up. Sobahr turned off the recorder. The same soft voice they had heard on the earlier recording gave away no clues, only instructions. Again it seemed studio quiet in terms of background noise. The location of the meeting place would be easily accessible from their present location and everyone in the room knew the hat and boot landmark, with the exception of Steve, who did not live in the area. Whoever had called knew there would be ample opportunity for surveillance from all directions. Not much chance for trickery. Darkness would be his only ally.

Jack stood visibly shaken. "Jason, I think I should be the one to go." All eyes immediately turned toward Jason.

"You're not going," Jason said softly. "We've been through this, Jack."

"You heard what he said," Jack retorted, his voice wracked with fear.

"They'll kill you, Jack," Jason said softly. "This is not open for discussion and you're wasting time."

"And they'll kill Jennifer if I don't show. You heard him."

"They'll kill her anyway, Jack. As soon as they have you, they will kill both Jennifer and Carol." Steve watched the interaction intently, ready to intervene at the slightest sign of trouble. Ben and Sobahr remained seated and watched in silence.

"And I suppose you think they won't kill you?" Jack asked sarcastically. "Then what, what have you gained?"

"Jennifer, Carol, and you will still be alive." Surprised by Jason's statement, Jack tried to speak but Jason continued. "And, as long as they don't get their hands on you, Jennifer will be safe. Now if I'm going to get there by nine-fifteen I have to leave. Give me the keys to the van." Jason extended his hand.

Jack looked to the others for support. Finding none, he hesitated for only a moment before handing the keys to Jason.

"Steve, let's go," Jason said, already on the move toward the door heading for the restroom.

Inside the restroom, Jason took off his shoulder holster, checked his Colt 10mm for a round in the chamber, put the safety back on, and put his holster and weapon in the satchel. Next he turned on the hot water, wet his hair, then took soap from the dispenser and ran it through his curls. "I hope this works," he mumbled to Steve. He ran his comb through his hair, slicking it back in the hope that when it dried it would help control the curliness. As he worked with his unruly hair, Sobahr entered with his hands full of electronic paraphernalia.

"Jason, this is very dangerous what you are attempting. At least let us put a wire on you. I have everything necessary." He held gear out to his friend.

"No chance, Sobahr. That'll be the first thing they check for." Then he looked at Steve. "Stay out of sight." Steve simply nodded, and without any further conversation, the two men left.

* * * * *

Steve dashed to his rental car and left the Columbia Tower parking garage. Jason walked directly to the rear of Jack's van. He opened the rear hatch and pulled up the carpet, opened the tire well and removed the spare. He placed his satchel in the well and replaced the cover and carpet. He doubted his captors would leave Jack's van in the open and hoped they would either take him in the van, or have him drive it and follow them. Either way his weapon would be accessible, providing the opportunity presented itself.

* * * * *

At nine-fourteen, Jason turned from Corson Street and drove through the open gate stopping the van behind the large structure shaped like a pair of boots. He rolled his window down and surveyed an empty lot, save the garbage and weeds that had accumulated over time. Jason sat alone with his thoughts in twilight darkness.

CHAPTER TWENTY-FOUR

Bad move, Jason muttered to himself. He had glanced into his side mirror just as the car pulled through the gate behind him. The bright headlights reflected off the side mirror directly into his eyes and blinded him. He tried to focus but had no time. In the next moment he heard several quick footsteps, then felt a cold gun barrel pressed against his neck.

"Don't move," a man's voice from the left told him. The passenger door opened and another man jumped into the seat beside him. Again, Jason felt the muzzle of a gun, this time pressed to his ribs. The same voice said, "Don't turn, don't even blink, or you're a dead man."

The man giving the orders removed the muzzle of his gun from Jason's neck, opened the car door, and slipped a black cloth bag partially over his head obscuring his vision. Jason heard the familiar screech of duct tape being peeled off the roll. He felt its sticky strength as the man slapped a sizeable piece across his mouth. Then the hood slid down and the drawstring tightened.

"Get out of the car—slowly," the voice said.

Do as you're told, Jason told himself. No sudden moves, nice and easy. You'll have all the time in the world. Discipline, discipline is the order of the hour. So far, so good. They haven't recognized me as an impostor and they haven't shot me—yet. He would offer no resistance, just collect information and worry about saving his ass later.

"Turn around. Put your hands behind your head and spread your legs." Jason followed the instructions obediently and felt probing hands patting him down. "He's clean, no weapon, no wire," a different voice said.

Jason deduced three people held him captive. Interesting, he thought. One car, three people. Jason had long ago learned to keep his mind active, constantly using his senses. Listen, look, smell, gather data no matter how insignificant, because one small detail could save his life.

His head was pushed sharply forward against the side of Jack's van, and his feet kicked farther apart."Put your hands behind your back."

Before Jason could respond voluntarily, both arms were jerked down behind him and his wrists bound with plastic wire ties so tightly they cut his flesh.

"Get him into the van."

In an instant, they grabbed him from both sides and literally threw him into the back of the van. The hatch slammed closed. Jason listened intently as two people entered the front, one through the passenger door, the other on the driver's side. The van's engine came to life, followed by the engine of the other car. He could hear the car tires spin on the decomposed asphalt as it backed up, turned around, and sped from the lot. Inertia rolled Jason from his side to his back as the van quickly backed in a tight arc, then pulled forward and made a right turn out of the gate.

Jason forced himself to his side, wedging his body between the back and the side of the van to stay off his back and minimize further damage to his wrists, the wire ties already sticky with blood. As the van made a quick left turn, a right, then another quick left, he had to push hard with his legs to keep from rolling again onto his back.

Experience had taught Jason the importance of keeping positive adrenaline flowing; he thought of his ordeal as a challenge, an adventure. Anything less could make him vulnerable. To maintain that mindset he tracked the turns and estimated distances to give him some clue as to his location. In less than a minute, Jason estimated they were on I-5 headed north. More minutes passed until the next direction change nearly rolled him on his face—a downhill then uphill sweeping turn to the right. Jason smiled to himself in spite of the pain. He knew that turn well—the I-5/I-90 interchange—the same route Wellington took after Dailey released him, the morning he went up like a Roman candle.

Jason had hoped to eavesdrop on his captors, to glean information, but there had been little conversation. Then, "We may have picked up a tail. See if you can spot it, about three cars back in the center lane."

Dammit, Steve, Jason said to himself.

"I can't tell," the man in the passenger seat said. "We'll know for sure in a couple of miles at the exit."

We must be somewhere around Issaquah, Jason guessed. So, Steve, we will soon find out if you remember your skills. During the days of the anti-terrorist team, all eleven of the men Jason had picked, along with himself, had trained with the Secret Service and the CIA, where they had learned all manner of surveillance, including how not to be spotted in traffic.

The van slowed. Jason could feel a slight downgrade and the veering to the right as the van exited onto the offramp. The van stopped then turned right.

"We got a live one," came the voice from the driver's seat. "It's the white station wagon, one car back."

"I got him," the passenger said. "What'll we do with him?"

"We'll see how persistent he is."

During the next few minutes Jason lost his bearings, as the van made countless right turns, left turns, stops. Off in the distance, a train whistle could be heard. It sounded to Jason as though it echoed through a valley, which would confirm they were in Issaquah. He felt strangely soothed by its wail.

"I think we lost him," the passenger said.

"Yeah, and we've wasted enough time doing it."

Jason could hear the whistle growing louder, which meant they were moving closer to the tracks. Within less than a minute, the van pulled to a stop and the ringing of railroad crossing bells sounded directly in front of them.

"I'll be damed to hell," the driver said. "That piece of crap car is back. I just caught a glimpse of him as he tried to sneak around the corner. Third car back in the line, the white station wagon."

Damn, Steve, why don't you wave a red flag? Jason thought. His silent cursing, however, was short lived. The van shuddered at the chest-throbbing resonance of the powerful locomotive as it closed on the crossing at break-neck speed. Long blasts of the whistle now came long and sharp, like a knife cut to the bone.

Without warning, the van lurched forward as the driver slammed the accelerator to the floor. Thrown violently towards the rear hatch of the van, Jason never heard the loud, crashing bang of the crossing gate splintering against the front of the van.

"Are you fucking crazy?" the passenger screamed. "That train nearly killed us."

"Yeah," came a cool reply, "but you don't see a white station wagon anymore, do you?"

* * * * *

Jason wished he could open his mouth to help sense the smell of where he might be, but he could only breathe deeply through his nose. It smelled like country woods to him, fir boughs in the cool, damp air. The two men led him, his head still bagged, up four stairs and across what seemed to be a porch. Loose boards complained sharply, heaving under their weight. Jason listened intently to the rusty squeaking of what he knew to be an old screen door, the jingling of keys, a key inserted into a lock, the song of dry hinges as a tired door opened to receive him. Just like the sound effects used on the old radio program *Inner Sanctum*, he thought.

Pushed violently from behind, he stumbled across the threshold, nearly falling, but catching his balance, landing on one knee. Stale air reeking of mold and mildew greeted them. The beeping of an armed security system was quickly silenced. Then Jason felt himself being picked up from both sides and hurled backwards into a stiff wooden high-backed chair. He winced with pain as the force of his weight drove his tied hands into the small of his back, the wire ties cutting deeper into his wrists, renewing the flow of blood. A man removed the hood giving him his first look at his captors.

Two men stood in front of him—both smaller than he, but both looked to be in good physical shape. Dressed alike in jeans, tee shirts and leather jackets, both had what looked to be about two days' growth of beard, giving them a seedy appearance. However, looking closer, Jason observed their clean clothes and neatly combed hair. The man closest to Jason had blond curls around his very tan and rather large, square face, blue eyes, and straight teeth. The other had a dark complexion with olive-pit eyes and slicked-back black hair.

Slick and Curly, Jason quipped to himself.

This had been the first opportunity for the two men to get a good look at their abductee. Jason could see their confusion as they realized the man sitting in the chair before them was not Jack O'Connor.

Curly's expression quickly changed from a smirk to per-turbed apprehension, then anger. "Well, Mr. Smart Ass, you just volunteered for some hard duty." He reached over and ripped the duct tape from Jason's mouth. Jason's face burned, as though half of his stubble had been removed by the roots. Waxing must be a real bitch! Jason thought.

"Who in the hell are you?" Curly demanded.

"I was about to ask you the sa—"

Instantly, Jason received a head-splitting blow to the left side of his face from the back of Curly's left fist. Before he could recover, Curly's powerful right delivered a second bone-crushing blow just below his sternum, nearly rocking him and his chair over backwards. Jason tried to protect himself from losing his breath by flexing his solar plexus, but to no avail. He gasped and struggled for just a wisp of air.

As Jason's chair rocked back, another crunching blow to the right side of his jaw sent him reeling back and crashing to the floor. He lay motionless except for his convulsing as he fought for a breath. His mouth filled with blood and he real-ized the last blow had caused him to bite his tongue deeply. Severely dazed and disoriented, he fought to remain conscious, knowing he needed to do something to defuse the situation.

What I need is a little time, Jason thought. He decided to fake unconsciousness. He rolled his body over onto his face, then went completely limp. Just when he thought he might take in a little air, he received a devastating kick to the rib cage. Again the coveted breath of air eluded him.

If this slime keeps this up, I will be unconscious, Jason thought. As his mind raced, he worked to control his reaction to the pain and somehow get control of the situation. He used all of his mental and physical discipline to continue his charade. Finally relief came when the two men grabbed him and jerked him up, then slammed him back into the chair. The abrupt movement of picking him up gave his lungs just enough stimulation to decompress and allow a little air to flow in. He sat in the chair, his head slumped forward with blood drooling from his mouth, and listened to their conversation, hoping to learn something, anything.

Slick spoke after a brief silence. "Now that you beat the dumb bastard senseless go call the man and find out what he wants us to do with him."

"I ain't calling the sonofabitch," Curly answered, "not after the last screwup. No way in hell I'm telling him we got the wrong man again! He'll hand me my fucking head. Besides, unless you brought the phone, it's still in the car."

"Christ! I'll drive to that Texaco we passed back there and find out what he wants us to do. I'll be back in a minute."

"If he comes around, I'll see what I can get out of him." Curly said, betraying an eager anticipation.

"Well, don't get carried away. Even if we don't know who he is, we want to keep him alive. He may be the only way we have of getting to O'Connor," Slick answered with a note of worry.

"Well, hell, we were supposed to kill O'Connor!"

"Not until we find out how much he knows and make sure the operation is secure, dumb ass. The man's gonna be pissed if we blow this again," Slick warned angrily. "You got it?"

"I got it," Curly said.

Jason listened intently as the door opened and closed. A moment later he heard Jack's van move down the gravel drive.

Jason's ploy had worked; now the time had come to take the offensive. He doubted that Slick would be away long. Since Slick and Curly had given Steve the slip at the rail crossing, he could expect no help. First priority, he needed to take inventory of his physical condition.

His swollen tongue would not be an impediment so the pain he could deal with, and the bleeding had begun to subside. Next he slowly and quietly took in a deep breath. Even the musty air felt good as he inhaled, until the pain in his ribs gave him the answer: bruised, one or two cracked maybe, but none broken. A sore jaw, but, again, nothing broken, and the major swelling around his left eye from the first blow he had taken should not cause him any grief.

He then focused his attention on his captors. They spoke only when necessary, did not use their names, and gave up no useful information. They had been well trained.

First, he needed to learn Carol's and Jennifer's location, the physical layout, and the number of guards. If he had time he would learn what these bozos were up to and what they thought Jack knew. He felt good enough to take control. The time had come to coax Curly into a mistake, and then rock and roll. He stirred in his chair as if coming around.

"Ah, he lives." Curly turned and moved toward Jason. "So, you still interested in being a smart ass?" he jeered with an arrogant smile.

"Nah, I give up."

Standing fully in front of Jason, Curly let out a nasty laugh. "You got a real smart mouth, Mr. Smart Ass. You don't give up, do you?"

Jason tried to look frightened, hoping to lure Curly a little closer. Slick could return any time, and if he were to alter his situation, it had to be now.

"Let's play a little game of question and answer." Curly reached his right hand around to his back pocket and took out a knife. As he did so, his unzipped jacket opened a bit on his right side, giving Jason a glimpse of the harness for a shoulder holster.

He waved the closed knife slowly back and forth in front of Jason's face. "Here's the way the game is played. I ask you, 'WHO THE HELL ARE YOU?'" In the next millisecond, a six-inch stiletto appeared with a loud ker-snap, less than a quarter of an inch from Jason's nose. "And now you TELL ME YOUR

NAME!" Curly snarled, attempting intimidation. His eyes resembled those of a psychopath's and the veins in his neck bulged like strands of blue rope.

Jason remained silent, focused only on Curly's eyes.

"Let me give you a piece of advice, Mr. Smart Ass. You read the papers? I did the dude in the parking lot last Sunday night. The poor sonofabitch barely whimpered. The only problem was that I did the wrong guy. So, my boss is real pissed, and when my boss is pissed, I turn into one mean sonofabitch, so DON'T FUCK WITH ME!" Curly continued to wave the stiletto slowly back and forth in front of Jason's face. "Now, one more time, or I'm going to cut your face apart one inch at a time. WHO THE HELL—"

Curly's eyes crossed with the shock of paralyzing pain as his gonads crushed against the hard bone of Jason's foreleg, which he shot powerfully upward, lifting him off the floor. Curly hunched forward involuntarily, and as he did, Jason quickly brought his forehead upward to meet him. He felt the sickening crunch of cartilage as Curly's nose gave way under the force of the collision, and a fountain of blood bathed both men. Unconscious, Curly draped over Jason like a worn-out bed sheet until Jason leaned forward, dumping him to the floor.

"Jason Brisben, Navy SEAL, retired, meaner sonofabitch," he said with satisfaction.

Jason stood in a brisk fluid movement and stretched out his back, ignoring the sharp pain from his ribs; he then knelt down, sliding his tied hands under his buttocks. In a smooth motion he rolled onto his back, first working one leg through his arms, then the other to get his hands in front of him. Moving quickly, he rolled Curly onto his back, removed a 357 Colt Python from the shoulder holster, and tucked it in his belt. Then he picked up the stiletto, sat back down on the chair, and held the knife between his knees to cut the plastic cable ties from his wrists. Before he could cut the ties, he heard footfalls rapidly climbing the stairs and crossing the porch. Jason dropped the knife, took the revolver from his belt, and leveled it on the door. The door burst open and Slick entered, his weapon held in a two-handed grip. Before he could evaluate the situation, two 357 magnum hollow-point rounds slammed into his chest, sending him backwards through the door from which he had come. Jason quickly ran to the porch to make sure Slick had come alone, and checked him for vital signs.

After freeing his wrists and finding the cuts to be superficial, Jason looked down at the still unconscious Curly, whose once handsome nose lay mashed across the center of his face. Jason lifted him into the chair and as he did, Curly began to regain consciousness. He removed Curly's belt, and lashed his wrists to the spindles on the chair back. Searching Curly's pockets, he found more wire ties and secured each of his legs to the legs of the chair. Curly would not yet be in any condition to give coherent answers, so Jason seized the opportunity to explore the main floor of the house.

He stood in an empty living room with the exception of two chairs, one of which held Curly. The room had what looked like an accumulation of fifty years of dirt and dust. Old rags or torn sheets, rotted by the sun, covered the windows. Glass-break sensors guarded the windows. "Why?" He wondered.

A single light bulb at the end of a wire hung from the ceiling provided the only light. He scanned the ceiling and spotted a motion sensor. He moved through an archway into what at one time could have been a dining room, also empty and equally as dirty. This room also had sensors on all of the windows. He moved through a swinging door into the kitchen and looked for a light switch, and located an old rotary switch near an exterior door. He gave it a twist and a low-wattage bulb came to life.

A high-backed, cast-iron sink with two faucets protruding through the back caught his eye. Its filth disgusted him as much as anything he had encountered in Vietnam. He turned the handle of the cold water faucet. Red, dusty air belched forth, then liquid rust splattered into dirt and stain-covered porcelain that smelled and looked more like an open sewer than a sink. He decided to let the water run, hoping it would clear while he finished his reconnaissance.

Three useable doors provided access to the room; the one through which he had entered, and the other one which had a couple of two-by-fours nailed across it, a door to the outside. The outside door and windows were alive with sensors. The ceiling also had wires connected to a second motion sensor. Another door led to a basement. A forth door opened into a bathroom that appeared to be in worse condition than the kitchen. The bathroom also had another door at the opposite end, and upon passing through, Jason found himself back in the living room, looking at a somewhat grotesque and grimacing Curly, still secure in his chair.

"Feeling a little better, are we?" Jason inquired. He received no response, only an attempt at an insipid smile. Another door in the living room piqued Jason's curiosity; he assumed it led to the upstairs bedrooms. "What's up there?" he asked pointing toward the door.

"Why don't you go up there and find out, hot shot?"

That sounded like a challenge, Jason thought. But rather than rise to the provocation, he returned to the kitchen to check on the water.

Although the water had cleared somewhat, it still did not look fit for human consumption, but he needed to rinse his face and mouth. Cold water would help slow the swelling. With the amount of blood in his mouth, he couldn't tell if the water was bad or not, but took care not to swallow. Jason looked at his reflection in the dirty kitchen window; the swollen bloody mess staring back surprised him. After a few minutes, he felt marginally better and dried himself with a portion of his shirt not covered with his or Curly's blood.

Once again in the living room Jason watched for Curly's reaction as he moved to the upstairs door. He received only a wry grin of anticipation. Upon opening the door, he exposed musty, wooden stairs that disappeared up into an unlit stairwell. Jason cautiously felt the sides of the stairwell hoping to find a light switch, but found none. The single light bulb from the living room did not provide light past the second step. As he surveyed the area, he remembered Curly's words, "Why don't you go up there and find out, hot shot?"

He dared me to use these stairs, Jason thought. A second before his foot touched the stair tread, he saw it. Suspended just an inch above the second step, the dim light from the living room played off a copper wire no thicker than a human hair. A trip wire. What in the hell is this place? he asked himself as he carefully backed out of the stairwell and closed the door. I'll check it out later, he reasoned. Jennifer and Carol first.

Jason dragged Slick's body from the porch into the living room. Slick had made contact with someone. No sense leaving a body out as a welcome mat, in case someone did show up.

Jason then turned his attention to Curly. "It's game time," he said. "We're playing Truth or Consequences and the rules have changed. I ask the questions and now you answer . . . and you will tell the truth," he said emphatically. "Now, before you say anything smart, think about this. I will not play 'fuck around' with you. You will answer me and give me the information that I want."

"Oh, fuck off," Curly replied sarcastically. "Ain't no way I'm giving you jack shit."

Jason's expression remained unchanged and his voice calm. From what he had witnessed to this point he knew these people were involved in deadly activities. Well-organized and disciplined, they would not give up information easily. Although he had taken Curly down, he would not be a push-over during questioning. Jason knew his interrogation could not be a drawn-out exercise; he would need to surprise Curly by inflicting intense pain, fear, and confusion to break him quickly. He'd have at most a window of fifteen to forty-five seconds in which Curly would spill his guts before regaining control and then clam up. If Jason's suspicions were correct about what lay at the end of the trip wire, Curly was not afraid to die.

"Let's go through this one more time. I ask—you tell the truth. I'll ask, where the girl and the woman are being held. I'll ask who's holding them and how many of them there are. Then I'll to ask why there's a contract on Jack O'Connor. That's the first three questions. Then we'll move on from there. So, are we ready?"

"Bite me, big man!"

Jason ignored Curly's last remark and spoke in a calm but emphatic voice. "Where are they holding the girl and the woman?" He reached to his back and brought out Curly's 357.

"What's that supposed to do, scare me?" Curly sneered.

"No. It's supposed to hurt you. It's called the consequence." Jason continued to speak calmly. "This is the last time I'll ask. I will count to three. If you don't tell me what I want to know, I'll put a hole in your foot that you could sail the Bremerton Ferry through."

"Up yours," Curly said, with a disinterested look.

"Where are they holding the girl and the woman? . . . . One . . . ."

The next instant a look of total horror and anguish spread over Curly's bloody face as his 357 exploded to life. He let out a deafening guttural scream as a 120-grain hollow-point bullet from his own gun slammed through his left foot. Blood boiled from the hole, forming a crimson river over the top of his neon-white athletic shoe. Dust from the walls and ceiling fell, creating a musty fog. Jason counted one, to let Curly know the only thing predictable in this interrogation would be unpredictably swift, intense pain.

Spittle spewed forth as Curly screamed, cursing and swearing at the pain's assault, his body quivering in agony.

"Where are they holding them, you slimy piece of shit?" Jason questioned him with eyes now ablaze. He no longer spoke softly as he fired his questions at Curly. He grabbed him by the throat lifting him and the chair off of the floor. "You're running out of time, tough guy," Jason continued. His face now only inches away from Curly's.

"I don't know," he lied.

Jason could see tears of pain and fear had replaced the once haughty, confident look in Curly's eyes as he returned him to the floor. "Last chance," he reiterated. "Where are . . . ."

"I don't know, I swear," Curly screamed, now begging.

"New game," Jason said, as he stuffed the muzzle of the 357 hard into Curly's already tender crotch. "It's called You Bet Your Balls. You tell me what I want to know or your jewels are going through the bottom of the chair." Jason pulled the hammer back hard, making sure Curly could feel it.

"Don't—don't. I don't know—I swear," he slobbered in fear as he begged.

Jason's instincts told him that Curly was ready to break. He pulled the muzzle away just as the hammer fell and the 357 exploded once again.

Terrified, Curly again screamed, still slobbering. "All right! All right! They're in Victoria."

Jason knew that the bullet slamming through the hard wooden seat of the chair would send shock waves of intense pain through Curly's still throbbing scrotum. "Where in Victoria?" Jason screamed back at him.

"I don't know exactly. It's an old gray house just down from The Olde England Inn, one, maybe two streets down toward the water, off of Lampson Street. It's right up against the fence of the military base."

"How many guards, and who's guarding them?"

"My partner, with one, maybe two others."

"Your partner, was he in the parking lot? He do the woman?"

"Yeah."

"How did you find O'Connor's daughter?"

"The kid's girlfriend went over to the O'Connor house the day after they gave us the slip. We followed her home and tapped their phone. The kid was calling from a phone booth in Oak Bay. We got a fix on her the second day."

"Why are they after O'Connor?"

"He knows something."

"What's he know?"

"I don't know, they never told us."

"Who's 'they,' and what in the hell is this all about?" Jason screamed, suddenly realizing he'd asked two questions in his haste to save time. Having nothing but disdain for this man who could kill a person and not know why, Jason vowed to inflict as much pain as necessary to learn who and why Jack had been targeted.

Jason recocked the revolver. As he did, he thought he heard the faint impact of a car door slamming over the loud ringing in his ears, caused by the discharging gun. Not knowing if Curly had heard the car door, he released the hammer and tucked the 357 in his belt. A look of relief crossed Curly's face when Jason left him and walked quickly away. Just as he entered the kitchen, Jason heard the front door open.

"Bill, he's in the kitchen," Curly cried.

"You stupid ass," the voice said.

"Bill, NO. DON'T! I didn't tell him anything! I swear."

A gunshot rang from the living room, then silence. This organization doesn't make allowances for screwups, Jason thought to himself. With gun in hand, he stood stone still, not breathing, listening for any sound to indicate from which direction trouble would come. Ringing ears impeded his hearing, but he knew his stalker would have the same problem. He waited for what seemed an eternity, hearing only the pounding of his heart. Then came the telltale squeak of the hardwood floor Jason had been waiting for. He was coming through the dining room.

Jason quickly moved to the basement door and swung it open hard, so it would slam against the kitchen wall. He then quietly slipped into the bathroom, closed the bathroom door, and waited. The trick with the door would hopefully make his stalker look in the basement or at least consider the possibility, which would buy Jason valuable time.

From the bathroom, Jason heard his stalker enter the kitchen, diving to the floor, a tactic to minimize himself as a target when he entered the room. This guy's good, Jason thought. He listened intently as he heard cautious footsteps toward the basement steps.

Jason moved stealthily backwards, inching toward the living room entrance, keeping his body facing the kitchen in case his ploy failed. With Curly's gun in his right hand pointed toward the kitchen door, he carefully felt for the door to the living room with his left hand behind. As his hand lightly touched the door, a creaking on the basement steps provided the break he'd been waiting for. Moving on the balls of his feet, Jason quickly opened the door and quietly slipped through into the living room. He gently closed the door and turned toward the chair where Curly's body slumped, motionless, covered in blood, with a single bullet hole through his head. The ruthlessness of the organization settled in on Jason. Human life meant nothing to these people.

Jason discarded his first impulse to make a break for the car. If he left his stalker unchecked, the assumption would be he had learned the location of Carol and Jennifer, and they would be moved before he could get to them. He needed to subdue and detain his stalker for later questioning.

The upstairs door looked to be his only option. Again, moving on the balls of his feet, he slowly opened the upstairs door and stepped up onto the second step, taking great care not to touch the trip wire. He quietly pulled the door to him, leaving it slightly ajar, then waited.

Some time passed before Jason heard any sound to betray the location of his stalker. It came again from the basement stairs. Apparently satisfied that Jason wasn't in the basement, the man moved cautiously out of the stairwell and through the kitchen entrance into the bathroom. Then again, total silence. The waiting tested his nerves. His body complained with pain from the beating Curly had inflicted, and his lack of movement invited a painful stiffness to settle in.

Jason's survival depended upon his ability to block out pain and all that might distract him from focusing on the capture of his unseen enemy. The continued uncomfortable roaring in his ears made hearing difficult. To fight the urge to strike, Jason drew on his former training, making the important transition from the hunted to hunter.

This guy is good, Jason reminded himself, Priority one: Outwait the adversary. In spite of his pain and his difficulty with hearing, he had taken control.

Ten minutes passed before Jason heard the bathroom door leading into the living room slowly open. At the sound, Jason exhaled in relief, then breathed slow and deliberately. Although he wanted out of his confining and dangerous quarters, he fought the urge to make his move prematurely. If this guy's worth his salt, Jason hypothesized, he'll place himself between the front door and the upstairs door, then check outside. He carefully slid one foot after the other to the back of the step to keep the toes of his shoes away from the trip wire. Then very slowly he crouched facing the door with Curly's 357 in his right hand.

"Let's get it on, you sonofabitch," Jason muttered softly. He rolled his left shoulder toward the door. With his head down and using his shoulder as a battering ram, he hurled himself forward through the door and out onto the living room floor. The door opened with such force that it hit the wall with crash.

A hail of bullets from a fully automatic Mac 10 rained just above his back, sending fragments of wood and plaster in all directions from the shredded doorjamb. As Jason's chest hit the floor, he skidded and returned fire, his outstretched arms holding the 357 with a two-handed grip. Firing once, then rolling to his right, he fired again while on his back. Continuing to roll, he pulled the trigger once again on his stomach, only to hear the hammer fall over an empty cylinder.

Jason's first bullet hit his attacker low in the abdomen. The second shot found its way squarely to the Adam's apple. The man died before he hit the floor. Jason picked himself up to one knee and studied the body for a moment.

"Jason, you can't get information out of a dead man, you idiot," he yelled aloud. Because the man had turned and fired when Jason exploded from the stairwell, he had no option but to defend himself. Jason knew to come out low; otherwise, he would have been cut in half by a clip full of 9mm rounds. He moved to the body and searched him. As he suspected, and as with Curly, the man carried no ID. All of his pockets were empty with the exception of car keys.

Jason went quickly on to Jack's van to retrieve his own weapon. Although the urgency to get to Jennifer and Carol quickly existed, he needed to learn why the place had a security system that rivaled Fort Knox. And why did these people want Jack dead?

Armed with a fully loaded pistol and a flashlight, he went back to the house and directly to the upstairs doorway. Using the flashlight to scan the stairwell, he spotted two additional trip wires, the second about halfway up the stairs, and a third near the top. All of the trip wires were suspended approximately one inch above the stair treads by small screw eyes. The wires then ran vertically up each side of the stairwell disappearing from sight as they entered the walls on the second story. "Well now," Jason said.. "Let's see what's so special about this place, and then get the hell out of here."

As he ascended the stairs, he took great care not to disturb any of the wires. The second floor had two rooms, one on either of the stairwell that at one time probably served as bedrooms in a cozy little house. The place where he stood no longer felt cozy, but ominous, cold, dangerous.

He checked the path where he would walk and then once again shined the light along the walls to make sure he hadn't missed any wires. He spotted three wires that ran through the walls into each of the rooms on either side of the stairwell.

Jason advanced slowly, taking cautious steps and shining the light in front of him on the floor, walls, ceiling, or any place that there might be any type of trigger mechanism or sensor. Three all-too-familiar objects caught his eye as he entered the room: pouches that usually contained plastic explosives, much like the ones he'd used in Vietnam. They lay on the floor against the wall at approximately the same spacing the trip wires had entered the wall on the opposite side.

He stood in front of enough plastic in this one room to obliterate an entire city block.

Several olive drab military crates, the type he recognized that were used to ship small arms, like M16's and ammunition, rested not two feet from the pouches. Stacked next to them were corrugated boxes void of any markings. He bent down and carefully examined one of the top crates, then slowly removed the lid which had previously been opened. One dozen brand, spanking, new M16's.

"One, two, three, four, five . . ." Jason counted twelve crates. "One hundred forty-four M16's. What the hell have we got going here, an insurrection?" Next he opened one of the smaller corrugated boxes that measured about six inches square and approximately eighteen inches high. The contents of the box looked to be a filter of some sort, similar to the water filter that he had under his kitchen sink at the loft. After looking in a few more boxes and finding the same contents in each, he counted them. There were sixty filters.

Puzzled, Jason took one of the M16s and one of the filters and went on carefully to the next room where he found another 144 M16's and another sixty filters.

Cautiously, he descended the steps to the main floor, set down the rifle and the box and went through the kitchen to explore the basement. After carefully negotiating the basement steps, which were also laced with trip wires, he finally stood on a rough concrete floor. An old octopus wood-burning furnace stood in the center of an empty basement. As he directed the flashlight around the basement, he counted another twelve pouches of explosives lining the basement walls.

Jason could not wait to leave the basement, the house, and the whole damn county.

CHAPTER TWENTY-FIVE

Jason quickly recognized his location and drove Jack's van south off the bluff towards Issaquah, then to I-90 towards Seattle. Just before the interchange, he pulled off an exit into a gas-mart and made two phone calls, the first to Tony at Hard-Ship Marine. The phone rang fifteen times before he heard a sleepy "Hard-Ship."

"Tony! It's Jason, get my boat in the water."

"What? Are you out of your mind? It's almost three o'clock in the bloomin' morning for Chri—!

"Tony! Shut up and listen. I've got a situation here. There are four lives at stake, so I don't need your guff." The phone went silent as Jason continued. "I'll be there in forty-five minutes. I want it fired and the oil temp at 190 degrees when I get there. Plot a course on the GPS through Admiralty Inlet to Fleming Bay. It's the lagoon just southwest of the military base on Vancouver Island, and then another to Oak Bay. And Tony, make sure the tanks are topped off."

"Jason, for Godsake, think about this! There's so much junk in the water after all the rain and warm weather you'll be lucky to make it halfway across Elliott Bay!" Tony was referring to drift debris brought into the water by spring runoff.

Tony had a valid concern, but Jason also knew he had no alternatives. It was a risk he would take. He knew no other way to get there quickly under cover of darkness. All flights could be easily monitored. Also, he would need of transportation once on Vancouver Island.

"I've got no choice, buddy. Just get it done! I'll explain it all to you when I get back. I'll see you in a few minutes." Jason hung up, dialed again and waited impatiently.

"Castellano."

"Joe, has Steve returned?" Jason asked anxiously.

"About half an hour ago. He said he looked for you as long as he dared after he—uh—missed the train, so to speak. You okay?"

"I'm fine. Joe, I have the location of Carol and Jennifer, but we'll need to move fast. Have Steve meet me at the Box Car in fifteen minutes. Tell him to bring his foul-weather gear. We're going for a boat ride. I want Dailey and Montgomery to meet us there as well. And Joe, rent a van and get Jack to Port Angeles. If everything goes well, I'll meet you there at the ferry landing sometime around dawn with his family."

Joe had no problem understanding Jason's instructions. "Foul-weather"meant full combat gear; being nighttime, it meant black and camo grease or hoods. He also understood to get to Port Angeles by dawn he would need to get started immediately because either the Bainbridge or the Bremerton Ferries had already made their last runs, making it necessary to drive through Tacoma.

"Will you stop at the cottage to pick up Dave for additional manpower?" Joe asked.

"There's no time. I have to get to Jennifer and Carol first. I don't know how much time I have before they figure it out and move them. Call the cottage and inform David I'm coming. Tell him not to say anything to Debbie in case I run into trouble. I'll see you in a few hours." Jason hung up and sprinted to the van.

* * * * *

Jason saw his car and a Seattle cruiser in The Box Car parking lot when he arrived. Steve climbed out of the Seville as he pulled to a stop. Thompson and Dolan exited the cruiser and greeted Jason and explained that Dailey and Montgomery were in Mukilteo on police business.

He acknowledged the information with a nod, then reached into his back pocket and handed Dolan the stiletto he had taken from Curly.

"This is the knife that killed Carston Jennings. I couldn't save the prints, sorry. It won't make much difference, though; the owner is in a house just north of Issaquah with a hole in his head. And just for the record, I didn't put it there. I've got something else here that might interest you." With the three men following, he walked quickly to the passenger side of the van, opened the door and handed Thompson the brand new M16.

"I'll bet there's a story associated with this," Thompson said with a wry smile as he visually appraised Jason's battered and swollen face.

Jason ignored the remark. "There are 287 more just like it. Give me your notepad." Thompson handed the M16 to Steve, then passed his notepad to Jason

"There is a house north of Issaquah up on the bluff above a new industrial complex." Jason gave an abbreviated description of what had transpired at the house as he wrote the directions, then handed the notepad back to Thompson. "Here's something else I found. Maybe you can figure out how it fits into this puzzle." Jason reached back into van and handed Dolan the box containing what looked like a filter.

"What the hell is this?" Dolan asked.

"Like I said, figure it out. But you ought to know that there are 119 of them. And they're well protected. You'll need the bomb boys when you go in there."

"Mr. Honeycut here told us what happened today," Thompson began. "With Dailey still up in Mukilteo . . ." He hesitated. "Mr. Brisben, in view of what's happened tonight, I think we need to talk to Dailey. This is some heavy shit going down here. Good God, man, we've got three more bodies to deal with."

Jason calmly said. "I'll be in your office by ten this morning. That's the best I can do."

Thompson took a deep breath, then sighed. "Brisben, think about this for a minute. We have three bodies, and from what you say, enough plastique to level Issaquah. If I go back without you, Dailey's going to have my ass."

"Look, these people are well organized, so you need to get up there fast. What you don't need is to spend two hours in an interrogation room with me. I'm acting in good faith and giving you everything as I get it. I didn't have to notify you. Now we've all wasted too much time. Steve and I are leaving to get Jennifer and Carol and reunite O'Connor with his family, so if you're planing on arresting us, make your move or get the hell out of the way."

"Come on, Brisben, it's not like that," Thompson said, with palms up in a pleading gesture. "You have to understand, we're in an awkward situation. If this thing gets out of hand, we're all in trouble. And by the looks of it, if your information is accurate . . . God, the feds were all over us after that damn car went up. This is military issue," he said pointing toward the M16 that Steve held. "We don't have any choice, the feds have to be notified. Dailey will need you"

Jason knew Thompson had a valid point, and now with the FBI involved, it could easily turn into an ugly situation for Dailey and Montgomery.

"I'm won't screw you over, Thompson. But you can't get to Jack's family before I can. You'll have to trust me on this. We'll meet at ten in the morning and I'll give you everything then."

"Where are they holding them? Can we provide some backup?" Dolan asked.

"They're close, but out of your jurisdiction. That's what I meant when I said you can't get to them as fast as we can. You have red tape. We don't. Now, we have to get moving."

Steve handed the M16 back to Thompson and moved along with Jason toward Jason's car, leaving the two officers.

"Jason?"

"Yeah?"

"Be careful," Thompson said.

* * * * *

"Stow the gear while I talk with Tony," Jason told Steve as he brought the car to a stop in front of Hard-Ship Marine. When they opened the car doors the rumbling resonance from Jason's boat could be heard as the two supercharged Hawk engines hunted for an even idle range. Some thirty feet below the nearly invisible, dark-blue boat lay in wait on coal-black water, exhaust condensation rising from its transom.

Tony appeared in the office doorway as Jason approached. "What the hell is going on?" he asked when he got a good look at Jason's badly beaten face.

"I'll fill you in when I get back," he said, as he gave his car keys to Tony.

"I hope you don't get yourself in trouble out there. Just slow down and take a minute for me to fill this thermos with coffee for you."

Jason knew at the speed they would be traveling there would be no chance to drink coffee, but it could be available for Carol and Debbie on their trip to Port Angeles.

"Thanks Tony, If all goes well I'll see you in a few hours, about eight o'clock."

Jason guided his stiletto-like craft away from its moorings and idled away from the marina. Steve went forward to stow the gear as Jason eased the throttles forward to bring the boat on step as they entered Elliott Bay, making a gradual turn north toward the Admiralty Inlet. When all had been secured, Steve joined Jason at the helm and settled into the bolster beside him.

"Hang on!" Jason yelled over the sound of the engines as they exploded to life. Steve grabbed the handles at the foot of the instrument panel and watched in amazement as the dual speedometers climbed in unison: fifty, sixty, seventy. At eighty-five miles an hour, Jason eased the throttles back to level off. The two tachometers vibrated steadily at 5000 rpm's.

"You okay?" Jason yelled at Steve over the roar of the engines and the wind. The partial cloud cover intermittently obscured the moon and stars, leaving little light to reflect off of the water, creating the eerie illusion of flying across a bumpy, black, void.

"We're going to die aren't we?" Steve shouted jokingly as he stared at the inky abyss in front of them.

"I hope not." Jason kept his eyes fixed on the instruments, paying particular attention to the GPS.

"What happens if we hit something?" Steve yelled.

"We'll die," Jason shouted back, laughing. Conditions, other than darkness, couldn't have been better: a two-foot chop to aerate the hull meant less resistance making it easy on the engines.

Steve left the bolster and went forward, returning several minutes later. He bumped Jason's arm to get his attention.

"What's up?

"You want some glasses?" Steve yelled, holding a familiar contraption in front of him.

"I'll be a sonofabitch," Jason said, overjoyed, at the night vision gear that Steve held out to him.

"I didn't know we'd be flying across the water at damn near a hundred miles an hour in this not-so-wonderfully-guided missile. Figured you might want to see where you're going."

Jason laughed. "Well, things are looking up. Here, take the wheel. Just hold it steady." Steve held the wheel with his right hand and hung on to one of the panic handles with his left while Jason slipped the goggles on and focused them. "Well, it looks like we can make some time," Jason shouted happily, taking the wheel back from Steve. He flipped the goggles up, checked the instruments, returned his goggles, and moved the throttles forward, then leveled off when the speed reached 100 mph.

"How fast will this damn thing go?" Steve yelled. The acceleration had forced him back into the bolster.

"About a 115, a 120, somewhere in that range."

"Shouldn't we be wearing life jackets?" Steve inquired.

"Hell, at this speed it won't make any difference, and besides, if we can-in, and end up in the drink, we'll only last ten minutes max. This water ain't like what we were used to in Florida. . . . You aren't enjoying this much, are you?"

"Well, listening to you doesn't instill a feeling of a long, healthy life." Steve had acclimated quickly to the ride, even without the luxury of the night vision. He had repeatedly placed his life in Jason's hands throughout his SEAL career without reservation.

Jason navigated the passage through the Admiralty Inlet then altered their heading to west by northwest for the straight shot to Victoria. Steve had noticed he could no longer see lights from land.

"Where the hell are we?" Steve shouted.

"We're about twenty minutes out, but it'll be a little rougher as we cross the tail end of the Strait." Steve looked ahead and saw nothing but blackness and heard nothing but the roar of the wind and the two relentless engines.

On schedule, Jason rolled the throttles back and turned on the exhaust baffles as they approached the entrance to Victoria Harbor. Continuing west past the entrance to the harbor, he brought the boat off step and moved in closer to shore to locate the inlet at the foot of Lampson Street. If he could find the right spot, it would only be four or five blocks to the house where they were holding Carol and Jennifer. Steve went forward into the cabin and began unpacking their gear.

Jason found the place he had been looking for and slowly eased the craft into the tiny lagoon. Fortunately, the small dock had not been removed during the winter, which would make getting off and back on the boat easy. He expertly worked the wheel and the throttles, spinning the boat around so the bow faced the open water in the event they needed to make a speedy retreat.

Jason turned on the cabin lights and moved forward. "First, we need to locate the house. I know about where it is, but I don't have an address. Fortunately, I've dined several times at the Olde England Inn and gone for walks afterwards in the evenings, so I'm somewhat familiar with the area."

He took a notepad and pencil from a drawer and made a sketch of the approximate layout of the streets. "If my memory serves me, I think the house is in this area," Jason said as he circled three houses. "We'll have to deal with the security and take things as they come."

"Nothing I like better than a solid plan," Steve said sarcastically.

"You got a better idea, Mr. Smart Ass?"

"Don't get testy. We've had worse."

"Yes we have," Jason said soberly. He continued to describe the lay of the land referring to the thumbnail sketch while they finished changing into black, donning weapons, and smearing on green and black grease paint. Once finished, they synchronized watches.

Jason said, "let's kick some ass."

"Just like the good old days!" Steve replied, with excitement in his voice.

* * * * *

Just one hour from the time they had left Seattle, they were running at a brisk pace toward The Olde England Inn, and Jason hoped their luck would hold.

They had gone three blocks up Lampson Street when Jason stopped to get his bearings. "I think it's down this way," he said, then turned east down a side street. As Steve followed, both men stayed in the shadows away from the streetlights. After two blocks, Jason stopped again. "Now this is where it gets sticky," he said, speaking softly. "Down at the end of this block is the west fence of the military base. I don't know if we're on the right street. If we have to, we should be able to move along the fence. I have no idea what we may run into. As far as I know, there are only two or three men watching them," he said, referring to Jennifer and Carol. "But, they've had plenty of time to bring in the cavalry, so let's be careful. I'd like to take two of them back for interrogation. Any others are disposable and we leave 'em. You wear the night-sight. From here on, we don't talk. Take it slow and quiet."

"You got it," Steve responded, with thumbs up.

They moved quietly into a yard on the north side of the street, then carefully worked their way east through one yard, then another, staying in the cover of shadows and shrubbery. Streetlights had stolen much of their coveted darkness making progress painfully slow.

Steve halted Jason. Using hand signals, he questioned which house Jason thought might be the one. They had two choices. Jason took a moment to study the two houses. He hypothesized: If I were hiding someone, would I use the house with a few short shrubs or the one with an abundance of tall shrubs that nearly obscured the house? Jason pointed to the house up a half a block and across the street, almost hidden behind the tall, unkempt bushes. Steve nodded his head in approval. If lucky, they crouched nearly across the street from Carol and Jennifer.

Jason and Steve drifted like smoke into the yard directly across the street from the house they'd targeted. Behind the cover of a laurel bush, Steve surveyed the yard and what little he could see of the house through the night vision. Jason waited impatiently at his side, his emotions churning at sudden thoughts of Carol, but forced himself to focus on overtaking her captors.

They faced an ill-kept yard, with shrubs untrimmed and an overgrown lawn riddled with weeds. The house sat back several feet from the street, far enough to make it difficult to even guess if it was gray, brown, or blue. Bushes toward the front of the yard and also around the foundation of the house made it difficult to detect sentries. They would be vulnerable crossing the street.

After some time had passed, Steve nudged Jason and signaled all clear. They darted simultaneously across the street and disappeared into the shrubbery. Steve again scanned the yard with the aid of the night vision. Jason felt the nudge of the all-clear on his arm and they moved toward the west side of the house closest to them.

Suddenly, Jason grabbed Steve's arm and they retreated to the cover of the shrubs. He signed to Steve the presence someone outside. Jason had detected a faint whiff of cigarette smoke. After checking again, Steve indicated his puzzlement. He could detect no one. Jason signed that he would move around the house and for Steve to wait for him to come into view from the opposite corner. Jason checked the wind. A slight breeze drifted from north to south with very subtle direction changes from time to time. He listened for crickets and the tree frogs; he would have to move slowly and quietly because when the critters stop singing it means something or someone is on the prowl. An alert sentry would notice.

Jason ghosted away, moving from bush to bush, a few feet at a time, melding from Steve's view into the shrubbery at the northwest corner of the house.

Steve waited, listening to leaves rustling in the breeze, crickets and tree frogs. The light breeze shifted again, this time swirling from the southeast. Steve only then caught a whiff of the cigarette smoke that Jason had detected earlier. It must be coming from the east side of the house, he thought. The side facing the base. At first impulse Steve considered changing his position for a better look. He thought better of the idea, how-ever, knowing Jason could take care of himself in most situations and devoted his attention to how they would gain entry to the house.

The house had rickety wood front porch that would be impossible to cross without the boards sounding an alarm. Maybe there would be a better way in. He would know when Jason reported.

After what seemed too long for Jason to be gone, Steve became a little edgy. The critters are still happy, so what is taking so long? he wondered. The breeze shifted, carrying faint traces of the cigarette smoke—and the pungent aroma of a cigar.

"Dammit," he said almost audibly. "There're two people out here."

Without hesitation, he backed away from his position and worked his way directly east until he came against the fence surrounding the military base. He hoped to find a vantage point where he could observe the east side of the house. He cau-tiously worked into a position between the fence and another one of the overgrown bushes. His suspicions were confirmed when he discovered two men standing in short shrubbery, one lighting another cigarette, the other smoking a small cigar, both armed with Mac 10's stuffed in their belts.

Steve detected the black shadow of Jason in between the house and the cover of laurel less than two feet away from the two men, who had no clue of his presence. Steve took his Browning from his shoulder holster and slowly moved into a position of advantage about ten feet away. He could hear the two men talking but made no effort to listen. Bringing his weapon up slowly and deliberately, he fired one round. The only sound was the zip of a bullet breaking the sound barrier on its deadly path. The man's head to Jason's left snapped back, his knees buckled, and he crumpled to the ground. Jason was on the other man from behind before he knew what had happened.

"You make a sound and you're dead," Jason whispered in the man's ear. He held him from behind, his hand clamped vise-like over the man's mouth. With Jason's knife at his throat, the man gave up all indication of struggle as he felt the cold edge of steel against his neck. In the next second, Steve appeared in front of them.

"What kept you?" Jason whispered.

"I got bored and took a nap," Steve whispered in return, as he disarmed and frisked their trembling victim.

"Looks like we found the right place," Jason said, barely audible. "Now my friend," he continued talking in the man's ear. "We need information. You get one chance. You blow it, you'll end up lying on top of your friend. Do you understand?"

The man nodded.

"How many men are inside?" he asked. "Don't try to talk, just use hand signals."

The man responded by holding up two shaking fingers.

"Now," Jason said, "I'm going to ask you some questions. If you don't tell me what I want to know or if you answer in anything above a whisper, you'll have a six-inch smile before you get half a word out. You understand?" Jason received an ever-so-slight affirmative nod.

"Where are they holding the girl?"

"There's two bedrooms to the right off the living room down a hallway. The girl is locked in the back bedroom and the redhead in the front bedroom."

"Weapons?"

"One Uzi, another Mac 10 and boot knifes."

"Entrance and exit?'

"Through the front. The kitchen door is boarded up."

While Jason continued the interrogation, Steve searched the dead man and cut his denim jacket sleeves into strips, then stood and faced Jason and the man he held. "Ready boss," he whispered. "We'd better get moving. We've only got an hour till daylight at best."

Jason slipped his left hand back over his informant's mouth and slid his right hand inside the collar of the jacket for leverage. With quick and hard pressure from his thumb knuckle, Jason pinched off the blood flow through the carotid artery. Within two seconds, the man lay unconscious against Jason. He maintained pressure for another second, then released his hand from the collar and supported the man from behind while Steve fashioned a gag from the strips he'd made and stuffed it into the man's mouth, tying it tightly behind his head. They laid him face down on the ground. Jason brought out two more cable ties that he'd taken from Curly and handed one to Steve. Steve bound their captive's ankles while Jason bound his wrists behind his back. They dragged him to the corner of the porch and propped him up against one of the vine maples. Steve took another cloth strip and bound the man by the neck to the vine maple trunks. If he struggled when he came to, he would strangle himself.

"You got a plan?" Steve asked in a whisper.

"There's only one way in. I guess we walk in through the front door like we own the place and deal with what comes."

"That's a plan?"

"You have a better idea?"

"Nope," Steve answered, quietly. "I'll go in first. You count to three and come in. No sense in both of us getting cut to ribbons. You ready?"

"Let's do it... Steve," Jason whispered. "I want to take two of these slimeballs back, but don't take any chances."

"Count on it," he whispered.

With guns in hand, they boldly walked onto the porch. Jason opened the front door and Steve quickly entered. "One, ... ah, screw it," Jason muttered to himself, as he went through the door. He saw Steve's back as he disappeared around what he thought to be the kitchen entrance. He had no more than disappeared when Jason heard something crash to the floor, then the zip of two silenced 9mm rounds followed by the muffled ker-thump of a body hitting the floor.

At the same moment, Jason heard a commotion in the front bedroom. He spun with his gun sighted toward the hallway and the entrance to the front bedroom. In the hallway was Carol and a man behind her, with his arm tightly wrapped around her waist and a knife at the left side of her throat. Carol was taller than the man holding her and Jason could only see a small portion of the right side of his head.

"Oh God, Jason," her voice quivered.

Jason showed no emotion, but his heart raged at the sight of her. Carol's hands were bound behind her. She had been beaten and looked exhausted and defeated. Her beautiful red hair lay dull and matted, her face bruised and puffy. Her upper lip was split and a mouse under her left eye made her to appear to squint. The shirt she had commandeered from Jason on Wednesday clung, dirty, wrinkled and torn, and her white Bermuda shorts were smudged with dirt. She had bruises on her long legs with partially scabbed abrasions on both knees. What angered Jason the most was the teardrop of blood forming on the apex of the knife as the man spoke.

"Okay, asshole, just like in the movies. Drop the gun or the bitch smiles from ear to ear."

Jason stood motionless with his gun pointed into the entrance of the hallway. Without hesitation, his 10 mm exploded with a deafening bang. Instantly, blood and brains spattered the left wall of the hallway. The man and his knife fell away from Carol.

"This ain't the movies, asshole." The hollow point bullet from Jason's powerful weapon had ripped through the only portion of the man's head that he could see. Carol stood motionless and trembling as he rushed to her. She collapsed into his arms.

Jason heard the hysterical screaming of Jennifer in the next bedroom at the same time Steve rushed to the couple.

"Why don't you get a silencer for that goddamned thing," he scolded. Firing a sidearm in close quarters did not sound at all like the romantic bass sound in the movie theaters but produced a sharp, painful shock to the ears. The thunderous blast had scared Jennifer.

"Stay with Carol," Jason commanded. Leaving her in Steve's care, he rushed down the hall to Jennifer's locked door.

"Jennifer, honey, it's Jason," he said, as he tried the locked door.

"No! Stay away," she screamed in terror.

"It's okay, honey. Nobody's going to hurt you any more. It's Jason. I'm not going to let anyone hurt you. Now stay away from the door. There's no key. I have to break the door."

"Don't! Stay away," a still terrified voice shrieked from beyond the locked door.

With his back braced against the hall wall, his left foot shot forward against the door near the handle. The breaking door jam allowed the door to swing open. Jason found Jennifer huddled in a dark corner, trembling and sobbing in fear. She tensed as he touched her shoulder.

"Come on, honey. You're going to be all right," he said, picking her up off of the floor. He hugged her quivering body as she buried her face into his shoulder, continuing to cry. "It's all right now. It's okay. Just let it out; let it out. You'll be fine," he consoled in a quiet voice.

Jason wanted to give Jennifer all the time she needed, but could not afford to. They needed to return to the boat and fast. Reinforcements could arrive any moment, and they would soon lose the cover of darkness.

"Okay, honey, let's get you and Carol to someplace safe, where nobody can hurt you. We have to leave now before any more bad guys show up, okay?" Without a response from Jennifer, Jason carried her out into the living room to Carol and Steve, taking care to shield her from the body and blood in the hallway.

"How are we doing?" Jason asked, concerned about Carol's condition.

"Good. We're ready to travel," Steve replied.

Jason looked at Carol and asked. "Can you make it on your own?"

"I'll be fine," she said soberly.

"Let's get the hell out of here," Jason commanded.

"You lead and I'll follow with the package," Steve said, referring to the captured man outside. He knew Jennifer would not permit herself to be pried loose from Jason's arms.

Once outside, Steve cut the rag restraint from the still unconscious man, and picked him up fireman-style for transport to the boat. Jason led the way, taking a route along the fence of the military base to the waterfront. When they reached the water, he led them west to the inlet where the nearly invisible dark boat lay quietly in the calm, early-morning water.

By the time they reached the boat, both Carol and Jennifer were cold and shivering. Below deck, Steve poured them hot coffee and got them into blankets. Jason deposited their captive unceremoniously in the port side passenger bolster and quickly cast off the lines and stowed the fenders. He brought the boat out of Fleming Bay and headed east toward Oak Bay and the rendezvous with David, Debbie, and family.

CHAPTER TWENTY-SIX

The cottage appeared deserted as Jason approached the front porch; with curtains drawn, only a hint of light escaped to the outside. He knocked quietly; almost instantly David opened the door.

"Everybody ready?" Jason asked, entering past David. He came to an ashen-faced Debbie. Horror stared at him as her eyes took in his bruised and swollen face resembling green hamburger.

"Where's Jennifer?" she asked, in fear-fueled agitation.

"She's on the boat, waiting for you." Jason had purposely used the words *waiting for you*, hoping to spark a sense of urgency for an immediate departure.

"How is she? Is . . . she all right?"

"She's fine," Jason replied with some impatience.

David interrupted, reading Jason's desire to get under way. "We're packed with what we can carry, the house is locked down. Mrs. O'Connor, would you please wake the children?"

Debbie seemed momentarily confused, looking first at David for no more than a second, then back to Jason before she followed the instruction and silently turned toward the bedroom.

During Debbie's brief absence, David took inventory of Jason's physical condition. "How'd it go? Looks like you've been leading with your face."

Jason had only partially wiped the camo grease from his face enroute to Oak Bay. The remnants of grease did little to hide the beating that he had taken. "I've been in worse shape."

"You learn anything while you were playing punching bag?"

Debbie appeared with Tommy in her arms. Ashley followed closely behind as if walking in her sleep.

"I'll brief you in Port Angeles," he answered.

*　*　*　*　*

Once clear of the rocks, Jason brought the boat up on step taking a heading due south. Five miles out, at speed and with exhaust baffles open, Jason nudged Steve in the bolster next to him. "Your sister still have that beach house in Manzanita?"

"As far as I know." Steve looked questioningly at Jason. "Are you thinking what I think you're thinking?"

Jason nodded. "You think it's available?"

"Should be. She usually doesn't come back from Arizona until the end of May. I'll make the call when we get to Port Angeles." Jason simply nodded his approval.

Debbie joined them at the helm and Steve went forward to make room for her in the bolster.

"How's Jennifer?" Jason asked, after she settled in.

"I don't know," she replied, almost in tears. "She just sits on her bunk all curled up in the blanket and won't talk."

"Was she molested?"

"I don't know, Jason. I asked Carol. She doesn't think so, but she can't say for sure. Apparently she had her hands full with one of those creeps."

"I know," Jason said. The night vision masked his sad and troubled face.

Debbie looked silently out into the darkness for some time before she had the courage to ask, "Did you find out why these people are trying to—" her voice choked with anguish and she could not finish the question.

"Not yet. But we're getting closer to finding the answer. And now we'll get you back together with Jack and to a place where they can't reach you."

"Damn you, Jason! That's what you said when you took us to your cottage."

"I know," he said sadly. "But we know how they found Jennifer and we can keep it from happening again. And Steve and David will be with you."

"So what the hell are we supposed to do, have two strangers living with us for the rest of our lives? Spend the rest of our lives terrified?" She hesitated briefly before continuing. "I'm sorry Jason I seem to be taking my frustration out on you. I know you've been worried about Carol too. For your peace of mind, they didn't get her. She wasn't raped."

"Thanks, I appreciate knowing that."

Without warning, Debbie's demeanor changed. "I almost forgot the reason that I came up here. Tommy is wide awake and he wants to help his Uncle Jason drive the boat."

Jason preferred to have him forward below deck, but he thought, what the hell, if everything goes well, we'll be in Port Angeles in fifteen minutes or less. The clouds had thinned and a brilliant pink glow was building on the east horizon.

"Well you'd better get him up here. We'll be arriving in Port Angeles soon."

Debbie reappeared moments later with Tommy. He moved forward in his bolster, flipped the seat in place, and sat back, tucking Tommy into his lap. Tommy had a million questions, especially about the night vision. Jason did his best to explain, then gave up, took off the cumbersome apparatus and held it up for Tommy to look through.

While Tommy jabbered incessantly, Jason looked over at Debbie, sitting in the bolster next to him, her medium-length hair blowing straight back. Her eyes looked almost vacant as she stared ahead with uncertainty toward the lights of Port Angeles.

In another few minutes Jason switched the exhaust baffles on and slowed the boat. Three miles out, he handed Tommy back to Debbie and asked her to send Steve to him.

A moment later Steve slid into the bolster next to him. "What's up boss?"

"The minute we're docked, call your sister about the beach house."

"Will do."

"How long do you she could let us use it?"

"If I explain the situation, as long as we need it. There's no reason she can't stay in Arizona."

"Well, if we don't find out what the hell is going on, it could take a while."

"We'll work it out."

"What do you want to do with the geek?" Steve asked, nodding to their now-conscious captive who sat bound to the bolster with a hood over his head.

"Just before we dock, get everyone on deck. Then take him below and lash him to one of the berths. I don't want Carol, Deb, or the kids to have to look at him."

As Jason carefully maneuvered his boat to its temporary moorings, relief spread across his battered face when he spotted Joe Castellano standing on the wharf.

"Looks like a successful trip," Joe yelled, seeing Carol, Debbie, and Jennifer, who, still wrapped in the blanket, clung to her mother. Ashley and Tommy stood behind, unaware of the peril in which their sister and Carol had been.

"Mission accomplished," Jason replied. "How's Jack?"

"Jack's fine; he's up in the restaurant."

David and Steve secured the boat while the O'Connor family and Carol made their way toward the restaurant. Jack bolted anxiously towards his family from the rear of the dining area, and as they entered, Tommy broke away from his mother and ran to his dad.

"Daddy! Daddy! Uncle Jason let me drive his boat! We went real fast and I got to see through night visor goggles and everything," Tommy reported jumping into Jack's open arms. "I could see in the dark, Daddy!"

A few moments of frantic commotion ensued with Tommy vying for attention and Jack and Deb's panic over each other and their obvious distress for Jennifer. When Jason arrived moments later, he took Carol's hand and led her into the empty bar area of the restaurant. The early breakfast crowd had not yet arrived and the only audible sounds came from restaurant prep work and Tommy's exuberance. An uncomfortable silence befell the two until Jason finally spoke.

"Are you okay? God, Carol, I've been worried sick about you."

"I'll be fine," Carol responded with somber coolness. "Jason, what is going on? What in the hell is Jack involved in?"

"I have no idea, and he doesn't either. All I know is that someone thinks he's a threat. They're bad, Carol, real bad, and whoever the hell they are, they're well organized."

"How in God's name did they ever find out where we were?" Then . . . "Jennifer. It was Jennifer wasn't it?"

"Bingo. We can't be too hard on her, though. She didn't know what was happening."

At that moment Jason's interest lay more towards learning about Carol and her condition, but she seemed to steer the conversation towards the immediate situation.

"Jason, I know you need to question me about what happened and you don't have a lot of time, so don't tiptoe around. Ask me your questions and then maybe we'll have a little time to talk." Carol's frankness surprised Jason. He had a sudden urge to hold her and tell her he loved her, but he followed her lead.

"Thank you for understanding," he said, taking her cold hands. "Honey, you're freezing. Do you want some coffee?"

"I'd rather have some hot chocolate. I had enough coffee on the boat." He immediately left the table in search of a server.

"I ordered some chocolate and a light breakfast," he reported upon his return. "I guess we might as well get started. Are you ready?"

Carol nodded and began. "I don't know if you noticed Wednesday afternoon, but Jennifer was in a real snit. Apparently, she wanted to take her best friend Jane along on our little spur-of-the-moment vacation. Then on Wednesday evening, she made a scene about her goldfish and who would care for them. It happened while you and I went shopping for groceries. Remember when we returned, Jennifer was on the phone? Debbie had let her call Jane to make arrangements to feed the fish. Thursday morning Jennifer sneaked out to call Jane again. That's where she had been when she came back during our breakfast. Remember?"

Jason explained what he learned from Curly and how they had found the phone booth. "That's what I meant when I said they're well organized. How did they pick you up?"

"Jennifer took off Friday morning to call Jane before she left for school. After a half an hour, I went to look for her. I saw her in the phone booth and headed towards her. When she saw me she hung up. About the same time, a white van pulled up and a man jumped out and grabbed her."

Carol trembled as she recounted her ordeal. "Oh God, Jason, all I could think of was Melanie. I saw the terror in Jennifer's face and I could only see my Melanie being kidnapped. The guy held something over her nose and mouth and by the time I reached them she was unconscious. I hit that sonofabitch as hard as I could in the kidneys and he went down. The next thing I knew, someone kidney-punched *me* from behind. I couldn't breathe; then I felt a crack on my head and that's the last thing I remember until I woke up in that dump where you found us."

"Did they give you any indication what they were involved with?"

"No, nothing. They didn't use names. Just 'Yo this' and 'Yo that.'

"I came around to find the slime bag—the guy whose brains you left all over the wall back there—pawing me. From what I could determine, he appeared to be the leader of the foursome. I found it interesting that the other three didn't seem that much afraid of him. When he tried to get the others to hold me down, the guy you brought back with you told him to fuck off because rape wasn't what they were there for. I suppose I should be grateful for that much. At any rate, I spent most of my time fending off the perverted bastard. Thank God you showed up. I don't think I could have held out much longer."

A waitress approached with their breakfast, and they sat in silence while they ate toast and bacon, Carol warming herself with hot chocolate, and Jason deep in thought over his coffee. From time to time he would glance at Carol, wondering if she'd become hardened from this experience. He vowed to do all he could to make sure she wouldn't.

"As far as I know," Carol began again, "Jennifer remained locked in that bedroom and was never let out, not even to the bathroom. I think they gave her some water once."

"Did they ever communicate with anyone? Any telephone, cell phone, radio? Did anyone come or go?"

"Not to my knowledge. But I was unconscious until just a few hours before you arrived. All I know is, it was after eight in the morning when we were abducted and dark when I came around." Carol's demeanor had softened somewhat, when she asked, "You have to go now, don't you?"

"Soon, but I want to know how you are. You have some nasty-looking bruises."

"I'll be fine," she reassured him. "What about you? It looks like you took a couple of pretty good shots. How are you doing?"

"It's nothing that won't heal in time."

Jason glanced at his watch; he needed to meet with Jack, Steve, and David and return to Seattle.

"Jason," she said, interrupting his thought. "While that man mauled me, I hated him and I wanted to kill him with my bare hands. When you killed him, I was elated. Now I feel guilty for *not* feeling guilty for my feelings. I don't know if this makes any sense to you. What I'm trying to explain is, I think I'm beginning to understand what you meant when you talked about people who can't live within the norms of acceptable human behavior, the terrorists you spoke of. And I believe I'm beginning to understand the inner struggle you've spoken about."

"Here's a couple of insights that might help you. First, you mentioned that you feel guilty about *not* feeling guilty for your feelings. That comment deserves a response. It's a perfectly normal reaction. Time will help you sort that out. You, in fact, have nothing to feel guilty about."

Carol stood and leaned over the table to Jason. "I know you have things you need to do, but before you leave, take this with you. I love you and I'm won't turn my back and walk away." She walked around the table and pulled Jason to his feet, hugging him and kissing him hard on the lips, too hard.

They both flinched from their bruised lips, then Carol pulled her head back and laughed.

They walked towards the main part of the restaurant to join Jack and the others.

"Jason?" Carol paused for a moment with an inquiring look.

"What is it?"

"Did you ever give any thought to the possibility that you might have missed back in that hallway and hit *me*?"

"I never considered it."

"I'm not quite sure how I feel after that response," she said squeezing his hand. "I was scared, Jason—I was terrified."

Jason thought for a moment. "When in a crisis, I focus on what needs to be done. When I saw you, I felt mostly rage. I wanted you out of that situation in the quickest possible way and acted on pure reflex and adrenaline. I never considered that I might miss. I took my shot instinctively. I would not have hit you.

"When you saw the man grab Jennifer, what was your first emotion? Probably fear. But when you went to her rescue, what were you feeling? Probably nothing. You were doing what needed to be done; you were operating on instinct and adrenaline. The same thing occurred back in the hallway with me."

"Thank you." Carol said thoughtfully. Jason's last statement helped her understand the depth of this man, and she marveled at how quickly he had embraced the art of communication. "I guess the only difference," she continued, "is that your rescue didn't fail—mine did."

"Whoa! Hold on a minute! These were two completely different sets of circumstances. We had time to get control of the situation. You didn't. You were faced with a situation in which you had no time for preparation. On the other hand, we had time to prepare and make a plan. We didn't just walk in like we owned the place, you know. We were in control, and we had some good luck." (He hoped she never would have a chance to talk to Steve about their so-called plan.)

"It didn't feel like you were in control when that knife was slicing into my throat. And what luck?" she asked in puzzlement.

"Hell, you probably saved my life." Carol looked shocked and started to speak, but Jason continued on. "If that creep hadn't been so preoccupied with trying to get into your pants, as Sean Connery said in *The Untouchables*, 'he wouldn't have brought a knife to a gunfight.' He screwed up. If he had cut your throat, you would have been useless to him as a shield and I would have shot him. He was bluffing, stalling, waiting for his two buddies to show up, but they were outside, one asleep, the other dead." Jason shrugged palms up, as if to say, it's just as simple as that.

Jason and Carol joined the others and after brief conversation, Jack, Steve, David, and Joe Castellano disengaged themselves and returned to the bar with Jason. As they settled in at a table large enough to accommodate them, Jason looked across the table and studied Jack for a moment, then asked, "How's Jennifer?"

"I don't know. She's not talking much. She feels responsible for this whole mess. We still haven't told her what's going on," he said morosely.

Jason's heart went out to his friend, but he could not think of anything to say that wouldn't sound patronizing. He felt frustratingly useless. Then he brightened as a thought came to him. "I'll be busy with Dailey, then with a bit of interrogation of my own for the remainder of the day," he said, referring to the man in the boat. "But if you think it will help, I'd like to bring a psychologist down to meet with Jennifer and your family tomorrow."

"Down where?" Jack asked. "Where are you taking us?"

Jason looked questioningly to Steve.

"Joyce said we can have the house as long as we need it."

"Who the hell is Joyce?" Jack asked. The puzzlement and frustration creased his face.

"Joyce is Steve's sister. And in answer to your first question, she owns a beach house in a little Oregon coast town, Manzanita. That's where David and Steve will be taking you when you leave here."

"I'm beginning to feel like a Bedouin." Jack said.

Joe Castellano interrupted. "Jack, look, I know you're feeling like you're being manipulated, and in a sense you are. But, it's obvious that you and your family can no longer remain safely in the Seattle area, and I think Jason's idea about a psychologist is a good one."

Jack barely gave Joe a passing glance, then looked hard at Jason, his body rigid against the increasing bombardment of bizarre circumstances over which he appeared to have no control.

"I'm beginning to wonder if we'll ever be safe again—and you think a shrink will help?" The second the words passed his lips, he realized he had been staring angrily at his friend, whose swollen and battered face bore testament to what he himself had been spared. "Oh—Jay, I didn't mean . . ." Jack could not finish whatever thought he been struggling with.

If wounded, Jason gave no indication of it. In an uncharacteristic display of affection, he reached over and said, "Believe me, Jack, I do understand, only I didn't have a family to worry about."

Jack quickly looked up from the sanctuary of his hands, and the instant their eyes met, the frustration melted away. In that brief unspoken communication Jack knew that Jason had told the truth.

Without further hesitation or preamble, Jason launched into the events of the last nine hours. "I've confirmed that they want you dead, Jack. They're not about to question you and let you go. They think you have learned something and once they can confirm whether or not you have shared that information with someone, they'll kill you."

"What the hell do I know?" he asked incredulously.

"That's the question of the hour, and what we have to figure out," Jason responded dryly. He relayed in accurate detail everything that had happened from the time Curly and Slick picked him up in Jack's van. Jason told the group about the weapons, the filters, and plastic explosives and that Curly had admitted killing Jennings.

"I don't know anything about guns or filters or explosives." Jack said with a pained look.

"I know, buddy. We'll just have to go over everything again and again until we find something."

"I have a question," David said. "Why did they just walk up and whack Jennings without asking questions when they thought he was Jack, and now all of the sudden they want to question him before they kill him?"

"Because they now know that Jack knows they're trying to kill him. They need to find out who, if anybody, he's passed their information on to," Joe interjected.

"Exactly," Jason confirmed. "Jack, I can't help but think that you've stumbled across something during your work activities."

"I have no idea what it could be," he said, irritated.

"That's my point. You've stumbled across something, seen something, or collected some data that means nothing to you, but has compromised someone or some project. Let's look at what we've learned. There's this thing with Pathmoor. We know: there is a connection between Comstock, Biddwell Die Casting, and Suter. We also know there is an abandoned house in Issaquah full of small arms and explosives. That's where they took me for interrogation, so you're connected in some way to that situation, either through Suter, Biddwell, Cervicon, or something we haven't stumbled onto yet."

"Now wait a minute," David interrupted. "Does anybody think this could be another covert government thing? I mean the stuff you found you just don't buy at your local candy store."

"That's true," Steve said, "but it doesn't feel right. From what little of them I've encountered, it's more like they're wannabes."

"I agree," Jason said. "They don't have the polish. They're disciplined and organized, but they're definitely not government. The people we encountered in Victoria were no more than kids."

"What are we talking here, a militia group?" David asked. Steve shrugged as if to say, "We don't know, you tell us."

"Jack, the night they killed Jennings, you got a phone message from Martin Cray. He said it was important that you call him. Did you ever find out what he wanted?" Jason asked.

"No, I didn't. Are you thinking there's a connection?"

"At this point, I'm not connecting anything, but I still think you stumbled onto something, during one of your onsite design exercises. I want you to think about how you approach your clients, the way you interface with them and survey the sites. Tomorrow when I come down to Manzanita, we can talk about it."

Jason looked at his watch, an obvious signal that he wanted to get under way. "Don't forget we have a good source for information that we haven't tapped yet sitting right here in the boat. I'll be interrogating him the minute I get him to The Kennel. And there won't be a mark on him when I turn him over to Dailey."

"Aaah yes, the old 'truth juice,'" Steve quipped.

Jason looked again at his watch and Joe responded to the action. "I think we have accomplished all we can for now. Jason obviously needs to get back. We won't learn anything more until he has a crack at our package in the boat. And you," he looked at David and Steve, "have a long drive ahead of you—about seven hours." He reached into his jacket pocket and removed an envelope, then passed it to Jack. "You'll need money when you get to Manzanita. There's two thousand dollars. Don't buy anything on credit. You are strictly cash only. And don't shop in the same place all the time. It'll be best if you and your family monitor your outside activities. You're not in seclusion, but use some discretion; David and Steve know the ropes. Now, if there's nothing else, let's call it a wrap. We all need to get going."

* * * * *

Before Jason left the restaurant, he bought a sweet roll and coffee to go. At the boat, he checked his passenger. After casting off, he idled slowly away from the port, then pushed the throttles forward bringing the boat up on step and cruised on an east-northeast heading. After traveling about ten miles, he dropped the boat speed, letting it settle to an idle and went forward to bring his prisoner aft. He removed the man's hood and freed his hands so he could relieve himself over the side, then led him to the port-side bolster. Jason tied him to the bolster at the waist and ankles with a length of rope, then gave him the coffee and roll, informing him if he so much as thought about trying anything, it would be the last thing he would ever do. Once again, Jason brought the boat up to speed and headed for

Seattle and his meeting with Lt. Dailey and Bob Montgomery. The bright sun and calm water held promise for a beautiful day. Ordinarily, Jason would revel in these conditions, but what spoiled it for him were the circumstances and the memory of Curly's words about Jack. "He knows something." He hoped his passenger would have the answer.

CHAPTER TWENTY-SEVEN

Lt. Dailey and Montgomery walked up four wooden steps and rang the doorbell of a charming white-framed two-story house in West Seattle. A young woman with short, platinum hair and enough rings in her left ear to supply a fishing tackle shop for a year answered the door. A mostly open, ugly-brown velour robe two sizes too large, draped her neon white body. Dailey would have stared at her overexposure had he not been exhausted. Montgomery stared anyway.

"Yeah?" she said. Her sour greeting gave the impression they were a great source of irritation. Dailey sincerely hoped they would be.

"Is Mr. Pathmoor in?" Dailey asked.

She turned without responding, partially closed the door and yelled, "Dad, there's someone here to see you."

"At this time of the morning? Who is it?" came an ill-tempered voice from somewhere within the bowels of the house. The house didn't have nearly the charm it had when they'd parked in front just minutes before.

The door swung open exposing an annoyed Richard Pathmoor. Surprise spread over his face, but he recovered and demanded, "What is it, Lieutenant? I don't appreciate having you interrupting my weekend at 8 a.m. on Saturday morning." Pathmoor wore a robe and slippers of the same color and vintage as his daughter's. A family dress code? Montgomery wondered.

"Well, Mr. Pathmoor, *I* don't appreciate having to be here at 8 a.m. on Saturday morning. This is my partner, Robert Montgomery. Now, may we come in or would you like to come downtown for our visit?"

Pathmoor flushed, started to speak, then reconsidered, remembering his prior encounter with Dailey. "Lieutenant, I have already told you that I have no knowledge of any attempts on Mr. O'Connor's life. And, I might add, I haven't heard from him since our conversation on Thursday."

"That's all well and good, and I appreciate your honesty, but you still haven't answered my question. Here or downtown?" Dailey persisted.

"Come in, if you must." Pathmoor's tone of voice made it clear they were about as welcome as a mother-in-law on a honeymoon. He led them through the house to a patio in the rear. "Wait here," he said curtly, "while I get some clothes on." He turned on his heels and vanished into the house.

They sat in cheap plastic chairs on a small patio in the midst of a tightly manicured yard. Three vibrant red azaleas set a spectacular contrast to the deep-green well-fertilized lawn. Flowerbeds filled with hothouse grown color spots of geraniums, petunias, and impatiens created an unexpectedly peaceful sanctuary.

Pathmoor returned quickly, still in his slippers but dressed in jeans and a tee shirt. He seated himself opposite Dailey and Montgomery.

"Now, what's so damn important?"

"Mr. Pathmoor," Dailey began. "As you have already mentioned this morning, you are well aware of Mr. O'Connor's situation." Pathmoor nodded. "Tell me please, when you last had personal contact with him"

"A week ago yesterday, I think. Yes I'm sure it was last Friday."

"And you had no contact with him over the weekend?"

"No."

"Sunday night, a man called O'Connor's home, claiming to be a co-worker. He said he needed to see him right away. Do you know who that might have been?"

"No, I have no idea."

Dailey and Montgomery both watched Pathmoor intently, looking for any sign of a reaction, no matter how subtle. The only thing they detected for certain was fear.

"That same night," Dailey continued, "Martin Cray called Mr. O'Connor's house and left a message with Mrs. O'Connor, saying he needed O'Connor to contact him. Do you know what that might have been about?"

"I have no idea, Lieutenant. I guess you'll have to ask him."

"Well, Mr. Pathmoor, that brings me to my next question. When I talked with you Thursday evening, you told me Mr. Cray was on vacation. I guess I need a little help on just where he went, along with dates, if you please."

"Well, er, uh," he stammered. "I don't know that. I just assumed he was on vacation because I hadn't seen him in a while."

Both Dailey and Montgomery caught the rapid blinking as Pathmoor answered the last question.

"Have you seen him since our meeting on Thursday, Mr. Pathmoor?"

"No."

"When was the last time you saw him?" Dailey pressed.

"I don't know exactly—maybe three weeks. Hell, I don't remember, maybe a little less. Since he retired, he just comes and goes whenever it suits him."

There it is again, Dailey said to himself, as the blinking became quicker.

"And you have no idea what was so important that he needed to call Jack O'Connor's home at ten o'clock on a Sunday evening?" Montgomery asked.

"No, I already told you. You'll have to ask him."

"Unfortunately, it's a bit of a problem," Dailey responded. Deep wrinkles furrowed his brow. "Not forty minutes ago, I received conformation that Martin Cray and his wife Martha have been identified as the victims of what's being termed for now 'a sailing accident.'"

"You're not serious! Is this some sort of joke, Lieutenant?" Pathmoor's face went pale with shock.

"No, Mr. Pathmoor, this is no joke. And it's very important that we find every bit of information about his activities prior to his leaving on this so-called vacation of his."

While Dailey spoke, Montgomery watched Pathmoor's face and body language for any further signs of his disingenuousness.

"What kind of sailing accident? What happened?"

"As I said, Mr. Pathmoor, only for the time being is it being called an accident." Dailey let his statement hang, watching his quarry intently until the full impact found its mark.

Disbelief, then renewed fear, spread across Pathmoor's face. He remembered Dailey's vocation. A homicide detective. Dailey had made that point very clear during their first meeting, and this time he had brought another detective with him. A wave of nausea swept through him as he realized the implications. He shuddered as he spoke. "You're not suggesting they . . . they . . . they were murdered!?"

"It's not a suggestion, Mr. Pathmoor," Montgomery said.

"What possible reason could anyone have for killing him?" Pathmoor asked, still in shock. "I mean, a boating accident can happen. What makes you think he was murdered?" In spite of the cool morning, droplets of perspiration formed on Pathmoor's upper lip and forehead.

"I will answer your last question first," Dailey said. "Yesterday morning, a ferry captain spotted what looked to be the wreckage of a boat west of Mukilteo. He radioed the Everett harbormaster who investigated and identified the wreckage as that of the *Miss Martha*, Cray's boat. The harbormaster called the Everett police chief, Craig Austin, who happens to be a personal friend of the Crays. Austin and I are also good friends; he called me for some help during the investigation because he didn't like what he saw.

"You see, Mr. Pathmoor, Bob and I spent the entire day on the water in Mukilteo picking up bits and pieces of boat wreckage. The harbormaster would like to write it off as carelessness, a propane explosion that could have been prevented. But Mr. Austin disagrees, and I concur. You see, Cray's boat, a forty-eight-foot sailboat, is—or—was too big a boat to be taken apart by a propane leak. Propane could have caused an explosion, all right, and there would have been an accompanying fire, which there was, but not enough. No, this boat was taken apart from stem to stern. As far as the Crays are concerned, they're bits and pieces as well. That's why it took so long for the ID.

"We, Bob and I, brought some of the wreckage back with us and did some testing. Guess what we found?" Pathmoor shook his head silently. Sweating profusely now, his eyes darted back and forth between Dailey and Montgomery. "Nitrates, Mr. Pathmoor, the same residue you would find from plastic explosives. So, you see, it wasn't an accident, Mr. Pathmoor. Martin and Martha Cray were murdered."

"Now, in response to your first question, Mr. Pathmoor: 'What possible reason would anyone have for killing Mr. Cray?' Let's look at that," Montgomery said. "We're trying to find out who would want Jack O'Connor dead. And quite honestly, so far, we're not coming up with a hell of a lot. But let me ask you this, with Martin Cray out of the way, who would be in line to take over Cervicon?"

"I... I don't know. I guess Jack O'Connor. I hadn't given it any thou—" Pathmoor started off slowly as if to be deep in concentration. Then, he once again seized what he perceived to be another opportunity to put O'Connor in a bad light. "Oh yes, I see what you mean. You don't suppose that he killed Cray—so he could take over the company?

"You mustn't forget," Montgomery interrupted, "that O'Connor is also a target. Now, who would be in line to take over if Cray and O'Connor were both out of the picture?"

"I wouldn't be surprised if all this stuff with O'Connor is just a smoke screen in an attempt to get control of—" Pathmoor stopped in mid-sentence as he noticed the two men staring intently at him with obvious disdain. Glancing back and forth between their penetrating gazes, he realized he had talked himself into another setup.

"Wait just a damn minute! You, you—" he stammered, his voice reaching the ridiculous squeak Dailey had remembered from their first meeting. "You don't think that I'm involved in this? You can't!"

"Sure we can," Dailey shot back. "And right now you look to be a pretty good suspect. You certainly have the motive—with O'Connor and Cray out of the way, you could have your way with Suter and Cervicon. A real coup d'état."

"You can't be serious!" Pathmoor sputtered.

"Why don't you give us an accounting of your activities, say, for the last two weeks," Montgomery suggested.

"I don't believe this. I don't have to put up with this shit, no way." Pathmoor jumped out of his chair and, shouting at the two men, he stood over them shaking.

Unfazed by the tirade, Dailey asked calmly, "Do you want to finish this here or downtown?"

Once again Richard Pathmoor's complexion, like a sickly chameleon, changed from scarlet to chalk white. Then, defeated, he returned to his chair. To the best of his recollection, he told the two officers about his activities during the last two weeks. He gave them names of people who could substantiate some of what he had given them.

Dailey looked at his watch occasionally. He wanted to wrap it up quickly as he an appointment with Jason in just over an hour. But Pathmoor was lying—and he wanted to know why.

"Last Wednesday, you had words with Mr. O'Connor. Would you care to enlighten us?

"What words?" Pathmoor asked, once again being caught off guard.

"Don't be coy," Dailey snapped. "We didn't just totter over here without doing our homework."

Agitated, Pathmoor replied, "I called him at Biddwell Die Casting in Portland. He's working on a job down there. I told him that I needed him back in Seattle to help with some business up here. He refused. In spite of what you think, Lieutenant, he's not all that easy to work with. Then you show up at my office and tell me that someone's trying to kill him. I haven't seen O'Connor since he left."

"What was your position at Suter?" Montgomery asked.

"Market research. I believe I explained that to the Lieutenant last Thursday. Why?"

Montgomery smiled, as if remembering some private joke. "How is it that a person in marketing would land a job as an operations manager?"

Pathmoor mustered some courage. "This is harrassment, pure and simple." Montgomery's observation apparently had struck a chord, but he stood his ground. "I think I've had enough of this. I want you out of my house, now! And, Lieutenant, if you're going to take me downtown, do it. I'll be happy to have my attorney to sit in."

Dailey doubted they would learn anything more.

* * * * *

"I want him watched," Dailey told Montgomery as they pulled from the curb. "I want men on him so close we'll know how many pieces of toilet paper he uses. He's dirty and I want him."

"We'll get him," Montgomery said. "Somehow there's a way to tie it all together. He lied about when he last saw Martin Cray."

"True," Dailey affirmed. "But, dammit, it still doesn't prove anything. We need proof! First thing Monday morning I want to get someone from research on this full time. I want a complete history—friends, jobs, bank records. I want to know everything about this guy. But until Monday, twenty-four-hour surveillance. When we get back, get Thompson and Dolan on him."

"Consider it done," Montgomery said. "You know, I was just thinking. Brisben seems to have some good contacts. Maybe he could nose around also. It couldn't hurt."

"I'm not so sure," Dailey countered. "After his little escapade last night, I think it might be time to put him out to pasture. This whole thing is getting out of hand. I get the feeling we've got storm clouds in the area—and he's a tornado who touches down whenever and wherever he pleases."

Montgomery fell silent. He liked Jason, but he knew the lieutenant had a valid point.

Dailey turned pensive during the remainder of the drive. They were to meet with Jason in fifteen minutes. What really had gone on out in Issaquah, he wondered. This man is walking destruction. How in hell would he explain all this to his captain? His mind filled with the gravity of the ramifications he faced for allowing a civilian to be involved in a case rapidly spiraling out of control. He pictured himself in a huge vortex:

Water was circling, then gravitating towards the bottomless black funnel-shaped hole at its center, and he was being sucked helplessly to oblivion.

* * * * *

Low fuel prevented Jason from making a hard charge back to Seattle so by the time the skyline came into view, he would hard pressed to make his ten o'clock appointment with Dailey. With the situation at the Issaquah and the rescue in Victoria, the die had been cast. With little consideration to the costs or consequences, Jason had made the transition from helpful citizen to vigilante, and there could be no turning back. To his way of thinking, Jack and his family were very high stakes; they were too much to risk.

He had contacted Ben DiAngelis at his home while enroute and asked for help. He needed Keller to sedate his prisoner when he arrived. He also need someone to watch him twenty-four hours a day. Much to his relief, Jason soon learned that Ben had picked up Pat Krieger and Miguel Macias at Boeing Field earlier that morning and taken them directly to The Kennel, solving the problem of having to find someone to watch their prisoner.

Jason also asked that Keller be available later in the day to assist in the interrogation of their prisoner. He would not allow Dailey access to his prisoner. Jason knew Dailey would be a force to reckon with, given his activities of the past sixteen hours and the tough interrogation awaiting him. But he also knew he could ill afford to be excluded, if he were to turn the prisoner over. The body count stood now at nine and he personally had been responsible for five of the deaths. Dailey would have little choice but to shut him out, or shut him down completely.

* * * * *

At The Kennel, Keller rose from his chair, across from the sofa where Pat Krieger and Miguel Macias were seated and accompanied Jason and the prisoner to the bedroom he had prepared. They laid the man on the bed, then cut the left sleeve of his jacket to expose his arm. This allowed Keller access to administer enough sedative to render the man helpless for several hours. Jason and Keller stood over him until the drug had a chance to carry him to the world of tranquillity. Jason removed the man's blindfold and Keller checked the man's pulse and pupils, whereupon he announced, "He's in there, but he won't be causing any trouble."

As much as Jason would have liked to reminisce with comrades he had not seen in over five years, his impending inquisition made it impossible. Pat Krieger, still a short, stocky man, appeared a bit rounder than Jason remembered. He had the same sparkling blue eyes and curly red hair, only now with sandy gray interspersed and the sheen of balding showing through. Jason embraced the still rock-solid man and commented on a new appendage that hung over his belt.

"Hey now, don't let looks deceive! My overdeveloped abs are bulletproof. I got a lot invested here," he said with a jovial smile, affectionately patting his belly.

"My concern is your ability to crawl on your belly without your butt being a target, since it looks to me that it might be up in the air a ways," Jason said, not entirely joking.

"Don't you be worrying about my ass getting shot off, pretty boy. I can still take care of it just fine." Pat's comeback brought a round of laughter.

Conversely, Miguel had not changed in the slightest. He remained tall and lean with impeccable posture, and the same dark complexion and shiny black hair now hanging to the base of his neck. His soft, dark, brooding eyes never really let you know his thoughts; his soft spoken and gentle appearance had deceived many.

"It's been a long time, Commander," he said softly. "How you been?"

The two men held each other's gaze for a moment, then embraced. "I've been well," Jason answered.

* * * * *

Other than being informed by Miguel of the death of Larry Bennett, the sixth remaining team member, Jason remembered little of the drive from Tukwila to Seattle. What he had done during the past hours came as naturally to him as birds take to flying, but how to justify it to Dailey? His preoccupation with the series of events burned through his mind and left little room for his short commute. How would he explain away the hole in Curly's foot? It seemed justifiable; he needed information and he got it. To the police it would be deemed torture. The fact that the sonofabitch had walked up to a perfect stranger and sliced his heart open, well, that doesn't matter. Even murderers have rights under the law.

Rights, laws, what the hell, Jason thought. He got out of the car and looked at his watch at ten minutes past ten. Ten minutes late for his inquisition. As he walked through the door, the picture of Lori Phillips and Carston Jennings lying in the parking lot flashed hotly through his mind once again. "And the creep didn't even know why he'd killed him," he said aloud. The man exiting the building turned and looked at Jason as if he were nuts.

CHAPTER TWENTY-EIGHT

The dull green, claustrophobic room had no windows, little ventilation if any, and irritating florescent lights. As Jason sat in the hard chair waiting for Dailey and Montgomery to settle, it hit him—his twenty-sixth hour without sleep. A mixture of fatigue and pain pressed in upon him making him acutely aware of his vulnerability. One side of his face throbbed and ached. When he moved his jaw, sharp pain shot to the top of his head like an electric current. Breathing was a painful necessity. With every breath, he felt Curly's foot attempting to penetrate his rib cage. The effects of the punishment Curly had inflicted were in full bloom, and what lay ahead for Jason would be mentally and emotionally taxing as well.

Lieutenant Dailey, armed with files, a notepad, and his tape recorder finally settled himself. Montgomery closed the door. They were ready.

"Why don't you begin?" Dailey said.

Jason began by telling them about Debbie's call on Friday morning and how they had waited for a phone call from the kidnappers. Then he launched into the details of the previous evening.

Dailey immediately interrupted. "Why weren't we notified when you got the call from the kidnappers?" He did not show any anger; he was calm. But his clear disapproval indicated to Jason the need to proceed carefully.

"The message we received said specifically not to notify you. We didn't know if there were leaks in your communication system or not," Jason explained. "It was the second time they had warned us, mentioning you by name, and there wasn't time to go around your switchboard to locate you. I assumed they got your name from Sam Wellington before he went up in smoke. I wasn't about to take chances."

Dailey looked unimpressed with the logic, but a motion of his hand signaled Jason to continue. He gave selective information up to the time he had met with Montgomery in the parking lot of The Box Car, then stopped.

Dailey made no response for several long moments. He did not look angry, as Jason had expected, but perplexed. His left hand stroked his scruffy beard and his eyes vacillated back and forth several times from the few notes he had taken to intense eye contact with Jason. Jason glanced briefly at Montgomery who also looked puzzled.

"Tell me once again about your interrogation of this man you call 'Curly,'" Dailey quietly asked.

Dailey's contemplative cautious demeanor unnerved Jason, and he became unsure of how much to tell. He knew Dailey would want to know all the details: the bullet hole in Curly's foot, the bullet hole in the chair. Naturally he hadn't told everything the first time around.

"He, I call him 'Curly,' told me he and his buddy did Jennings and Phillips in the parking lot, obviously an attempt to impress me. Then he beat the shit out of me for a while; he got sloppy; then I beat the shit out of him for a while. About that time his buddy came in through the door flashing his gun and I popped him. I tied Curly to the chair and went into the kitchen to clean up. When I came back, I roughed him up some more and he told me where Jennifer and Carol were. About that time, another one of his buddies showed up, someone I hadn't seen before. I hid; he came in and popped Curly; I hid in the stairwell, and, like I said, the guy started shooting up the place. I got lucky and came out low and hit him with two rounds. After checking the rest of the house, I set Curly's piece by his body when I left."

Jason realized that he had trapped himself. He knew during the investigation the police would quickly learn that Curly's weapon had been fired at least six times, not the four he'd claimed. He had hoped to blame the hole in Curly's foot on the guy who killed him; and what about the hole in the chair? He waited for the question. It never came.

"Let's talk again about the armor that you found upstairs," Dailey directed. He remained calm, but his air of frustration betrayed a hidden agenda.

Jason described the weapons, explosives, and filters in detail, information that he knew would leave Dailey no choice but to bring the Feds into it. That would complicate Dailey's life as well as his own. The Feds would want to know how he had stumbled onto a large cache of arms, and Dailey would have problems with the Feds well as his boss.

After nearly two hours the room became a stifling, stench-filled sweatbox. Jason was soaked, and tired, and sore, and most of all, confused. Dailey's passive manner did not make sense. He fully expected the third degree by a cranky policeman in the throes of a full-blown tirade. Has he gone soft? Jason wondered. Not likely. The only facial expressions Dailey or Montgomery exhibited communicated confused frustration.

"How did things go on Vancouver Island?" Montgomery asked.

"Things went well," Jason answered, determined to divulge a minimum of information. "We went into an area just west of Victoria, extracted Jack's daughter and Carol, then split. Jack's family is reunited and Carol's with them."

"Where are they now?" Montgomery inquired.

"Safe," Jason responded.

"And you met no resistance?" Dailey asked. He continued to fondle his beard with his left hand and doodled on his notepad with the other.

"Minimal," Jason replied.

"Minimal?" Dailey questioned suspiciously. He rubbed his lips with the backside of the fingertips as if in deep thought. Jason sat, waiting for Dailey's next move. A few seconds passed. "Now, refresh my memory, Mr. Brisben. What kind of a weapon did you say you killed Curly's friends with?"

"Lieutenant," Jason began, with no attempt to mask his irritation. "I've told you twice now, Curly had a Colt 357 Python. I used his weapon. My fingerprints are all over it. I don't know what game you're playing, but why don't you get on with it? I'm hungry, I'm tired, I'm damn sore, and I want to go home and get some sleep."

"We don't have the weapon, Jason," Montgomery said. Dailey immediately spun his head around, giving his partner an angry look.

"What the hell are you talking about? What do you mean you don't have his gun?" Jason quickly leaned across the table. His eyes flashing between the two men across from him.

"Sorry, boss," Montgomery said. "I just figured it was time to get this moving." Dailey, angry at towards his partner, said nothing.

"Will someone tell me what the hell is going on!" Jason shouted and rose from his chair.

Dailey stared at Montgomery a bit longer as if to make his point. Then he slowly turned to Jason who now stood leaning across the table above him. Dailey looked up at him.

"We found no 357 Colt Python, Mr. Brisben. We found no other 357 magnum, no Mac 10, no bodies, no 120 filters, and no 244 M16's."

A look of astonishment swept over Jason's face. "What the hell are you talking about, Lieutenant? I was there! I didn't just dream this up." Jason slowly sat down. His frustration mounted as he looked back and forth between Dailey and Montgomery. "What gives! Come on, talk to me, dammit!"

"The place was cleaned out, Jason," Montgomery said. "Cleaner than an operating room."

"Well, not quite," Dailey interrupted. "We found some blood stains that they'd made a hurried attempt to clean up and enough nitrate residue to give our sniffer dog terminal hay fever. We found holes in the stairwells for the hardware for the trip wires, and the door jamb and the door to the upstairs were shot up just as you said." He paused for a moment, then shrugged. "So, what do you think happened?"

"What do I think happened!" Jason said, shocked at the question. "How the hell should I know? How long did it take you to get up there?" Jason suddenly realized his last question sounded like an accusation. He needed to calm down and think clearly. Dailey had put him through two and a half hours of questioning, when he could have told him right off what had happened. If it had not been for Montgomery, he would probably still be getting grilled. His instinct told him Dailey was cutting him out of the information loop so he felt justified in his decision to take his prisoner to The Kennel.

"You have to remember, Mr. Brisben," Dailey began, "it's not as simple as just driving straight up there. That territory is out of our jurisdiction. First we had to get the cooperation from the authorities in Issaquah. They arrived first on the scene at 3:45. We arrived at 3:59. The place was clean when they got there, and they encountered no traffic headed their way when they went in."

"So how did they get the place cleaned out so quick?" Montgomery questioned.

Jason sighed, his head clearing. "The only thing I can figure is they intended to take Jack up there to question him, then kill him. When they found me instead, they probably didn't want to chance being compromised so they cleaned house. They could have been scrambling to get a cleaning crew together at the same time the new guy came back and capped Curly. It would probably have only taken four or five men twenty or thirty minutes to clean the place out."

"Did you see any traffic on your way out?" Dailey asked.

"No, none to speak of. I was nervous about that because Jack's van would have been easy to spot with its front end all caved in. I only saw two cars until I got to I-90. I didn't see any trucks—and it would have taken a good-sized van to haul all that stuff."

"Why they didn't torch the place after they cleaned it out?" Montgomery mused.

"They may have wanted to, but ran out of time. They could have had spotters to watch for cops," Dailey said quietly.

"We'd've seen 'em coming out if they had cut it that close," Montgomery said.

"Not necessarily. If they had spotters like the lieutenant suggested, they probably went out through Redmond."

"Well it doesn't matter how they did it. The fact is, they're gone and we're left with an old house full of stale air," Dailey snapped, now back in his cranky form. "We got nothing."

Jason breathed a sigh of relief. If they had cleaned out the Issaquah house, they had probably cleaned out the Victoria house also. That should cut the hassle factor for him to about zero. But once again, Dailey changed direction and caught him off guard.

"I need you to bring O'Connor in."

"I'll be perfectly honest with you, Lieutenant. I can't bring him in. He hasn't arrived at his destination. And I wouldn't bring him in if I could."

The look between Dailey and Montgomery confirmed to Jason he was now on the outside. "Believe me, Mr. Brisben, I understand how you feel. But you have to understand our position." Dailey went on to explain all of the things Jason had already gone over several times in his mind: Dailey's boss had forbidden him to let a civilian get involved. The FBI had become involved—by law they had to be notified of the car bombing. The M16 Jason had given Montgomery earlier that morning would also have to be turned over to the Feds. It would be done later today.

"Brisben, I like you and I realize your only goal in this whole mess is to protect your friend and his family, and I appreciate that. In a sense we've had a stroke of luck here. We found no bodies in Issaquah, so I think we can keep you out of this mess. But I won't be able to do that much longer if you're out there mucking about. As far as the Feds are concerned, you probably would rather they didn't know you've had any part in this, but, and make no mistake about this, if they get wind of your involvement, they'll slap you with obstruction of justice. And there's one other thing. If you screw me over, I'll be all over you like green on grass. It is imperative that I meet with O'Connor. Do we understand each other?"

"Perfectly, Lieutenant." Jason appreciated Dailey's little speech. And Dailey was right about the Feds. Jason also knew the lieutenant's case was a long way from being solved, and that meant he still needed Jason's help. In fact, he could tell Dailey had been somewhat disingenuous, just as Jason had been and would continue to be. From here on out, it would be a subtle chess match—information traded for information gained. Dailey needed O'Connor, and Jason had him.

"I'm glad we have an understanding." Dailey said, sounding pleased. "Then let's get back to business. I need you to bring Mr. O'Connor in," he repeated.

"No way in hell, Lieutenant," Jason said without hesitation. He knew Dailey needed information. Dailey had found something and withheld the information. The chess match had begun. "He's safe now, and that's the way he's going to stay."

"May I remind you, Mr. Brisben, that you thought O'Connor's family would be safe before, and look how that turned out," Dailey snapped.

Jason fell into an instant rage, and struck back with a cruel accusation. "You two in this room were the only ones I told about his family being at Oak Bay, Lieutenant. And your people were supposed to protect Lori Phillips. Safe? Don't you talk to me about safe. Like I said, he's safe and he'll stay safe. Unless you have a damn good reason, he is staying put."

Dailey turned crimson. He jumped out of his chair and looked down at Jason. "How's this for a reason, mister. I'll march your butt into a cell and you can sit on your proverbial hard ass until you tell me where he is."

"Go for it, Lieutenant," Jason shot back, shooting to his feet with such force his chair flew back, crashing into the wall. The two men now came nose to nose. "Not without a damn good reason."

"Dammit, you two!" Montgomery shouted, slamming his fist to the table. "For Crissakes, look at you. You figure we got time for this shit? The people we're looking for sure as hell do! Why don't you tell him, Lieutenant? It'll be a real kick in the nuts for him to read about it in tomorrow's paper."

Jason glanced at Montgomery and then quickly back to Dailey, the policeman's face still inches from his own. "Tell me what, Lieutenant? What is so important that's worth risking bringing Jack back into the city?" A long silence followed.

"Tell him, Mort, or I'll tell him myself," Montgomery said as if giving an order to his boss. Dailey did not speak. His eyes still locked with Jason's, and Jason saw nothing but stubborn determination looking back.

"You shut your damn gob, Bob," Dailey shouted, hotly, his face crimson.

"Tell him, Lieutenant." Montgomery repeated once again, but this time in supplication. Again a palpable silence followed.

"Mr. Brisben," Dailey finally began, his stare still intense but with a somewhat softened voice, "the bodies of Martin and Martha Cray were found yesterday up out of Mukilteo in amongst the wreckage of their boat. They were murdered."

Jason felt a twinge in his knees and his breath left him as surely as if he had received a blow to the solar plexus. He held Dailey's gaze momentarily, then turned to pick up his chair and sat down with his head in his hands. What does this latest development mean? he asked himself. Did Cray stumble onto the same thing that Jack had? Now the phone call from Cray took on new importance. But what the hell did it mean? Which part of the puzzle? How would he ever fit the pieces? he wondered. Exhaustion pressed heavily in on him. The body count now stood at eleven, and none of the men in the room had any idea of where this mess was headed.

"What happened?" he asked quietly.

Dailey recapped the details of the previous day, related the details of the morning's meeting with Pathmoor, and then told Jason he and his partner both thought Pathmoor was involved.

"At the very least, he lied about when he had last seen Cray," Dailey said. "That, Mr. Brisben, is why I need to talk to O'Connor, and quickly."

"It's too risky," Jason insisted. "Lieutenant, why does he have to come to Seattle? If I can arrange for you to talk to him on a secured line, wouldn't that be satisfactory?"

"I suppose it would. But how do you propose to do that?"

"At the offices of Castellano, DiAngelis, and Partner. I can set it up for tomorrow."

"I hoped talk to him before then," Dailey said.

"Can we agree that it's an acceptable alternative to my bringing Jack back to Seattle? Because, under the best circumstances, it would be impossible to get Jack back here before late tomorrow evening. So do we have a deal?"

Montgomery sat back in his chair, shaking his head in amazement at the way Jason had maneuvered the situation. Dailey tugged the ends of his beard again, thinking. His gaze never left Jason. He appeared to be weighing every aspect of the offer, looking for pitfalls, hidden conditions, or a trap of some sort.

"No strings attached, Lieutenant," Jason offered, as if reading his mind.

"I guess we have a deal. How soon will I be able to talk to him?" he asked without hesitation.

"Three o'clock tomorrow afternoon. That's the best I can do."

Dailey accepted the time without argument but asked, "How soon will you be able to contact Jack?"

"I honestly I'm not sure, Lieutenant," Jason said, artfully sidestepping the issue. "Jack won't be at his destination for several hours yet." Then Jason played what he hoped would be his trump card for getting out of the interrogation room. "If I'm to be able to make any of this happen, I'll need get started coordinating it all."

"Understood. You're free to go." Surprised, Jason stood.

"Oh, Mr. Brisben, just one thing before you leave," Dailey said. Jason glanced questioningly at Montgomery who immediately shrugged as if to say, "I have no idea." "Just so you don't think we're totally incompetent," Dailey continued, "we found a couple of curious things up in Issaquah."

"What were they?" Jason asked, guessing the direction Dailey would take.

"We pulled up a couple of sections of the floor and it seems as though ballistics removed a 38 slug from each section. Looks like they could have been fired from a 357. And to top that off, one of the samples had a lot of blood on it and tissue and bone fragments in the hole. You have any ideas on that?"

"Not a one, Lieutenant."

* * * * *

Too many things and too little time in which to do them consumed Jason's weary mind as he rocketed vertically to the forty-third floor of the tower. Getting the partners to finish ferreting out every shred of information that existed on Pathmoor and Comstock became the number one priority. Now Martin Cray would be added to the list. There had to be a common thread linking the threesome. When they found the link, they might be able to tie it to Issaquah and possibly the reason why Cray was killed. Then there would be hope for Jack. Jason began to think, the more information he acquired the less he knew.

Next, he needed to contact Laura, and persuade her to give up her relaxing vacation for an all-expenses-paid work trip to Manzanita, Oregon, for God only knew how long. It looked to be a tough sell.

The interrogation of the prisoner at The Kennel had been scheduled to begin as soon as he finished his business with the partners. Jason remained hopeful that his prisoner would unlock the riddle, and looked forward to joining Keller and the rest at The Kennel. Damn, he thought, I wish I weren't so tired.

CHAPTER TWENTY-NINE

In the pre-dawn darkness, the black abyss of the Columbia River snaked along several hundred feet below them as Jason drove across the Longview Bridge, enroute to Manzanita, Oregon. He glanced over at Laura and smiled. She was sound asleep now, her seat reclined, oblivious to the real estate passing beneath them. His smile remained as he turned his attention back to a road disappearing beneath the hood of the rented Lincoln Town Car. Jason's smile turned to a chuckle as he recalled the heated negotiations preceding her reluctant agreement to accompany him.

He hadn't been able to reach her until nearly ten o'clock the previous evening. She had just returned from an exhausting hike in the Olympics, which, he felt, ultimately worked to his advantage. The fact that she had planned to begin a long-awaited vacation on Monday had not worked to his favor. Only after he explained what had happened to Jennifer and Carol, described in great detail Debbie's condition, and assured her that she was in no danger, did she consent to accompany him to Manzanita. Laura, being a woman of principle, sounded offended when he explained he would be paying her by the hour from the time he picked her up and until he returned her home. Or maybe it was the five a.m. departure time that offended her.

As darkness began to relinquish its hold on the dawn, Jason felt only somewhat rejuvenated after five hours of badly needed sleep, but he hoped for more rest once he arrived in

Manzanita. As he looked back on the previous day's activities, with the exception of the news about the Crays, it had not been a bad day. He had rescued the girls and taken one prisoner who yielded a wealth of information. He had an interesting interview with a friend of Ben DiAngelis. He now had a competent counselor along for the O'Connors. And Dailey had not successfully cut him out of the loop, although the lieutenant thought differently. Jason finally had a plan. There were now enough pieces to begin fitting the puzzle together. Yes, it had been a pretty good day, he thought.

* * * * *

A busy five hours began from the moment that Jason entered the partners' offices. He gave the three men a detailed report of his meeting with Dailey and Montgomery. He explained that he was being cut from the information loop and laid out his plan for making it difficult for Dailey to do so.

"We need more information on Pathmoor and Comstock, a complete workup on Martin Cray, ASAP. Dailey will be going after the same information, but he'll have no chance of getting it before some time Monday afternoon. We can get the jump on an overworked police department and feed select parts of our information to Dailey before he has his conversation with Jack. Maybe we can keep information flowing both ways, using Jack as the go-between."

"We have the complete report on Comstock," Ben began. "We've also done some investigating of our own. According to the report, Comstock disappeared shortly after leaving Suter. However, our investigation shows Comstock has remained involved with several militia groups. The trips to Idaho," Ben explained. "I called a friend who's been in and out of some of the organizations and he's agreed to come to the office this afternoon."

At four-thirty, a bald, muscular man wearing surplus fatigues arrived at the partners' offices. Ben introduced him as Bud Rockwell and after being seated, Ben asked him to impart his knowledge of George Comstock.

"I first met Comstock when I was a member of the WSFF— the Washington State Freedom Force," he began. "Comstock always seemed to have a chip on his shoulder, a nasty-ass attitude. He hung around the younger recruits. I think it made him feel like kind of a leader. Anyway, a couple of years back, we don't see him any more," Rockwell remembered. "Rumors were he'd been asked to leave, something about not having the same goals as our organization.

"When I was a member, the WSFF just wanted to stay as far away from government as possible. This guy Comstock wanted to mix it up with 'em. The guy was a real nut case. About six months later, I heard talk around he'd been courting some outfit in Idaho and, as rumor had it, same thing happened. He got the old polished boot to his ass. Funny thing, each time an outfit showed him the door, he'd take couple of the younger recruits with him.

"Didn't hear anything for a while. Then a friend of mine who hunts regularly in Idaho with fellas from some of the groups, told me that he'd heard a walking haystack had started a group on a little island," Rockwell said, referring to Comstock. "It's supposed to be off the southwest tip of Lopez Island. I did a little checking on my own—Diablo Island. I guess it's a little thing about ten to twelve square miles. Anyway, sure sounds like Comstock. I think he's got his own military camp out there. The guy's a real loose cannon."

"I know where Diablo Island is," Jason acknowledged, then changed tack. "What would someone like Comstock be doing with a bunch of filters?"

"Water filters, probably," Rockwell answered. "Comstock's got a little side business going, from what I hear. I guess he's some kind of a wizard with chemicals, makes water filters, sells 'em to the survivalist camps. He's got 'em convinced that the government will poison their water when they want to go after 'em. Preaches a lot of paranoia, that guy does, but I guess the filters are damn good. Can filter a minnow fart out of a reservoir, from what I've been told."

Jason dared not show his elation at receiving their first solid bit of information. "Thank you, Mr. Rockwell. If you think of any additional information, you can contact Ben. You've been very helpful." With that Rockwell understood he had been dismissed and left the office.

"I want to know who owns that house in Issaquah and get me all the information on Diablo Island you can," Jason directed. "But prior to that, we need detailed workups on Pathmoor and Cray; complete financials, real estate holdings, work history—any and all information we can compile. I'll conference-call with you Sunday morning from Manzanita, then decide what information we'll give to Dailey. Joe, you're a big brute, we'll use you for our intimidation factor. You'll be the courier and deliver the information to Dailey no more than two hours before he calls to talk to Jack. It'll be a much-appreciated surprise to Dailey, and Jack will corroborate much of the information and hopefully it'll open up the conversation for some good dialogue. We can feed him new information from time to time and just maybe it'll stimulate him to be more talkative. If it works, we may be privy to information Dailey would otherwise hold back." A sound strategy, everyone agreed.

* * * * *

Keller ushered Jason into the bedroom where his captive lay on the bed, again blindfolded. The blindfold prevented any possibility of Keller being recognized. The man had been mildly sedated and lay passive with an IV in his arm. Keller had just administered sodium Pentothal. After several minutes, Keller took the covering from the man's eyes. He looked relaxed and coherent.

Jason began the questioning while Keller monitored the IV and stood by with more of the Pentothal if needed. Todd Monroe; came from Connecticut; his family had money; he'd been a student at University Of Washington; he dropped out five years ago; lived on the streets in Seattle for two years; settled in a militia camp near Pocatello, Idaho; met George Comstock a year later. Jason recorded the two-hour session, which would enable him to go over it with Jack, David, and Steve Sunday morning. He also made a copy for the partners. Keller would see that they received it later that evening.

With the interrogation completed, Keller checked Monroe's vital signs and the two men left the room. As they walked down the hall toward the living room, Keller turned to Jason. "Now it's time for a long overdue physical examination. You look like hell."

In spite of Jason's aggravated protests, Keller spent the next half-hour examining the exhausted gladiator. At the conclusion of his examination, Keller pronounced Jason badly bruised and suspected a hairline fracture in his jaw. He would be sore for a while, but Keller had seen Jason in worse shape. He sent Jason home to the loft for a long overdue shower and much needed sleep.

* * * * *

Rain came in heavy sheets as Jason and Laura entered the east end of Astoria. Laura had just begun to stir. She sat up, bringing her seat back with her. "Where are we?" she asked, blinking several times, trying to focus.

"Oregon," Jason replied.

She looked over at Jason with a sarcastic expression. "Really. So what area of the famous Oregon sunshine are we driving through?"

"Astoria. You hungry?"

"Starved." Laura laid her head back, letting a long yawn escape. She looked around the interior of the car, puzzled for a moment, then asked, "You have a beautiful Cadillac, why rent this car?"

"If I need to return to Seattle in a hurry, which I probably will, I'll be able to leave you with transportation."

"How will you get back, if you leave me the car?"

"Hitchhike," he said without hesitation. She took his answer to mean none of her business and did not press.

After they stopped for breakfast at the Astoria Red Lion, they had been on the road only a few minutes when Laura asked, "You feel like talking? I mean, as long as you're paying me you ought to make good use of your time. Right? I know we scheduled an appointment for you two weeks from Tuesday, but there's no reason we can't have a session sooner. How far are we from Manzanita?"

"Fifty, sixty miles," he answered.

"Sounds like we'd have time for a full session," Laura said.

Jason thought for a moment and his mind went blank. While Laura had been sleeping, his brain had been racing in review of the past two hectic days and thinking forward to the meeting with Jack. None of it had a thing to do with why he had first sought Laura's help, the question of how to get where he thought he wanted to be in his personal life. He could not think of a relevant thought—until he remembered the night at the cottage with Carol and their brief reunion in Port Angeles. Those two encounters had stimulated the question: What is it that I really want?

"I think I need to learn what it is I want or expect from the rest of my life," Jason said thoughtfully.

"Do you have any ideas what you're searching for?" Laura asked. "I don't mean specifically, but in general."

Although Jason's eyes remained focused on the road, a deep searching occupied his thoughts. "I guess I would have to say a sense of fulfillment, the knowledge that I've accomplished something with my life."

"Jason, that's not an original goal you've come up with. Sounds very normal. Let me ask you this. What in your life has fulfilled you? And don't try to tell me nothing."

"I'm proud or was proud when I was serving my country."

"And that was fulfilling?"

"Yes."

"So?"

"So, what?" Jason asked in frustration.

"So what's the problem—that's not enough?" Laura questioned. "Fulfillment, I mean."

"So I'm not doing that any more. Things have changed," he said.

"Ah." She had been able once again to lead Jason to the path of discovery, and although it had not quite registered yet, he had stumbled on the right word.

"Ah, what?" Jason questioned.

"You said the key word. Think about it," she said, still leading him.

"What? Things have changed?"

"Yes, things have changed," Laura encouraged. "Now, I want you to take a couple of minutes. Think about what it is that's lacking in your life. Is it internal or external?"

Jason thought for a moment. "I'm not quite sure what you mean." He puzzled the question, then started thinking out loud. "In the service, you're too busy to think about being fulfilled, even though when I look back I was, very much so. Everything's done according to someone's direct orders, by the clock or by the book. When I finished a job or mission, I was satisfied. Now, I . . ." Jason hesitated. "Oh—now I understand what you're after. I guess the question to me is, am I looking for something to replace the career, or do I want to find fulfillment *within*?"

"Bingo! So now what? Where does that leave you?" Laura, had noticed a difference in Jason from two years ago. He thought on a much deeper level than he had in the past. Although much of his intensity had remained, his acute anger had not—a good sign. Now her goal was to guide him to a place where he understood that the future is not something to be conquered. He had not answered, so she asked again, "Where does that leave you?"

"Frustrated. That's where it leaves me. I have mixed feelings."

"About?"

"About what I'm doing right now. About Carol. And I thought this thing with Jack would make me feel like I did in the good old days, but it hasn't. Oh, I get a rush from the challenge, but it's not where I want to be long term. I think I would like to have a meaningful relationship with Carol, but it scares the hell out of me. A couple of nights ago, I remembered what you said about observing, but I've been too busy lately."

"The observing part is excellent. But the first two items on your list are external, outside fulfillment. It doesn't matter what you fill your life with, Jason; you have to be contented with *you*. Now, if you're talking about having a woman in your life for the completion of the union of oneness, then that's a different subject. Okay, we only have time for one of the two subjects—your choice. Do we talk about your being fulfilled within yourself, or having the completeness of a union?" Laura asked. "And I'm assuming the latter includes Carol."

Jason thought for several miles before he spoke. "I'm not sure how to separate the two. I thought I was comfortable in my life, until this thing with Jack, and now I'm no longer sure."

Jason's thoughts flashed back to the night he stood on Jack's deck, and to the morning after at the loft when he watched the ferry land and the early morning of musing at his cottage. "Maybe I wasn't as happy as I thought, because over the past several months I've recognized a yearning for something and I have no idea what it is . . . . As I think about it now, I'm beginning to think I'm lonely. So, if I'm reading you right and I am looking for completeness in a mate, I need to have my emotional ducks in a row or I'm liable to place the demands and expectations on my mate for my fulfillment. Or something like that."

Laura leaned her seat back into the reclining position again and closed her eyes. She smiled and said, "You've found your way, Jason. All that's left for you to do now is observe. Your decisions will be based on your observations, and more often than not, they will be the right decisions, providing you're honest with yourself."

Jason had found his way with minimal coaxing. He did not respond to Laura, but pondered as he drove, wondering how he had been able to concentrate on his personal situation in the midst of all of the turmoil of the past week. But he had. He looked over approvingly at the now dozing Laura, and was thankful for her gift to him. The light of understanding had explained his feelings. And with understanding came a rush of peace filling him slowly and releasing the pent-up anxiety that had accumulated over past years.

He now understood his insecurity had blocked communication. He could not worry about nor be responsible for other people's reactions to his opinions. In the context of a relationship, he need no longer feel attacked by others' views nor defensive of his own. These insights not only gave him hope for a long-term relationship, but also an inner confidence that had eluded him for so long. Jason understood that his transition would not be instantaneous but would evolve as he became more comfortable with himself. He would no longer be looking to the past for fulfillment. And the future? Fulfillment in the future would be a journey to anticipate with renewed interest.

CHAPTER THIRTY

The ocean came into view just prior to the Cannon Beach by-pass. During the miles that had passed, Jason had made the transition from the thoughts of his personal pilgrimage to those of the situation at hand. He had reviewed the morning's agenda several times, making sure that nothing would be over-looked. They were fifteen minutes from the beach house, a good time to wake Laura, as the scenery to Manzanita would be quite beautiful.

* * * * *

The beach house, a hexagonal structure, created a unique form nestled in among the trees on a bluff that dropped off sharply to the rocky shore below. Although the rain had stopped, a misty fog combined with wood fire smoke hanging in layers below the chimney composed a romantically gray scene, a perfect watercolor against a lush green backdrop. Tommy could be seen from one of the many upper windows and waved frantically upon hearing the car's approach down the tree-arched gravel drive.

"What an unusual house," Laura commented as they rolled to a stop. Her hazel eyes danced with an energized interest, taking in the surroundings and the wild surf pound-ing only a few feet below. Jason had no more than opened his door before Tommy burst from a door in the lower portion of the house. He bent over and scooped up the boy on his way around the car to open the door for Laura.

"My lord, this is a beautiful setting!" she said, climbing out of the car and taking in the view. "That house," she reiterated, "it must have a hundred-and-eighty-degree view. How long did you say you were paying me for?" she laughed.

"As long as it takes," he responded cheerfully, then steered her toward the lower entrance.

The threesome ascended a spiral staircase leading to the main floor. Framed windows set two feet above the floor extended to the ceiling, which vaulted from six sides towards the center some sixteen feet above. As Laura had suspected, an exquisite panorama lay before them on all sides.

Tommy struggled to pry himself loose from Jason in order to show off the Yosemite Sam puzzle he had put together. Carol and Debbie, still in their robes and slippers, padded around in the kitchen area, cleaning up after breakfast. When Jason extricated himself from Tommy's attention, he introduced Laura to Debbie. As Laura and the women exchanged polite but tentative pleasantries, Steve entered through the sliding door off of the kitchen.

"Where's David?" Jason asked, now concerned with the business of security. Steve, understanding, responded by wagging his thumb toward the sandy beach a quarter of a mile south of the house. Jason saw the figure running hard, heading away from the house towards Manzanita for his morning exercise. "Jack is in the shower, the two girls are in the downstairs bedroom. The property's situated on the side of this mountain that traverses down to a rocky shore with a small beach appearing only at low tide. David and I checked the perimeter when we arrived," Steve reported, pointing toward the drive. "That's the only way in. Two sides of the property are against the mountain and are protected by trees and impenetrable undergrowth. And, of course, in the front we have this twenty-five-foot brush-covered cliff," he said, as he made a sweep of his arm across the front of the property toward the ocean. "It'd take some determined people to get in here."

"Rest assured, they are," Jason countered. "Let's get the luggage." Jason did not speak again until they reached the car. "When Jack's finished with his shower, we'll talk. A lot has happened since Friday."

As Steve continued to press for new information, Jason looked up to see Carol, who smiled down at him. Preoccupied with Steve and matters of strategy her smile did not get returned with the warmth in which it had been given. Her exuberance faded as she sensed the tension in Jason's forced response.

"How are you doing?" Jason asked when Carol intercepted them in the lower portion of the house. Steve continued on with the luggage to give them a moment of privacy.

"I'm doing well, considering," she answered, flashing a bright smile. "I had a very good sleep last night, which surprised me. Jack is very antsy, Debbie is still uptight, but better, and Jennifer is sullen and keeps to herself most of the time. I would have to say, given the events of the last four days, everyone is doing better than one would imagine."

Jason had not expected such an enthusiastic response. He looked into her tentative, searching eyes and realized how glad he was to see her. Carol took him by the arms, pulled him to her, and laid her head on his shoulder. "I'm so glad you're here," she said softly, then kissed his neck and clung even tighter.

Jason steeled himself against her embrace; needing to remain focused, he did not respond in kind.

Carol instinctively knew there must be some new burden that he carried and did not press him. "Will you have time to rest while you're here?" she finally asked. "You look tired."

"I am tired. I'm hoping for at least a couple of days' rest," he whispered, feeling a combination of weariness and remorse for not being what Carol needed him to be at the moment. "It depends what happens up north. Carol, there are some new developments—I have—"

"Shhh." She tenderly put her finger to his lips. "I know. You're not here for a vacation and you have much to do. But when you have time to rest, I want to be there."

Jason slowly pushed her away and held her at arm's length. "The R and R definitely includes spending quality time with you."

"Oh?" she looked at him with a coy smile. "And just what does quality time include?"

* * * * *

Jack sat stunned and paled at the news of the Crays' deaths. Jason had thought long and hard of a way to bring the news gently and had found none. The four men sat in silence for several minutes in the largest of the downstairs bedrooms, allowing Jack a moment to assimilate the news.

Jason reached over and put his hand on Jack's shoulder. He was rigid with anger. "I'm sorry," were the only words Jason could think to say and they sounded shallow. He knew Jack had considered Martin a friend, at least until he had brought Pathmoor to Cervicon. They had struggled for twenty-one years together, building the business into a leader in the industry.

"I need to get up there," Jack said in a quiet, determined voice. "I can't let this company go." He sat on the edge of the bed, his head bent down, his forehead cradled in his hand. When he looked up, he slowly shook his head and closed his eyes tight in a failed attempt to fight back the tears. "I can't let that bastard Pathmoor get his hooks into a company he has no stake in."

"He's not going to get your company," Jason assured him. "Dailey and Montgomery think he lied about when he last saw Cray—and they now have him under surveillance. The partners are working on it too. So don't worry about your company. There's no way he'll get it. Let's get all the information before we make any decisions about returning to Seattle."

With the issue of Jack's returning to Seattle temporarily circumvented, Jason quickly launched into a synopsis of his last meeting with the partners. He explained in detail about the information being sought on Pathmoor, Comstock, and Cray, and the plan to get the information to Dailey this afternoon. Also he explained Jack's role in keeping the line of communication intact with Dailey and how the information from the partners would play in it. He also related what Rockwell had told him about George Comstock.

"Now that it's confirmed Comstock is involved, we know where to focus our attention," Jason went on. "Before the end of the day, the partners will have all the available information on Diablo Island in addition to what we learned from our prisoner.

Let's listen to what our Mr. Monroe had to say." Jason set out the tape recorder and played back the interrogation.

Jason's voice, relaxed but metallic sounding, emanated from the speaker of the compact machine.

"Can you hear me?" Jason asked.

"Yes.

"Are you comfortable?"

"Yes." The man's voice was clear and relaxed without a hint of anxiety.

"What is your name?"

"Todd Monroe."

"How old are you?"

"Twenty-five."

"Where were you born?"

"Bridgeport, Connecticut."

"Did you grow up in Connecticut?"

"Yes."

"When did you first leave Connecticut?"

"After I graduated from high school."

"Where did you go after you graduated from high school?"

"Seattle."

"What did you do in Seattle?"

"Went to college."

"Where did you go to college?"

"University of Washington."

"Did you graduate?"

"No."

"How long were you at the University of Washington?"

"Two years."

"Why did you leave school?"

"I didn't like school and my grades weren't very good."

"Why did you go to the University of Washington if you didn't like school?" Jason continued to ask easy questions in order to keep Monroe relaxed.

"My dad graduated from the University of Washington. He wanted me to go there."

"What did you do after you left school?"

"Worked odd jobs, just knocked around. Sometimes I lived on the street with people I met."

"What were their names, these people that you met?"

"I didn't know all their names, but Tosh Williams and Jim Anderson were the ones I was closest to."

Jason now confident of Monroe's comfortable demeanor, launched into the meat of the interrogation. "Did you ever meet a man named George Comstock?"

"Yes."

"How did you meet him?"

"Tosh and Jim heard about some militia groups in Idaho and wanted to check them out. We went to one in Hayden Lake, Idaho, then one in Pocatello. We met George Comstock at the camp in Pocatello."

"Describe the camp in Pocatello."

"It was just a bunch of people, men mostly, who were banding together to form a community trying to protect themselves from a government that continues to degrade our freedoms and increase our taxes. The politicians continue to de-fang our military, close facilities and then spread our resources so thin we couldn't put together a competent fighting force in a crisis. We just want to be prepared."

Properly brainwashed, Jason thought, listening to the canned statement. But he could not disagree. He also noted that Monroe said *we*, which indicated to him that Monroe had been converted. "Were they armed?"

"Yeah. We got to do a lot of shooting and practical survival exercises. It was kind of fun." Jason recognized practical survival exercises, as a politically correct term for combat training.

"Tell me about George Comstock. When did you first meet?"

"About a year and a half ago he showed up at the camp. Quite a few of the personnel already knew him. He stayed for a couple of months and then we didn't see him for a while. About ten months ago, he showed up again. Tosh and I were out on an exercise when our instructor came and got us and took us to the office. Comstock was in the office when we got there. He asked us if we wanted to join an organization of patriots that were really interested in saving this country and not just going through the motions. He told us it was a camp he started for that specific purpose. Tosh and I thought it would be fun and good experience, so we said yes."

"Then what happened?"

"Then, he told us to pack our gear and meet him back at the office in half an hour."

"What happened to your friend, Jim?"

"Jim left the camp about a month before."

"Why did Jim leave?"

"He told us he thought some of the guys were nuts and didn't want any part of it any more. The last time I saw him was about two days later when he left."

"What happened when you and Tosh returned to the office?"

"They blindfolded us and loaded us onto a helicopter and flew us to a new camp on an island somewhere."

"What did you do at the new camp?" Jason asked.

"We learned hand to hand, small weapons, how to make bombs, how to handle plastique. We learned how to survive with no gear, just clothes, boots, and a belt."

"Did Comstock tell you and your friend what all this training was for?"

"We didn't have much contact with Mr. Comstock. We only saw him from a distance from time to time. The only ones we had contact with were our instructors. They told us we were training to save real Americans and when it came to fighting, we would be prepared to kick ass."

"Who was in charge of this camp?"

"I don't know. There was a building in the compound we were never allowed to go near. Mr. Comstock would go into the building whenever he came to the camp. I think whoever he met in the building was in charge."

"Do you know his name?"

"No."

Jason stopped the tape and said, "When we interviewed Rockwell, he believed Comstock owned the camp. And our friend here, Todd Monroe, said as much when Comstock asked him to go to 'this camp of his.'"

Steve said, "But, an island isn't cheap, nor is arming a camp like that. So where'd the money come from?"

"There's a lot of money in drugs," David interjected. South American armies have been financed with drug money. Do the Contras ring a bell?"

"It's a thought," Jason said as he pressed the play button again. "Take notes; it gets better."

"Have you ever killed anyone?" Jason asked.

"No."

"Would you kill someone?"

"If I was told to."

"If you were to kill someone, who would give you the orders?"

"One of the instructors, or somebody higher up."

"How did you get to Victoria?"

"I don't know that I've ever been to Victoria."

Learning that Monroe didn't know where he was when he had been captured came as a surprise to Jason. "How did you get from the camp to where you were captured?"

"My instructor told me that I had been chosen for a mission, said it was real important. Tosh and I were flown to somewhere near to where we were captured. We were met by two guys in a white van and taken directly to a house."

"What were the two men's names?" Jason interrupted.

"Greg and Carlos." The name Carlos stirred Jason's memory. Carlos sounded as if he might have been Curly's partner, the one he said was watching Jack's daughter, the one that Lori Phillips described as her attacker.

"What day was this?"

"Late Thursday night."

"Did they tell you what the mission was?"

"Only that we had to help guard a house and watch some people."

"Were you told who these people were or why you had to guard them?"

"No."

"When did the people show up at the house?"

"About eight-thirty in the morning."

"Who did Greg and Carlos bring to the house for you to guard?"

"A girl about twelve or thirteen and a tall woman. They were both unconscious. I was kind of disappointed."

"Why were you disappointed?"

"Because I thought it would be someone important."

If you only knew, Jason thought. "How did you communicate with the people who were giving the orders?"

"By cell phone and radio; a lot of houses were without phone service because of the storm last Saturday night."

"How were the prisoners treated?"

"Okay. They were unconscious for quite a while. When the girl came too, she just cried most of the time. I tried to give her water once, but she didn't want it. Carlos told me to stay away from her. So I did."

"Was Carlos in charge?"

"Sort of. I didn't much care for him though, and he was hanging around the woman a lot after she woke up. He slapped her around some and asked if I wanted her. I told him to knock it off because that wasn't what we were there for. He just laughed and told me to buzz off. I stayed away from him as much as possible. Greg and Carlos argued about the way Carlos was treating her."

"What happened the morning that you were attacked?"

"It was late, some time around four o'clock in the morning. Earlier we received a radio message to stay alert and that we may have to move the girl and woman. I went out to relieve Tosh, he was kind of groggy. I think he might have been sleeping. Anyway, I told him that something was up, we needed to stay sharp. We were having a smoke, when, out of nowhere, Tosh took a hit in the head. Then before I knew what happened, someone had me from behind. I panicked. I'd never seen anyone get killed before. When these two guys questioned me about who was in the house, I told them everything they wanted to know. That's the last thing I remember until I woke up on a boat."

"Did you see who killed Tosh, or do you have any idea who they were?"

"No."

"Do you know where you are right now, or any of the people around you?"

"No."

Jason then turned the questions towards the camp itself, probing for information that would somehow unlock the key to their ultimate goal: finding out why they wanted to silence Jack O'Connor. He asked questions that pertained to the personnel's daily activities, and heard once again of their strong emphasis on covert combat drills, training with explosives and survival. The island "Diablo" seemed appropriately named. Then he asked Monroe if he had ever left the island prior to his experience at the house in Victoria.

"Yes."

"What did you do when you left the camp?"

"We were transported by helicopter to an airport, then taken to some kind of chemical plant to work."

"Do you know what airport you were taken to?"

"We were always blindfolded for the trip, but just before we landed, they took the blindfolds off. I think it was Boeing Field."

"Where was the chemical company?"

"I don't know. We were always picked up in a van. It didn't have any windows in the back, so we never saw where we were going, but it wasn't far from the airport."

"What type of work did you do at the chemical plant?"

"Mainly just load sacks of fertilizer on pallets and then onto trucks that came to pick them up."

"Were there any names on the bags or the trucks?"

"No."

"How many trips did you make to the chemical company?"

"Two."

"Were others from the camp transported to the chemical company to work?"

"Yes, some of them stayed for weeks at a time. The longest I ever stayed was two days."

"How big is the plant?"

"I don't know. The part that I worked in was about half a city block. The rest of it was off limits. Armed guards, the works."

"Were you or the others ever paid for working at the plant?"

"I never was. I don't know about the others."

"Why did you only work at the plant two times, when others worked there more?"

"Tosh and I were training hard to move up in the ranks. We believed in what the camp stood for and wanted to help achieve the goal."

"What are the goals of the camp?"

"Have a strong and lethal fighting force, organize protest marches and demonstrations, educate people through meetings and underground newspapers and magazines, and surgically remove corrupt people from business and government."

"Have you ever heard the name, Jack O'Connor?"

"No."

"Richard Pathmoor?"

"No."

"Martin Cray?"

"No."

"How often have you seen George Comstock in the last week?"

"Once at the chemical plant on Monday and twice at the camp during the week. The last time was Thursday night. He came to the camp just before Tosh and I were sent away to guard the house."

"Has Comstock been there more than usual this past week?"

"Yes."

"Has there been a lot of activity this week, more instructors or other personnel coming and going?"

"Yes."

"Do you know anything about water filters?"

"Yeah. We use them all the time at the camp. The water on the island is real bad. Can't even drink it if it isn't filtered."

Jason stopped the tape. Since he had been present during the interrogation, he was more interested in the other men's reactions and comments rather than listening to the taped dialogue again. Jack's passivity surprised him. Jason understood he was still reeling from the news of the Crays, but he also expected Jack to be more attentive to the information they had discovered.

"So, what've we got here," David began," a bonafide terrorist camp with a buncha brainwashed zombies?"

"There're three things we now know for sure," Jason answered. "First, these people have made no provisions for screw-ups: case in point, Wellington and Curly. They were eliminated without any interrogation. As far as anyone farther up the food chain knew, these two guys may or may not have given up information, but they were capped without bothering to find out. They take no chances. And the interesting thing is that the trainees, like our friend Monroe and even an instructor like Curly, apparently are unaware of the consequences for failure. The other thing we know for sure is that the instructors, based again on my personal experience with Curly, aren't in the know either. Jack, when I questioned Curly, who was obviously not a trainee, he had *no idea* why you were on their hit list."

"How far up the food chain do you have to be, before you get to be in the know?" Steve asked.

"Good question," Jason answered. "Which brings me back to the third and most sinister bit of information we've learned. These zombies, as Dave appropriately called them, apparently do not question their orders, or need justification for killing someone. Orders come down and are simply carried out by these brainwashed fanatics. I can handle the part about a strong and lethal fighting force, holding protests and demonstrations, educating people through meetings and underground newspapers and magazines, but the part about surgically removing corrupt people in business and government scares the hell out of me. And Jack, I think you stumbled into the latter."

Jason waited a moment for a response. Jack did not respond; he simply stared blankly ahead. Jason then explained the partners were looking for a chemical company within a ten-mile radius of Boeing Field. It would be another piece of information for their morning report.

Jason again turned to Jack. "Well now, we know who, but we still don't know why. Jack, anything coming to you, anything at all?"

Jack slowly looked up at Jason and shook his head. "I have no idea."

"Who gives a shit about the why any more as long as we know who," David interrupted. "Let's get on it now and bust some balls."

"And to what end?" Jason asked disapprovingly. "There's still too much that we don't know. Jack has inadvertently stumbled into something big. This damn thing is like an octopus with tentacles reaching in all directions. We might be able to hack off a couple of arms, but there'll be six left to carry on. There's an armed terrorist camp on Diablo Island, a chemical company, and Suter. We don't know what part Pathmoor's playing in this, or why Cray was hit. We need more information. Let's break for lunch and wait for our conference call with the partners."

* * * * *

A palpable tension presided during lunch. Jennifer remained sullen; Jack silently moved food from one side of his plate to another; Debbie, though attempting an upbeat mood, let her anxiety filter through a brave façade. The obnoxious banterings of David and Steve fell upon unamused ears, and soon they too fell silent. Even Tommy, who typically noticed little beyond his four-year-old world, sensed the tension and fell unusually quiet. Carol, Ashley and Laura maintained normal conversation as best they could.

After lunch Jennifer retreated to her room and Tommy and Ashley returned to another jigsaw puzzle. Carol brought bottled beer to the table for the men. Sensing important business lay ahead she simply bent over and kissed Jason on the cheek and returned to the kitchen to help the others.

After a few uncomfortable minutes of sparse conversation, Steve took his beer and asked David to accompany him on a walk of the perimeter of the property.

Jack looked across the table and out the window at the angry surf, sipped his beer and worried, the little die-cast part between his fingers that he had gotten from Biddwell. He hadn't uttered a word since lunch.

"We have to talk, Jack," Jason said quietly.

Jack glanced at him for a second, then shifted his gaze back to the heavy surf without a response.

"C'mon, Jack. This isn't helping," Jason persisted. "I know this situation with the Crays is tough and you're frightened for your family, but we need your help. We're getting close. We just need a couple of pieces and we'll be able to start completing this puzzle."

Jack's gaze returned to Jason. His eyes held tears of rage.

"What the hell is with you?" he asked in a guttural tone through gritted teeth. "You have ice water in your veins, or what? This is just a great adventure to you, isn't it? My family has nearly been ripped to pieces, a twenty-one-year relationship with a friend and owner of the company that I've poured my life into has just come to an end, and you sit there as if nothing's happened and tell me we have to talk. I'm scared shitless, I can't think straight, and you want to talk? Go to hell, Jay!"

Debbie may not have heard what her husband said but she instinctively knew their friend needed help with her husband's mood. She moved behind Jack and bent over, wrapping her arms around him, and kissed the top of his head. In a loving embrace, she held him without uttering a word. Jack didn't respond. In the midst of the turmoil, Debbie now fought to keep the situation under control. But without seeming to notice, Jack returned his gaze to the cold, gray surf that accurately reflected his inner anguish and rage.

Jason could not argue with Jack's comments. He had wrestled with those very issues. The previous Monday night, Carol had accused him of the same thing. In the past forty-eight hours, he had killed three men, he had been in a life-threatening situation near Issaquah, and again in Victoria. He had walked away unshaken. Just another day at the office, as Carol had put it to him. He had prepared himself mentally to deal with it. He was a warrior and that's what warriors do. And yes, he admitted excitement, and adrenaline had flowed like a narcotic.

Jack had no way of knowing that Jason too carried fear—a fear of losing a part of his life he had been searching for, a true friendship. He suddenly realized how important it had become to him. But even more important was the glimmer of hope for a fulfillment that did not include the adrenaline flow upon which he had been so dependent in the past.

He felt bad that Jack's friends, the Crays, had been killed, not merely because their lives had been taken away, but because he knew what Martin had meant to Jack. He tried to not to press him, even though time had become critical.

Debbie, in spite of the stress she'd been carrying, continued to hug her husband and simply said in a soft tone, "He needs your help, honey. We need to help him and trust him, in order for him to help us. We'll pull through this."

Jason noted the way that Debbie had spoken. She had used the term "we" instead of "you," which made her an equal part of the equation. She projected no hint of accusation in her prodding.

Jack, still rigid, turned to Jason and said, "We probably ought to get downstairs."

CHAPTER THIRTY-ONE

Jack closed the door of the lower bedroom. He remained standing and leaned against it with his head back and eyes closed. Even though he had recently showered, he appeared disheveled, a reflection of his inner exhaustion. David and Steve were already seated. Jason sat on the bed next to the portable telephone and speaker setup. He punched in the partners' phone number and they all listened intently to the speaker as it rang.

"Castellano."

"It's Jason, Joe. What do you have for us?"

"Plenty. We've been working around the clock. We're all here and I have to tell you, the storyboard has a completely different look. I know you'll want to make contact with Dailey shortly, so we'll work off your agenda. That way, we'll be prepared to back you up with the information that you'll want us to feed him. We can deal with the rest later, but I'm assuming you'll want to get some of this new information to Dailey ASAP."

"Comstock?" Jason queried

Ben's voice came over the speaker. "Nothing really new on him. He was a ghost until we received the information from Monroe. We've now two places to look—the island and the chemical company. Since yesterday, we've done some checking and we came up with three chemical warehouses or chemical distributors in the south Seattle area that you laid out. I've put surveillance in place on all three. I talked with Keller about twenty minutes ago at the hospital. When his shift is over, he's going back to The Kennel to have another session with Monroe. He wants to try for more details on the warehouse. Maybe get a quick fix on the right one. Other than that, that's about it for Comstock.

"—Oh, there's one other item of interest. We had a call from Bud Rockwell this morning. Seems as though Fort Lewis took a hit on some small arms about three months ago. The information's been sketchy at best, but as near as he could tell, it sounded like case lots of M16's. Sobahr will have some of his people check on it first thing tomorrow. Again, we have to be real careful on this one, Jay; we don't need the military or the Feds snooping around. Also, Keller is making arrangements for a stealthy chopper to do a night recon over Diablo. You want in on it?"

"Let's see how it plays out, Ben. I'd like to get a couple days' rest. Keep me informed."

"Understood."

"Pathmoor?" Jason asked. He stole a glance at Jack as he said the name Pathmoor. Jack still leaned against the door, his head now hung down with his chin against his chest, appearing not to look at anything and still worrying the little die cast part between his fingers.

"Pathmoor," Joe's voice now came over the speaker. "Now that's where the board takes a turn. Our friend is living beyond his means, and I mean w-a-a-y beyond. A year ago he brought home 48K from Suter. Here is a brief synopsis. His annual salary from Cervicon is guaranteed at sixty-two five."

At that statement, Jason looked up as he heard a metallic sound and something skittered across the tile floor. Jack's and Jason's eyes met as Jack bent over to look for the little die casting. As Jason retrieved it and handed it to Jack, he could see a seething hatred behind Jack's eyes. Jason knew Jack only brought home fifty grand a year.

"That sonofabitch," Jack muttered, just loud enough to be heard.

Joe, unaware of the episode, continued on. "Now on the surface everything looks okay, but we added things up and here's what we found. He's putting ten percent into his retirement. He has $6,993.97 in a savings account at SeaFirst. His mortgage payment is $1,325. He is paying $650 in monthly support for a six-year-old boy from his second marriage; divorced a year and a half ago. He has a car payment of $462 per month. He's taking care of a daughter from his first marriage: private school, clothes, food, utilities. From all appearances, our man's on the edge."

Although Jack just stared at the floor, Jason saw the clenched jaw and flushed neck with muscles and veins protruding.

"A lot of people are on the edge, Joe," Jason reminded him. If you're headed somewhere with this, get on with it," Jason said, mirroring Jack's frustration.

"December 12th of '94," Joe continued, "Pathmoor bought 800 shares of Microsoft at 63-1/8 per. Cash transaction. The beginning of April of this year, he bought a forty-two-foot sailboat at a drug confiscation auction, paid 50K for it. Cash transaction. Has it moored up in Anacortes; the damn moorage is costing him $235 a month. He has no discretionary funds and his savings account hasn't fluctuated more than a thousand over the past two years, and $500 of fluctuation just happened to be the additional amount needed to make the stock purchase."

"Offshore funds?" Jason asked.

"Not that we can find," Ben interrupted. "That's the first thing we checked. The man has a big-time sugar daddy. Once I got into my investigation of Suter, I didn't need to waste more time on trying to find Pathmoor's additional income."

At that comment, Jack's head snapped up and his eyes looked directly at the speaker. He had, in spite of his appearance, been listening intently.

"At first everything looked normal until November of last year, November 28th to be precise. I found a withdrawal for a cashier's check in the amount of 50K. The only notation my access could ferret out was a memo for an allocation for consulting fees. That in itself did not seem unusual, but a funny thing happened on my way through the calendar this morning. The transaction happened five days short of one month after Pathmoor landed at Cervicon. Fifteen days later, our Mr. P dumps a wad he doesn't have into Microsoft stock. Now don't get your water boiling just yet. March 29th of this year, Suter earmarked another 50K for consulting fees: the same procedure. Ten days later, Mr. P spends a tad more than that for his dreamboat and hides it up in Anacortes. We three kings think we found Mr. P's sugar daddy."

"What in hell am I in the middle of?" Jack asked, then rested his head again against the bedroom door.

"I truly understand, Mr. O'Connor, that this must be extremely difficult for you." Sobahr's voice now came from the speaker. "And I regret we cannot allow you a little time to adjust to the loss of your friends, especially after hearing about it just this morning. Please forgive me, but we must press forward with our investigation." Sobahr paused, but Jack said nothing. "Have you had any contact with the men who make financial decisions such as those Ben just described? So far we have Hugh Saltzman, Abel Sloan, and A.J. Suter. Would you know of any others?"

Jack, leaning against the door with his head tilted back, closed his eyes momentarily, then stared at the ceiling thoughtfully.

"I'm not sure I know many of the players at Suter, at least in the financial arena. My main contact was Hugh Saltzman, the general manager, but I'm not sure he'd have the clout to make that type of draw. Abel Sloan is the president. I had limited contact with him, and as of late, none of it very friendly. He certainly would. He's the one who's pushing Pathmoor's buttons about short-cutting the security designs. Of course, there's A.J. Suter, the founder and chairman of the board. Nice man. I've only met with him on two occasions. I suppose there may be others with the authority to write checks and make draws, but I wouldn't have any way of knowing."

"I'm sure our Mr. Pathmoor would know," Jason interjected.

"Ah yes, I see what you mean. Are you suggesting then, that you are planning to pay Mr. Pathmoor a visit?" Sobahr asked.

"No, not at all," Jason answered quickly. "I'm already treading lightly with Dailey. I bet when we give him this information, he'll not wait before he questions him again. And, if we play our cards right, I think he'll share the results."

"Yes, yes, I see. But is it not possible that we might miss out on the connection to the munitions in Issaquah if you do not speak to Mr. Pathmoor personally?"

"I'm not so sure there's a connection, Sobahr. I've given considerable thought to that and have come to the conclusion that it doesn't make any difference if Pathmoor's involved. We know the Issaquah house is connected with the camp on Diablo. If Pathmoor's involved with that, we'll find out soon enough. And, if he's not supposed to be involved, or he's stumbled onto it, or onto anything he shouldn't have, he would have been dead long before now, particularly in view of what we've seen so far. We'll let Dailey field this one."

"Oh yes, yes, once again I see what you mean. Then we must give this information to the lieutenant before our meeting." Sobahr became animated with excitement.

"Hold your camels, partner," Joe interrupted. "There're probably a couple of other things we need to talk over before our meeting with Dailey. Question, Jason: I assume there will be no mention of our friend at The Kennel to Dailey."

"Correct," Jason answered. "For right now we'll leave Dailey with Pathmoor and sweeten the pot with information on Comstock."

"Comstock? You're giving him Comstock?" Joe asked surprised.

"We'll concentrate on Diablo Island and keep Dailey busy with Comstock. After we give him the Comstock info, I don't think he'll be so tight-lipped. Just don't give him anything that will connect Comstock to the Island or Issaquah."

"Okay, we have enough on our hands. And speaking of Diablo, we're having a hell of a time getting the information on who owns that damn island. Whoever they are they're well insolated. We'll keep you informed."

* * * * *

Jason suggested they take a forty-five-minute break before the expected conference call with Dailey, who would be making his contact from the offices of the partners. The upstairs was off limits while Laura conducted a counseling session with Debbie, Jennifer, and Carol. David and Steve left to walk the perimeter. Jason and Jack elected to remain in the bedroom. Jason stretched out on the bed alongside the phone equipment, while Jack sank tiredly into one of the chairs.

Jason turned his head towards his friend. "I want to say something profound or comforting to you, but I have no idea what it should be. Jack, I've never had to deal with the grief that comes with losing a friend, so I can't say that I know how you feel. I've lost buddies from time to time, but in my business it's to be expected, and I've worked hard not to become attached to anyone. I know this sounds like a contradiction, but I think I'm beginning to understand how you feel about Martin Cray. You're my first attempt at a lasting friendship, and I can only imagine what I would feel if I lost you."

"You know. You've just forgotten," Jack said quietly. He turned to face Jason. "Debbie told me about your second wife being killed." Caught off guard, Jason started to speak, but Jack cut him off. "Carol told Deb the day they talked."

Still shocked, Jason reflected a few moments before speaking. "It was a lot different, Jack. I hadn't learned to love yet. I'll admit it was different than losing a buddy. She was beautiful and we had sex like there was no tomorrow, but love— maybe if we'd had more time—" Jason's voice trailed off, taking on a dream-like quality as he remembered, trying his best to relate the feelings. "There was no history, no bond. I don't know, maybe I'd have learned to love. I guess it was like having something taken away from me. I was angry, but I don't think I grieved."

Jack realized this was the first time Jason had talked about anything of significance in his past. He felt honored as he began to understand the man's commitment to their friendship. Also, he realized what a slap in the face his outburst upstairs must have been. "Jay, I'm sorry about what I said to you upstairs," he said contritely. "I had no right to—"

"Apology accepted," Jason replied. He understood the legitimacy of Jack's outburst, one spawned by fear. But he wasn't quite sure how he felt about sharing the private details of his past. Does it make me feel vulnerable? he wondered. It shouldn't. A friendship is based on trust, isn't it? He closed his eyes and drifted in weary thought.

Jack also closed his eyes, sensing Jason's need for rest. He would gladly give him that, even if it were only a few brief minutes.

* * * * *

All were together again in the lower bedroom when the call came through from the partners' office with both Dailey and Montgomery present.

Dailey, as always, curtly got straight to the point. "My God, Brisben, how did you and your pack of friends here come up with all the information on Pathmoor and Cray so quickly?"

"Lieutenant, we're in the computer age," Jason answered with a wry smile. "We call it networking."

Dailey did not find humor in the flippant response. "Well you and your friends are scaring the hell out of me. All right, let's get to it. Is O'Connor there with you?" Jack answered and Dailey began speaking directly to him. "I am assuming by now, Mr. O'Connor, that you have been apprised of the situation regarding both Richard Pathmoor and the murder of the Crays. I'll start with the Crays. How long have you known Mr. Cray?"

"Over twenty years. I went to work for him right after he started Cervicon in 1974 and I've worked with and for him ever since."

"Would you have considered yourself a good friend of Cray?"

Jack hesitated briefly before answering. "Yes, I would say so." Jason, observing Jack's facial expressions and body language, knew the hesitation came as a result of his thinking about the deterioration of their relationship, which began after the surprise hiring of Pathmoor.

"Did Cray, as a friend, ever explain to you of his reasons for hiring Pathmoor?"

"He knew I liked designing and being out in the field. He felt that I would be of more value to the company doing what I'm good at and what I love rather than being stuck behind a desk. He told me this rather unexpectedly when he informed me about the hiring of Pathmoor. He also assured me Pathmoor wasn't my boss. Of course, Pathmoor doesn't see it that way."

"I understand. Did you ever talk to Mr. Cray about the way things were going with Pathmoor?"

"I mentioned it once. He didn't seem concerned, said it'd probably smooth out in time. It never has. I was reluctant to bring it up again because things never seemed the same between us."

Jason watched Jack intently and saw the pain in his eyes and heard the grieving beneath the words as he spoke to Dailey. He understood the guilt Jack felt at having been angry with his friend Martin for not confiding in him. Although the situation had been beyond Jack's control, it did not lessen the feeling of guilt or make the grieving any easier.

Dailey also must have sensed the emotions stirring in Jack. "I apologize for having to ask you all of this under these circumstances, but it's necessary . . . Mr. O'Connor, I want you to think carefully, because this may be important. When was the last time that you saw Mr. Cray?"

"A week ago last Tuesday, I think."

"Please be precise, if you can."

Jack hesitated, then responded. "It had to have been. I was out of town most of that week from Tuesday afternoon on."

"You never saw him again before he made his call to your home last Sunday night?"

"That's correct, Lieutenant. I'm sure because, as I said, I spent most of that week out of the office. And, as I mentioned before, Martin hasn't had regular hours since Pathmoor arrived. I went in briefly Friday morning before I left for an appointment, but he wasn't at the office."

That matched with what Pathmoor had said. Dailey paused, then spoke again. "We, Bob and I, believe Pathmoor lied when we asked him about the last time he'd seen Martin Cray. You said that you saw him last Tuesday. Pathmoor said that he hadn't seen him for at least two weeks. Is it possible that Mr. Cray would have been at the office and not had contact with Pathmoor?"

"It's not likely, Lieutenant. Pathmoor used every opportunity to complain about my lack of progress on the Suter project. The past few months he's had much more contact with Martin than I had."

"Mr. O'Connor, I don't want to ask the following questions, but you must understand, it has been alleged that you may have a possible motive for wanting Mr. Cray out of the way." Jack went scarlet and started to speak, but Dailey talked over him. "I will need you to account for your activities over the past two weeks. Please understand I will be required to supply this information."

Jack, outraged at the implication, responded angrily. "Lieutenant, I can account for every minute of my time for the last year if you like. Marcy at the office can provide you with all of my appointments: dates, times, and trip notes. I keep a log of my activities in office hours and when I'm not at the office, I'm at home or with my family. The only exception to that in the last month was last Sunday night, and, if I recall correctly, you were there."

"Please understand, Mr. O'Connor, I have to ask and confirm this to my captain."

"Here's more information that will further confuse the issue," Montgomery interrupted. "Somebody is looking for information—not only from you, Mr. O'Connor, but from Mr. Cray as well."

"What do you mean?" Jason asked.

"Cray's house has been broken into and ransacked," Montgomery continued. "Somebody's looking for something, something documented in some fashion."

"What the hell could someone be looking for at the Crays'?" Jack yelled in frustration.

"I thought you might be able to help us with that," Montgomery said.

"Me!" Jack said with incredulity, then looked at Jason puzzled.

"Hold on a minute." Joe Castellano interrupted. "Montgomery is right. If Cray's house has been searched, there's definitely physical evidence of some kind. Apparently Cray had it, and whoever these people are think you know about it, Jack. Cray must have realized what he had. In all probability that's why he called Sunday night."

Jack, still processing the new information, asked, "Is it possible that Pathmoor might know what it is?"

"Only if he's involved deeper than we think," Jason answered. "Like I said before, those who are not supposed to know what ever it is, or not supposed to be involved are dead."

"That's a good point," Montgomery offered. "Pathmoor looked frightened when we told him about the Crays. Maybe he's dabbling where he doesn't belong."

"It may be a good time to pay him another visit," Dailey said. "We know now that he lied when he said he hadn't seen Cray for two weeks. If what you say is true, he probably saw him a week ago last Tuesday and lied about it. There must be a reason."

Jason seized the opportunity for his contribution. "While you're at it, Lieutenant, ask him what he knows about George Comstock."

"Who in hell is George Comstock?" Dailey inquired.

"At this point, Lieutenant, we're not sure of a whole lot. We know Comstock worked in the shipping department at Suter. He also worked at Biddwell Die Casting. He's kind of disappeared. Ben has a file on him."

The men in the bedroom could hear the shuffling of papers in the background over the phone's speaker. During the muted conversation from the partners' offices, Jason took the opportunity to evaluate the new information.

His mind raced at the implications of the search of the Cray's house. All Jason could think of were more questions. If Pathmoor had the same information as Cray, did it connect him to Comstock? It didn't seem right that Cray would be involved with Comstock. Or did it? Would Pathmoor knowingly be involved in the murder of the Crays? No. From what Jason had learned of Pathmoor, he didn't think he would have the stomach for that type of activity.

Closer to the truth, Comstock may have learned that Cray had learned whatever it is Jack didn't know he knew, and Comstock punched Cray's ticket. That made more sense. But how did he make the connection? The questions and suppositions continued in an endless stream, and Jason decided to stay with what he knew and hoped the rest would fall into place. In his mind there were still two separate issues: Pathmoor was not the threat to Jack. Comstock was. He had already learned that from the interview with Monroe and his encounter with Curly. Pathmoor simply muddied the water, probably without knowing it. Pathmoor had blindly stumbled into more than he had bargained for.

As Jason pondered, he came up with an idea of how this situation with Pathmoor could possibly be twisted just far enough to eliminate Pathmoor from the equation and then they could gain information on what Cray had learned and whom it threatened.

"Lieutenant," Jason began, "we know Pathmoor is nothing but a low-life. What if we work him to our advantage? With any luck, he'll beg you to lock him up for his own protection."

"I'm listening."

"You've told us he looked frightened when you told him about the Crays. Now let's put the fear of God into him."

"And just how do you propose we do that?" Dailey asked dubiously.

"You said that you were sure he lied when you asked him about the last time he saw Cray. Ask him about his stock and his boat. Ask him about Comstock. We think that Comstock is mixed up in this equation somehow. Press him."

Jason briefly recapped some of the information on Comstock, stopping just short of telling him about Monroe and Diablo Island. He explained to Dailey about Comstock's army career, his short stint at Biddwell Die Casting, the employment at Suter and then his sudden disappearance.

On several occasions, Dailey tried to interrupt with questions, but Jason talked over him, and assuring him that the information was sound. He hoped he had done the right thing. He would rather have personally interrogated Pathmoor himself, but he knew that would be impossible.

"Lieutenant, the way I see it, there're only two possibilities: one, Pathmoor is involved with whoever killed Cray and knows what the hell is going on, in which case he has nothing to fear, or so he may think. The very fact that you have contacted him may change that. Seems like when you talk to people lately, their life span dramatically decreases.

"The second possibility is that he doesn't know squat. But he lied about the last time he saw Cray. It'd be your job,

Lieutenant, to make him think that whoever we're dealing with knows about him. Then all you need to do is walk through the body count to date in graphic detail. Tell him about Carston Jennings bleeding to death in the parking lot and about Lori Phillips being snuffed in the hospital while under guard.

"Even though you weren't there, you can tell him about Curly being blown away by one of his own because he screwed up. Tell him about how Samuel Wellington was turned into a piece of toast for nothing more than being questioned—and you might add that the guy never said a thing."

As Jason continued to speak, he became impassioned, taking on the sound of a wound-up Southern Baptist preacher. He brought a frightening perspective to the singular events of the past seven days. Everyone, including Jason himself, having been focused on bits and pieces of specific events, had lost track of the overall picture. As Jason laid it out now, it looked like a black hole.

"Ask our Mr. Pathmoor what Martin Cray might have known, Lieutenant. Impress upon him that everyone who has either stumbled into this mess or been a part of it and screwed up has wound up looking at the sky through a six-foot-deep dirt filter. I'll bet you your last raise that he'll squirm like a salted slug and be more than happy to talk to you about when he last saw Martin Cray. Who knows? You might get lucky and get some information on Comstock."

"You've painted a pretty ugly picture," Dailey said quietly.

"It is an ugly picture, Lieutenant. So, you up for this one? Think it'll work?"

"Based on what we saw yesterday, I think it will," Montgomery said. "He's on the edge, it won't take much to push him over."

"You think this Comstock is the key to this mess, Brisben?" Dailey asked.

"He's involved somehow, Lieutenant."

"Well, Pathmoor's not stupid. He'll want an attorney and then turn into a mute."

"That's his point, boss," Montgomery said, having picked up on the psychology of Jason's idea. "We make Pathmoor an offer: protection for information. All we have to do is go through the litany of corpses, then convince him that we won't be able to protect him if he's on the street. We can always make the deal sound better than it is."

A groan rose from the speaker. "I wish I'd taken my early retirement," said Dailey. "Brisben, the day you talked me into letting you in on this, I knew I'd regret it. Just for your information, I'm not real big on cutting deals to slime. I'm also not too keen on promising something that I can't deliver, doesn't matter how slimy they are. I guess that's beside the point now, isn't it? Also, before I go harassing Pathmoor again, I think it'd be prudent to talk to someone over at Suter. If I'm going on a fishing expedition, I'd kinda like to know what kind of bait I'll be using."

"The man to contact at Suter would be Hugh Saltzman, VP and general manager," Jack offered. "He can provide any information that you'd need."

"Why do I get this gnawing sensation that I'm not in control of this damn investigation?" Dailey asked in frustration.

All eyes shifted to Jason, whose expression changed to just a hint of a grin. David and Steve understood the wisdom of Jason's strategy not to be completely forthright, viewing the manipulation of Dailey and withholding of information a necessity. If Dailey and Montgomery were to get wind of Monroe or Diablo, they would have no choice but to let the Feds take control. And no one wanted that.

Jack, however, saw Jason's withholding of information as dangerously wrong, even with the additional information he had given Dailey. He gave his friend a penetrating stare, but said nothing.

"So, when can I expect you back in town, Mr. Brisben?" asked Dailey.

"I'll be returning to Seattle midday on Tuesday."

"You contact me the minute you arrive," Dailey commanded. With that, the call ended.

After David and Steve left the room, Jack asked, "Jason, why are you being dishonest with Dailey? I don't like it. It makes me uneasy."

"I have no problem sharing what I know with Lieutenant Dailey, Jack. But if I gave him all the information I have, he would have to turn it over to the government."

"Well, what if he does?" Jack asked. "It seems to me, that would be the safest way out of this mess."

"For who, Jack? Maybe for the government, but certainly not for you. We're about 95 percent on who but we're nowhere on the why. If the Feds get involved, you may never be safe."

"How in the hell do you figure that?" Jack asked in frustration.

"How well did they handle Waco or Ruby Ridge? If the Feds get involved, they may shut the island down, no problem. A lot of people could get killed. Or, on the other hand, because of media pressure, nothing may happen. It might just turn into a standoff. With either scenario, you'll be in danger."

"Why would I still be in danger if the operation is shut down?"

"Because, Jack, we may never learn the why, and until we do, we can't effectively bring this thing to a close. Until we know why, and also get close enough to the organization to find all parties in the know on this, we'll run the risk of some straggler out there somewhere looking for revenge. Don't forget this whole thing started because someone thinks you know something that can jeopardize whatever it is they're into. Please trust me on this Jack. I promise you, I'll give Comstock to Dailey, but only if it works to our advantage. As you've witnessed, the partners and I can move faster than the police or the government. Just remember, Jennings and Phillips are dead, Wellington is dead, the Crays are dead. Since just a week ago tonight, there's a pile of bodies stacking up that Evel Knievel couldn't jump his motorcycle over."

CHAPTER THIRTY-TWO

Jason had been lying down almost an hour when Carol entered the room, quietly closed the door, and padded to the bed. "Did I wake you?" she asked as she climbed in next to him.

"No," he answered in a voice full of both preoccupation and fatigue. It had been a long day, and he had not recovered from the lack of sleep from the previous week. The few brief hours of the preceding night had not satisfied the deficit. Delivering the news about the Crays and the mental fencing with Dailey had effectively drained his energy.

After his conversation with Jack that afternoon, he had contacted Keller and made arrangements to be picked up Tuesday at the Nehalem Airstrip, then gone upstairs to join Jack and the others.

Laura had just finished a session with Debbie, Jennifer, and Carol and, by the looks of all parties, it had gone well. While Debbie started dinner in the kitchen, Laura took Jason aside to report.

Jennifer would be fine. The fear and terror would eventually subside, maybe in two or three months, but the guilt of betraying her family and putting them at risk would take longer. Laura worked diligently with her on that issue, impressing upon her that she had not been told of her family's situation and had no knowledge of the risk. To her credit, Jennifer had flatly stated that she wasn't sure it would have made any difference.

"I'm not sure I would have believed you, Mom; I probably would have done it anyway," she said. "I think I just wanted my own way." She shook her head in disbelief and once again apologized. "It was so stupid. I'm so sorry."

Jennifer, in the midst of difficult adolescent physical and hormonal changes in her transition to womanhood, communicated a mature honesty to her mother, Carol and Laura, and most important, to herself. Her parents could be proud of her and the values they had mirrored to her.

The episode in Victoria had released a myriad of demons from Carol's past. Seeing the abduction of Jennifer renewed the nightmares, the mental images that tortured her. Not knowing what had happened to her nine-year-old daughter was worse than knowing the worst. Laura assured Jason that Carol, too, would be fine, but again, it would take time and patience.

Debbie for some inexplicable reason seemed to be doing well, her anxiety having somewhat subsided. Laura hypothesized that Debbie's family being together provided comfort to her. She had suppressed a great deal, but for now she appeared rather content, a good sign.

Laura's report, the events of the past week and speculation on what lay ahead were what took Jason away from Carol as he lay next to her. Alone with his thoughts he fell into an exhausted stupor. Then sleep.

* * * * *

Jason felt Carol draw close and felt the warmth of her body and breath on his neck. He opened his eyes to find sun streaming through a crack in the curtains.

"Are you with us?" she asked softly into his ear.

He remembered nothing of falling asleep. The aroma of fresh-brewed coffee filled the room. Carol had already been up and made the coffee. He turned his head toward her and slid deeply into her green eyes as he tried to orient himself. I love this woman, he said to himself, then asked for the time.

"Eight-fifteen," she answered. He raised his head and kissed her gently on the lips. She had showered and brushed her teeth; she smelled fresh.

"How are you?" he asked quietly.

In a honey-sweet voice she answered, "Fine." He knew better. She was frightened and vulnerable, and reliving the horror of the past.

In a time past, he would have taken her physically as he had so many women over the years, roughly and with pain, not worrying nor even caring about her spirit or soul. Even with his last wife, he had not taken time to learn what lay beneath the skin. They were reckless, taking their fill of the days. They drank and danced and made love with abandon. He took no time to get to know her and, as it turned out, their future held no opportunity for him to do so.

But this time it will be different, Jason vowed. He knew Carol hungered for reassurance and protection just as she had from her husband after the loss of their daughter. Instead, she had received rejection and abandonment. He knew that fear made her vulnerable. I want Carol to know it won't be like before, he thought. I won't abandon her. I will stick with her and protect her. When we make love it will be for the right reasons. The commitment of love draws what is right.

"Do you want to talk about it?" he asked timidly.

Carol blinked with surprise. "Talk about what?" Her look transformed into one of bewilderment as she raised up on her elbow.

Jason reached up and tenderly touched her cheek with his fingertips. His eyes betrayed his bravery, but his courage did not falter as they maintained eye contact.

"This is hard for me, so just let me talk for a minute, before I lose my nerve. Funny, I asked you if you wanted to talk and now I want to do all the talking.

"I won't abandon you. I know you're frightened and this thing that happened in Victoria not only scared the hell out of you but it also stirred up old memories. I just want you to know I'll be here for you, just to hold you, reassure you, whatever you need. I don't want you to think our lovemaking is the only glue that holds us together. There's a lot more here than that. Don't get me wrong. Lovemaking with you is something special, but it's more important to me that you're okay."

Her eyes welled up. "You bastard," she sobbed.

Jason wanted to ask why she said what she had, but some new instinct allowed him to hold his tongue. He did not know how to respond and hoped she would say more. She laid her head on his chest and continued crying. He simply held her and let her cry. After several minutes, she spoke in between sobs.

"I was angry with you for this whole mess. I hated you in Victoria because of the memories of Melanie and my inability to control the situation with Jennifer. When I woke up in that house with that ugly sonofabitch drooling in my face, you got blamed for that too. I knew without a doubt that if and when I ever got to see you again, I would scratch your eyes out.

"When that jerk had me in the hallway and you turned around, I wanted to run to you and have you hold me. But it seemed as if you didn't even see me. You looked hard like stone. Then I understood the kind of job you'd been doing all those years and what you've been struggling with." Her gaze held his. "I saw you as the warrior, Jason.

"And . . . and now you've said things to me that you've never said before. You want to have a . . . a relationship. You want to spend the rest of your life with me. I'm scared to death of you and yet I'm drawn to you like a magnet. I don't want to fall in love with you, Jason; oh hell, who am I trying to kid? I already have."

Carol raised up again and rested on her elbow. She took the sheet and wiped her eyes and nose. She looked hard at Jason through her puffy, bloodshot eyes.

"What scares me is that one day you'll go see a friend or try to help somebody and some slimy creep will do to you what you did to that bastard in Victoria. I don't want to live in fear, Jason, fear of you one day walking out the door and me never hearing from you again. It's happened to me once and I don't want to try living through that again. I can't.

"And now I'm really mad. I came in here last night wanting to make love, thinking at least it would feel good, give us a release, a momentary escape. And you fall asleep on me. Then this morning, when you do wake up, you want to talk and dredge up all this garbage."

Jason reached up and lightly brushed a few strands of her crimson hair from her eyes. "It was important, wasn't it?" he asked, searching her face for some clue about how to proceed. "I mean talking about how we feel? I understand how you feel about things. I just want to know where we go from here?"

A look of astonishment came over Carol. "You understand," she said, "and now you want me to decide where we go from here? That's fair!"

"I'm sorry. You misunderstood. I'm part of this equation. This is something we both have to decide. And no, it's not fair. We are both in this situation. I didn't plan it and you sure as hell didn't plan it, but here we are."

He reached his arm around her and gently pulled her to his chest again. "We are where we are," he said, kissing the top of her head and inhaling the perfume of her hair. "I'm tempted to say this is the way I am and if you can't accept me, then walk and don't look back. And if you did do that, I wouldn't blame you. But that's not fair either, because it puts the responsibility solely on you and I think I have responsibility here also. I don't think I can change overnight, but maybe we can evolve. We both have to understand that I'm going back to Seattle tomorrow. I don't know what lies in the future and you don't either. So what would happen if we simply trust and step ahead one day at a time and let our relationship and our lives evolve? I can promise you one thing, I won't go out of my way looking for trouble."

"But you won't run from it either," she said quietly.

"No," he answered. You're right. And I can't predict the future. I know . . . the normal way of doing things seems to be 'plan your life, your education, your finances, your children, and family,' but stop and think for a minute. What are we really in control of? Hell, look at Jack. He's the epitome of a planner and look what's happened to him. He may not have a company to go back to. All I'm saying is, life is a journey with detours and pitfalls, it's evolution being lived out. I don't want to make decisions about the rest of our lives based on what's happened this last week. Do you think that we can take it slow, let us progress and see how it turns out? I know it's asking a lot, but I don't want to screw this up and lose you."

Carol remained silent and after a time of lying together in silence, she said, "I don't know what to say."

"You don't have to say anything."

"I had all of the reasons why our relationship won't work memorized, and now . . ."

"There are many reasons why our relationship might not work," Jason interrupted, "but the question is, is it worth fighting for? And this isn't as one-sided as it sounds. You have some issues playing into this situation. It's going to take both of us putting 100 percent into it."

"I know," she said softly.

"So, you want to think about it?"

"No. I just want it to happen." She raised up again and kissed his forehead.

"It will," he answered, "with commitment and a lot of patience. Oh, by the way, in case you're wondering, I would have liked nothing better than to make love to you earlier, but I thought we'd have a better chance for success in our relationship if we had this discussion."

"The discussion is finished isn't it? I fail to see the problem."

* * * * *

At Suter in Chehalis, Dailey explained to Hugh Saltzman that he needed to ask some questions pertaining to alleged improprieties regarding Richard Pathmoor.

Saltzman, a tall man with a head of snow-white hair, and an iron-grip handshake, carried an air of professionalism about him. His white shirt and summer wool trousers were meticulously pressed, but in spite of his appearance, he had a way of putting one at ease with a disarming smile.

"Lieutenant, I can't believe that anyone from the Suter organization would pressure Pathmoor, or anyone, to influence the standards of the security system. I've been very impressed with the work Jack O'Connor and Cervicon have performed. I have been aware of the delays and the financial ramifications, but that's certainly not any of Mr. O'Connor's doing."

"Mr. Saltzman, last week when I questioned Pathmoor, he admitted to hiring on at Cervicon to speed the project along."

Saltzman shook his head "I'm appalled to think someone at Suter would be involved in compromising our security.

Pathmoor must be acting on his own. I assure you, gentlemen, you will have Suter's full cooperation in your investigation."

"The name George Comstock has come up during our investigation. Apparently he's an ex-employee of yours. Do you happen to have any information on him?" Montgomery inquired.

"The name isn't one I recognize, but we have over one hundred and thirty employees here." Saltzman pushed the intercom on his desk. "Katharine, get a hold of Human Resources and have them locate a personnel file on a George Comstock, please. Oh and Katharine, find out where he worked and have his supervisor report to my office with the file immediately. Thank you."

Within five minutes, a gray-haired man in his middle fifties entered Saltzman's office with Comstock's file in hand. Saltzman introduced him to Dailey and Montgomery as Carl Fortner, the shipping manager and Comstock's former supervisor.

"Mr. Fortner," Dailey began, "tell me about Comstock as an employee."

"Comstock wasn't a problem employee, per se, or disruptive, but he wasn't highly motivated either," Fortner emphasized. "We have six loading bays, eight forklifts, and fifteen people in shipping on two shifts, so I don't have my eye on them 100 percent of the time."

"I am assuming that Comstock worked days," Dailey guessed.

"Yes."

"Who hired Comstock?"

"Hiring is handled through our personnel department. Department heads put in requests for the manpower they need, and if there isn't a hiring freeze, you get what you need. I simply put in a requisition and bingo, Comstock showed up four days later. As I said, Comstock as an employee wasn't much to write home about, but he did get the product out the door."

"Would someone have recommended Comstock for the position or did he have a friend here at Suter?" Fortner gave a noncommittal shrug, but something in his eyes said he had more to tell. "I ask only because, according to our information,"

Dailey said, "George Comstock was discharged from the US Army for dealing drugs and also was suspected of dealing drugs in his previous job before coming to Suter. I guess my question would have to be how in hell did he get hired on at one of the nation's top drug companies with that background?"

"I don't know," Fortner replied, again with a shrug, and glanced away, breaking eye contact. He did not appear to be shaken or concerned by Dailey's question. "As I said, I don't hire. I just run with the people they give me. I guess you ought to be talking to the people in personnel."

Suddenly an air of electric tension filled Saltzman's office. While Fortner looked bored with the questioning, Saltzman radiated shock.

"Those are some serious charges, Lieutenant," Saltzman said, his voice husky with anger. "And dammit, man," he said turning toward his shipping supervisor, "I don't think you have a grasp of the severity of what Lt. Dailey has just implied. If what he says is true, we have some serious problems here, and I expect you to be a damn sight more cooperative."

Saltzman's charge effected little change in Fortner's expression, nor did he appear intimidated by the general manager. Once again his lack of response baffled Dailey. Obviously he knew more about Comstock than he let on. The dilemma that faced Dailey was one of jurisdiction. He had no legal authority as a police officer. He could only hope Saltzman would provide the leverage.

"Let me add a bit of perspective," Dailey interjected. "I'm in the midst of a murder investigation up in Seattle, actually several murders." Fortner suddenly lost his bored and passive demeanor.

"Murder!" Saltzman exclaimed. "Lieutenant, I'm confused, I thought this interview was about Pathmoor's possible unethical business practices and your wanting some background information on Comstock. Did I miss something here? When did we make the transition to murder?"

"I'm sure by now you have heard of the death of Martin Cray, and, just a week ago now, about a couple in Seattle stabbed to death in a restaurant parking lot."

"I read about both in the paper," Saltzman interrupted. "Cray's terrible boating accident. But I don't understand the connection with the parking lot incident."

"You're just a little out of your jurisdiction, aren't you, Lieutenant?" asked Fortner sarcastically.

"Dammit, Carl," Saltzman snapped, "this isn't about jurisdiction; it's about people who've been killed, so you'd damn well better act like it matters. I'm not liking what I'm seeing. If you value your position, you'd better get your act together. Have I made myself clear?"

"Perfectly." Fortner's eyes danced with rage.

"Excuse me, Lieutenant," Saltzman said, turning his attention back to Dailey. "As I said, I'm a bit confused. Are you saying that Martin Cray was also murdered?"

"Our being here is a bit more than routine," Dailey admitted. "It won't be long before the press prints the facts. The explosion that took place on Cray's boat did not qualify as an accident. We need help, and there are people who have information we can use. Pathmoor, for one, and we are in contact with him on a regular basis, but Comstock is another story. We seem to be unable to locate him or anyone who knows much about him. Any help you gentleman can provide will be appreciated."

Saltzman, still reeling from the news of Martin Cray's murder, looked at Dailey. It him took a moment to speak. "And you think there is a connection between the parking lot murders and Martin Cray, and Comstock is involved?"

"Don't know. At this point, we're not sure but it would be helpful if we could speak to him."

Saltzman nodded his understanding as he reached for the telephone. "Well, the one we should talk to is Pam Devlin our Human Resources Manager."

Saltzman stood at his desk and pushed the intercom button. "Katharine, please send Pam Devlin in."

"I'm sorry, Hugh," the voice from the speaker said, "Pam is off for the day. She has a doctor's appointment."

"Lieutenant, it appears we won't be too much help today." Saltzman turned toward Fortner and instructed him to talk with his people in shipping. "See if you can learn anything about Comstock. Maybe someone will know how to contact him. Take Detective Montgomery with you," he added.

"Yes, sir," Fortner answered sharply. His face flushed as he glanced at his watch, then walked from the office leaving Montgomery to follow.

Saltzman spoke immediately after Montgomery closed the office door. "Lieutenant, I apologize for Carl's behavior. I don't appreciate the vagueness with which he answered your questions.

"These questions you've put to me are frightening because there are only two people in this organization who are at a higher level than me: Abel Sloan, the president, and A.J. Suter the company founder. I'm not quite sure whom I can trust at this point, that is, if Pathmoor's story is true. Lieutenant, I would appreciate the opportunity, or the time, that is, to make some discrete inquiries into this thing with Pathmoor. I'd also like to interview Pam Devlin and get answers on how Comstock, a drug dealer, was granted employment here at Suter."

As Saltzman spoke, Dailey observed a frightened sincerity. But he decided not to ask Saltzman about the coincidence of the two 50K cashiers checks; he would wait and confront Pathmoor first.

Dailey handed Saltzman him his card. "We would appreciate any help that you can provide, Mr. Saltzman. If you should come across anything of importance before your interview with Ms. Devlin, please call the precinct number. They'll page me if I'm not in. Detective Montgomery or I will get right back to you."

* * * * *

Now Dailey and Montgomery stood before Pathmoor wishing they had taken more time before confronting him. He would rather have conducted a thorough investigation at Suter. To his way of thinking, a lot more information would have been beneficial at this moment, such as Pathmoor's contact at Suter. Who would benefit from a compromised security system? Who were the people outside of Suter that would stand to gain: Pathmoor? Comstock?

The fact that he was involved in an investigation over which he had no control also plagued Dailey. He had been called to a murder scene shortly after midnight last Monday morning. By Monday afternoon, he had rebuffed Jason Brisben's offer to assist in the investigation. And now? Now, exactly one week later, he stood again in front of Richard Pathmoor—with the sense that he had been led and manipulated by Jason Brisben's spoonfed leads. Also it seemed to him that Jason evidently had a great deal more information than he shared. The Issaquah house particularly bothered him. What had really gone on out there? And Comstock? Where did all of the information on him come from, and how much did Brisben really have? What had gone on in Victoria? Jason had kept him busy since the rescue of Jennifer O'Connor and Carol Dunsmure. Then why, as one of Seattle's finest, hadn't he waited in order to pull the loose ends together? Damn! Nevertheless, they were there, weren't they—he, Montgomery, and the nervous, Mr. Pathmoor.

Dailey started with a plan to unnerve his adversary by asking questions in three areas. This time, Pathmoor sat cowering behind his desk, his bravado gone.

"Mr. Pathmoor, does the name George Comstock mean anything to you?" He watched carefully for any indication of a lie (a wasted effort in that Pathmoor rarely told the truth, until he trapped himself.)

"I don't understand," he replied, not answering directly, obviously surprised and confused by the question—the effect Dailey had wanted.

"It's a simple question," Montgomery, abruptly interrupted. "We know he worked at Suter. Are you going to pretend that you didn't know him—or at least know of him—when you worked there?"

Pathmoor looked for help from Dailey. "No, I don't recognize the name." The man had the look of a trapped animal, which heightened Dailey's attack.

"We know that George Comstock worked at Suter from December of '93 to November of '94." Dailey, his eyes blazing like lasers, leaned across Pathmoor's desk, their faces only inches apart. "A six-foot-plus, three-hundred-pound behemoth.

Now don't give me any bullshit that you didn't know him. Suter only has a hundred and thirty-some employees. I can't believe that he worked there for damn near a year and you didn't at least know of him?"

"Why should I have contact with someone who worked in shipping?" Pathmoor shot.

"Why indeed?" Without diverting eye contact with Pathmoor, Dailey spoke to Montgomery. "Interesting. Bob, I didn't say anything about shipping. Did you mention anything about shipping? Because if you didn't, how the hell did our Mr. Pathmoor here know that George Comstock worked in shipping? Would you care to clarify that for us?"

Dailey reveled in the look on Pathmoor's face and the ensuing silence. Dailey had just hit his stride, now at his best, the infighting of interrogation. More information from Suter would have been helpful, but that only would have removed the fencing, the drama of uncertainty. Pathmoor's face had given the lieutenant what he wanted. Pathmoor was trapped like an animal in a hole. The first one to speak would be the loser.

"I . . . I'd just seen him a couple of times out on the shipping dock," he stammered. "That doesn't mean I knew him."

The rodent panicked and darted from his hole, on the run with the wily old fox at his heels.

"Go on," Dailey told Pathmoor, his face still only inches away. He watched silently as his crumbling adversary self-destructed before his eyes. He would have felt sorry for the little rat, if he hadn't despised him so much.

"Go on? What's to go on about? I saw him—all right? So what?" He tried to look away, but with Dailey's face so close he had nowhere to look.

"'So what,' Mr. Pathmoor, is that we're in the midst of a murder investigation. You do remember that, don't you? We know about Comstock's involvement with drugs. We know that Comstock is somehow connected to the Carston Jennings murder in the parking lot. We suspect he is involved in the murder of the Crays. And we are pretty damn sure that you know him, or know a lot damn more than you're letting on. So let's try this once again. I want to know what you know about George Comstock."

"I told you, I just saw him in the shipping area a couple of times." In that, Pathmoor seemed quite adamant. "And this is becoming tiresome, Lieutenant."

Dailey had no hard evidence to link Pathmoor or Comstock to any of the murders. He only knew that bodies were stacking up like cordwood. But he saw this as a chess match with Pathmoor in trouble; still, Dailey had nothing to move to the endgame. But he could read Pathmoor's fear. What was he afraid of? What did he know?

Montgomery took a turn, "We've been to Suter. We've talked to Hugh Saltzman, to Carl Fortner, and Pam Devlin. We have Comstock's personnel file," he lied, "and it's a curious thing, Mr. Pathmoor, it doesn't mention a thing about him having a drug problem. Not to mention, selling them. How do you suppose he landed a job at Suter with a background like that, Mr. Pathmoor?"

Pathmoor flinched when Montgomery stated that they had been to Suter. "I have no idea. I was not in charge of hiring at Suter. You must remember my area of responsibility: market research."

Dailey allowed his instincts to direct his attack. The rat would tire soon, and to quicken the process, he turned him in a different direction.

"Let me help you get a handle on the overall picture. When I met you last week, you told me that you came to Cervicon to expedite the approval on the security system at the new Suter plant. And no, I don't buy the story that you, out of the kindness of your heart would leave your job at Suter to do them a favor by pressuring Cervicon into doing a schlocky job of security."

Dailey quizzed, "So they wouldn't lose money, as you claimed? I'm not at all convinced that's the real goal. So that leaves me with a whole truckload of questions, mister. One being, who at Suter stands to gain by a compromised security system? Certainly not A.J. Suter. He would have more to lose than money from bad publicity due to lax security. He'd be out of business. That's too great a risk for someone who's spent his whole life building his dynasty."

Dailey and Montgomery watched intently for any sign of a reaction in Pathmoor—another flinch, a tick of the eye, anything at all.

"How about Hugh Saltzman?" No perceptible reaction detected, and Dailey guarded against showing any disappointment. "Carl Fortner," again nothing. "The president, Abel Sloan?" Dailey barked. Ah, there it was: Pathmoor's eyes flickered downward for but an instant before he could recover and once again lock on his inquisitor's penetrating stare. Dailey immediately resumed the chase affording no time for recovery, leaving the despicable rodent no other direction but headlong into his jaws.

"You see, Mr. Pathmoor, we know you're dirty. We're sure of it. You have lied to me from the start. You've lied to us about your last contact with Martin Cray." At that, Pathmoor simply closed his eyes. With Dailey's face still only inches from his own, he had no other option. "You lied about the real purpose of your going to Cervicon. You're a piece of scum. You've confirmed that only too well. Tell me, Mr. Pathmoor—please tell me about the two payments totaling one hundred thousand dollars you received from Suter." Pathmoor could not escape the jaws of the fox.

In defeat, he slowly shook his head, letting it fall forward from sagging shoulders into his hands. "I want an attorney."

"Of course you do, Mr. Pathmoor, of course you do."

CHAPTER THIRTY-THREE

A heavy overcast, followed by a penetrating mist so typical of the Oregon coast, defeated the afternoon sun's warmth and light. Jason and Carol walked back toward the beach house, looking like a pair of wet dogs, their frolic on the beach cut short by the elements. A quarter of a mile from the house, Carol pointed toward one of the large windows. "What's that light?"

"A strobe light. It's a signal from David or Steve that something's up." Unknown to Carol, Jason had been aware of the signal for some time. In truth, the weather had not caused their return.

"What do you think it is?" Carol asked with worried anxiousness.

"Don't know, but I'm sure I'll find out soon enough." They walked briskly to the beach's end, then clambered over the rocks and driftwood to the trail that disappeared into the undergrowth and ultimately led up the bluff to the house. Ferns and Oregon grape, laden with mist, swabbed the couple at their passing. By the time they arrived at the house, they were soaked to the skin.

Carol went to their room and toweled off while Jason met with David and Steve. When he returned, his expression confirmed her fears. She knew their time had been cut short.

"When do you have to leave?" she asked, failing to mask her disappointment.

"Keller's on his way in a helicopter. He'll be here in an hour or so."

"What's happened? He wasn't suppose to come until tomorrow." The fear she had described to him that morning as they lay bed could not be disguised. She looked to Jason for a response. Dread chiseled her face as if it were sculpted in stone.

"The partners think they've located Comstock. David and Steve will stay here with you and the family. I have to meet with the partners."

"Shouldn't that information be turned over to Lieutenant Dailey?" Carol asked, trying not to sound accusing.

Jason understood her concern, but chose not to debate the issue. He also would not lie to her either.

"Dailey will get bogged down in red tape and procedures. We can move a hell of a lot faster than he can."

She shuddered as a fear-induced chill breathed through her body. This new development terrified her, but she knew she would have to release him to what he needed to do. The fear and pain of it were hers alone to deal with.

Jason felt her coldness and her trembling. He took her into his arms to warm her, but he had nothing to say to quell the fear. He just held her, taking in her anxiety.

After a few minutes, she pressed herself loose from him and locked the bedroom door. She returned and took his hands, led him to the bathroom, and turned on the water in the shower.

"I don't have a lot of time, sweetheart."

"I know you don't . . . but right now I'll settle for the little that we do have."

Words were of no value. Jason simply held Carol and allowed her to absorb what little protection he could give her in what their time would afford. After a while, Carol took the soap, handed it to Jason and guided his hand over her body. He returned the soap to the tray, then slowly ran his hands over her slick contours. She drew him to her. They remained locked together, steam turning the small bathroom into a cleansing sauna. Briefly, time stood still. Time enough for two souls to become one.

* * * * *

"Have any trouble coming in with all this soup?" Jason asked Keller as they lifted off.

The doctor waved his free hand across the panorama of instrumentation spread before them. "Not a bit, man. Ain't all this modern technology grand?"

Jason watched Steve drive the Lincoln away from the Nehalem Airstrip as the ground rapidly dropped away beneath them. He felt a twinge of longing and wished Carol had come to see him off, but he understood why she hadn't. He continued to watch the silver car diminish in size until it disappeared from view as Keller banked sharply to the left, taking the helicopter west over the ocean. At about a thousand feet, he dropped the nose and headed up the coast through the mist and clouds. Jason could see the beach house as only a faint shadow through the heavy mist and felt remorse at what he had left behind.

"You all right, buddy?" Keller asked, looking intently out at nothing but gray, then taking a quick glance at the instruments.

"What? Oh, yeah. Why aren't you at the hospital?"

"I took some vacation time. I can't let you have all the fun." He glanced over briefly at Jason, then back to the business of flying blind. "I'm still pissed about Lori Phillips, and according to the partners, you're spread way too thin on this damn thing, buddy, so I figured you could use another body. And besides, I haven't done any ass-kicking for a long time. Now I'm gonna ask you one more time. You okay? You act like you're not all here."

"I'm fine." Jason answered, now understanding Keller's concern. He just needed a little time to get focused and hoped the return trip would be enough. "How'd they locate Comstock?"

"A combined effort. Krieger sat in on my session with Monroe. We now have a detailed description of the camp. One thing Krieger picked up on was that the Diablo personnel were being ferried back and forth to Boeing Field by chopper, so he staked it out. While he checked out Boeing Field, I got a call from the partners. They seemed to think an outfit named Patriot Chemicals looked promising. Seems as though they're extremely profitable. They move a considerable tonnage through the place. About three times as much as the competition."

Jason's eyes were closed, his head pressed against the seat headrest. A jolt of turbulence made him open his eyes and turn his head toward Keller.

"The funny thing is," Keller continued, as he worked the ship to find smooth air, "the competition has two to three times the manpower and they're turning over less product. Patriot claims only seven employees."

"So they're using labor from the camp, not paying them, and funneling the profits to the camp to build an army."

"Sure looks that way."

"About the same time I'm learning all this, Krieger spotted a Huey come in and drop off half a dozen men. They were packed into a van with no windows, just like Monroe said."

"And Krieger followed it to Patriot Chemicals," Jason cut in.

"You got it! So Krieger rented a pickup and did a little snooping, pretending to be lost with a delivery for a business down the street. While he's talking with some dude, a door from a side office opens, and our boy catches a glimpse of someone the size of Sasquatch. Said the Neanderthal looked about six-six and close to four hundred pounds."

"Sounds like we found the missing link," Jason said, referring to Comstock.

"Looks like it." Keller fell silent as he continued to deal with increasing turbulence.

"The other news you'll be interested in hearing, " Keller began again, "is Dailey and Montgomery took Richard Pathmoor in around three o'clock this afternoon for questioning. As far as we know, he hasn't asked for an attorney, at least not yet. I checked with Joe about twenty minutes before I picked you up. I guess that leaves us with a few decisions to make. You want to talk to the partners first? You want to try to make a night run up to Diablo tonight or you want to go back to The Kennel and make a plan on hitting Comstock?"

Jason considered this new information. He knew the first priority should be getting hold of Comstock, but it would be tricky now that Dailey knew about him. Conversely, if Jason, were to give up Comstock now that he knew his location, would

Dailey provide any information in return? Not likely, he thought.

The camp on Diablo Island he would leave as an open option. Jason sensed the camp lay at the root of the situation, but now more than ever he would need to exercise patience. "Let's see what we can find out about Pathmoor; then we can decide how to handle Comstock," Jason said, thinking aloud. "No sense going to The Kennel. Let's go directly to the partners for a reality check, then hit Dailey before we make any decisions."

Keller simply nodded, retaining his stoic vigilance at the controls as the now violent ride continued through seemingly impenetrable gray.

*　*　*　*　*

Once at the precinct, they took Pathmoor to an interrogation room. Montgomery explained to him that he had not been arrested, only brought in for more questioning; and he assured him he could have an attorney present at any time.

Dailey, holding a manila folder, seated himself directly across from Pathmoor, while Montgomery stood, leaning against the wall next to the door. Pathmoor's eyes shifted expectantly back and forth between the two detectives as Dailey slowly removed photographs from the file folder and studied them briefly. His facial expression gave no hint of his thoughts while slowly sifting through the lot of them, then turning a select few face down in front of Pathmoor. Pathmoor's eyes nervously flitted between the backsides of the photos and the hard stare of Dailey. Montgomery looked relaxed continuing to observe from the wall.

"Well, Mr. Pathmoor," Dailey began, "a lot has changed since I spoke to you about the attempts on Jack O'Connor's life. Now, I realize you have requested an attorney—and you're certainly entitled. But before you exercise that right, I think you'll want to hear me out. Are you agreeable to that?"

Pathmoor continued to look back and forth between the photos and Dailey's now passive stare before he responded weakly, "Just what is it you have to say, Lieutenant?"

*　*　*　*　*

After landing at Boeing Field in heavy rain, Jason and Keller drove directly to the partners' office where Jason learned that Dailey was still questioning Pathmoor. "If that's the situation, we might as well make use of our time to develop a strategy for a recon of Diablo," Jason suggested.

"Speaking of Diablo," Ben said, "a closed corporation named Federal Free Incorporated, purchased the island three years ago from United Resorts Unlimited. URU originally purchased the island in 1990 with the intention of building an upscale resort. Unfortunately the island lived up to its name by proving to be inhospitable. Below a shallow surface of topsoil, there's nothing but rock and very little water, and what water there is is undrinkable. The only access to the island is by boat, float plane, or helicopter. There's not enough suitable area for even a small airstrip. URU's market research determined that the costs of trying to make the rock an appealing vacation destination didn't pencil out when weighed against a limited clientele and decided to cut their losses. They sold to Federal Free in '92 for 6.2 million. My efforts to research Federal Free yielded a big zero. The officers of the corporation don't seem to exist."

* * * * *

Dailey dispensed with further head games and went after the information he wanted. "As you'll notice, the recorder isn't running." He nodded at the machine and paused briefly for effect, then plowed ahead with a blend of bluff and factual information. "On November 28th of last year, a cashier's check was drawn from Suter Pharmaceuticals for, of all things, consulting fees. We know you received fifty thousand dollars in November of last year, and used it to buy your 800 shares of Microsoft stock at 63-1/8. You were $500 short for the transaction and drew the balance from your savings at SeaFirst bank. March 29th, guess what? Another cashier's check for another fifty thousand dollars! April 8th of this year you bought, from what I'm told, a pretty nice sailboat. That cost you another 50K. Let's not fence, Mr. Pathmoor, I'm playing it straight with you, because I've got a truckload of bodies piling up and I'm running out of time for getting answers."

"Yes, I understand that, Lieutenant," he said weakly. "But just because I've made some purchases doesn't prove anything. Doesn't mean I—"

"Stop!" Dailey shouted, rising from his chair. "I don't want to hear anything unless it's why Abel Sloan is paying you off." Dailey only guessed at Sloan, but given the reaction he'd received from Pathmoor when he previously mentioned the name, he took the chance.

Pathmoor gasped at Dailey. "How did you find out?" he quavered.

"You have a short memory, Mr. Pathmoor. My partner and I," Dailey nodded toward Montgomery, "are detectives.

"We also know you lied to us when we asked about when you last had contact with Martin Cray. Now, again, before you say anything, I want to stress that I'm not interested in your dirty little schemes, but I need information. And the information you give me now may damn well have a bearing on how much time you have left on this earth."

Pathmoor's eyes widened with a new and confused fear.

"Indulge me in an abbreviated history lesson," Daily continued. "A week ago last night, someone killed Carston Jennings and attacked his companion, Lori Phillips. Phillips looked like she might make it, but she was murdered in the hospital last Tuesday night. That same night we learned O'Connor's house had been placed under surveillance, and we went out there and hauled a guy named Samuel Wellington in for questioning. Kind of like what we're doing with you. We had to release him for lack of evidence and an hour later he died when his car exploded. If you're counting, that's three people dead. Now, during all this, one of O'Connor's daughters and a family friend were kidnapped. A friend of Jack O'Connor's took the kidnapping real personal and last Friday night, he ascertained the location of the daughter and friend— at a cost of three more lives. Early Saturday he rescued them. While all these fun and games were going on, Martin Cray, his wife, and his boat go up like a Roman candle. Our morgue is getting pretty crowded, Mr. Pathmoor. That's a body count of eight, just in case you've lost count.

"And the only names we've come up with, are yours, George Comstock, and Abel Sloan."

"I swear to you, Lieutenant, I don't know any thing about any killings," Pathmoor pleaded, shaking uncontrollably.

Dailey slammed his fist to the table with a crash that even startled Montgomery.

"Your swearing don't mean shit to me, mister. I wouldn't trust you with my granddaughter's loaded diaper. Now! Why did you lie about when you last saw Cray? Why has Sloan given you one hundred thousand dollars? What's the money buying him or you—besides stocks and boats?"

Pathmoor began to blubber, crumbling like a rotten log in the rain forest.

"What I want, mister, is information. There's a link here. Martin Cray called, needing to talk to O'Connor about something important. Just an hour or two later, someone connected to Comstock killed Carston Jennings mistaking him for Jack O'Connor. So far, we haven't been able to locate anyone who's seen Comstock or knows his whereabouts. The people we've found, who have had contact with him either directly or indirectly as of late, *are dead*. It doesn't take a rocket scientist to figure out that you're either in tight with him or he hasn't gotten around to punching your ticket yet. And I emphasize the word *yet*."

Shock washed over Pathmoor's face, as he understood the danger he faced.

Dailey, reading the awareness in his eyes, capitalized on the situation. He turned the pictures of Carston Jennings up and threw them in front of Pathmoor, followed quickly by those of the car bombing, then the wreckage of Cray's boat. "That's what's been happening to the people involved in this, mister. Take a look! Take a damn good look!

"Here's the deal: You tell me what I need to know and I give you protection. You continue to jerk me around and I'll personally throw your ass back on the street, with maybe a few hints that you rolled over on Sloan and Comstock. Then, Mr. Pathmoor, we'll just see how long you'll last. Now, I'm going to ask you one more time. Why is Sloan so generous with Suter's money?"

The expression on Pathmoor's face told Dailey that he had finally hit his mark. For a moment Dailey thought the man would vomit.

Dailey pressed the record button, stated the date and time, that he was interviewing Richard Pathmoor with regard to the Carston Jenning's case and that Pathmoor had waived his rights. Pathmoor did not object nor could he remove his eyes from the photographs lying before him. Pale and terrified, he began to talk.

"As I told you, I went to Cervicon to facilitate getting the security system expedited." He hesitated for a moment, apparently reconsidering what he wanted to say. "Well, that's not entirely true. Sloan came to me with an offer to go to Cervicon not only to expedite the system, but also to learn how the security system functioned."

"In exchange for what?" Dailey pressed.

"I would be paid $50,000 when I got hired at Cervicon and another $100,000 when I confirmed the expedite and learned the system."

Montgomery interrupted. "What difference would learning the system make? If Suter owned the system, they would know how it functioned."

"That's true in theory, but Cervicon is not only supplying the system, they're also contracted to staff and manage all security for Suter. Nobody at Suter would know the system's capabilities."

"Why were you paid the second 50K if the job wasn't complete?" Dailey asked.

"I gave Sloan what information I could on the system and told him the design would be completed by last Friday. I needed money for the boat and moorage. He only gave me another half until the plans were complete and O'Connor agreed to the concessions. Said he didn't trust me for all of it."

"Smart man," Montgomery said wryly.

It became clear to Dailey that Sloan's primary objective was to know how to compromise the system rather than to expedite it. The expediting appeared to be a smoke screen.

"Why does Sloan need to compromise the system?"

"You must believe me, Lieutenant, I don't know."

For once, Dailey believed Pathmoor's answer. He pondered the possibilities: Comstock had dealt drugs. Could Sloan be his source? He decided to initiate an investigation of Abel Sloan as soon as he finished his session with Pathmoor. But first he wanted to know why Pathmoor lied about when he'd last met with Martin Cray. What more did Pathmoor have to hide?

"So the expedite has just been an excuse to compromise the security system all along," Dailey stated.

"I suppose so," Pathmoor answered.

"You suppose so," Dailey mimicked back with disgust. "Was Cray aware of the pressure that you were applying on O'Connor to get the job finished?"

"Not until a few weeks ago." Pathmoor, finally admitting defeat to himself, spoke in a matter-of-fact way, without flinching or flitting his eyes. He understood that further evasiveness would buy him nothing. "I realized three weeks ago O'Connor would not compromise on the design and I wouldn't be able to deliver on my commitment to Sloan. Until then, I hadn't mentioned anything to Cray. Two weeks ago, I panicked and went to Cray and told him that I felt O'Connor had caused real problems with the Suter project."

At that, Dailey raised his eyebrows, and Pathmoor realized too late that he had admitted to another lie, but he continued on.

"During the week prior to this mess, I met with Martin Cray on two occasions. He told me he would look into the situation."

"Why did you lie when I asked you about the last time you'd seen Cray?"

"When you came to my office, I knew something had gone wrong. The Friday before—"

"You mean the Friday before the Jennings murder, Friday May 12th?" Dailey interrupted for clarification.

"Yes. O'Connor had been in that morning, then left for an appointment. Cray arrived at Cervicon just after O'Connor left and told me he would be in O'Connor's office to review the project. He stayed there most of the day. I found him there again Saturday morning when I arrived. I asked him if he had any ideas on how we could wrap the project up quicker. He told me he wouldn't change a thing, and concurred with O'Connor's decision, but said he'd keep working on it for a while. About 1:30 in the afternoon, he stormed into my office holding a cassette tape and asked me if I had seen any of the videos that Jack had taken out at Suter."

"What videos?" Dailey asked, surprised.

"It's not uncommon for O'Connor to stash remote cameras and recorders in strategic places in order to observe activities, employee traffic, areas that could compromise overall security. Cuts down on system tune-ups after installations. He had several tapes on the old Suter plant as well as some on the new construction in Issaquah. At any rate, Cray had one of the tapes when he came to my office. He looked anxious and asked me if I had looked at any of the tapes from Suter at Chehalis. I told him no and asked why, but he just said not to worry about it and left my office. A few minutes later he left the building and that's the last time that I saw him."

Dailey looked across the table at Pathmoor with disgust. He could have used this valuable information a week ago. He had no words to describe the loathing he felt. Dailey rubbed his face vigorously, to give himself time to clear his mind and control his anger. As he did so, a thought struck him and he abruptly turned off the recorder and left the room, leaving a surprised Montgomery to watch over Pathmoor.

Dailey nearly ran to the detectives' office and picked up the first available telephone to call Hugh Saltzman.

"This is Katharine, Lieutenant. You just missed him by twenty minutes. I'll try to connect you through to his car phone."

"Thank you, Dailey said. He cursed while waiting and was about to disconnect when he heard "Saltzman."

"Mr. Saltzman, this is Lieutenant Dailey. Can you tell me if Martin Cray had contact with Sloan a week ago last Saturday or anytime after?"

Saltzman paused before speaking. "That would be May 12th. I can't say for sure. I'm sure security would know."

"I've been interviewing Richard Pathmoor for the last several hours. We've just learned Abel Sloan was working with

Pathmoor on a scheme of some sort to compromise the security system."

"Dammit!—Lieutenant, I just left Sloan's office not a half an hour ago. Apparently, Carl Fortner packed up and left the plant shortly after you questioned him. I figured Fortner was the inside man on the drug thing. I went to Sloan about it. Now it all makes sense as to why he seemed so guarded. It's just after five; I'll head back to the plant. I'm only fifteen minutes away. I'll try to catch Sloan's secretary from the car and find out if Martin Cray made any visits after the 12th."

"Do that and see if you can locate Sloan as well. We'll need to talk to him. I'll notify the Chehalis authorities. I think it's time to bring in both Sloan and Fortner for a chat."

After he disconnected, Dailey contacted operations and identified himself. "Do we still have anyone on the Pathmoor house?"

"No. We pulled the detail when you brought him in," the officer answered.

"Call dispatch, get someone out there, and get the Pathmoor girl the hell away from that house. If she's not there, find her. And put someone back on that house until she's found."

Dailey disconnected and leaned back in the chair, sifting through the recent information. He had confirmed Pathmoor's culpability in providing classified information about the security system. In his naiveté and greed, Pathmoor had deluded himself into believing he had a place of importance. Dailey knew without a doubt that when Sloan had what he wanted, Pathmoor would end up like the rest. What could have been on the tape that Cray had discovered in O'Connor's office and why, if incriminating, hadn't O'Connor brought it to light? And where did Comstock fit into the puzzle?

* * * * *

Upon his return and without any explanation, Dailey sat down, restarted the recorder, and resumed his questioning.

"After Martin Cray left Cervicon, did you look at the tapes?"

"Yes."

"And?" Dailey asked in exasperation.

"I only looked at parts of a couple of them. I didn't see anything on them that looked important: tape of the clean rooms, packaging areas, halls, entrances, exits, that sort of thing."

"Do you still maintain that you had no personal contact with George Comstock?"

"Yes."

"Do you know if Comstock had any relationship or contact with Sloan?"

"No."

"When did you last have contact with Sloan?"

Pathmoor hesitated. "Abel Sloan called me at home Sunday just after noon and asked me if I had viewed any of the tapes O'Connor had taken at Suter. He sounded upset, so I told him I hadn't. He asked me if I knew where they were and I said that I did. He told me to gather all of them together and ship them to him first thing Monday morning. I said I didn't think I could do that because Martin Cray was reviewing them. He interrupted me and ordered me to do it. Then he hung up. So Monday first thing when I came in, I packed them and shipped them to him UPS."

Dailey stood, red faced. "Book this vermin into protective custody, then meet me at my desk," he told Montgomery.

CHAPTER THIRTY-FOUR

Dailey had called the offices of the partners with an urgent need to speak with Jack and would not divulge information about the nature of his call. Jason, Keller, Krieger, and the partners sat at the large rosewood conference table in the situation room, impatiently waiting forty-five minutes for the return call from the beach house.

Jason had quickly contacted David at the beach house to instruct him to record the conversation and to use his personal cellular phone for all communication with Dailey since he wouldn't be able to trace the call. Jason instructed that the call be recorded for his review immediately upon completion.

Jason hoped the report from the beach would come soon, as he had only fifteen minutes before his appointment with Dailey.

Prior to Dailey's call, they had completed a detailed layout of the camp on Diablo Island using the information provided by Monroe. Jason, Keller and Krieger planned a carefully executed reconnaissance for later that night using Jason's boat for transport, rather than a fly-over, which would not yield the precise information Jason wanted.

While waiting for the report from Jack, Pat Krieger gave a detailed description of Patriot Chemicals and the surrounding area, information Jason could use as bargaining chip in the sharing of information with Dailey, depending on his mood.

* * * * *

Jack, David, and Steve were gathered in the lower bedroom, when David put the call through to Dailey and handed the cell phone to Jack. David had rigged the phone to the recorder, and monitored the call through an earpiece.

As usual Dailey came straight to the point. "Mr. O'Connor, I've just spent the last two hours with Mr. Pathmoor. He informed me that you made some video tapes of the Suter operation."

"That's correct, lieutenant, what about them?"

Dailey went on to explain that Martin Cray had been reviewing the tapes during Jack's absence.

"Apparently, Mr. Cray found something on one of the tapes that greatly disturbed him. Do you have any idea what that might have been?"

"I don't, lieutenant," Jack said, puzzled. "There are several tapes and I actually only viewed one that dealt with a specific clean room. With all the pressure I've been under lately, I haven't had a chance to review them. I'd be glad to have a look, see if anything raises a red flag."

"I'm afraid that won't be possible," Dailey said. "It seems as though Mr. Pathmoor sent the lot of them off to Suter."

"What! What the hell—lieutenant, I want that sonofabitch arrested," Jack yelled in rage. "I want to know what the worst possible thing is that you can do to that bastard. I—"

"Mr. O'Connor, I'm sure that Mr. Castellano, or Mr. DeAngelis, can better advise you on how to—"

"Lieutenant, I want—"

"Mr. O'Connor, please! I understand your anger. Pathmoor is in custody, but right now I have multiple murders on my hands. I need some help here. Do you have any idea at all, does *anything* come to mind that could remotely be of help?"

"No, lieutenant, I don't," Jack said quietly.

* * * * *

At the conversation's conclusion, Dailey looked up from his desk in disgust. It galled him to have to go through Jason to have contact with Jack and he was not naive enough to think that by the time Jason arrived for their meeting, he wouldn't already have the latest information on Pathmoor. It also frustrated him to have learned nothing new from Jack. He vigorously rubbed his face and realized he was developing a nervous habit. Well I deserve one, he thought.

Phones rang incessantly and the detectives who responded to the calls talked louder and louder to overcome the self-perpetuating din. In the midst of the racket, Dailey struggled with getting things straight in his head before Jason arrived. His session with Pathmoor and the issue with Sloan had altered the way he viewed the case. It was not about the deadline nor about lost revenue. It was about drugs, with Pathmoor as nothing more than a pawn. With security compromised, Sloan would have the ability to run drugs out of the plant undetected.

Another thing puzzled Dailey. If Cray confronted Sloan with a tape, where was it now? The Cray house had been ransacked; Cray must have hidden the tape.

The ring of his telephone startled him. He shook his head to clear his thoughts and lifted the receiver. "Dailey."

"Lieutenant, this is Hugh Saltzman. I'm back at the plant and have just finished a conversation with Sloan's secretary. Sloan left the office just minutes before I returned. He told her that he would be out of town for a few days. She said he took his passport. I called his home. His wife expects him home at any time and knows nothing of any immediate travel plans.

"Another point of interest, Lieutenant: According to Security, Sloan came in on Sunday morning. That is not too unusual. However, security also said that Martin Cray paid him a visit.

"Also, I contacted Pam Devlin from Human Resources at her home. I asked her about George Comstock and who had performed his background check. She told me Sloan had personally told her to hire him and that he would take care of the paperwork. The only information on him is what is contained in his file, which is precious little, as you know.

"I'm trying to contact Suter and let him know what's happened. Then I'll nose around Sloan's office, see if I can find anything more."

"Call me if you do," Dailey said, then disconnected and punched Montgomery's extension number. "Bob, any word on the Pathmoor girl?"

"No, not yet. We've got a car at the house and I just added Thompson to the detail. Thompson's solo, with Dolan on vacation."

"Well, get on his ass! I want that girl found!"

Minutes later Montgomery ushered Jason and Joe Castellano to his desk. Jason had brought Joe in case issues of obstruction of justice should arise.

Dailey eyed the lawyer with something that bordered on contempt. Now well into the evening, Joe looked fresh, his white shirt still crisp and accented by rubies in gold cufflinks. After ten hours in the office, he still looked ready for a bout of corporate litigation. Dailey knew why Joe had come.

"Well, Lieutenant," Jason began, "what's the latest on Pathmoor?" The three men crowded chairs near Dailey's desk and seated themselves.

"Mr. Brisben, I'm not at liberty to tell you what we learned from or about Pathmoor."

Jason had known this time would come and a decision would have to be made—give up Comstock and hope Dailey would trade information, or walk out and work on his own. If he were to walk, Dailey would have grounds for charging him with interfering in a murder investigation. He glanced briefly at Joe whose facial expression suggested, "It's your call."

Jason also faced the issue of limited resources. He did not have the manpower to take on Comstock and deal with the camp. He looked back to Dailey; their eyes locked as they now engaged in mental fencing.

Dailey is no fool, a good cop, Jason mused. Thrust—parry—thrust . . . watch his eyes. Jason Brisben! This is about Jack O'Connor and his family; it's not a game. It's not about your selfish pride or winning. It's about what's best for Jack. You can't do it all, he said to himself.

Dailey also entered the contest of wills as he tried to stare Jason down. What's this man know, he wondered. He's calm; he's got something. Dammit! What the hell is it? Why won't he help me do my job? Who am I trying to kid? Hell, he's given me 90 percent of what I do have, him and his partners. Is that what bothers me? No. What bothers me is, he has more information! I can see it. This man is not beaten. And there it is. Is that what you want, to beat this man? What about Jack O'Connor? Isn't he supposed to come first? This man and I need to work together.

"Lieutenant."

"Mr. Brisben."

Both men began to speak at the same time, but Jason forged ahead. "Lieutenant, I'm not here to bullshit you. You're trying to catch the murderers of Jennings, Phillips, and the Crays. I'm trying to protect Jack as best I can. You're spread thin. I'm spread thin, but as you know, my people and I can move rather quickly. We both know now Jack doesn't know anything. Sloan, Comstock, and whoever else is involved thought Jack had learned the same thing that's gotten everyone killed." Jason paused. "Joe, give him the file." Joe slid the file across the cluttered desk to Dailey.

Dailey and Montgomery looked at one another, then back to Jason. "What's this?" Dailey asked.

"We've located George Comstock."

* * * * *

"Although we gave up some information on Comstock, we gained a great deal," Joe explained, standing in front of the board. "We were allowed to hear the taped interrogation of Pathmoor. Now we are able to clear up some of the unknowns, and, I'd like to add, we gained a much-improved relationship with Dailey." Joe went on to impart the information they had gleaned from Dailey and Montgomery including the latest news: Sloan's disappearance.

"I know this all seems a bit of a mish-mash," Jason began, "but a lot of this I've dumped in Dailey's lap. We still, of course, will focus on Jack and his family's safety, but there's something bigger at stake here, something imminently dangerous going on, out on that island."

"Why do you say 'imminent'?" Krieger asked.

"Because they're showing signs of panic," Jason answered. "Cray found the tape on Saturday, May 13th. According to Suter Security, Sloan met with Cray Sunday morning. The hit in the parking lot went down Sunday night. The last person to hear from Cray that we know of was Jack's wife. They're fast-tracking, trying to stop the bleeding from an information breach.

"We won't know why until we check out that island, and that, my friends, we do tonight. And while we're there, Joe and the boys will be preparing a good layout of the Patriot facility for Dailey. He'll get it first thing in the morning. Their tentative strike date is set for tomorrow night."

"Hell, we might run into Comstock on Diablo," Krieger said. "He might've gotten spooked and run for cover with all this stuff with Cray and Sloan."

"It's possible," Jason said. "I'm sure Sloan gave him a heads up. Remember, though, nobody's seen him since last October, so he probably feels pretty safe at Patriot."

Jason launched into his plan for the reconnaissance of Diablo Island. "First, and most important, we make no contact with anyone on that island. They can't know that we've been there. Don't take anything. Don't touch anything. Full black, night vision, infrared insulation, the works."

For three hours, Jason, Keller, Pat Krieger, and Miguel Macias went over and over the layout of the island and the camp. Sobahr had gone to The Kennel and relieved Miguel so he could be present for the briefing. The prime directive was to gather information. Jason had described what he had found in the Issaquah house. In his opinion, the weapons, ammunition, and filters he had seen at the house would not be found at the Patriot Chemicals facility, but at the camp. They were also to get a count on all weapons and their locations, a personnel count and their locations, and an accurate assessment of the security system. And then, get the hell out. "Without being detected," he stressed.

No one had questions so Jason called Tony at Hard-Ship Marine and instructed him to get his boat in the water.

* * * * *

The nearly invisible, cobalt-blue boat idled slowly, lying low in the water, as Jason maneuvered as close to the island as he dared. A little over a mile offshore, they would paddle an inflatable to the beach. Jason had chosen to go ashore on the opposite side from the island's boat dock and private ferry landing. The island had its own ferry for transport of the camp's trucks and heavy equipment, but Jason chose to stay away from the camp's access road and infiltrate from the backside.

Jason gave the signal for Miguel to drop the anchor, and then he killed the engines. He positioned the boat so they would be paddling against the current going in, so if something were to go wrong, they would not have to fight the current while making a hasty retreat. The inflatable was equipped with a motor, which would be used only in an emergency. Once anchored with lines secured, Krieger and Keller lowered the inflatable over the side and discharged the bottles which inflated the craft in little more than ten seconds. Then all were over the side and under way, paddling furiously.

"Shit, it looked a lot flatter on the map," Krieger complained, once they were ashore.

Miguel laughed. "Probably 'cause it was on a flat piece of paper. Hell, time you get done with this run, your fat belly might fit under the fence."

"Cut the chatter," Jason whispered. "From now on, hand signals. No voice communication. We follow the plan and no screwups."

They were due south of the camp in heavy timber and underbrush. They had rough terrain and dense vegetation to negotiate before reaching the camp perimeter.

"Remember, these steep draws will get you disoriented, so watch your compasses. From here we go due north. The third draw over has a rock north face. When we come up against it, we'll head due west for two hundred yards. It should bring us right to the southeast perimeter. Any questions?" Jason asked. Everyone remained silent. "Let's move out."

They had not traveled twenty feet up the rocks before they came upon a hostile warning: a white sign with bold red letters attached to a steel post.

POSTED
PRIVATE PROPERTY
ABSOLUTELY NO TRESPASSING
NO HUNTING
NO FISHING
PROPERTY PATROLLED
VIOLATORS WILL BE PROSECUTED

"Real friendly group," Krieger muttered to himself.

Surreal is the only word to describe night vision, eerie blue-green shadowy shapes in the midst of a somewhat muted depth perception. They made their way up the side of the second draw; about one-half mile into the trek, heavy dew-covered undergrowth made progress slow. The wet vegetation helped mute the sound as they passed. Jason looked from side to side. He could see Keller and Miguel intermittently to his right through the trees. Krieger moved in and out of his vision on the left. All moved in a staggered line fifteen to twenty yards apart.

They broke over the top of a ridge heading down into the third and final draw. Jason wondered how the others felt. He kept himself in great shape, working out regularly on the weights and often running several miles a day. He had plenty of strength, plenty of wind. But the beating he had taken caught up with him. Every breath felt like a knife twisting in his badly bruised ribs. He remembered a time when he had relished pain, even embraced it. But somewhere along the way, he had changed. This was not romantic, not fun or macho anymore, but pure agony. Even as they headed down, and going became easier, it didn't feel better. It felt worse.

The rock face came into view and the line of men made a sweeping turn to the west. As they descended, they encountered a steep incline and Jason endured a higher level of pain. For the first time since the beatings from his father, he wished the pain would stop. The thought sobered him for two reasons: He had been focusing on the pain, not on the mission. That could get him or one of his comrades killed. Second, he hadn't thought about his father and the hatred that had burned within him since he had joined the service. No matter how perverted the logic, that hatred caused him to measure worthiness by the amount of pain he could endure and how tough he was.

Right now he hurt like hell, and he didn't feel all that tough. This is a bad time to be sorting this out, he thought as the southern corner of the fence line came into his vision. He needed either to get his head back into the mission and off his discomfort or get out, now. For his own safety and that of his men, he had to make the decision, and do it before any of them entered the camp.

A buffer zone had been cleared around the perimeter of the camp. The incline became steep and his comrades sprinted those last fifty yards, so they wouldn't be caught on open ground. His ribs transmitted sharp, burning pain as his lungs sucked in air pungent with the scent of wet ferns and fir. The bittersweet scent seemed a bit like life to him. The bitter he knew all too well, but the sweetness of the past had been victory, conquering, enduring. Now the sweetness seemed absent.

As he closed on an eight-foot-high fence, another of the large warning signs that had greeted them on the shore loomed at him. Reading the sign a second time made him acutely aware of an indisputable fact: Three men had accompanied him for no reason other than that he had asked. It was his plan, his responsibility to endure the pain and to lead his men. The pain must be secondary.

As he slid through a hollow under the fence, he knew he would be okay. His ability to function under adverse conditions had not diminished. He could still block the pain and focus on what he needed to do: lead the mission.

The compound lay another half mile from their present position, which meant they were once again on the run. From the information Keller had gleaned from Monroe, they learned security would be light because of the camp's inaccessibility. Also the few motion detectors and closed-circuit cameras could easily be avoided. They all carried sensors that could detect electric current, much like a sophisticated stud finder.

Jason had two concerns: first, random patrols with no time patterns; second, camp personnel with night vision. Although the camp's equipment would not be as sophisticated as that of Jason and his men, it still would level the playing field to some extent. Jason's group wore black nonreflective insulated clothing and hoods, making them hard to spot or pick up by heat sensors.

The invaders were also equipped with closed-circuit communication, an earpiece, and a microphone. These were to be used only in an emergency.

Each man had a specific area of the camp to check and they would make no contact with one another until they returned to the beach. They were only armed with Glock 20's, which were light 15-round 10mm mostly composite—meaning plastic—side arms. The objective was to get in and out undetected. If there came a need to use weapons, the mission would be a failure.

According to Monroe's information, the compound consisted of: an office, three barracks, a kitchen and mess hall, the stores and armory, stockade, powerhouse, two well houses, a hangar for three helicopters, a motor pool building, and an underground concrete bunker. A boathouse attached to the dock on the extreme west side of the island had been placed off limits on this trip.

There were an estimated 140 personnel, and they ran a self-sufficient camp. The island had a landing pad, and they generated their own electricity with wind and diesel, with storage. There were three wells on the property, two of which were active and one in reserve. All the water was filtered with filters manufactured on the island. They raised crops in small garden plots where soil permitted, and raised and butchered their own livestock as needed.

Jason assumed responsibility for the reconnaissance of the office and stores; Pat Krieger, the hangar and bunker, Keller, the barracks; Miguel, the generator and electricity delivery-system and the wells. Jason wanted to know everything about the camp, especially what kinds of records were kept and who the players were. He wanted to know about their supplies and weapons, how many and what type. Without an electrical system the camp would be incapacitated. He wanted to know how to disable it. The same held true for the water supply.

Something bad was going on in this place and Jason needed to know what and who was behind it. So far, eleven people had died in a five-day period in order to protect something. Nobody knew what, but everything pointed to the camp. This was no weekend survivalist camp. Within fifteen hours, Dailey would be arresting George Comstock, and once that occurred, Jason knew that if anyone even suspected the camp had been invaded, nothing would be the same tomorrow. Any evidence would be quickly hidden or destroyed.

The first building came into view. Jason stopped to survey the layout and check for sentries. Again, Monroe's information proved accurate—it looked just as he had described. As Jason moved stealthily to the northeast, he could see the low profile of the office building with the stores building partially blocked from view by the number-three barrack building. It proved to be a well-planned layout, with the office in the building farthest from the only road in, which would take the longest to reach in a frontal attack or an attack from either side. Under attack, office personnel would be afforded the longest amount of time to destroy records and documents, with the barracks providing a buffer. Access from the north and northeast would be impossible due to sheer rock cliffs dropping to the water; the camp was nearly impenetrable.

Jason cautiously moved forward, scanning a full three-hundred-sixty degrees. He caught the shadow of movement to his right; there, then gone. When in stealth mode he did nothing quickly, including stop. He slowly went into a crouch, waited and watched. He saw it again after a moment and recognized Keller.

Keller had nearly reached the corner of the first barrack when Jason saw someone approaching from the backside of the building. If the person continued on his present course, he would eventually trip over Jason. And if he went around the side of the building toward the front, he could possibly end up behind Keller. The first impulse of the unseasoned would be to pop the guy. But then you would have a camp full of geeks looking for their comrade by morning. Jason understood the discipline of the mission and waited out the situation.

The man continued on a course toward Jason just as Keller passed from his view at the corner of the barrack. He then stopped directly in front of Jason not thirty feet away and proceeded to light a cigarette. This presented a problem. Jason was in the open with no cover and could only hope to look like a rock, a stump, or anything but an intruder.

He saw that the man did not have night vision, was unarmed and only partially dressed in a tee shirt and fatigues, which meant they were not on alert status. A good sign, given what had happened in Seattle during the past twenty-four hours. Damn, Jason thought, I'm in the middle of an enemy camp and I've run into an insomniac out for a midnight smoke.

After fifteen minutes and the second cigarette, the guy casually unzipped and proceeded to relieve himself. Jason wanted to look at his watch. He couldn't. His Friday night injuries throbbed and stiffness set in from lack of movement. He needed to move. He couldn't. He wanted to laugh about his situation. He couldn't. His frustration mounted.

* * * * *

Miguel set out to confirm the location of the wells on the map and determine the quickest way to cut the power supply, which in turn would incapacitate the water supply. Once the wells were charted, he would move on to the generators. Upon arriving at the second well, Miguel correctly surmised the lay-out would be the same: power running underground and coming up through the floorboards of the well house, then by conduit up to a switchbox mounted on the wall. The pumps were submersibles so the only equipment in the pump houses was the filter systems, the plumbing networks and heat tape to keep pipes from freezing.

* * * * *

Pat Krieger first checked the motor pool and the chopper landing pad, which sat near the east perimeter cliffs some two hundred yards away. A hangar large enough for three helicopters stood nearly empty with only one bird in residence. Krieger had seen another that had carried the personnel to Patriot Chemicals. If a third bird existed, it was off somewhere.

The motor pool and hangar shared a common wall. Krieger saw nothing of note in the motor pool: two army surplus, two-and-a-half-ton transports and couple of pickups. Scuff marks on the floor indicated that two pieces of heavy equipment, a backhoe and a CAT, also shared lodging, but were absent. Krieger took a quick second look before heading off toward the bunker and made note of the cleanliness; all tools and toolboxes sparkled and the painted concrete shown with a waxed luster.

The low concrete bunker located next to the pistol, rifle, and live-fire ranges contained the camp's munitions. Shortly after the entry to the concrete structure, Krieger made two observations worthy of note: one, the organization—everything was neatly stored and labeled. Second, from what he could determine, there were only two calibers of the small arms ammunition in the place: 9mm Parabellum and 7.62mm. The 9mm, he knew to be for side arms and submachine guns and the 7.62mm for rifle and machine guns. No matter where he looked, a single round of a different caliber could be found. Even the belted rounds for machine guns were 7.62mm.

One large area was devoted to the manufacturing of ammunition. Two multi-stage automated bullet-swage presses for making the bullets stood surrounded by tubs for each caliber. The 7.62's were lead-core, boat-tail bullets similar to hunting ammunition, 160-grain, the kind that leave an eight-inch diameter of destroyed tissue that is impossible to repair. And the 9's were also lead-core hollow-points, also deadly. On impact, they expand to the size of a nickel. Five-gallon buckets of pills in the two calibers too numerous to count lined the walls. Several twenty-five-gallon barrels of brass casings for both calibers sat waiting to be charged. Behind a solid steel door in a separate magazine, Krieger found five-pound barrel after barrel of powder.

"This is a nightmare. These assholes could hold off the whole United States freaking Army," he muttered. Krieger closed the magazine door and walked to the opposite end of the bunker and got a second shock at what he saw: tank LAWs rocket launchers, hand-held Stinger anti-aircraft missile launchers, and grenades. "What the fuck," he said aloud before he could catch himself.

* * * * *

Miguel, after checking the wells, had moved on to the powerhouse and seen all he needed for his assessment. Although he had not gone to inspect the individual wind generators, he saw where the leads came into the small building and connected to the transformer and relay system. The power could either be routed directly into use or into the battery storage system. The same held true for the two-diesel generators.

The diesel generators were silent, and from the gauges, Miguel determined the slight breeze was not sufficient to run the wind equipment. The camp ran silently from the battery supply.

He took a minute to admire the simple but efficient operation. It had been well thought out. As he left the powerhouse, he spotted the low profile of another building just to the northwest of his location. From the briefing and the diagram, he remembered and recognized the location of the building. It should be the stockade, he thought. Rather than directly returning to the beach, he decided to have a look. He renavigated around the motion detector that guarded the powerhouse and headed off to do a little additional exploring.

A lone pine tree concealed both a motion detector and video monitor guarding the stockade. Miguel could not detect any electrical activity and assumed that he would find the stockade empty. As he entered, an inner wave of heaviness pressed in on him. The stockade itself appeared to be a rather simple building, and at one end there were two separate steel bar cages with a single-barred door to each. He found no plumbing and no bunks, just four-sided cages.

At the opposite end of the building Miguel found something that made his hair stand on end. Memories coursed through his being of a time when he, David, and Steve, had rescued Jason from an apparatus much like this. In its simplicity stood a well-designed table for torture. He stared at the wooden bed set at a forty-five degree angle with manacles to hold the victim spread-eagle. He took inventory of sinister electrodes that, when in use, were taped to the victim's body: the temples, armpits, bottoms of feet, the testicles, and the most vicious and despicable of all, a probe that resembled a catheter, all black with a tiny silver tip. They all led to a small wooden table and were connected to the black box with the switches and dials that controlled the voltage. He saw the telltale stains from hemorrhages and involuntary voiding from unconscious, naked victims.

Miguel, so wrapped in the horror of the moment, failed to hear the slight creak in the floor behind him.

"You wanna take it for a spin?" said a voice from behind him in the dark.

* * * * *

Keller had just finished his count of the second barrack and begun his exit through the end door when someone entered through a side door. He froze as the man quietly walked to a vacant bunk toward the center of the barrack. He shed his unlaced boots and fatigues, then slid silently into his bunk and turned on his side facing away from Keller. Keller, his heart pounding, stood motionless for ten minutes barely breathing before he could move silently out the door.

Once outside, he breathed a sigh of relief and wondered how he had escaped without someone hearing the loudness of his heartbeat. He took a minute, allowing himself time to calm a bit before heading to the third and final barrack. To this point he counted a total of ninety-seven sleeping personnel. Two bunks in the previous barrack had been empty and after the late arrival, the second barrack had been full. Armed with that knowledge, he knew if there were patrols about, they would have generated from the third and final barrack, which increased the odds of running into someone. This is not fun anymore, he told himself as he entered the final building.

* * * * *

Jason, because of his unfortunate holdup, chose to reconnoiter the stores and armory first, then finish with the office on the return to the beach. He reminded himself not to hurry. Rule one: Don't try to make up lost time. Being in a hurry causes mistakes. Even so, he found it difficult to move slowly. He, too, found the sensing devices inactive. It seemed odd the security would be so lax, but this gave a good indication that Comstock and his crew back in Seattle did not seem alarmed.

The stores and armory were under one roof in what appeared from the outside to be a large barn, with a formidable partition separating the two. The first area that Jason entered looked to be a well-stocked supply depot: tents, blankets, rations, boxes of dehydrated food, camp tools of every description. They could survive indefinitely. He moved along toward the armory partition, scanning from right to left all the way while making mental notes of the supplies. Then, bingo, he recognized a neat stack of corrugated boxes—the filters he had seen at the Issaquah house. He counted one hundred ten.

At the Issaquah house he had counted one hundred twenty in all. Since he had taken one of them, that left nine unaccounted for. He filed the information into his memory and proceeded to the armory.

A large sliding door allowed access to the armory, and, after passing through, Jason stood stunned at the amount of armaments: racks upon racks of every kind of small arms imaginable at the ready. A regiment of men could file through on the run and pick their weapons of choice. Too many for him to count, he did a cursory estimate.

A four-foot aisle separated two rows of racks, each row two racks high. The high-power stuff sat on the lower racks: sniper rifles, assault rifles, grenade launchers, and the heavier machine guns. The upper racks held the light machine guns, submachine guns, side arms, and a few shotguns. Jason also noticed, with the exception of the shotguns, all the weaponry used only two calibers of ammunition: 7.62mm or 9mm.

The armory contained enough firepower to supply a major training facility—or start a war. Maybe both, he thought. At the far end of the building, on what looked to be a loading dock, he saw the familiar cases of the M16's that he'd seen just three nights before in Issaquah. It dawned on him that he saw no M16's or any weapons on the racks that would accept the smaller 5.56mm ammunition. So why steal the M16's?

He had seen enough of this place. Enough to scare the hell out of him and add more to the mounting number of questions. Maybe he would find the answers in the office.

* * * * *

Miguel stood frozen, the chill of surprise and panic coursing through his body. He had compromised the mission by being there and now he had no way out. The voice in the dark came from between him and the only exit and he had no way to get an accurate fix on his adversary's location.

"Don't even think about moving," the raspy voice whispered.

Miguel slowly began to turn. "I'm going to kill you, you sonofabitch."

"Yeah, well I hope you packed a lunch," Pat Krieger whispered in return. "What the fuck are you doing here?"

"Same thing you're doing here. Now let's get the hell outta here. Jason'll kill us both, if he finds out."

The second time Krieger had spoken, Miguel had recognized his voice, but it had been a dangerous, stupid act on both men's part. An overreaction by Miguel could very well have gotten one or both men killed, not to mention the fact that they could have jeopardized the entire mission. This time they had been lucky.

* * * * *

The pungent aroma of fresh coffee and cigarette smoke greeted Jason as he stole through a side entrance to the office building, not a good sign. He had no knowledge of the floor plan, because Monroe had never been in the office. According to him, only trainers and higher-ups were allowed access. Somewhere in the rooms that lay ahead, Jason could hear muted conversation. He had entered from the north end of the building into a type of catchall room where odds and ends were kept out of sight. He fervently hoped that he would remain out of sight. He planned to head south from his present location at the north end, through the office, out the south end, and to his rendezvous on the beach.

With great caution, he stealthily inched forward into a hallway, every step bringing him closer to danger and the intermittent voices.

He entered a room to his left. Inside he found a wastebasket, file cabinet, chair, and a desk with a computer. It would be too risky trying to log on, not knowing if it had been networked to other computers or a server. He found the file cabinet locked. The first room denied him information.

Moving again out into the hallway, Jason removed his night vision because of light emanating from the doorway to what appeared to be a large room from where the voices came. Quietly, he approached the opening. His choices were limited, not knowing the positions of the people in the room. To find out, he would have to look through the opening and, if spotted, the operation would be lost. The best he could do would be to remain in the hallway and try to glean information from the conversation. But that too would leave him exposed.

He retraced his steps and exited through the same door that he had entered. He circled the building and tried the door at the south end of the building, and found it locked and bolted. To his chagrin, he realized he would get no answers this night, and began a careful retreat to the boat.

CHAPTER THIRTY-FIVE

After several miles of idling, keeping the boat low and quiet, Jason pushed the throttles forward, forcing his comrades back in their bolsters. Once again the boat knifed effortlessly through the water on the return to Seattle. The team members had been waiting on the rocky shore when Jason arrived. There had been no discussion of the mission prior to their departure. Even as they paddled the inflatable to their boat, they remained silent. A full debriefing would take place once they returned to the partners' offices. Even though they each had signaled a "thumbs up" the mission a success, unanswered questions still raged in Jason's mind.

One other encounter with camp personnel had occurred during Krieger and Miguel's return to the rendezvous point on the beach. They had stumbled upon three men and a back-hoe. The men appeared to be resting around the silent machinery, talking and drinking beer. Whatever the task, it looked like they had finished for the night. Miguel had noticed the men were older, not young like Monroe. Since he and Krieger were late for the rendezvous, they decided against moving closer to determine what the men were doing out in the woods at nearly four in the morning. It would be discussed during the debriefing.

* * * * *

A disheveled and cranky Dailey walked to Montgomery's desk; Montgomery had become accustomed to Dailey's untidy dress and demeanor. In a rare and random act of kindness, Dailey brought two cups of coffee, one black and one with enough cream and sugar to give off a repulsive aroma. He gave Montgomery the black.

"What the hell is that?" Montgomery asked pointing to his boss's coffee.

"My coffee."

"You don't like cream and sugar."

"That's the point. I'm trying to cut back on my coffee. Makes me shaky, makes me grumpy."

"The coffee was doing that? Damn. Maybe we could get you a patch." Montgomery's chair squeaked and groaned as he leaned back and carefully sipped the hot brew. "Maybe we could find you a kinder, gentler blend."

"Just give me the damn information," Dailey commanded, ignoring his partner's attempt at levity at 6 a.m. He seated himself in the chair beside Montgomery's desk. "Anything on the Pathmoor girl?"

"Thompson picked her up this morning about one-thirty. We got her over to Family Services. I informed Pathmoor half an hour ago. I think he finally realized his ass isn't worth much if he hits the street. That's something else we need to deal with. Probably should get with Legal to discuss his options."

Dailey nodded at the news about the girl, but gave a wave of dismissal about Pathmoor's legal situation. "How's the raid on Patriot shaping up? Do we know for a fact this Comstock character is still there?"

"Still set for tonight right after dark. SWAT's been briefed. We're doing our own surveillance in conjunction with theirs, but it'll be their plan to design and execute. As far as we know, no one fitting Comstock's description has left the premises. We've checked with Brisben's partners. The word from them is Comstock's still holed up. Speaking of Brisben, we gonna let him be there for our little raid?"

"No," Dailey said thoughtfully and sipped his coffee. "While we're on the subject of Brisben, I gotta tell ya, he's scaring the hell out of me, him and those partners. They're connected to a light-speed network." He looked off into space as he thought, then took another sip of coffee. An instantaneous grimace spread across his face. "Damn, this is terrible." He dropped the remainder into the wastebasket.

Montgomery grinned. "I hear what you're saying, but he gave us practically all of the information that we have."

"That's just the point, Bob, the guy is playing us like a damn Stradivarius," Dailey returned. "He's just giving us enough information to keep us busy. And, quite frankly, I don't think he's wanted to give us as much as he has. He's got something else going on and I don't mind telling you, it scares me."

"He could have gone off on his own and done just as well, given his connections. I think he's trying to stay out of trouble, considering his past and all, but he definitely wants to be involved. You think this has anything to do with all this government crap he was involved in a while back?"

"Hell, I don't know . . . I need some real coffee." Dailey got up and started toward the coffee machine. "This ain't a mystery, it's a freaking nightmare."

* * * * *

"So what d'ya think, boss?" Miguel asked.

Jason turned toward Ben. "You hear anything from Victoria?"

"Not a thing."

They all had gathered around the conference table in the situation room for the debriefing. "I think they were digging a grave," Jason said, in answer to Miguel's question. Miguel and Krieger had just finished describing the men with the backhoe they had come across at the camp. All heads turned toward Jason with quizzical expressions.

"Think about it. Dailey and crew didn't find the three bodies in Issaquah. Ben's had discreet feelers out regarding the house in Victoria. The police, after an anonymous tip, found blood in the kitchen, on the hallway wall and floor, but no bodies. They didn't find the body outside. Those six bodies have to be somewhere, and I'll bet they ain't at Tranquil Acres. And, from what you said, Miguel, the guys weren't the young bucks. They were older, probably officers of the organization. I don't think most of them know what's really going on out there. Monroe doesn't seem to know."

"Just what do you think is going on out there, Jay?" Joe Castellano asked.

"It's a hell of a lot more than our little songbird at The Kennel knows. They definitely have a small army out there and we already know they're fanatical. But there's more to it. We know the guys we've been dealing with consider themselves to be freedom fighters. I think they've been brainwashed enough to do whatever they're told. We know they have no compunction about killing on command."

"So they're a terrorist group?" Ben asked.

"At least. But there's more. They have some sort of master plan and apparently they think Jack stumbled onto it. They're making a real effort to take out any threat. I think something was planned for the near future and now they're trying to move the schedule ahead.

"I've thought a lot about those M16's this morning. They're not using them. Everything they use is 7.62mm, NATO rounds. They're either trading them or selling them. It's the same with the drugs, same with the filter business. They're using it all to finance their mission, whatever the hell it is. After thinking about it, all of the guns and filters looked ready to be shipped off somewhere—they were not being received or stored as I originally thought. With this blowup at Suter Pharmaceuticals, and Abel Sloan running off and hiding like Comstock, I'm thinking Suter's been the source of a significant amount of their income. My guess is with everything coming down, they might try to fast-track."

Jason shrugged. "Just a hunch. One thing is certain, they're not too excited out at the camp and Comstock must be feeling pretty secure because he's not moving. But I'll bet his panties'll be in a wad after Dailey and his boys hit him tonight."

"What about that? They gonna let us in on that?" Krieger asked.

"No." Jason answered. "I phoned Dailey before we started this meeting. Too much of a liability he says."

"You think they'll get him?" Keller asked.

"Nope," Jason said smiling.

"You thinking what I think you're thinking?" Keller asked, as all the puzzled faces turned toward Jason again.

"You bet your ass."

* * * * *

Jason, along with Keller, Krieger, and Miguel, sat in the dark, nursing their second beers, watching a portion of Boeing Field that from all outward appearances seemed devoid of activity. Jason retreated into his thoughts. The he more he thought about the way he had handled the Comstock situation, the more he thought he had made a mistake. After being on the island, the whole series of events had taken on new meaning and he had possibly given the key to Dailey. No matter what happened tonight, Dailey would be close enough to the link that he'd have no choice but let the Feds take control.

His thoughts were abruptly interrupted by the sound of small arms fire less than a mile away. The others quickly stashed their beer cans and remained alert. Dailey's move on Comstock at Patriot Chemicals was apparently not going smoothly. Within a few seconds, automatic weapons could be heard accompanied by the muted thump of gas grenades being launched.

Jason set his beer down and crouched behind the crates with his comrades. "Shouldn't be long now," he said motioning toward the helicopter they had been watching. A man had just run from the hangar behind the bird, heading for the cockpit. As he ran, he looked over his shoulder in the direction of Patriot Chemicals at the sound of a large explosion. He clambered aboard and the engine began to whine as it spooled up.

"Sounds like it's getting ugly," Keller said.

"Dammit, why didn't I handle it?" Jason said, his face awash with genuine remorse at giving up Comstock's location. "All right, get into position." All four men, as if on cue, turned on their personal communication systems and adjusted their earpieces and microphones. They were armed with HK-MP5SDs, silenced 9mm submachine guns equipped with laser sights. Krieger and Miguel left to skirt around and flank the helicopter. Jason and Keller moved along in the shadows toward the front.

Light emanating from various buildings and security lights eliminated any need for night vision, but not enough to inhibit the effectiveness of the laser sights. Jason preferred laser sights in that they were not only accurate (wherever the little red dot landed would be where the bullet struck), but they were a great deterrent to resistance: When the adversary saw the dot on his chest he knew without a doubt he had nowhere to hide.

"How many you think there'll be?" Keller asked.

"This bird will only hold ten or so, but my guess'll be Comstock and a driver. I think whatever his escape route might be, it'd be pretty low key. I'd be willing to bet he was on his way out before the shooting ever started."

They only had to wait a few minutes before a camouflaged Chevy Blazer rolled up the frontage road and turned into the hangar drive. As it came to an abrupt stop in front of the hangar, a man that Jason had recognized from the description extracted himself with great difficulty from the driver's seat. He looked like a four-hundred-pound, six-foot-six bag of Jell-o. He ambled in a fat swagger toward the waiting helicopter.

"Looks a lot like wishful thinking, doesn't it?" Keller whispered, as they both looked at Comstock, then back to the helicopter. "Bird looks smaller than it did a minute ago. Kinda reminds me of The Little Engine That Could."

"Yeah. Well he ain't gonna have to say 'I think I can,'" Jason whispered back, then said into his microphone, "It's time to bag this mountain of shit. Let's do it."

Comstock had no chance to think when Krieger and Miguel appeared out of the dark and confronted him. In the past, Jason and his team had honed the unfair advantage to perfection, and in the time they had been apart they hadn't lost a bit of their timing. Comstock was approached from opposite sides in a quick and decisive move. The man had a laser dot on his forehead and another on the center of his chest. Walking appeared to have been quite an effort for him, let alone making any sudden moves. He had no options for escape and he knew it. He stood motionless and showed absolutely no emotion as Miguel moved in to pat him down. Krieger stood his ground and kept the dot on Comstock's chest, hoping that he wouldn't have to shoot him. He knew if Comstock went down, they would probably never get him up. And Jason had made it perfectly clear they needed him alive.

"Hands behind your head, fingers interlocked," Miguel growled. "And don't even blink or my friend'll be makin' you look an awful lot like a leaky bag of puss." Comstock remained stoic and calmly did as he was told. Miguel found him unarmed and secured his hands behind his back with wire ties. It took three sets of ties before Miguel felt certain Comstock would remain secure.

At the same time Krieger and Miguel dealt with Comstock, Keller trained a laser dot on the pilot's forehead as Jason climbed through the co-pilot door and stuffed the muzzle of his HK against the side of the shocked pilot's head. He dragged him from the cockpit by the nape of his neck and secured him while Keller crawled into the cockpit to kill the engine. Then Jason and Keller, on either side, quickly steered the pilot to where Comstock stood guarded.

A rage began to well in Jason as he approached Comstock, the man responsible for the chaos and pain in the lives of his friends, the creator of the terror in the O'Connor family, the one responsible for traumatizing a thirteen-year-old girl and Carol. The closer he came to Comstock, the more enraged he became. The only thing that kept him from shooting his knee-caps off was the fact that he needed some questions answered, and he doubted that even all four of them would be able to carry him. Well, there still might be time later for his knee-caps, he thought.

"So, if it isn't the missing George Comstock," Jason said, his hate palpable.

"Who the fuck are you?" Comstock asked, in a voice like garbled gravel.

"I'm someone you'll wish you'd never met. Krieger, you and Miguel come with me and this bag of shit. We'll take the Blazer. Doc, take the fly-guy in my car and we'll see you at The Kennel."

Jason turned to steer Comstock toward the Blazer when the area was suddenly bathed with light.

"Police! Drop your weapons!"

CHAPTER THIRTY-SIX

"Damn you!" Jason screamed with his face twisted in crimson rage. His white-knuckled fists were clenched on the table in front of him, the veins in his neck looked as though they would not withstand the pressure. "How can you in good conscience tell me you can't divulge any information regarding that pig? If it hadn't been for my help and my friends, the O'Connors and Carol Dunsmure would be dead right now. And you wouldn't know fuck all about it!"

"I know I'd be upset if I were in your place," Dailey responded, "but I can't give you any information until we learn something about this situation ourselves. And I certainly can't have you in on our interrogations. My captain would crucify me."

Jason slammed his fists on the table, barely this side of sanity, and stood to leave. "That's pure bullshit, Lieutenant, and you know it."

"Brisben, what is it with you? Let us play this out. We've got the kingpin now. Give us a little time. Be thankful your friends are out of danger now."

"If you knew—" In his anger, he almost told Dailey about how much he didn't know, then caught himself. "Lieutenant, you ain't got shit!" Jason turned and walked from the interrogation room, somehow having a sense that Comstock would give up little information, if any.

As Jason walked down the hall to the elevator, he realized Dailey had been very lenient with both him and his comrades, and for that he should be grateful. They all could have been arrested for illegal weapons, interfering with a police investigation, obstruction of justice and probably a few other things if he'd given enough thought to it. His frustration, however, stemmed from still not knowing the why part of this nightmare.

According to the sketchy information that Jason was able to pry from Dailey, the raid at Patriot had turned into a blood bath. Two police officers on the SWAT team had been wounded, one critically. The people at Patriot had not fared nearly so well. Six men were killed by the Seattle police and at least another half dozen had committed suicide. Apparently some sort of an alarm had gone off when Dailey and Montgomery walked through the front door and asked for Comstock. In the meantime, someone in the warehouse caught sight of a SWAT cop and opened fire; from then on the situation rapidly deteriorated. During the firefight, Comstock made his escape through a tunnel that took him nearly two blocks from the fracas, enabling him to get to Boeing Field, where Jason and crew intercepted him. Jason knew any terrorist worth his salt always has an escape plan. Preoccupied and suffering from sleep deprivation, Jason had not noticed he had been followed from the time of his last meeting with Dailey. When Dailey had been notified that Jason and his pals looked to be lying in wait for someone, he ordered in reinforcements. Jason and his men walked free only because Dailey understood that Comstock had been a gift from him.

The massive explosion and the fire that followed had destroyed the office and much of the storage area at Patriot. The whole fiasco raised a firestorm of questions to which no one in the department had answers. And, there were no survivors from Patriot to ask. Jason knew there would be no information.

The press had swarmed, feeding a frenzy of paranoia with the usual speculation and accusations of a cover-up. Once again the why remained a mystery.

Dailey's frustration level with Jason had peaked, heightened by the suspicion that he'd held back information that might have prevented the disaster. And his captain wanted answers as to why he had walked into an ambush. It had been a shitty day all around.

* * * * *

Jason, aware he was being followed when he returned to the partners' offices, was too tired and angry to care. Dailey already knew where their offices were, so it really didn't matter, but he warned the others to use caution when traveling to The Kennel.

Jason recapped the events of his confrontation with Dailey and reported what useless information he did get. At four-thirty Wednesday morning, Krieger and Miguel left and headed back to The Kennel assuring Jason they would take care to lose their tail. Exhausted and temporarily stymied, Jason returned to the loft and again, didn't care if they followed. Keller decided he would return to the hospital. If he were followed, it wouldn't matter.

Faint light from the breaking dawn sparkled off a light Elliott Bay chop as Jason entered the loft. Barely visible, the phenomenon appeared almost magical, like millions of tiny fireflies dancing in celebration of a new day. He paused and watched for a few brief moments. Too weary to fully appreciate the spectacle, he dragged himself to his room, stripped, showered quickly, and poured himself into bed, hoping for a better day in which to celebrate—just like the fireflies of Elliott Bay.

* * * * *

If frustration were money, Dailey, Montgomery, and the whole Seattle police department would be millionaires. Three hours of intensive interrogation of two men had yielded nothing. Comstock's pilot sat silent and rigid under everything Seattle's finest threw at him. The man would not talk. They knew nothing about him. He carried no identification, and the helicopter registration numbers showed it to be registered to another dead man.

They faired no better with Comstock. For nearly two hours, Dailey screamed questions until he was hoarse. Comstock simply sat, draped like a giant beanbag over a chair, and looked bored. His passive expression never once changed. When asked about Jack O'Connor, he had no reaction or response. They received the same icy stare when asked about Pathmoor, Martin Cray, and Abel Sloan. Out of sheer exasperation, Dailey charged Comstock with murder, conspiracy to commit murder, and drug trafficking. They mirandized him and his response, "Fuck you," were the only two words he spoke. When asked specifically if he wanted an attorney, he again calmly responded, "Fuck you."

Dailey turned to Montgomery and barked, "Get him the hell out of here! Dammit! I should've let Brisben have him."

Montgomery opened the interrogation room door and motioned to the guard as he brought Comstock to the door. His large body brushed both sides of the doorjambs on the way through. The guard and Montgomery escorted him down the hall toward the elevator as Dailey looked on in disgust. He felt nothing but dread as he headed toward his next order, a meeting with his captain.

* * * * *

"With Patriot Chemicals destroyed and Comstock behind bars, I see no reason why I can't return home. And besides, with Martin gone and Pathmoor in jail, I need to get back and run the company."

"Jack, listen to reason. Nothing has changed," Jason said. Nine o'clock a.m. seemed too early to be embroiled in this heated conversation.

"God Almighty, Jay, what do you mean nothing has changed? It sound's like everyone's dead and Comstock's in jail. What more do you want?"

"There's an armed camp out on that island with a 150 fanatics looking to do something, and before you're going to be safe, we need to find out what the hell it is."

At this point, Jason found it difficult to keep his anger under control. Why couldn't Jack see it from his perspective? He didn't want Jack feeling like a prisoner, but he had no choice.

"Jack, just give it a few more days. Please. I don't want to have to tell David and Steve to sit on you."

"Go to hell, Jay." The line went dead.

Jason looked at the receiver and slammed it to the cradle. In a sense, Jack was right, he thought. How long can I expect him to hide? I asked for a few days. How can I be certain of a time frame when I still have no idea what's going on?

He picked up his coffee and sipped contemplatively, rehashing the events of the past week and trying to make some sense of it. After a time, he realized his coffee had gotten cold and he returned to the kitchen for a refill. He sat on a barstool, leaned his back against the island and looked out over the bay. As he blew steam from his fresh coffee, he pondered his next move. In the silence, he could hear the quiet tick-tick-tick from the pendulum of his prized clock, a reminder, perhaps, of the urgency he felt while on Diablo, a feeling that something was about to happen and not knowing what or how to deal with it. Would the new development with Comstock stop or accelerate their plan, what ever it was? He sipped his coffee until it too became cold, then set it down and walked to his office in preparation for a call he thought he would never make.

"Admiralty," came the voice from his handset.

"Lieutenant Commander Brisben, calling for Admiral Fitzgerald."

"One moment please."

Jason felt hot. After spending nearly an hour going over every aspect of the situation again and again, he could see no other way. After much agonizing, he asked the questions: Am I willing to risk everything again? What about Carol? What about—?

"Brisben, m'boy," came a low, chesty, southern drawl. "It's been a while. You almost missed me. Just on my way to lunch and I'm damn near an hour late at that. What can I do for you?"

"Admiral, how far are you from a secured line?"

"This is gon'ta take a while, isn't it?" Fitzgerald asked cautiously.

"Yes, sir, it will."

"About ten minutes. Give me a number."

Jason replaced the handset. His thoughts now were of Carol, and whether he was making the right decision. He felt numb inside and almost sick to his stomach. He had indeed changed. Leaning back in his chair, he put Carol out of his mind and visualized Fitzgerald's square, bulldog face and flabby jowls. The sharp ring startled him.

"Brisben."

"Fitzgerald here. Now, what's going on?"

"Sir, I'm calling from Seattle, and from all indications, we've got a sensitive situation here."

Jason went on to describe the events of the past week and a half. He went into great detail when it came time to describe the camp and the armaments. As he summarized, the admiral interrupted.

"Well, Brisben, it sounds like something that needs to be turned over to the FBI."

"With all due respect, sir, I disagree. There isn't enough time. It's my opinion they're fast-tracking. If you'll permit, I see one of two scenarios: By the time the FBI gets their shit together, the campers'll be doing whatever it is they've been planning to do. Or, the FBI will charge in like bulls in a china shop and there'll be a Waco standoff which will give the campers time to cover up whatever it is they've been planning."

"So what is it you want from me?" The Admiral sounded guarded.

"I want permission to pull the remainder of my team together. I want six canisters of Z gas. I need three suppressed Galil sniper rifles with night scopes. And I need to go in and find out what these hamburger heads are planning and then remove the threat. Of course, we'll turn all arms and information over to you. No one will know that we've ever been there."

"I suppose, this is all predicated on you and your fire pissers not getting caught. Besides, you know the drill, Brisben. The Secretary of State and the head of the Security Council will have to be briefed on something like this."

"In my opinion, sir, I feel they're too close to the President. If, as you say, something were to happen, it would be ugly for our Commander-in-Chief. Looks to me like he already has a full plate with his bimbos and extracurricular activities in the Oval Office. Besides, I don't mean to be disrespectful, sir, but by the time those two constipated limp-dicks make a decision, Armageddon will have been over for two years."

"Point taken." The Admiral laughed heartily. "Uh, Brisben, my boy, you seem to gravitate to trouble like a fly to horseshit."

He laughed again, then composed himself and suddenly turned serious. "Sounds like you've given this a lot of thought."

"Yes, sir. I have."

"You realize, of course, what you're getting into. There won't be any cover for you; you'll be totally on your own."

"Yes, sir. I know. And as you well know, I've been there before."

"Yes, I do know, and I guess it surprises me you'd want'a to go there again. Last time you were lucky. This time . . . ." His voice trailed off. "I suppose I should be honest with you. I'm not totally surprised at your call. Apparently you gave McNairy's name to a Seattle detective as a reference. He called to verify. He also called to get information about your connections. It kind'a sounds like you've been busy. Scaring the living shit out of the good lieutenant, you are. And McNairy didn't tell him a whole lot that would put him at ease. And of course our friend McNairy still has a burr up his ass from the heat he took after your last cleanup expedition. He considers you to be something of a hothead."

"Well, I came home one night and found my wife's brains all over the bedroom. I took care of the cleanup. He sure as hell wasn't watching our backs, now, was he?" Jason said, hotly. "Anyway, I called you because I know you will get me what I need with a minimum of BS."

"What you really want is someone to run interference for you in a political pissing contest."

"What pissing contest? You outrank him."

"Jason, you have been away for a while, haven't you? I still have to work with the sonofabitch. Now, what is it you really want?"

"I want the ban on contact between team members abolished. I want the supplies I listed."

"When do you supposedly need this, uh, favor?"

"I'm not in any particular hurry. By the end of tomorrow would be fine. You can have a package flown to the Naval Air Station at Whidbey Island. Keller will fly up and pick it up."

"In case you've forgotten, Brisben, I don't walk on water. And what the hell am I supposed to do with 150 bodies?"

"Shouldn't be that many, if everything goes well. A hundred forty will be sleeping through the whole thing; that's what the gas is for." Jason replied, matter-of-factly. "We get the people in charge, the ones making the decisions, the rest will fold and disappear. We'll record everything so your ass will be covered. Admiral, you know me, and what I'm trained for—I'll cover our tracks. When the Feds move in, it'll all be laid out for them. Once they see what's out there, they won't be advertising it. I'm not blowing smoke, Admiral. Whatever these people are planning could make Oklahoma City look like a nursery rhyme."

Jason felt confident Fitzgerald would help. The admiral had always been a strong ally, someone he could trust.

"Jason," Fitzgerald said, now sounding somber, "I know that you have good instincts, but I hope for your sake this is what you say it is. I'll see what I can do. No promises. We'll talk later."

"Thank you, Admiral."

"Be damn careful, m'boy." The connection broke off.

Jason slowly returned the handset to the cradle. A long sigh escaped as he leaned back, his fingers interlaced behind the base of his neck. When he closed his eyes he realized he had been holding his breath and his palms were covered with perspiration.

He wondered if it had made the right decision. Protecting Jack had turned out to be something quite different than he had anticipated. Jason reminded himself that he wanted into this party. He had trained hard to learn how to deal with terrorist activity, but thought it was all behind him after the team debacle—until now. He could not let it go, knowing he and his team could handle it better than anyone. They were the best and this was too big to walk away from.

"Oh God, Carol," Jason groaned with a burning recognition. He had just done what she said he would do, and he heard her broken-hearted, fearful voice say the words, "but you won't run either." Now he fully understood the lies he'd lived—that nothing really mattered or that he couldn't be hurt—the lies he'd disguised behind anger so well for so many years. The thought of losing Carol, he finally admitted, hurt like hell. He also realized something else unexpected: He felt Carol's pain, and this time, it mattered.

With his head still leaning back, he slowly opened his eyes and stared at a cobweb where the ceiling joined the wall. Normally, he would have immediately stood and brushed it away, but he just stared at the cobweb and wondered if Carol could forgive his decision.

Jason had no idea how long he had stared at that cobweb. It hadn't really mattered. He removed his hands from behind his head and massaged his tired, itching eyes. He had spent enough time lamenting his personal life. As if turned by a switch he focused his attention to the one piece of business that still needed to be addressed. He picked up the phone and dialed Keller's pager number.

When Keller called, Jason spoke without preamble. "How soon can you come to the loft?"

* * * * *

Some forty-five minutes later, Jason told Keller about his conversation with Admiral Fitzgerald. The doctor listened to his friend patiently, but wondered why the information necessitated his coming to the loft.

Sensing Keller's puzzlement, Jason said, "Tom, I asked you here because you're the only one on this exercise who stands to lose. Krieger, Miguel, David, Steve, and I have all been down this road. We know the risks involved. You have a great career and you love your work. If this thing turns sour, if something happens out on that island, you may never work again. I'm giving you the option to walk away from this. You know, and all of us would agree, it'd be the smart thing to do."

Jason had voiced a valid concern. Fitzgerald's warning had been very specific. If for any reason something went awry and Jason or any of his team were caught, even if it were in the name of national security, they would become scapegoats once again. For Jason and the rest, it would not be a catastrophe, as they had been in and out of covert operations all along. But for Keller, it would destroy a brilliant career.

Fire burned in Keller's eyes. "Along with five other people, I spent eight hours suturing Lori Phillips together. We nursed her minute by minute for another thirty-six hours until she looked as though she would make it. These psycho bastards offed her, Jay. I want their asses. I know the risk, and I'm in. Subject closed."

Jason nodded, "That's it, then. I'll need you to fly up to Whidbey to pick up a package as soon as Fitzgerald calls. How're you sitting with the hospital?"

"I'm off for the duration. You've got me for as long as you need me. When do you figure he'll have it together?" Keller asked referring to the gas and weapons.

"It'll be late back there by the time he puts it all together. I doubt if he'll be able to get it on a courier before morning their time. I'm supposed to hear confirmation later today. In the meantime, I think we should meet at the partners and rough out a preliminary strategy for a return to the island. How and when we move will depend on what information, if any, Dailey is willing to share about Comstock."

"When do you want to meet?" Keller asked.

"Later this evening. That will give everyone time to get some long overdue rest. I'll call you with a time. And Tom— thank you."

"When we bust these a-holes, it will have been my pleasure."

* * * * *

The sun melted behind the Olympic Mountain Range in spectacular fashion, burning brilliant color through a partly cloudy sky. Jason watched the spectacle from his living room as he sipped single-malt scotch, not enjoying either as much as he usually did. He wanted this thing with Jack to be over. He had hung up from yet another argument and Jack had mercilessly stung him, accusing him of having a battle of egos with Dailey, using himself—Jack—as the pawn. There had been a bit of truth in that, and it hurt. But it wasn't as it seemed. Jason had spent a considerable amount of time learning how to discover terrorist activity. What Jack stumbled into looked to be a motherlode. If Jason's instincts proved true, his own life or the lives of his men would be a small price to pay.

His thoughts turned to Carol again. While he had always instinctively been concerned with his survival, he had never looked past surviving from one event to the next. For the first time, he felt he had a future—and he wanted to live it.

The telephone interrupted his ruminations. He set his tumbler of scotch on the coffee table and strode to his office. "Brisben."

"Fitzgerald here. There will be a package leaving for Whidbey at 0600 tomorrow. It should arrive before 1200 hours. It'll have Keller's name on it. Make sure he has his reserve ID with him.

"Now for the good or the bad news depending on your perspective: With the incident in Oklahoma just a month old, I've reintroduced the issue of anti-terrorist teams. I have to tell you straight out, Brisben, I've a received heated response, both for and against. I haven't mentioned word one about this little exercise you're involved in, but if it's as you say, and there is truly a crisis to be thwarted, I just may be able to get your commission reinstated, and what's left of your team just may be back in business."

Jason stood stunned. To be vindicated after five years was more than he had ever allowed himself to hope for. "I don't know what to say, Admiral."

"Don't say anything. My ass is already hanging out a mile, m'boy, because I've laid some very preliminary groundwork, so don't you dare burn it."

"With all due respect, Admiral, there are five other asses hanging out here. Mine and yours makes it seven. I'll be careful."

"Brisben—you do that. And good luck." The line went dead.

* * * * *

The odds of six men invading an armed camp of 140-plus brainwashed fanatics seemed insurmountable. But it did nothing to quell the enthusiasm of Krieger and Miguel once Jason relayed his conversation with Fitzgerald; they were a team again. Miguel quickly called the beach house and handed the phone to Jason so he could be the one to impart the information to David and Steve. Jason wished he could have shared in their excitement, but it somehow seemed different when his personal sacrifice was so great.

When Jason concluded his conversation, he launched into planning the invasion of the camp. "To neutralize the odds, we'll place two canisters of Z gas in each of the three barracks. It's nothing more than a sleeping gas and it'll render the troops unconscious. They'll sleep through a nuclear explosion. Once that's accomplished, we'll have the freedom to get the information we're after. Resistance should be minimal. We take prisoners, and there are not many who can resist my charms when I want information; it's just a matter of persuasion. Once we get what we want, I'll notify the Navy SEAL team at Poulsbo and let them clean up. Depending on the political mood, the government or the Navy will be heroes and we'll maintain our anonymity. It's perfect. So let's get some rest and tomorrow we'll make a finite plan and divvy up the assignments."

* * * * *

There was that sound again. The young black man had been lying on the bunk in the holding cell for several hours, listening to the tearing of fabric every few minutes. Fear and nausea had kept him awake after being arrested for stealing a car. An "A" student who had never been in trouble before had done it as a dare. Stupid! Stupid! Stupid, he thought. The tearing stopped and he finally drifted off.

A few cells down the row, George Comstock sat hunched over at the foot of his bunk, putting the finishing touches on his project. Two dim night-lights struggled against the darkness in the holding area, barely illuminating his naked body. He had torn and braided his orange detention coveralls into a substantial rope.

Two hours before, he had finished his second session with Dailey and Montgomery, and much to Comstock's pleasure, had netted them nothing. Comstock knew, however, the train had somehow been derailed and he and his pilot had now become liabilities. But the mission was still safe. Nobody knew about the camp and only six people other than himself knew about their mission. The pilot did not know the mission, but he did know the location of the camp.

Comstock slowly lifted his obese body with much effort, as he did with every movement he made. He lumbered the two steps to the bars of the adjoining cell and whispered, "Bill—Bill." His pilot stirred in his bunk, then raised his head and looked around sleepily. "Bill, c'mere, I need to talk to ya."

The man quietly rose and stepped to the bars where Comstock stood. In an uncharacteristically quick movement, Comstock reached through the bars and grabbed his pilot's chin with one hand and the back of his head with the other and rotated it powerfully and quickly. The sickening muffled crunch of the man's neck as it snapped seemed to echo in the darkness. Comstock slowly and quietly lowered him to the floor. Then he took the rope he had made and looped it through the top frame of the bars and tied it off securely, then tested it with his weight.

When satisfied that it would support him, he fashioned a slip noose, lowered it over his head and tightened it around his neck. He turned and leaned his back against the bars and relaxed his knees letting the rope tighten around his neck. Speaking inwardly to himself, he cursed his country, its leaders and the bureaucracy with its out-of-control government. The dim light became dimmer. His last thoughts were of the plan he had helped create and the satisfaction he felt. It was in motion and could not be stopped. Everything went black . . . the quiet became nothing.

CHAPTER THIRTY-SEVEN

The telephone once again woke Jason from a sound sleep at 5:30 a.m. In the midst of all the turmoil, he had not slept well and it felt to him as if he had just dropped off. After a bit of reorientation, he sleepily answered. "Brisben."

"Jason, this is Bob Montgomery. I'm sorry to disturb you so early but I wanted you to know before you heard it on the news. George Comstock murdered his pilot, then committed suicide during the night."

Jason, now wide awake from the sudden adrenal rush, had somehow known that Comstock wouldn't give up any information, but he hadn't expected this bit of news. Deep down he hoped he would have had access to Comstock. More than once he reveled in thinking about interrogating him. That possibility had just instantly vanished.

"These people are fanatical!" he mumbled out of frustration.

Not hearing him, Montgomery asked, "What's that?"

Jason ignored the question. "How did he do it?"

"Prelim, looks like he broke his pilot's neck through the bar. He made a rope from his coveralls and hung himself . . . thought you'd want to know."

"Thanks I appreciate it . . . uh—Bob, how's the lieutenant handling it?" Jason asked, trying to collect his thoughts and make some semblance of intelligent conversation.

A coolness crept into Montgomery's voice. "Well, Jason, to put it bluntly, not very well. The captain wants answers, and soon. He's wanting to know what the hell is going on, and he's putting a hell of a lot of pressure on Dailey to get his shit together and find out. The media is out of control on this thing now. I don't have to tell you the rumor mill will be in full form in a matter of hours if we don't give 'em something solid. How's Dailey? He's pissed. And quite frankly, I can't blame him. Just a little side note: He thinks you're holding out on him and to be honest, so do I, for what it's worth. And by the way, we never had this conversation. Give us a call if you have anything that'll help." The line went dead.

Jason stared at the receiver momentarily, then returned it to the cradle. Ah, yes, "Guilt—the gift that keeps on giving," he thought. And well deserved. But how to handle it? If he went to Dailey now, Dailey would be forced to turn the information over to his captain. No, he decided, as difficult as it was, he would wait. But, would waiting help? No matter when Jason gave him information, chances were Dailey would still have to take it to his superior.

With Comstock's information going to the grave with him, it became more important that Sloan and Fortner be found. Formulating a game plan required more information, information that neither he nor Dailey had. He needed more to work with.

* * * * *

Later that morning, Jason struggled with another dilemma. He had received a phone call from Jack at the beach house in Manzanita.

"Jason, I'm coming home. The thing about Comstock is all over the news. With him out of the way, I see no—

"Not a good idea, Jack." Jason's patience with his friend had all but expired. Just because Comstock—"

"Jay! I will not argue the issue anymore. I'll agree to leave the family here, I'll no longer tolerate being held prisoner. Steve let me call Cervicon to check on things and everything is in turmoil without Martin. I need to get back—"

Jason leaned his head back and closed his eyes as Jack continued on. I'm sick of listening to this shit, he thought.

"Alright, Jack! Enough! Come back. But you'll stay with me until we get this sorted out. And that is *not* negotiable."

Jack started to say something but never finished the first word. "Jack! Not another fucking word! Now, let me talk to Steve."

"I'm sorry boss, the guy's out of control," Steve said, when he came on the line.

"I probably would be too, given the situation," Jason answered. I want you to leave the Lincoln at the beach house and you and David bring Jack by the loft. He'll be bunking with me. That way I can take him to work and pick him up. If you leave within the hour you'll be back this evening."

"See you tonight boss."

After hanging up Jason retrieved his coffee from the kitchen counter, and slowly worked his way to the living room.

If I were in his place, I would do the same, Jason thought. Funny creatures we men are, what we consider the "priority." As he sipped his coffee, he thought of an oath to his country he had taken long ago and how he had put that oath before anything else. Now, some twenty-five years later, he realized his commitment was still just as strong. It had been his marriage, then and apparently now, even after the failure of the anti-terrorist program. Could he really fault Jack for his commitment, even though it seemed like suicide? The day before, he, too, had made a choice, not unlike Jack's, when he chose to contact Admiral Fitzgerald.

He reflected upon his life. During his service career, he'd had a notorious reputation for having some kind of a death wish. He had developed incredible survival instincts and skills, but still, he had reveled in the death battles. When confronted about being insane, his stock response was, "I play the game with vigor." In retrospect, he wasn't so sure. Was he so filled with anger that he didn't care if he lived or died? Wasn't that an act of cowardice simply camouflaged as bravery? And what about today? Was his plan to invade Diablo Island any different? Wasn't it just another reckless adventure?

No, not this time. This time it's necessary. He could see some type of terrorist activity shaping up out at the camp. The evidence confirmed it. In Vietnam he'd seen enough terrorist activity to last a lifetime. But just last month, a truck bomb had ripped the Alfred P. Murrah Federal Building in Oklahoma City, killing over eighty people and leaving dozens more injured. In February of 1993 at the World Trade Center parking garage, another bomb exploded, leaving six killed and a 1,000 injured. Still, the United States to this point, had remained relatively free from terrorist activity. But for how much longer? Jason would do anything to keep that kind of activity from U.S. soil, including the giving of his life. He and his men had trained for this, and that is not suicide.

Jason had hoped to have something to look forward to. He thought of Carol and having some semblance of a normal life. But how could he expect her to brave the kind of uncertainty he had to offer? He needed to talk with her, and soon. What a dichotomy, calling and telling her that he wanted her in his life, and in the next breath that he had just been reinstated into his anti-terrorist team. Jason knew he had to release her, and the thought of it hurt like hell.

* * * * *

Later, Jason sat once again in his office in front of the telephone. The telephone seemed such a cold instrument, but he knew the call must be made. He wished at that moment he could be with Carol. He felt remorse that once again he had made a commitment without allowing her input. How was that fair? How did that work into the shared decision-making process? Jason remembered the fear and pain in Carol's eyes the morning he left Manzanita and he still felt her pain as he thought about making the call.

He tipped his head back as he finished a can of beer, then went to the refrigerator for another. Without hesitation, he popped the top and took several long swallows before reaching for the wall phone.

Jason had not been prepared for Carol to answer the telephone; she picked up the hesitancy Jason's voice conveyed.

"Jay, just tell me what's going on."

Jason took a deep breath and told her about his conversation with Admiral Fitzgerald. "This is something I have to do. It's not just about protecting Jack any more and that's about all I can tell you for right now without placing everyone in more danger. But I just want to—"

"Jason," Carol interrupted.

"Wait a minute. Let me finish. I just need to . . ." He tried to regain control of the conversation but to no avail.

"Jason listen to me. It's all right. You don't have to explain. I understand and I know you love me. And I want you to know that I love you. But trying to change you would destroy who you are and would become a source of resentment. Jason, just know I loved you like no other. Now go do what you must. And Jason, I know this sounds trite, but please, be careful and don't be worrying about me. Concentrate on what it is you have to do.

"Steve talked to his sister before he left and the house is ours for as long as we need it. Laura and I will be staying on down here for a couple of weeks. We'll talk then." Without warning, Carol disconnected and the line went dead.

Jason looked at the handset in disbelief. This had not been the way he had envisioned the conversation should go. He had so much he wanted to say to her and it frustrated him that he never had the chance. He realized Carol needed to protect herself from the conversation that would have been inevitable, his explanation of why he had to continue what he'd started. The anguish in her voice had told the truth even though her words had not. And he knew it to be unfair and selfish of him to expect her to endure the instability of his choice. The team had again become his "wife"; he'd simply been separated for five years. Carol understood this. She had not wanted to be his fatal distraction, causing him to worry about her while fighting for his life.

Numbly, Jason finally hung up the phone, questioning his choice. This time he had given up something precious. His breath left him as if he had taken a blow to the solar plexus. A wale of grief involuntarily escaped his chest, and he openly wept for the first time in over forty years. Vivid memories of Debbie saying she felt her heart was breaking, and the look on Jack's face at his arrival to The Kennel, flashed before Jason, as he experienced the loss and emptiness of a breaking heart. For the first time in his life, Jason Brisben hurt too much to be angry.

Jason remained with his back against the kitchen island and stared sadly out at the water, as the sun traversed the afternoon sky and finally faded behind the Olympics. He started at the security door buzzer; David and Steve had arrived to drop off Jack. Anxious to reunite with Krieger and Miguel, the two team members did not stay long.

Jason welcomed Jack as enthusiastically as he could given his apprehension, then busied himself with the preparation of dinner. As Jack looked on from a barstool, Jason could tell the man had something on his mind. Into an uncomfortable silence, Jack finally spoke.

"You must think I'm an ungrateful idiot." Jason looked up as Jack continued on. "So much has happened lately I obviously haven't been thinking too clearly. I know I've questioned your judgment and said things that sounded illogical, and I want to apologize. I don't want to go on about it, but I hope you can accept the fact that I know I blew it."

Jason understood Jack's expression of regret, but he also thought he knew why Jack's mood had improved so dramatically. With Comstock now out of the way, he thought he would have nothing to fear. With Pathmoor behind bars, he could get back to Cervicon and hopefully pick up where Martin Cray had left off.

Jason had no problem forgiving Jack for things said, born of fear, frustration, and grief. But Jason did not believe Jack was out of danger. That possibility would still have to be dealt with on a day-to-day basis; and so as not to spoil his friend's mood, Jason did not mention it.

"Not a problem. I would have acted no better." Jason did not bring up the subject of Diablo Island or any of the latter developments for the simple reason that he didn't feel like talking. They both retired after a simple meal of bacon, lettuce, and tomato sandwiches and Guinness.

They awoke early the next morning and Jason fixed a breakfast of Spanish omelets and coffee from a French press. Jack ate little, his appetite curbed by his excitement about returning to work. Jason drove him to Cervicon at six a.m. and returned to the loft.

It had been a little over twenty-four hours since Jason had learned of Comstock's death, and the early-morning conversation with Montgomery weighed heavily on his mind. Dailey's frustration must be palpable, he thought. But what to do about it? If I level with him and tell him what I know including what's on that island, will it ease his mind or increase his frustration? Jason wondered. Demands to questions that Jason knew the Seattle Police Department could not answer were splayed across the morning *Times* like a bold, black indictment. For better or worse, Jason made the call.

At seven o'clock in the morning, Jason expected to leave a message for Dailey and it surprised him when the lieutenant gruffly answered his telephone.

"Good morning, Lieutenant. I'm surprised you're in at this hour."

"Well, I'll tell you what, Brisben, I haven't been getting a whole lot of sleep since I ran into you down at that Pandora's Box Car. And it doesn't appear that it'll get much better from here on out. My boss and I had a real informative conversation with an Admiral Fitzgerald yesterday. It cleared up a lot of things about you. But you have to know we lowly city cops don't care for outsiders mucking about on our turf. So with that said, what the hell do you want at this lovely hour?"

"I thought it would be good for us to talk, Lieutenant."

Dailey let out a sarcastic guffaw. "Now there's a novel idea. I get a call from some admiral telling me that you may be coming across some sensitive information and we're not to interfere, and now all of a sudden you want to talk after damn near two weeks of holding out on me. That's rich, son, real fuckin' rich."

Stung by the comment, Jason began to react hotly until he realized he could now tell Dailey what he knew. There would no longer be a need for the continual fencing.

"Look, Lieutenant, I didn't know Fitzgerald would call you, but now that he has, I'd like to have an opportunity to give you the information that I have. You can't share it with anyone, but at least you will have some peace of mind knowing that there's more going on than a murder in a parking lot."

"Dammit, Brisben, I've got five bodies in the morgue. There are supposedly three from Issaquah and God only knows how many others from Victoria. I know damn well that this mess is more than a murder in a fucking parking lot."

Jason, kicking himself for the stupidity of his last statement, could not fault Dailey for his sarcasm.

"Okay, Lieutenant, I deserved that, but can we get past the way I've handled this and talk? Even though it's a little late, there is information that I can share that will help you understand." That didn't sound much better, he thought.

A long silence, then a heavy sigh came from the receiver. "Oh, hell, when do you want to do this?"

"Now, Lieutenant. I can pick you up in ten minutes."

"I'll be ready."

CHAPTER THIRTY-EIGHT

Lt. Dailey stood waiting in front of the Public Service Building as Jason pulled to a stop and opened the passenger door. The seat in his Seville screeched and chirped as plush leather enveloped Dailey. The lieutenant eyed the interior analytically.

"So, what'd this hunk of Detroit iron set you back?"

"Well, it's more aluminum and plastic than iron and not so much Detroit any more, unless the Rio Grande has moved farther north since I last looked at a map. About fifty, in answer your question. Then I spent another ten on some engine and suspension tweaks."

Dailey shook his head slowly, an unreadable expression on his face. "I must be in the wrong business."

Conversation began slowly with both fencing, neither wanting to have been bested. Finally, as if by some external prodding, Dailey produced a document and handed it to Jason as they waited at the stoplight on the end of the Tukwila off-ramp.

"What's this?" Jason queried.

"It's the official request from your buddy Admiral Fitzgerald not to interfere or hinder your investigation of possible terrorist activity in the Seattle area." Jason only glanced at the document, then handed it back to Dailey as the light changed. "If you'd take the time to read the damn thing, you'd see that it's not exactly a request, if you get my drift."

With all the media pressure, Jason understood Dailey's and his captain's reaction to the directive.

"So, would I be out of line if I asked you where the hell you're taking me?" Dailey asked sarcastically.

Jason didn't let the dig slide. "Lieutenant, believe it or not, we're on the same side. I have two choices. I can give you all the information that I have, but with that comes problems. You can't reveal any of it, even to your captain. Or I tell you nothing, and we carry on as we have for the past two weeks. Obviously, this mess overlaps into your investigation and I understand that it's awkward. What's your preference, Lieutenant? You want to be uncomfortable with me, and not know, or do you want to know and be uncomfortable with your captain and the media, and have to keep your mouth shut?"

"I'm already uncomfortable, Brisben. What the hell difference does it make now?" he responded, with an edge to his anger.

"Because what I tell you now, you may never be able to reveal," Jason answered hotly.

"Well, Brisben, sounds like you're on the horns of a dilemma. Why don't you knock off all this cloak and dagger shit and make a decision. One way or the other."

"I need a commitment, Lieutenant. I have to know that you'll keep this information in confidence until we or I get to the bottom of whatever is going on. And it might take longer than the media or your captain is willing to wait," Jason said, his patience wearing thin.

"You aren't getting a commitment, son. Maybe you'll just have to trust that I have a modicum of common sense."

The gauntlet had been thrown. As Dailey said, Jason had to make the decision. He had in the beginning intended to take Dailey to The Kennel, tell him about Victoria, introduce him to Monroe, and tell him about Diablo Island. But now his pride stood in the way. He did not like Dailey's challenge, and he had the most to lose.

Dailey interrupted Jason's thoughts. "You still haven't told me where you're taking me."

"You're about one minute from finding out." The decision had been made.

Dailey looked sideways at him but said nothing. At the end of the block, Jason turned the car into the gravel drive and parked beside the rented van and Taurus station wagon.

Jason turned off the ignition, shifted in his seat to face Dailey, and began telling him the chain of events from the time that he arrived on Vancouver Island the previous Saturday morning to the present. He gave the details of the rescue and told about the prisoners being held captive inside the house. As Jason spoke, Dailey's mind raced frantically on how the Seattle Police would possibly explain away even a small portion of the information. Even though he had some satisfaction in Jason divulging his secrets, a part of him wished he hadn't been told.

Jason continued on, revealing the information gleaned from Monroe, about being recruited by Comstock, the camp on Diablo Island, the work force at Patriot Chemicals and, finally, what he and his men found during their early Tuesday morning trip to the island.

"It's a well-armed camp, Lieutenant. There is too much out there; it's too well-financed. This is one of the best laid out and well-funded terrorist training facilities I've ever seen, and there's a plan in motion. I don't know yet what it is, and that's what I have to learn—and damn quick. Do you think for one minute, Lieutenant, Comstock committed suicide because of being suspected of murder? The minute you arrested him, he knew he had become a liability and he removed himself, just like everyone else who has been compromised. He wasn't above it. Lieutenant, these people are fanatical. You ever wonder why there weren't any survivors from Patriot Chemicals?"

Dailey sat motionless and quiet, his expression unreadable, trying to assimilate the new information and make some determination of what to do with it.

Dailey looked at Jason a moment longer before answering. "Of course I've thought about it!" He went silent again and turned a contemplative gaze out the windshield. Turning slowly to face Jason again, he asked, "How much time do you need?"

Jason shook his head slowly. "Lieutenant, I don't know. I'm planning another trip to the island, but now with Comstock dead and Patriot down, our next trip won't be a cake walk."

"So why'd you bring me here?" Dailey asked.

"To meet Monroe. Let you see that when I have the time to extract information, I'm not the bloodthirsty thug you think I am. Introduce you to the team, to—"

Dailey held his hand up. "Not necessary." A troubled expression washed over his face. "It's not necessary, son. I don't want to go in. I have no need to meet your team. And I don't particularly care to know as much as I do."

Dailey both envied Jason and resented him. Jason had the freedom to get it done without the encumbrances of departmental procedure. But Dailey also had empathy for him, because Jason was alone and always would be, because his chosen vocation was a sinister, uncompromising, unforgiving bitch. He reached into the inside vest pocket of his rumpled sports jacket and removed a cassette tape, which he handed to Jason.

"What's this?"

"It's our interrogation of Carl Fortner," Dailey answered, with neither pride nor sarcasm. All spirit of competition had vanished and only grave concern etched his face.

"I thought—"

"Thought Fortner and Sloan had disappeared?" Dailey finished. "Sloan is still at-large. With the aid of the Hoodsport Police, Thompson and I picked Fortner up last night several miles above the campground at Lake Cushman. He'd been hiding out with his family in their fifth wheel, scared out of his mind. I think he told the truth. Have a listen."

Jason placed the tape in the car cassette player. Dailey had been right. A frightened Fortner answered the questions put to him without ambiguity.

"Sloan had delivered Comstock to me at the shipping dock with instructions to put him to work preparing product for shipment. I had no idea where he came from and knew nothing about his background."

Dailey and Jason listened for nearly forty-five minutes with nothing of significance coming to light, until: "After a couple of months, I noticed that Comstock'd been doing a lot of special packaging for Abel Sloan."

"Do you have any idea what the packages contained?" Dailey asked.

"No. You have to understand, I don't know squat about drugs. I just shipped the stuff. Every morning I get a shipping schedule complete with bar codes. It comes to us in boxes already packaged up with the lids open. We do a count, so many . . . yada, yada, yada . . . and match the numbers to the ship sheet. We sign it off as a completed order, fill any air space with foam, seal the box, put an address label and the bar code onto the box, and send it down the conveyer. We UPS almost everything. Most of the time it's just bottles of pills, but once in a while we would get vials. Those we shipped in special containers, the kind you could drop from thirty thousand feet and whatever was in them wouldn't break. The vials, I've been told, contained serums ranging from the ultra-expensive to the ultra-dangerous.

"About a month before Comstock disappeared—I mean, one day he never showed for work and we never saw him again—" Fortner went on, "I got a chance to see what he put in one of the packages that went to Sloan. It contained bottles of capsules and three vials. That's all I can tell you. I don't have any idea what was in the packages, and with all the shit that's coming down right now, I don't think I want to know."

"When did you last see Sloan?" Dailey asked.

"About ten minutes after you left the plant on Monday. I went to his office and asked what was going on. He told me to forget that it ever happened and pack up my family and disappear. I tried to ask him again, but he just screamed at me, told me to keep my mouth shut and get the hell out of town . . . . What the hell is going on?"

"The less you know the better off you'll be," Dailey answered.

Jason stopped the tape and replayed the last portion, deep in thought as he listened.

When he stopped the tape again, Dailey asked, "Mean something?"

Jason thought several moments before answering. "Not sure, Lieutenant. The more I learn about this mess, the less I know. One thing's for sure, Sloan and Comstock had something going: drugs, arms, using Diablo camp labor at the chemical plant. Looks like it all went to funding the camp. But for what? Eleven people have died and I'm not sure anyone knows why, except Comstock. It's obvious Fortner doesn't know anything."

Jason restarted the tape, but heard nothing more of any use. When the tape finally came to an end fifteen minutes later, Jason looked at Dailey. "Thank you, Lieutenant."

Dailey nodded his acknowledgment. "It looks like you've some big fish to fry, son. Question is, now what?" Dailey sat quietly for several minutes, then asked, "What can I do to help, I mean without getting my ass further in a sling?"

Jason, surprised by the offer, did not respond immediately. Then, "I have a man in there," he said nodding toward the house. "We can't turn him over to you without opening another can of worms. There're only six of us to return to that island and we'll be spread thin. I need someone to watch him. You have someone we can trust?"

Dailey shook his head, then stopped as a thought struck him. "Dolan! He's on vacation. He has a little fixer-upper in South Seattle—took some time off to work on it. It's worth a try. It's just a few minutes from here."

Jason started the car and backed from the drive. "Lead the way."

* * * * *

Jason pulled to a stop in front of a 1940's-vintage bungalow. The exterior displayed fresh paint and a yard in transition with the rubble of in-process interior remodeling discards piled against one side of the house.

"You should have seen it when he first bought it. A sorely neglected dump it was," Dailey said as they left the car. "That young hellion sure has the energy. He's doing it all himself and it's looking pretty damn good."

They climbed the two steps to the small front porch. Jason and Dailey looked at each other with dread in their eyes as the lieutenant rapped hard on the door. Each man knew what the other need not state. Jason instinctively recognized the odor from Vietnam, and Dailey also, from too many encounters in his line of work. Although faint, the scent of decomposition was unmistakable. Dailey nodded toward a silver Honda Prelude parked at the curb. "It's his."

Dailey tried the doorknob and found it locked. Without a word, Jason pushed Dailey aside and put his foot to the door with such quickness and force the door flew open with the jamb exploding into splinters. The odor, no longer faint, hit them like a hot impenetrable wave. Both men fought to control the involuntary reflex to retch as they went from room to room, searching for what neither wanted to find.

Jason turned left into a kitchen dinette area that appeared to be the most recent subject of Dolan's remodeling attention. The tools on the small dining table seemed to be of the plumbing variety and one of the cabinet doors under the kitchen sink hung open.

"In here," Dailey yelled. "In the bathroom." Dailey had caught sight of a leg splayed out of the bathroom doorway centered between two bedrooms. He stood with his arm braced against the doorjamb, looking down at Dolan who appeared to have been dressed for his project of the day: long cut-off jeans and a weightlifter's tank top, the type with the sides ripped out to make room for overdeveloped lat muscles.

"Use the phone in my car," Jason told Dailey as he gently laid his hand on his back. "I won't touch anything."

After a moment Dailey slowly turned and retraced his steps to the car. Jason watched his retreat compassionately and then turned his attention to the dead police officer on the floor. He bent down on one knee and studied the corpse that lay before him. The man had been a dedicated bodybuilder. His shoulder muscles were developed to the size of cantaloupes and his trapezius muscles radiused into his thick neck like steel straps. His quads were ripped and pushed tight against the cut-off denim. The color of his skin had turned a pasty gray, defying the hours spent in the tanning booth. The sight of his face brought about another wave of nausea. Blow flies had already done their work, having laid their eggs in his wide-open eyes, nose, and mouth. His contorted face revealed great pain or surprise, or both.

Jason backed away and carefully looked at details of the surroundings and the condition of the house, being careful not to touch anything. He saw no sign of a struggle. As he walked through the house, windows were closed with no evidence of a forced entry. The bedroom he found neat and orderly, the bathroom relatively clean, for a bachelor. Returning to the kitchen, he observed new untaped wallboard on the walls and what looked to be a newly installed dishwasher. He looked once again at the tools on the table and nearly succumbed to the temptation to handle them. Something gnawed at him. What am I supposed to see, he wondered.

About the same time Dailey returned, Jason heard sirens off in the distance.

"I called it in to our precinct and called the coroner. We don't need an ambulance. You touch anything?" Jason simply shook his head. "You see anything?"

"Beats the hell out of me, Lieutenant; I didn't see anything suspicious. The guy looked like Hercules. I can't believe he just dropped dead."

"Well, I've got Callon Henderson on the way. He's my pathologist of choice. We'll know something today. I'm calling in a favor on this one. I just want to know what killed him," he added remorsefully, then walked to the front door to meet the cruiser that had just pulled up out front. Thompson showed up a minute later, followed shortly by the coroner's wagon.

Callon Henderson, a tall, frail-looking man resembling the cartoon characterization of Ichabod Crane, walked through, carrying a black medical bag. Dailey immediately led him to the bathroom. Henderson bent down over Dolan, took a brief look, then he turned to Dailey, Thompson, and Jason, all crowded into the narrow space.

"Do you mind? How about a little breathing room? I promise I won't steal him."

About twenty minutes later, Henderson came out onto the front porch. "Bag him," he said to his assistant and a uniformed officer.

"What do you think?" Dailey asked.

"If I had to say right now, I'd guess a heart attack."

"Bullshit," Thompson said. "He was the most fit man in the department."

"Well, dammit, that's why I ain't saying right now. It's a guess, just a guess," he returned hotly. "Ask me in a couple of hours. Then maybe I won't be guessing." He stomped off the porch, then turned back to Thompson, "Gimme a ride back so I can get set up. The kid can bring Dolan back in the wagon."

"Take me back with you," Dailey said. He turned to Jason, "I'll see if I can find a replacement to watch your friend, Mr. Monroe." Jason nodded. "I'll call when I learn anything about Dolan."

Jason turned and walked back into the house. He didn't have particular reason for doing so—maybe just frustration, or disappointment that someone else had died. He wrote it off to paranoia and only stayed a few minutes.

* * * * *

Jason returned to The Kennel and informed his comrades about Dolan. After several minutes of useless speculation, they spent the remainder of their time forming a strategy for the invasion of Diablo. Steve, Pat, and Miguel took their assignments, then revisited the plan several times discussing ways to minimize risk. When all appeared to be satisfied, they unpacked the equipment Keller had delivered earlier.

Later that afternoon, Jason returned to the partners' office where he retreated to the situation room alone. The partners were off on business, and the office staff had left for the day. He sipped scotch and perused the storyboard, laboring over the chronology until his eyes burned. He had all the information on Pathmoor. Fortner proved a dead-end of sorts. Sloan he knew to be involved somehow—and he had gone missing. Jason went through every scrap of information they had on Comstock, his service career, the trail he left through Idaho, the die cast shop. And now the behemoth had killed himself at the worst possible time. SPD, as far as he knew, found nothing at Patriot Chemicals. He had found nothing in Victoria, although he hadn't spent any time looking, and Monroe had given up everything he had.

The information took Jason all the way back to the Sunday night at The Box Car parking lot, with nothing jumping out at him as he had hoped. "Damn. Dammit!"

"Sounds like you're in a good mood," Tom Keller said as he entered.

"I'm just frustrated with this damn mess. By the way, thanks for the package from Whidbey."

"You're welcome. They told me when I called The Kennel that you'd be here. So, have you heard the news?" Keller asked with his brow furrowed.

"What news?"

"It's all over the TV and radio. Senator Bronson, his two daughters, and his housekeeper were found dead about an hour ago at their estate on Mercer Island. Cause unknown."

"What the hell? What the hell's going on, Tom, some kind of epidemic of people dying of cause unknown? You heard about Dolan, didn't you?"

"Yeah, when I called The Kennel."

Jason turned silent for a moment and looked out the window at Elliott Bay. "You want a drink? I found Joe's stash of some damned fine scotch."

"Sounds good. Neat—two fingers."

Jason walked to the bar and poured an inch of scotch in a tumbler, then caried it to Keller who asked, "You thinking the deaths are connected? The Bronsons' and Dolan's, I mean?"

"I don't see how they could be," Jason said quietly.

"Good. For a minute I thought you were going paranoid on me."

Jason folded back the white panels exposing a 32-inch TV and turned to channel 5. The special news team reported from the studio, but also broadcast updates from the field team at the gates of the Bronson estate every few minutes. Jason returned to his chair and watched. The two slipped into silence with the exception of the droning on of few facts and much speculation from the talking heads on the tube. The telephone rang, giving them a welcome break.

Jason pushed the mute button on the remote and answered. "Castellano, DiAngelis and Partner."

"Have you seen the news?" Dailey asked.

"We're watching it as we speak," Jason answered, putting the call on the speakerphone.

"Well, you can kiss good-bye any help in regard to finding a babysitter for Monroe. Every available cop in the state is being called in."

"I thought as much," Jason said. "I know you probably have your hands full, Lieutenant, but did you get any information back on Dolan?"

"I knew you'd ask me that. Henderson never got a chance to finish. They pulled him out to the senator's estate. Got real testy when I tried to pump him for information. You saw how he reacts to not having all his information together. Doesn't know what to think, said Dolan's heart just stopped for no apparent reason. Said his heart looked like a big charley horse."

Keller nearly flew out of his chair. "Lieutenant, this is Tom Keller. Can you get ahold of Dr. Henderson? It's really important. It sounds like the same symptoms Lori Phillips exhibited when I examined her. She was the woman—"

"I know who the hell she is," Dailey snapped. "I'll give you his pager number."

Keller paged the coroner four times before the phone rang. He grabbed the receiver, but before he had a chance to speak, an angry voice blared form the speaker.

"Henderson. Who in the hell is paging me?"

"Doctor, this is Dr. Thomas Keller, I'm the head of ER at St. Francis'. I had a case ten days ago, a female stabbing victim, whom I believe was murdered. She exhibited the same symptoms that Officer Dolan did. I need to talk to you about your findings."

"I don't have any findings yet. Who the hell you been talking to?" Henderson asked angrily.

"I just spoke to Lt. Dailey and—"

"Dailey's a damn blabbermouth. I'm not ready to come to any conclusions. Call me in a couple of days."

"We may not have a couple of days, Doctor. In a couple of days, we may be up to our eyeballs in bodies."

"I'm already up to my eyeballs in bodies." Henderson, stubborn and unyielding, sounded as if he were about to hang up.

"Dammit, I'm trying to help you save some lives, you ornery sonofabitch!" The veins in Keller's neck protruded like blue ropes as he screamed into the receiver. "All I want is two minutes of your fucking time. Just answer three questions." Keller expected the line to go dead, but it didn't and he blurted out the first question. "Did Officer Dolan have any needle marks?"

"Not that I could find."

"Toxicology?"

"Prelim showed negative."

"So it's possible that whatever did this was ingested orally."

"Well, if it wasn't injected, that doesn't leave many options, now does it? What are you suggesting, that someone invented a new heart disease? 'Cause it sure as hell wasn't natural."

"It's looking like something along those lines, Doctor."

"Well, if that's the case, you'd better get hot on the trail, Doctor. I've got four more Dolans out here staring me in the face. Now that's just between you and me. Capiche?"

"Doctor, just one more question. Were there any needle marks on the senator or his family?"

"Not that I've found to this point." The line went dead.

Jason stared at Keller in disbelief. He suspected something would soon rear its sinister head, but he had not expected this.

"Get Dailey on the phone," Keller said impatiently. "We're going over Dolan's house with a finetooth comb and a microscope."

* * * * *

Dailey arrived at Dolan's house only moments after Jason and Keller. "Mind telling me what we're looking for?" he asked as the three men stepped onto the porch.

"It's possible Officer Dolan was killed by the same substance that killed Lori Phillips and Senator Bronson and his family," Keller said as they entered the house. "When I talked with Dr. Henderson, he said he found no needle marks on Dolan or the senator and his family. That means whatever this concoction is, it had to be ingested. Dolan was a bodybuilder. He probably used protein and carbohydrate supplements, vitamins, sports drinks. It could be anything. And, Lieutenant, it's invisible. I couldn't identify anything in Lori Phillips' body that showed unnatural. And neither could Dr. Henderson."

"If that's the case, then how do you know this, whatever it is, exists?"

"Because, what it *does* is unnatural," Keller said with vehemence.

"If this is murder, shouldn't this place be swept for fingerprints?" Jason asked.

"Don't ask me why," Dailey quickly answered, "but I called in a team right after the coroner's crew left. Here, put these on." He pulled latex gloves from his jacket pocket, handed them to Jason and Keller. Jason shrugged and walked toward the kitchen. "Anything edible, huh?"

Keller walked the opposite direction to the bathroom. He went directly to the medicine cabinet looking for pills, mouthwash, anything at all that could be ingested. He had found a small box in one of the bedrooms and began gingerly loading contents of the cabinet for transport, being very careful not to disturb any latent fingerprints that may have been missed by the crime team.

Dailey, in the kitchen, involved himself in the same process. He first went through the refrigerator. Milk, a two-quart jug of Gatorade, cooking sauces, half a package of sliced chicken breast all went carefully into a box.

Jason moved more as a spectator, seeing the activity, but not fully aware. Instead he had plunged himself into finding a logical reason for Dolan to be embroiled in the situation. As far as he could remember, Dolan's only connection had been the pickup of the kid who had watched Jack's house and he had accompanied Thompson the night they met after the ordeal at the Issaquah house.

It could be outright murder, or God forbid, something Jason feared most, terrorist activity. But how? What was the vehicle? And how did Dolan fit? Jason looked at an overstuffed rocker and sat down, closed his eyes and visualized the storyboard once again.

In the background he heard Dailey and Keller talking in the kitchen.

"Look at all these new appliances," he heard Keller remark. "Looks like the dishwasher's the latest addition to the remodel endeavor."

Jason thought about what he had just heard. Appliances, remodel. His eyes opened wide as a fleeting memory passed through his mind. "I've got it!" he said as he jumped out of the chair. He ran into the kitchen past Keller and Dailey to the cabinet door, still ajar below the sink. "It's here," he said as he opened both doors fully and looked under the sink.

Both men looked at him blankly. "What?" Dailey asked.

Jason rose and walked back to the kitchen table and picked up a work light from the tools scattered on it. Then he returned and shined the light on the plumbing under the sink. "This is what we've been looking for." He focused the light on a water filter. "This is the filter I brought from Issaquah and passed along to Dolan and Thompson. There's no way of knowing when, but apparently, somewhere along the way, Dolan figured as long as he was remodeling, he might as well have a water filter. Lieutenant, get Dr. Henderson on the phone, if he's still at the senator's house. See if there's a water filter anywhere on the premises."

Jason remembered the exchange in The Box Car parking lot and the way Dolan had longingly looked into the box at the filter. He stood and faced the two men, but spoke to Keller.

"Tom, I'm remembering something Bud Rockwell said. He said, 'Comstock made water filters and sold them.' A filter that, as he put it, 'could filter a minnow fart out of a reservoir.' Think it could filter something into the water? And if his filters are as good as Bud Rockwell said, couldn't they filter out all of the material that you would normally detect, and just leave the bad stuff?"

Dailey gave pause, then moved rapidly to the front door.

Keller paled as the magnitude of Jason's question settled upon him. "Tell the people out there not to drink any water," Keller yelled after Dailey. Looking anxious, he turned his full attention back to Jason. "How many of these damn things did you find?"

"Two damned many," Jason said, soberly. "I counted 120 filters at the house in Issaquah. I took one, and this is it. When we were on Diablo Island, I found 110. Somewhere there are nine of these things, and I think one of the nine is out at the senator's house. Here's something else to think about. It's been three days since we were out there. If you're a praying man, you'd better be praying there are still 110 at that camp.

"I'll get this one out of here and send it along with Dailey." He nodded toward the space under the sink. "You take my car, go to The Kennel, and get the team together and meet me at Hard-Ship Marine. Steve knows the way. Dailey can drop me at the loft, then take this thing to the lab. I'll let Jack know what we've found, collect my gear and rendezvous with you at the boat." He handed Keller his car keys as Keller ran toward the door.

Jason nearly had the filter removed when Dailey returned. He poked his head under the counter where Jason lay on his back.

"Henderson had already left the scene but he said he'd send someone back to check. How you coming?"

"Just about have it. One more fitting and it'll be out."

"Don't spill any of that shit on you," Dailey cautioned.

"You don't have to say that twice . . . I got it." Jason slid out onto the floor, holding the filter carefully to the side. Once on his feet, he set the filter on the counter where they could take full advantage of the new kitchen lighting. It looked like an ordinary water filter with the exception of a clear plastic housing on the side of the cylindrical shape near the top. "It looks like there is some kind of mechanism in there, could be some sort of a metering device," he said. He held the filter up to the light for a better look and looked through the mechanism housing. "It almost looks like there are a couple of electrical contacts in there—Wait a minute! Son-of-a-bitch!" The blood drained from Jason's face. "Jack has one of these parts."

"What? What parts?" Dailey asked impatiently.

"Look here." Jason rotated the filter half a turn, then held it up to the light again so Dailey could see through it. "See those two gold-plated brackets with the nubs on them?"

"Yes."

"Those are detonating devices. Remember, Jack was at a die cast shop in Portland?" Jason asked rhetorically. "They make these things. It's a little aluminum die casting. They gold plate them for conductivity and then they plate a thin coat of rhodium over the top. The stuff is conductive and real hard. It's used for durability. These are actually detonating contacts for smart bombs. Look again, see how those two nubs are in contact with one another? I think I'm right. It's a metering device. Jack picked up one of these little contacts; I've seen him fiddling with it. Biddwell Die Casting sells these things to some defense contractor. Biddwell had a break-in a couple of weeks ago. Now I think we know why Comstock went to work for Biddwell. It's all making sense now. Remember the part in his service record about being in the chemical warfare group? It's all beginning to fit."

"I remember. I understand the chemical part and Comstock's part in this, but there's no electricity to this thing. How the hell does it work?"

"We'd have to take it apart to be sure, but a camera battery could provide enough power to work a simple mechanism, and something as simple and even more compact than a garage door opener could activate it."

"Holy Mother Mary, this could be a real nightmare!"

"It'll get a hell of a lot worse if I don't get to the rest of those filters."

* * * * *

At ten-fifteen, Jason opened his door to a dark loft. A wave of numbness washed over him. Jack should have been there by that time. Jack would not be working this late, he reasoned, and he became angry again for allowing him to return to Seattle. He continued the self-berating until he found the note Jack had left on the island counter, inviting him to meet him and a client of Cervicon at Cutters. A sigh of relief flowed from deep in his chest. He collected his gear, and planned a quick stop at Cutters on his way to Hard-Ship.

On Jason's way out the door the phone rang.

"We have three more fatalities," Dailey said. "Three men from the weekend custodial at the state capitol building in Olympia. Thank God it's the weekend," he continued. "At least the place can be shut down without too much fuss."

"Lieutenant, get to the partners," Jason advised. "That way you can keep up with our progress from there. We'll stay in touch."

"It's looking like you've been a bit busier these past two weeks than you've let on."

"Well, Lieutenant, that will give us something to discuss over scotch for years to come. Talk to you soon."

"I hope you renegades are as good as you think you are."

"So do I, Lieutenant."

"Good luck, son."

"Thanks. I'll take all we can get."

* * * * *

Jason, usually smiling and impeccably dressed whenever he dined at Cutters, burst through the door on a dead run. The night manager, Darrel, lingering with two customers near the hostess counter, looked shocked as Jason approached. They could see by Jason's expression, and all-black jumpsuit that something was terribly wrong.

"You have a Jack O'Connor here with a client. Could you show me to his table?"

"I could, if he had shown up."

CHAPTER THIRTY-NINE

There comes a time in a man's life when an event of great magnitude rends the soul, a time, if only for a moment, that brings one to a precipice facing the chasm of despair. Jason, less than an hour before, had received a blow that brought him face to face with failure: He had failed to adequately protect his friend. The deep sense of loss, the frustration and helplessness of not having time to at least investigate Jack's whereabouts, overwhelmed him. But innocent people were dying, and, after all, Jack had made the choice to return to Seattle. He would be another of the casualties.

Jason had no choice but to continue on with the mission without taking time to look for his friend. The senseless slaughter of innocent people had to be quelled. The rationale seemed sound, but it didn't make it any more palatable. The loss this night was twofold: He had resigned himself to losing Carol, a relationship he had truly desired to nurture into fullness. The transition had come to an abrupt end. He was a warrior. But he no longer reveled in it—and hadn't for a long time.

Alone with his thoughts, insulated from his comrades by darkness and violent wind, Jason mercilessly piloted his boat across rough water at nearly 100 miles per hour. He realized he must not look into the chasm. He had purpose in his life. It would not bless him or his soul, but it did have value. And for a brief time, it would have to be enough. His memory retreated to the video he had watched not quite two weeks ago. Now feeling a great sorrow and sense of loss, he thought he had an understanding of the man who committed suicide in that movie, or, more accurately, whom the man represented—individuals who had nothing in their lives to help them transcend the chasm. Suicide, the supreme act of selfish cowardice, he had always felt, was the result of utter despair. But now, he realized, there were two more possible origins for the act: fear, of which he knew little, and anger, of which he knew a great deal.

He continued to blink moist, burning eyes tightly as he backed off the throttles, slowing the boat.

"Ten minutes," he said into the microphone of the PCD. "Let's make this real quiet, just like last time." Jason forced himself to focus, because what lay ahead would most certainly be a different scenario than what they had encountered early Tuesday morning. With the advent of Comstock's murder-suicide, combined with the latest developments in Seattle and Olympia, the camp promised to be something other than a cake walk. He could not allow himself to be distracted by other events over which he had no control.

Someone had launched an all-out terrorist offensive; although no one had yet claimed responsibility, the filters proved Diablo Island as the point of origin. The ultimate goal would be taking control of the filters.

The camp had ground support for at least two, maybe three, helicopters and also the two boats and ferry at the opposite side of the island. Their first objective would be to incapacitate all transportation. The second would be to secure their office and obtain the locations of targets and the remaining seven filters that were no longer at the camp, and then collect the remaining 110 from the stores. To accomplish this safely, canisters of nonlethal gas would be discharged among personnel in the barracks eliminating the possibility of a large confrontational force.

Krieger and Miguel were responsible for the dock, motor pool/hangar, and landing pad. Once all transportation was disabled, they would take out the power supply. Keller and Steve had responsibility for the three barracks, then they would move to the stores and secure the filters. Jason and David would take the offices, as they both had experience with encrypted computer programs. With the electricity down, Jason believed any information stored on computers would be safe. He and David could move in quickly, neutralize any opposition, and secure all records. Their mission on the island had been designed to take no longer than two hours.

On this trip they would be heavily laden and penetration would be much slower. Each pair would have a sniper rifle with twenty-round magazines, and each man a fully automatic HK MP5SD with 200 rounds, sidearms with 50 rounds, and, of course, a survival knife. The strategy in all cases was one man would move in to do the work, while the other covered with an automatic sniping rifle at long range. In addition, each man would pack a canister of gas to the center of the island. When the teams split up, Keller and Steve were to shoulder the six canisters of gas on their own.

From the information given by Monroe, the camp patrols would be two-man teams.

"Kill any man on patrol," Jason ordered. "I want them sniped in pairs, I don't want surprises from the rear. We use deadly force against any personnel we encounter with the exception of the sleeping or someone of rank. Anyone who looks to be in authority we take alive for interrogation."

As before, the instant the anchor dropped, the men were over the side and paddling. While under way, they had pulled on their black hoods, adjusted their night vision, loaded and locked their weapons, and checked their personal communication systems. Their body armor was covered by black, insulated jump suits. The weather was cooler this trip and each man could see his breath. They would be easier to spot with either night vision or infrared even though the suits were designed to counteract the technology. They would need to be alert, a tough task, moving with speed and over eighty pounds of arms, ammunition, gas, communications, and night vision.

* * * * *

Miguel's voice came quietly over the earphones. "Movement at ten o'clock." The six men went silently on their faces as if their legs had been cut from beneath them. "Hundred yards, in the thicket," his voice still calm. In the early morning quiet, the men heard only their labored breathing. Three sniping rifles came instantly ready with safeties off, and six pairs of eyes scanned in the direction of the bramble thicket. Keller, to the far right, and Krieger to the far left, spotting nothing, began scanning 180 degrees to their respective sides, a precaution against a surprise from the sides or rear.

No breeze, no sound even from the crickets. Something had disturbed them, a confirmation that someone or something had been moving ahead of them.

"We wait three minutes," Jason whispered. "If nothing moves, Steve and Miguel, move in fifty yards apart. And stay low." Keller, Krieger, and David manned the sniping rifles. The others would move forward under the watchful eyes of their partners.

They checked their watches, then waited. Waiting for Father Time in an anticipatory mode is much like watching a glacier flowing down a frozen mountainside. Three minutes seemed like an eternity . . . and then, Steve and Miguel inch-wormed off in the direction Miguel had indicated.

They had lost five minutes since Miguel's signal, time they could ill afford. From Jason's perspective, the reign of terror had begun, which meant more filters would be needed in strategic locations. Jason and his team had only one element in their favor. Their adversary did not know the filters had been discovered. For the team, moving swiftly was critical. But at point of execution, moving swiftly and moving undetected always opposed one another.

"I got it." Steve and Miguel had moved only a few yards when David spotted movement again. "Range ninety yards, eleven o'clock moving west from the thicket—fucking bobcats, two of 'em," he said.

"Way ta go, Don Juan," David said referring to Miguel.

"Cut the chatter," Jason said.

"What a waste of adrenaline," David said, continuing his banter.

"Repeat. Cut the chatter!" Jason's second directive went unchallenged. He located the movement in the direction David had indicated. There they were, two bobcats lazily serpentining with their noses to the ground, seeking the scent of prey. Their unguarded movements indicated no immediate threat in the area, human included.

"Move out," Jason said.

Once on the move, the rhythm of their stride soon returned, as did their pain from the loads they carried. Although the diversion had given them a brief respite, the stress of the mission would continue to draw their energy.

Again, the posted perimeter of the camp came into view. Everyone came to a halt, allowing time to scan for patrols. After a brief pause, it appeared safe to proceed.

They moved to the spot they had used on the previous trip and slipped quietly under the fence one at a time. All members guarded one another vigilantly—while one passed under the wire, the others scanned 360 degrees. Once all were safely on the other side, they broke into their designated teams and headed toward their prearranged objectives.

Jason and David had traveled about fifty yards when David tugged Jason's arm and signaled him to turn off the PCD.

"What's up?" Jason whispered.

"I just want to make sure you have your head together," David said. "You look like a man with too many things on his mind, other than what we're about right now."

Jason, even knowing David had been right would, not allow the challenge. "I'm together. Now let's get moving." He turned away toward the compound.

David took his arm again and spun him around. "Look, boss. We're just a half step this side of a fucking suicide mission, and I want the guy who's covering my ass to have his shit together. You broke the first rule. Don't get involved. You did it twice. You did it with Jack and you did it with that red-headed amazon back at the beach. Damnit, Jay, get it together."

"Now you listen and listen good, I've got one thing on my mind, and that's getting those fucking filters and the location of the seven others. Standing here listening to you piss and moan ain't getting it done. If you ever do this again, I'll hand you your fucking head."

"That's what's got me worried, boss. If you were on top of your game, it'd been done."

Jason turned away saying, "Get your voice on and let's do this thing." As he moved in the direction of the compound, he fought to control his anger. He couldn't fault David. He was angry, not so much with himself, but at the situation over which he had little control, other than to do the right thing as best he could. And his best would not happen while lamenting the loss of Jack and Carol. David had been right. He had lost that bulletproof barrier that had made him impervious to most everything.

The three teams had been out of contact with one another for some time when Jason and Dave heard Keller's voice in their earpieces.

"Patrol headed your way, boss. Two, packing, and they can see in the dark."

As if they had rehearsed it a thousand times, Jason and David stopped instantly, then ever so slowly began their crouch. No sudden moves to draw attention. They were in an area that afforded little cover: sparse cedars, a few stumps, and short, grazed grass. Both Jason and David were down, motionless on one knee, eyes straining into the eerie green depth of night vision. The crickets off in the distance chirped out their syncopation, then slowly they ceased. Something had disturbed them.

Humans, those who do not hunt, have the misguided notion that only humans will disturb wild life. Not true. Deer and elk when stealing about on the forest floor will set squirrels and a variety of birds to chattering off defense warnings. In the night, happy crickets go silent. On this island at night, there could be more natural predators about other than the bobcats: cougars, and coyotes, all stalking, looking for their unsuspecting prey. Jason and his men knew all the warning signs of nature. They knew them without thinking about them; it had become instinctive. Any one of them could, under favorable conditions, smell a deer or an elk from one hundred yards, or the body odor of a frightened man from twenty-five yards. Tonight the forest was alive with predators, the most deadly of predators—man.

Jason and David continued searching the darkness, but saw nothing. Periodically, David brought up his Galil and scanned the real estate that lay ahead through the telescopic sights. Nothing. The most difficult part of any operation was the wait. Patience and sniping are synonymous, waiting for your adversary to appear in your sights, or a slow calculated stalk.

Jason considered sniping his most loathsome task in warfare, even though a necessary part of war, and effective. It is a demoralizing stratagem. The effect of a bullet coming from nowhere wreaks terror into an unsuspecting enemy, and is nearly impossible to defend against. It seemed to him such a cowardly way to fight. But in reality, he knew better. Rule number one: In war there is no such thing as an unfair advantage. War is about killing and there are no provisions for second place. And in this war, if they could not snipe their way to their objective, then came rule number two: Attack with violent and ruthless surprise, designed to terrorize the enemy and create the false notion that they are up against a much larger force. That is accomplished by kill, quickly move, kill, quickly move, kill. In this business, one had to believe, and rightly so, that sniping was saving lives.

With time now running short, Jason and David would soon have to go on a stalk, a slow and dangerous option. They could become the hunted, if they weren't already. Jason knew if Keller and his team had any kind of a tandem shot, they would have taken it. He also assumed they had continued on to their objective. Getting the personnel in the barracks into a good sound sleep was a high priority. Jason and David were on their own now, against an unseen enemy.

"This sucks," David muttered quietly. "I feel like a fucking duck in a gallery pond."

Jason's anger burned. He had given an emphatic directive prior to the mission: Keep the airtime to an minimum. He said, "If you don't shut up, I'm going to shoot you myself."

"Now I really feel secure, boss."

Jason couldn't believe David defied him yet again, and nearly responded, but he had more important business.

"We've got company," he said. "About 150 yards back in the perimeter of the trees. There're two, only one visible now."

"I got him," David whispered quietly.

"Remember, we take 'em in pairs," Jason cautioned. "There's another one, left, about ten yards, still in the trees."

"Well, let's hope he pokes his face out, so he ain't late. What the—?" David had no sooner started his bantering when the man in his cross-hairs lurched to the right and dropped from his sight picture. At the same instant, the man in the trees for whom Jason had been searching also fell forward from behind his cover and lay on his face motionless.

Keller's voice could be heard in their earphones. "Thought we'd lend a hand, boss. Looked like you were a bit bogged down."

"Thanks. You'd best get on with playing sandman. We'll check out the sleepers up ahead, then rendezvous at the canister drop."

Resistance had been lighter than Jason had expected, but intuition told him it would not remain that way. Jason and David worked their way to where the bodies lay. Upon examination they were relieved to find the opposition only equipped with walkie-talkies and early model night vision. Walkie-talkies indicated no monitored contact with the office. A good sign. The first man had been shot nearly from behind, the bullet entering slightly from the right, highcenter back, at the base of the neck, and exiting through the left collarbone. With his backbone obliterated, the man died instantly. The other had been taken more from the side, high in the neck at the base of the skull; he also hit the ground dead on arrival. Keller had shot high out of the chest area as if he were concerned about body armor. They had none, also a good sign.

Krieger and Miguel made their canister drop and encountered no enemy personnel until they reached the landing pad and hangar/motor pool building. They had, with stealth, gone previously to the dock and ferry landing and rigged the two boats and ferry motors with explosives. The intent was to save that equipment for the evacuation of the island after the mission had been accomplished. However, if anyone from the camp tried leaving by water, they would not.

Little had changed with the hangar/motor pool facility. Five vehicles were parked outside: the two pickups, the three two-and-a-half-ton transports and also, the large backhoe that Krieger and Miguel had spotted on their return to the boat Tuesday morning.

A cursory recon of the perimeter of the one large building and yard turned up negative in the way of patrolling personnel. However, light accompanied by muffled voices came from behind a partially open sliding door. The twosome tipped their night vision up from their field of view, allowed a moment for their eyes to adjust, then stole past the opening. There were three men visible: one performing what looked to be routine maintenance on a flatbed truck and two by a coffee pot having a cigarette break. The two by the coffeepot had sidearms that hung from military-type holsters at their waists. Krieger and Miguel assumed they were a patrol that stopped by for coffee. Bad timing for them. The man with his head under the hood appeared to be unarmed.

Krieger quietly set his Galil against the partially open door. Then he and Miguel gripped their MP5's in both hands and quickly moved through the opening. Miguel felt a twinge of guilt as he went in. These were just kids, he thought. How unfair. But the apprehension vanished instantly as one young man reached for his sidearm and the other reached for one of the assault rifles that leaned against the shelf on which the coffeepot rested. Short bursts from the 9mms cut the young men down before their hands fully gripped their weapons. The mechanic dove toward his toolbox. Krieger spun to the left and opened up with another short burst before the mechanic could reach what he was after. He tumbled against his roll-around toolbox knocking it over with a loud crash as the tools spewed forth from the drawers in all directions. He rolled off the right corner of his toolbox and lay still on the floor among the tools in which he probably had taken much pride. All three lay dead. Krieger and Miguel quickly hid the bodies in an office between the garage and hangar portions of the building.

The two men swiftly prepared to disable the equipment. Toward the dark end of the hangar, two helicopters sat at rest: the Huey, a twin to the one impounded at Boeing Field, and the other, a Bell Cobra Attack helicopter, equipped with a three-barrel 20mm Gatling gun and forward-looking infrared for laser target tracking.

"These people are more dangerous than we thought," Miguel said grimly.

They directed their attention first to the aircraft, then to the ground transportation. The engine cowlings were removed and they set about their work efficiently and quietly. Once the aircraft were disabled, they moved on to the trucks and even the backhoe. Thirty minutes after their arrival, they were ready to move on to the generator house.

After turning off the lights and replacing their night vision they went out through the sliding door. Krieger bent down to retrieve his sniper rifle when he took a hit to the back that propelled him instantly to the ground. The zzzz-whack of the bullet was followed closely by the report of the assault rifle from which it came. Another round ripped through Miguel's jumpsuit right at the waist, tearing the fabric and just grazing his body armor. All in the same movement, he turned and went down facing the direction of fire just in time to see the muzzle flash, the bullet singing only inches from his head. The report followed at the same time he returned fire.

Krieger, although having the wind knocked from him by the impact of the bullet to his body armor, managed to roll to the right and return fire at the same time as Miguel. They were under fire from three men less than 75 yards away and rapidly advancing. Bullets impacted wildly all around them. Miguel drew first blood. The lead man piled into the dirt nearly tripping the man running too closely behind him. These young adversaries, now unnerved by return fire and seeing a comrade go down, began firing indiscriminately without taking time to aim. They had never faced targets that shot back. In the midst of a hail of wild bullets, having survived many such encounters, Krieger and Miguel quickly dispatched the remaining two, unshaken by the exchange.

Jason did not need Miguel's report—"This mission just turned to shit, boss"— to know that it was so. He and the rest of the team had heard the automatic weapons fire and known it was camp personnel, because all of the team weapons were suppressed with silencers.

"Any casualties?" Jason asked, concerned only with his two team members.

"Negative," Miguel responded. "At least not the good guys. We are up and on our way." They left on a dead run to the power plant, no longer needing to continue the slow quiet strategy. Every available man would be on the prowl and the power plant would be a priority to protect.

The firefight had occurred a bit too soon, on all three counts. The alarm had sounded. The camp was still under power. It would be several minutes before Krieger and Miguel would be able to disable the power plant. Jason began to hear fire coming from one of the barracks, something had gone wrong there as well.

Steve had placed his canisters first and had no problem with his barrack. Keller's had also placed canisters in the second barrack without incident. But there had been a problem with the regulator on one of canisters in the third and final barrack. Only 75 percent of the gas had been distributed into one end and there had not been sufficient time for the gas to take its full effect. Thirty half-coherent troops were trying to get through the door at the sound of the alarm.

Keller and Steve were laying a hail of fire into the exit in an attempt to discourage the men from exiting. They hoped to contain them until they were overcome. If any were to leave through the entrance in their semi-coherent condition, they would be one step short of death.

Fortunately, minimal return fire from the barrack allowed Steve to lob a backup canister rigged with a charge through a window close to the exit. Upon detonation, it released its full contents. Within three minutes the return fire ceased. Only four men had made it through the doorway, and only a few steps beyond. They took no pride in that small victory, other than the fact that thirty men's lives in the gas-filled barrack had been spared.

Jason knew the patrols would rally to the two main focal points: the power plant and the offices. He and David had no choice now but to hit the offices head-on and quickly if they were to have any chance of obtaining information on the locations of the remaining filters. While en route, he directed previously discussed contingencies: "Steve, Krieger, and Miguel need cover." Someone needed to watch their backs while placing charges at the power plant.

"I'm on my way."

"It's time to be bigger than life, boys. Keller, make a circuit. And keep your head down. You're our ticket out of here."

Keller's new priority was to make a circuit and create as much noise and as many diversions as possible with flashbang distraction grenades and claymores. The claymores were to be placed in traffic lanes where the patrols might travel from point to point. They would shred anyone unfortunate enough to trip them. The purpose of the flashbang grenades was twofold: create the illusion of a large force and at the same time divert patrols into the paths of the claymores. The desired effect would be demoralizing confusion.

"Got your backside, boss." Keller began his circuit of the camp.

Krieger and Miguel came under heavy fire and were pinned down a hundred yards from the power plant, and roughly twenty-five yards apart in an area that afforded little or no cover. The camp layout had been well planned.

Coming upon the situation, Steve after a brief evaluation, skirted around to the left. Krieger and Miguel were drawing fire from two positions. Steve worked into a location where he could get a clear shot at both positions, move, and strike again. He still had eighteen rounds in the sniper rifle he had taken from Keller. With the enemy preoccupied with Krieger and Miguel and he with his suppressed rifle, he would be nearly impossible to spot.

Fortunately, Krieger and Miguel were in a very shallow swale. They could not take a direct hit, but neither could they raise their heads more than a couple of inches making it impossible to return fire. But the camp personnel could not advance on them either. However, it would not take them long to figure out that one man could keep both of them pinned down while others could skirt around and take them out. Had camp personnel been more experienced, such a tactic would have been automatic.

Steve knew he did not have a lot of time. "Hang on, boys, The Shadow is here," he said as he found the second of two positions that he liked. He would fire from the second position first, then fall back to the first. That way he would be assured of knowing where to go without having to think. He settled in and took his sight picture.

The muzzle flashes of his enemy blared brightly in his night vision as he found his first target. His fingertip touched the cool trigger and lightly squeezed, delicately increasing the pressure until he felt the recoil. He quickly looked through the scope before moving to the second target some ninety yards farther away. He saw a man wiping his partner's blood off of the side of his face. The split second of horror and indecision allowed Steve to take him out also.

He quickly found a target in the second group. Sixteen rounds left, he said to himself, as he squeezed off another round. Fifteen rounds left.

One of the men in the second group must have had some experience and heard the direction from where the bullet had come. He turned toward Steve, lay over the body of the man next to him, and began firing in his direction. The bullets landed surprisingly close. Steve backed up and moved to the right toward the first position he had found. The enemy now fired in two directions. The second two fired across the face of the single man left from the first group.

"They're distracted," Steve said to himself. "Roll to different positions. Stay low and get ready."

Once Steve settled in again, he turned his attention to the remaining member of the first group. The man alternated his fire back and forth, from where Krieger and Miguel were, to where Steve had been. Exhale slowly, squeeze. Fourteen rounds left. The first group had been eliminated.

As Steve turned his attention back to the second group, he heard from Krieger. "We're set."

The two men in the second group had divided their fire. One fired at Steve's first position, the other fired towards Krieger and Miguel's position. Steve had him in his sight. Breathe slowly, squeeze, recoil.

"Go," Steve said quietly into his mouthpiece. Krieger and Miguel came up out of the shallow swale. While the remaining man tried to locate Steve, Krieger and Miguel both found the man in their sights, squeezed off, and it was over.

Steve stayed in his position while his comrades quickly advanced to the powerhouse. The charges were placed in the battery storage, the diesel generator, and in the relay system. He could hear the low resonance of the diesel generator, which meant the camp was also recharging its battery storage. Krieger and Miguel were inside for less than a minute when they suddenly emerged on a dead run under his watchful eyes.

Thirty seconds later, one half of the powerhouse ripped apart from the explosion, and the drone of the powerful diesel engine ceased. The camp had no power nor the means to recover it.

Jason and David encountered fire from opposite ends of the office building, David on the south end and Jason on the north. They had made little progress in their attempt to gain access when the power went down. The firefight at the powerhouse had been audible throughout the camp, and according to the chatter, Jason's team had not suffered casualties.

At least that's accomplished, Jason thought. Combined with the powerhouse skirmish, the ruckus that Keller was making, and the fire that he and David came under, it sounded like a formidable invasion. The only problem: The longer it took to secure the office, the more time they had to destroy valuable information.

"Let's blow it," Jason said. "David and I need some cover. Krieger, Miguel, we need some silly putty ASAP. North, south. I want the ends off the office building."

"Steve, we'll need some cover," Jason directed.

"We're on our way."

En route to the office building, Krieger, Miguel, and Steve came under fire as they passed in close proximity to the stockade.

"I'm hit!" Miguel said, as he took a 7mm round to his right shoulder. It slammed into him like a 2,800-foot-per-second sledgehammer and spun him around with such force his weapon went flying and he found himself lying on his back. Although his whole body was racked with a numbing pain, he managed to roll to his stomach, gain control again of his 9mm HK MP5 with his left hand, then lie perfectly still. Movement would draw fire. "Not a good night in the woods, boys," he said weakly. "Shit."

Krieger laid down a blanket of fire while Steve tried to determine number and positions of the enemy. "How bad?" he asked Miguel.

"Bad. Right shoulder and it's a hell of a leak." He needed to control the bleeding and to do that he would have to move. If he continued to lie still, he would bleed to death in a matter of minutes. "Keep those fuckers' heads down, boys. I have to get this stopped or tomorrow ain't gonna be happenin'."

Steve caught sight of a muzzle flash adjusted for a right-handed shooter and squeezed off.

"These guys are good," Krieger said. "They're moving around on us; they're dark and they can see. How many you make?"

Steve was unable to confirm a hit on his last shot, but he very seldom missed. He had not seen the target other than a muzzle flash. "Three, maybe four, can't tell for sure. Maybe one less by keying off a flash."

Miguel removed the strap from his HK. He rolled onto his left side with the strap under his left arm then wrapped the strap around his right shoulder, using an emptied clip pouch for a compress, and cinched it tight. Fire from several directions continued. He heard two rapidly fired bullets fly over his head in the direction where he thought Krieger was hunkered down.

"Suppressed bogey, two-thirty, right over the top of me," Miguel said. "Fucker thinks I'm dead." The words had scarcely left his lips when a bullet impacted only inches from his head. Dirt from the bullet's impact ripped through his hood and ricocheted off his night vision.

"Somebody tee off on that motherfucker. He don't think I'm dead anymore." Ignoring the shoulder pain and now the pain and blood from his face, Miguel began rolling to his right with hope of finding cover.

"I got him," Krieger said. A millisecond later, Miguel heard the tell-tail zzzz of Krieger's return fire off to his left. "A hole in one," he said.

Numb and dizzy, Miguel laid his face on the cool ground and listened to his heartbeat roaring in his ears. His face throbbed with pain and his black hood became sticky with blood. The three-minute firefight going on around him registered as dreamy background noise in the staticky roar of his heartbeat. Krieger and Steve were taking fire from at least three directions. Like their adversaries, they would fire, change positions, and fire again—a chess match in which everyone was a pawn and everyone wore black.

Miguel opened his eyes and tried to focus. The bullets seemed to have stopped, or was he dreaming? Not sure if his eyes were actually open, he thought he saw something: a low black form moving slowly to the left of him about twenty-five yards away.

"Where are you guys?" he asked weakly into his PCD. If he were able to shoot at all, he sure as hell did not want to have a friendly-fire fatality.

"Six o'clock, seventy-five yards from you," Steve said.

"Eight o'clock from you, fifty west of Steve," Krieger responded a second later.

"What's up?" Steve asked.

"Bogey at nine o'clock from me. He's in a little bit of a hollow. Can you make him?"

"Negative." replied both men.

Under excruciating pain, Miguel rolled to his right side. Since his right arm was useless, he tried desperately to gain control of his MP5 with his left hand. He raised slowly and fired a short three-round burst, then another and another. Three rounds were all that he dared risk, lest his weapon climb out of control.

The man had been hit, but not severely. Surprised and wounded, he turned to return fire toward Miguel. Miguel, a sitting duck, continued to fire short bursts. His enemy returned fire only briefly before he jerked violently toward his left, then lay still, face down in the dirt. He had risen just a little too far, which afforded both Krieger and Steve unobstructed head shots.

The skirmish ended. It had lasted four valuable minutes. Both Steve and Krieger rushed to Miguel to administer first aid and make him as comfortable as possible. Then they left on a dead run toward the office to help Jason and David in their bid to gain access to the office. Keller would be sent to aid Miguel.

Jason and David laid down heavy fire covering Steve and Krieger as they placed heavy charges of C5 plastique at opposite ends of the office building. The two men worked with exacting precision as bullets from Jason and David impacted merely inches over their heads. Once the charges were placed, they made a hasty retreat to good cover. The charges were all set to detonate at precisely the same time which would create maximum confusion but controlled damage. They did not want the inner offices or the computers to be damaged.

Moments later, what sounded like one large explosion removed approximately eight feet of each end of the office building and all of the windows. The dust had not begun to settle before Jason and David were up and on their way into the building. But this time they did not go in through the ends. In unison, they bounded the four wooden steps to the front entrance that Keller had been guarding.

Small arms fire burst from the interior. David took a hit in his left forearm. The resolve of the few men who remained alive had not diminished after the explosion. Men hid down both hallways tucked behind doorjambs. These were not inexperienced recruits. These that remained, although concussed and disoriented by the explosion, were fierce, seasoned warriors, determined to fight to the death. Ten years ago David would have reveled in this kind of action, but no longer. He wanted it to be over.

David pulled back and ministered to his arm. "It's superficial," he said after quick examination. What now?" he asked.

The answer became obvious when Jason pulled two grenades from his jumpsuit. David laid fire into the hallway on Jason's side. Jason lobbed one grenade, then another, just beyond the open doorways. Seconds later the openings and hallway were filled with shrapnel. They repeated the procedure down the north hallway on David's side, but Jason avoided the office where the computers were.

The second the shrapnel cleared, Jason was up and running down his hall and dove into the first opening. He saw a leg disappear behind a desk as he hit the floor and rolled. Instantly he fired a volley close to the floor and heard a gasp of pain. He fired again and heard the man's weapon fall to the floor. He got up, checked the room and behind the desk. The man lay dead on the floor, blood leaking from a combination of shrapnel and bullet wounds.

"Room's clear, I'm coming out," Jason yelled.

Steve apeared in the entrance area with David. Steve covered the north hall and David covered Jason's back as he returned to the south hall to secure the next room. The rooms beyond the second doorway had been destroyed by the blast. They were close to success now. Jason could nearly taste it, but it was no time to let stragglers escape. Jason ordered Keller and Krieger around the back to keep anyone from exiting through any of the rear windows.

Another grenade preceded Jason before he entered the second room. But this time he pulled the pin and counted to two before pitching it into the room. Two sets of feet could be heard scrambling about the same time as the detonation. Whether they were trying to get to it to throw it back into the hall or run from it, Jason did not know. In any event, the plan had been to hold the grenade long enough so that the occupants of the room would have precious little time to deal with it. It worked. The offices of the south hall were now secure.

The offices off the north hall followed suit. Five minutes after Steve and Krieger's fireworks, the office building was secure. Now they could safely take custody of any hard copy records and the hard disks from the computers. Jason sent Krieger and Steve to the stores to check on the filters. Keller remained hidden outside to snipe stragglers.

* * * * *

Miguel, in and out of consciousness, dizzy and disoriented, was becoming dehydrated. He knew he needed water and soon. Only a few yards from the stockade, he thought to look there. Weakened from tremendous blood loss, he nearly fell on his face when he stood. Walking loomed as a nearly impossible task and staggering the few yards to the stockade seemed to take more effort than he could muster. The low sinister building appeared to be moving along ahead of him as his faltering steps took him slowly and painfully forward. Miguel thought he heard another firefight, but it was off somewhere else. He didn't care. He only wanted something to drink.

What had taken him only minutes seemed much longer to his disoriented mind. He had made it. He slung his MP5 over his left shoulder and tried to open the door. It was locked. He leaned his weight against the door to rest, turning the knob again and again in sheer frustration. It gave way under his weight and he spilled into the room sprawling onto the concrete floor. It had not been locked at all. He lay on the floor and laughed at himself in his delirium.

Once again with much effort he staggered to his feet and looked around for water. He flinched when he saw a still figure sitting in a chair off in the far corner. He fumbled pathetically to bring his weapon up to defend himself but to no avail. The man in the chair simply sat and watched Miguel fumble with his weapon, without care or emotion, not seeming to notice his presence. It took a moment for Miguel to notice the slightly forward cant of the head and the dark stain on the shirt that had flowed down the side of his neck originating from a single bullet hole to the head.

Miguel started once again when he looked left to the torture table and saw yet another man. A man barefoot and stripped to the waist. Electrical leads were affixed to his chest and the bottoms of his feet. He stared towards Miguel through eyes enlarged with fear. He did not speak or cry out. If he could see at all in the dark it must have been a sight, Miguel dressed in black, wearing his night vision, black hood, radio, and microphone, his shoulder shot to hell.

"Jack?" Miguel asked.

Adrenaline, the all-powerful drug, kicked in with full measure. Miguel no longer felt any of his own infirmities. He went to Jack and unstrapped him from the table.

"Jack, it's Miguel. How about we get you the hell out of here?" Layers of skin came off with the leads as Miguel removed them. Jack flinched but said nothing.

Although conscious, Jack was disoriented from the electrical shock. He dropped to his knees when he tried to stand. The pain from the burns on the bottoms of his feet must have been excruciating, but he made no sound of complaint. Miguel supported him with his good side enough to get him to a chair.

"Hang in there, buddy; we're gonna get you out of here. I've got Jack, boss, I've got Jack," he said into the mike. He could hear occasional chatter in his earpiece, but no response. He repeated the message, but again, no response. He tried to adjust his mike wire and found that it had been torn loose when he fell through the door.

Miguel could not get Jack's shoes on over the burns on his feet so he bound them with towels. With that accomplished, he helped him into a jacket he found lying in a corner.

"I'm thirsty," Jack said, weakly. "Water over by the cage." He motioned to the cell next to the table.

Miguel found a tin cup and filled it with cool water. As he carried it to Jack he remembered his want of water had led him here. He patiently let Jack drink his fill, then returned for his own.

Pumped full of new resolve, Miguel returned to Jack and hoisted him from the chair to support him with his left shoulder. "All right, let's get the hell out of here."

* * * * *

Ten men had died defending the office. Two objectives now remained: gather information and find the filters. Jason and David surveyed and located four computers and one server in three of the remaining offices. The quiet was almost unsettling as they worked with quick precision, opening each of the cases, and carefully removing the hard discs. Even if the discs had been erased, valuable information could still be retrieved.

Jason had completed his task of extracting the disk from a lone computer in one office while David worked in another room. When he finished, Jason moved to the largest of the three offices where there were another two computers and the server. He had begun removing the case from the server when David joined him a moment later and immediately started on the first of the two remaining computers. In five minutes, Jason had another hard disk in his hand. He turned to David and saw that he had nearly completed the removal of another disk.

"I'll let you get the last one," he said. "I'll start checking for hard copy."

"Be my guest," David responded. "Another five minutes and we can be off this fucking rock." He worked efficiently, ignoring the wound in his forearm, the hasty bandage now showing crimson. David, as did Jason and all his men, had a very high pain threshold. Impervious, masochistic, some said.

"You need to take time to look at that," Jason said.

"Doc can take care of it later."

"Suit yourself," Jason answered, as he opened the file cabinets. He found nothing of importance in the first so he went on to the second when Steve reported from the stores.

"We've got 110 filters, boss."

Jason breathed a sigh of relief. The feeling of success was exhilarating, or, at this point, half success. They still had to find the location of the missing seven.

"You've got fifteen minutes to move and hide those things. Fitzgerald's cleanup crew can pick them up later."

"Roger that. They'll be invisible in fifteen minutes."

Jason continued to rifle through the second file cabinet and found nothing of use: bills and receipts for staples, diesel fuel, equipment parts. All information could be confiscated and sifted through at a later time.

After several more minutes of finding nothing of immediate value in the paper files, Jason turned his attention to an old black walnut desk. He had to jimmy open the drawers. In the center drawer were the usual—pencils, pens, paper clips, rubber stamps, and an inkpad. In the middle of the drawer toward the rear he found a manila file folder. Jason picked up the folder to check the contents and found it empty. As he discarded the folder he caught sight of two objects that lay hidden under the folder. They sent a choking wave of nausea through him that nearly stopped his heart. The Belgian-made 9mm Browning high-power he recognized immediately, the gift he had given Jack eleven days before, and, next to the pistol lay the little die casting of his that had been worried to a bright polish.

"He's here," Jason said weakly.

"Who's here?" David asked as he put the last of the hard drives in a canvas pack.

"Jack's here. The Browning and this little die casting are his."

Jason's mind raced with questions. Where was he? Was he in the stockade? He felt sick at the thought that he might have been in the parts of the office building destroyed in the explosion, or God forbid, in one of the offices where he'd pitched a grenade.

He spoke into his mike, "I want the camp searched for Jack O'Connor. He's here. Find him."

Even though a frustrated Miguel heard the directive that Jason had given through his earpiece, he could not respond because of his broken mike. He and Jack were making painfully slow progress toward the office building. At their rate of progress they were another ten minutes away. Jack could barely hobble with his badly burned feet that now bled freely, and because he was terribly disoriented, Miguel did not dare leave him alone. Miguel himself, not in much better condition, was fading from continued blood loss and shock.

Jason left the office and went to search the building. He frantically ran from office to office to examine the bodies to make sure none of them was Jack. His anxiety lessened only slightly at not finding the body of his friend. He then commanded David to check the rubble at the north end of the building. "I'll check the south end."

David took the packsack containing the hard drives out of the building to keep them from getting damaged while rummaging through the rubble of the explosions; he then proceeded to the blast zone at the north end of the building.

Jason returned to the larger office where he had found the die casting. He completely searched the desk for anything to do with an interrogation or any other of Jack's belongings. He found Jack's wallet and stuffed it in a leg pocket of his jumpsuit on his way to check the rubble at the south end of the building.

As he passed the next office door, he noticed something peculiar. He poked his head into the office and looked to his left about ten feet away to the wall at the north end of the room. Then he returned to the hall and walked to the main office, poked his head through the doorway and looked to his right at the south wall. It also was about ten feet. The problem was that he had counted eleven paces as he walked the hallway. At roughly three feet per pace that would be approximately thirty-one feet. There was ten feet of floor space missing.

He ran to the file cabinets placed in a row against the wall and slid them away looking for an opening. Nothing. He ran to the adjacent office and looked at the floor to ceiling bookshelves that covered one third of the wall. He pulled on one side of the bookcase. It would not budge. He tried the other side with the same results. As a man possessed, he began throwing the contents from the shelves until he found what he had been looking for. Jason pulled the latch and the left side of the case released. After swinging the heavy structure fully open, he entered an eight-by-fifteen-foot room.

A man sat in total darkness at the end of the room and looked back at him from behind a wooden desk.

"Where's Jack O'Connor," Jason shouted.

"He's in a safe place," the man answered calmly. "And you are?"

"I'm the one holding the gun," Jason said impatiently, keeping his MP5 trained on the man. "Now, I'll only ask you one more time, where is O'Connor?"

"He's in our little stockade, keeping Abel Sloan company, although I don't think Abel much cares at this point."

"Doc, get to the stockade; check on Jack!" Jason said anxiously into his PCD. "If he's injured in any way, I'll personally rip you a new ass," he continued, barely able to contain his burning anger. "Now, who the hell are you and why were you trying to kill O'Connor?"

"My name is irrelevant in answer to the first part of your question, and we apparently made a mistake, to answer the second. O'Connor was working on the Suter security system and inadvertently video-taped a sensitive part of my operation."

"Comstock supplying drugs to Sloan," Jason interrupted.

"You seem to be well informed, Mr. . . .?" The man waited for Jason to supply his name, but he was ignored once again.

David, hearing Jason speaking with someone, entered the room and stood several feet to the left of Jason. He said nothing, until he recognized the man behind the desk.

"Mr. Hargrave, we meet again. You're a long away from the die cast shop aren't you?"

Jason purposely said nothing to avoid revealing his surprise. He had not met Hargrave when he visited Jack at Biddwell. David and Steve had seen Hargrave at Biddwell on several occasions while they were watching over Jack.

"I'm afraid you have me at a disadvantage, sir. Your voice is familiar. I can't see in the dark but obviously you can," Hargrave replied.

"And that's the way we're going to keep it," David returned.

Jason rapidly pieced the puzzle together in his mind. But a loose end still eluded him.

"If you faked the break-in at Biddwell just to get to O'Connor, why did you try a hit in Seattle?"

"Ah yes, an unfortunate breakdown in the chain of command. Our Mr. Comstock took matters into his own hands a bit prematurely. I would have taken care of O'Connor when he arrived in Portland. But Comstock, being a bit impulsive, fouled up my plan. O'Connor seemed to have gotten wind of the mistake because he was a bit elusive his first night in Portland. Then, of course, the two bodyguards showed up. Was that your doing as well, Mr. . .?" Once again, Jason did not respond to the request for his name.

After a moment, Hargrave continued, "As far as faking the break-in at Biddwell, it was an opportune time to disrupt the flow of detonators and other components critical to the production of Patriot Missiles being shipped to the Kuwait defense system. You folks stumbled onto an operation of major proportions."

"So it's not simply a case of drugs and filters that funded this operation."

"Hardly," Hargrave answered, with a stifled snigger. "As I said, you have no concept of the magnitude of what you're involved with."

"Oh, I think I do, Mr. Hargrave. Keeping things stirred up in the Arab countries is nothing new. But slowing the flow of arms into Kuwait will be nothing more than an irritation."

"Ah, yes, but an irritation nonetheless," he said, a note of humor in his voice.

His cavalier attitude angered Jason.

"We've wasted enough time," he said impatiently. "I want the locations of the filters."

"You have been busy. My compliments. They're around, strategic places—the Washington State Capital, Oregon State Capital, a couple of senators' homes. They're in enough places to make a profound statement. But you're a bit too late. By now they're already doing their dirty work or soon will be. You'll not stop them. Just a little sweet revenge for Iraq."

Awareness came upon Jason; Hargrave calmly and freely revealed sensitive information. Why? He would only do that knowing the information would go no further. Just as he realized this, he was distracted by Keller's voice in his earpiece.

"We've got Jack, Boss."

"Say again," Jason requested. But he never heard Keller repeat the message. The front of the desk exploded as a full load of 00 buckshot ripped through the desk's wood and impacted Jason fully in the chest. He was upended and flying backwards when the second round from the twelve-gauge shotgun struck. He crumpled to the floor, unable to breathe, the wind knocked from him by the impact of the first round.

One of the rules that the team followed was two men never stood close together in a confrontation situation. For that reason David had purposely positioned himself several feet away. At the first blast, David opened up with his MP5. A flurry of 9mm rounds struck Hargrave in the chest, arms, neck, and face sending him backwards out of his chair and against the wall. He slid down the wall and came to rest, sitting on the floor, staring blankly and lifelessly into the darkness.

Although Jason's body armor protected him from buckshot penetration, the tremendous impact had broken his ribs. This was not the first time that he had had to deal with having the wind knocked completely from him or the ensuing struggle of simply fighting to suck a wisp of air to keep from passing out. But something else was wrong, terribly wrong. His legs felt as though they were being attacked by thousands of needles from the inside, much like a limb that has gone to sleep and is just getting the circulation back. His whole body screamed with pain and at the same time felt numb as if it had received an electrical shock. But the realization that he could not move terrified him. The only parts of his body that he could move, as far as he could determine, were his eyes.

David immediately came to his side and it only took a moment to recognize that his comrade had been gravely wounded. The most obvious injury was the blood boiling from his femoral artery. Jason desperately tried to speak but he could not. He was paralyzed, helpless.

While David tended to his friend, he failed to notice the slow movements of Hargrave who, now shielded from view behind the remains of the desk, also had been wearing body armor. The round to the face had removed most of his jaw, and another bullet had struck his lower neck and collarbone; blood sprayed from his carotid artery.

In his last act of defiance, Hargrave quietly removed a wireless detonator from his jacket pocket. He lifted the safety lever and pushed the button that lay below. A flashing red LED warned that the device had been armed. He pressed the button a second time. Both Jason and David heard the quick chirp of the detonator and knew there was no escape. Jason felt no more pain and nothing other than a sensation of heavy weight pressing in on him. Then blackness. Then nothing.

CHAPTER FORTY

Jackie Kennedy sunglasses covered Carol's eyes, shielding them from bright sun that blazed through the early morning lavender haze. They also served to hide the redness and dark circles caused by three days of crying. As she stood at the graveside, Jack, still on crutches, supported her with Debbie on the opposite side. The words of Reverend Scott had been little more than insignificant background babble. As the small funeral party turned and walked toward the mortuary limousine, she did have a slight recollection of his saying something about the sacrifices of brave men, and "No greater love . . . ."

Her resentment at being here had been in the forefront of her thoughts. If it were not for the prodding of Dr. Keller, Debbie, and Jack, she would be where she wanted to be, which was home. Keller and Jack repeatedly told her that Jason would have wanted her to be here. But what if he does come out of his coma while I'm not there? she worried. She did not want to be in Arizona; she wanted to be at Jason's bedside, willing him to live.

Keller, who had been the first to get to Jason and David, had carried Jason from the clutches of the hellfire that had followed the explosion. He explained that when David knelt beside Jason to check his condition, he had inadvertently but effectively shielded him from the blast. David had been killed instantly.

Keller had stayed with Jason for the twenty hours that followed, through all of the examinations and the fourteen-hour surgery. Immediately following, he filled Carol in on all of the details of what had happened—Jason's status and the prognosis of a team of four specialists. He explained that Jason was in critical condition and severely concussed. The injury to his lower back proved even more serious. From what had been determined, the first round of double-ought buckshot had hit Jason fully in the chest. Although the body armor had protected him from the force of impact, it had broken several ribs.

The second round had hit him in the groin area. For the most part, the groin pad had also protected him. His reproductive organs were badly bruised, but intact. However, the more serious problem was several pieces of buckshot had hit his right thigh and one had ricocheted off of his hipbone and lodged in his lower spine. The buckshot had been removed during the surgery, but he would not speculate as to whether Jason would walk again, if he, in fact, regained consciousness.

Carol had not left Jason's bedside until practically forced to attend David's funeral. Only a total of eight people attended the graveside service: Reverend Scott, Carol, Jack and Debbie, Keller, Steve, Pat Krieger and the one remaining team member whose name Carol did not care to know, although he looked as if he too had been seriously wounded. The three members of Jason's anti-terrorist team and Keller were the pallbearers and had dressed in their all-black night gear.

For Carol, seeing these men stoic and devoid of emotion unsettled her, and she sought no contact with them. Not that she did not want to honor the man David DuPonte, who had saved Jason's life; but her only interest was to return to Seattle as quickly as possible to be with Jason.

Steve Honeycut had quietly followed her to the limousine. "Carol."

She removed her sunglasses and turned to face him.

"I'll be here for a couple of days taking care of David's affairs. Then I'll return to Seattle. In the meantime, if there is anything I can do for you or if there's any change in Jay's condition, please call me." He handed her a card with a phone number.

She searched his eyes looking for some emotion, and, not finding any, she wondered what kind of men these were who could not allow themselves to grieve at the loss of a colleague. Had these men's country turned their souls and spirits to granite? Was Jason also lost to the ice of his conditioning, never to return? She had taken some time in her thoughts before her delayed response.

Steve had already started to turn away when she said, "Thank you. I'll be sure to call you if there is any change." He nodded and walked away.

Jack struggled with his crutches, but still helped Debbie and Carol into the back seat and closed the door. Then he hobbled to Steve and his friends and spoke briefly to them before making his way back to his side of the car. The limousine pulled away from the little group, leaving the cemetery behind and speeding its passengers to the airport.

* * * * *

Two and a half weeks had passed since David's funeral, and Carol's vigil continued. Jason had made arrangements with the partners for Carol to be provided for in the event anything should happen to him. This he had done prior to his first trip to Diablo Island. She had quit her job at The Box Car, and stayed with Jason twenty-three hours a day, sleeping at his bedside, holding his hand, talking to him, shaving and bathing him, leaving his side briefly each day to shower at the loft before returning. Only because of Keller's influence did the hospital grant her the courtesy.

Jason's body functioned on his own now, with the exception of receiving nourishment intravenously. But his being unconscious for this long worried the doctors. Tests showed his brain was functioning, he was breathing on his own, and his muscles responded to stimulation. He simply would not wake up. The doctors were baffled.

Carol was terrified. Her worst fear had been that Jason would leave one day on some dark, secretive quest never to return, destination unknown, just as it had been with Melanie. Now her heart broke a little more each day as she watched Jason's body atrophy. She never knew from one day to the next what to expect. Her first emotion had been one of anger because of the hurt he had caused her, then came resentment toward Jack for being the cause of the whole episode. Both, she came to realize with Laura's help, were the normal combination of grieving and feeling sorry for oneself. But that had passed and now she simply loved him as best she could.

Carol returned from the loft at 10:30 p.m. not even knowing the day of the week, and once again took Jason's hand as she had so many nights before. She sat beside his bed and laid her head on his chest to ponder the things known, and wonder about the things unknown that had shaped the man she loved. As she closed her eyes, John Lennon's song *Imagine* wafted through her being as first exhaustion, then sleep, took her.

* * * * *

The most prevalent were sounds that resembled pounding surf far off in the distance. Through the misty images and dreamy sound, a man and woman danced on the beach. The image slowly changed to the hallway rescue of Carol, then changed again and again back in time, farther back each time until just a green jungle remained. Only the soft muffled sounds of surf and surreal music were constant. There was a spirit's view of hovering through the lush green landscape until a village appeared in a clearing.

Three helicopters sat at the farthest end of the clearing away from the huts. The engines were spooling up and rotors had just begun to rotate. A group of SEALs were milling around and some were boarding in preparation for another insertion. Villagers moved about in normal fashion—a common occurrence in small villages. Children scampered here and there, darting in and out around the aircraft, giving flowers and fruit to the warriors as they always did. One of the SEALs had just taken a coolie hat filled with flowers and fruit and passed it to one of the men on board one of the choppers, a welcome treat for their journey.

Seconds later, the helicopter exploded in a fireball, then, in a second, another was engulfed as well. Dismembered bodies of children and soldiers flew through the air landing thirty to fifty feet from the explosion. Simultaneously, torrents of automatic weapon fire erupted from some of the huts. The remaining helicopter lifted off to get above the melee and to give cover to the few SEAL survivors who now returned fire. It was a smoky, bloody mess with innocent villagers hopelessly caught in the crossfire.

A lone warrior in the center of the clearing raked the clearing and village huts, cutting down anything or anybody that moved with a dragon's breath of automatic weapons fire. A little girl ran towards him with flowers in a clay pot and was nearly cut in two by the hellfire that spewed from him. The helicopter also rained death on every square inch of the village around him. Within a few short minutes, it ended. The only sounds were the wailing of a few surviving villagers and the whomp of the rotors as the chopper sought a safe place to land. The pungent smell of chordite and the blood that saturated dust and dirt completed the stench of death.

The warrior dropped his weapon and slowly walked to the little child. He knelt before her, gathered her into his arms and carried her off, disappearing into the jungle. As he carried her toward the bright light at the top of a hill, he remembered that, not too long before, he had watched this little girl holding a huge blossom that she had picked from a tree. Unaware of being observed she had lifted the blossom to her face and inhaled its sweet perfume. This little being reveled in the richness of life in the midst of her abject poverty, her spirit touched by something beautiful that had not yet been destroyed by the hell around her in which she lived. Dancing, she had carried the flower and presented it to her father with loving excitement. He had tenderly stroked her head as he took the flower. Her father also appreciated beauty in the midst of hell.

The warrior, now sobbing at the top of the hill, held the child to the light—then she was gone. With his arms outstretched to the light he waited, pleading to the light. But it was not his time. He slowly turned and walked from the light. With empty arms covered with the blood of innocence and a breaking heart, he walked from the light. He had many times gone to the light and many times returned. This time was different. This was the last time he would journey to the light. The many times before, he had turned away knowing that it was not his time; but this time the warrior not only had accepted forgiveness but he had forgiven himself. He need not return.

Carol woke with a start because of the pain in her hand, the hand that held Jason's. Her hand was being squeezed in a quivering, vice-like grip. She thought it would be crushed, and bit her lip to keep from crying out. She raised her head and noticed Jason's right hand was clenched into a fist; it too shook. His lower lip trembled and she watched a tear roll from the corner of one of his eyes. She sensed the inner anguish but also the release in the shuddering body that now gripped her. She knew in her spirit that they had shared this dream.

Carol watched and cried with Jason for what seemed a long time. Her hand turned white from lack of circulation, and she had almost rung for the doctor, but decided against it. This was a spiritual time for the two of them, not to be interrupted. And because of what had just happened to them, she knew deep in her soul that Jason was on his way back.

It had been nearly an hour since she had awakened. Without any further warning, Jason's eyes opened. It took several minutes for him to focus. Then through a parched throat he whispered, "It's over."